The Color of Tea

A Novel

Hannah Tunnicliffe

Scribner

New York   London   Toronto   Sydney   New Delhi

Scribner
A Division of Simon & Schuster, Inc.
1230 Avenue of the Americas
New York, NY 10020

Originally published in 2011 in Macmillan by Pan Macmillan Australia Limited
as *The Colour of Tea*

First Scribner trade paperback edition June 2012

For information about special discounts for bulk purchases, please contact Simon & Schuster Special Sales at 1-866-506-1949 or business@simonandschuster.com.

The Simon & Schuster Speakers Bureau can bring authors to your live event. For more information or to book an event contact the Simon & Schuster Speakers Bureau at 1-866-248-3049 or visit our website at www.simonspeakers.com.

Designed by Carla Jayne Jones

Manufactured in the United States of America

1   3   5   7   9   10   8   6   4   2

Library of Congress Control Number: 20122009165

ISBN 978-1-4516-8282-3
ISBN 978-1-4516-8283-0 (ebook)

For Matt

I found you and now I know

Contents

Contents

Contents

Prologue

e arrived in Macau at the end of the Year of the Golden Pig. Apparently a golden pig year comes around only once every sixty, and it brings good fortune. So when we came to make Macau our home, at the backside end of this golden pig year, there were fat, pink pigs dancing in bank ads, sparkly cartoon pigs wearing Chinese pajamas hanging in the local bakery, and tiny souvenir golden pigs for sale at the post office. All those pigs around me were comforting, with their full snouts and chubby grins. *Welcome to Macau!* they snorted. *You'll like it here. We do!* I was willing to accept any good luck a golden hog could throw at me.

Macau: the bulbous nose of China, a peninsula and two islands strung together like a three-bead necklace, though by now the sand and silt have crept up and almost covered the silk of the ocean in between. Gobbled up, like most everything in Macau, by Progress. Progress and gambling. This tiny country, only twenty-eight square kilometers, once a sleepy Portuguese outpost, is the only place in China where you can drop a coin into a slot or lay a chip on kidney-shaped lawns of soft, green felt. The Vegas of the East. Bright lights, little city, fast cash.

We stepped off the ferry from Hong Kong on the eighth of January 2008. The date had a nice ring to it. A fresh start, a clean slate, a new beginning. We arrived with suitcases full of the light, breezy clothes usually reserved for the brief but seductive British summer. We were full of naïve optimism about our new life adventure. My Australian husband and his red-haired, blush-of-cheek English rose. We were babes in the woods.

The January winter was bitter in more ways than one. It was one of the coldest on record, and we were freezing in our bright, thin clothes. Every morning the sky was the color of milk. The apartment had no central heating, and it took us some time to realize we needed a dehumidifier. The walls started to bloom with a dark mold, which spread like a growing bruise, and I couldn't feel my fingers in the evenings. It was the kind of damp cold that settles deep in the marrow of your bones and refuses to budge.

This is where I will start. Our life in this cold month, before the Year of the Rat began. When we couldn't run any longer from realities; when life hunted us down and found us. It followed us all the way from Melbourne to London, London to Macau. All that running, and still we were discovered, no longer able to hide out in the meaningless details of our life—who is making breakfast and could you remember to pick up the dry cleaning.

It was time to find a life for myself. To make something out of nothing. The end of hope and the beginning of it too.

L'Arrivée—Arrival

Sweet and Smoky Caramel with Salted Buttery Cream Filling

his is the kind of trip my mama would make. Getting on a bus in a foreign place, the language a sea of meaningless nonsense, the script even more baffling; alone, save for the rows of faces turned and staring. She would love this. Dark eyes gazing over the red hair and pale skin. The warm, crowded bodies jostling unself-consciously against one another as the wheels hit scars in the tar seal. Instead I am nervous and feel slightly seasick, holding tight to my handbag and making useless apologies in English for getting in the way. I feel, as Pete might say, like a spare prick at a wedding.

Macau is framed in the grimy window. We drive over the bridge from Taipa Island to the peninsula, as though driving directly into the white and soupy sky. The bus makes several stops, braking late so that people fall into one another like skittles. No one complains. We pass the Lisboa casino, painted the orange of a bad cocktail with circular sixties-style windows. Then the gleaming new Grand Lisboa, which seems to erupt straight out of the ground in the shape of a pineapple, angular petals fanning high in the sky. The bulb of its base illuminates like a large convex television screen, flashing advertisements, fish, rolling coins, special deals. Passengers get off, wearing identical white shirts and black trousers. As they push past me, I squeeze my handbag into my side, feel the square edges of my guidebook press against my ribs.

Weaving into the central part of town, the roads become narrower and harder to navigate. Most of the buildings are old apartment blocks, washed gray with age, dark stains dripping from window frames and fading clothes hung carefully from miniature washing lines. Mopeds dart waspishly in and out of the traffic while men sit on the pavements, slurping noodles from plastic bowls. They barely lift their heads at the noise: exhaust pipe belches, car horns, the metallic protests of brakes. The temperature is slowly turning today. Finally defrosting. I unwind the scarf from around my neck and jam it into my bag. I am hoping to end up in San Malo, but not being able to speak Cantonese, I cannot ask anyone for directions. At least I can be sure that no one will try to strike up a conversation with me. That's a small sweetness.

I keep my head turned toward the window, looking for the landmarks I have read about. We turn in to a neighborhood where black-and-white Portuguese cobblestones are arranged in thoughtful swirls and waves. There are historic buildings instead of apartment blocks and sparkling casinos. Trims are a creamy white, façades candy pink or lemon yellow—Easter egg colors. Less vivid than the photo in the book, but I recognize it.

"San Malo!" the driver calls out, and I leap to my feet, bumping against people who stare at the color of my hair rather than look me in the eye.

There is a thrumming of tourists, each group lugging bags of souvenirs and following a man or woman in a wide-brimmed cap waving a yellow flag. I can see over the crowds, dark heads hovering around my chin. I promised Pete that I would get out of the apartment today, explore this new city we live in. My excuse for staying in has been that I should wait for the delivery of our sofa, which somehow didn't arrive with the rest of our furniture. But we both know that is not what I am really waiting for. Earlier in the week he caught me in the bathroom, reading *What to Expect When You're Expecting*, sunk deep in a tub of hot water. He did a double take and then pretended not to notice, turning his hazel eyes away from me, idly suggesting I go see some sights, get out in the "fresh air." Now I realize I have become so used to hiding away in the apartment, anonymous, that I am finding all the people and attention overwhelming. I slip down a side street away from the chatter and gawking and bustle and try to find the temple mentioned in the guidebook.

Soon I am in front of tall wooden doors painted with two warrior-like gods, eyes bulging and long beards flying and curling. The noise of the crowds has grown quiet; the black-and-white cobblestones here are faded and chipped. It is as though my feet already knew the way, stumbling across it like this, so easily. I pause at a manicured potted tree by the entrance. Its needles shiver. Smoky fronds of incense whisper out of the doors, and I walk up the small steps even while my head and heart are unsure. It is dark inside and filled with statues and gold, fruit and pictures. Candles drip honey-colored wax onto the concrete floor. Above my head the incense is burning, dropping from the ceiling in thick saffron coils like strange golden snakes. A cat leaps out past me, a patchwork of black, ginger, and white. I gasp, and it turns to look back at me, round-eyed. Someone inside snorts.

"That's just Molly. She lives here." The language is English, but the voice is Chinese.

I have to squint to make out the figure in the dim light— a young woman in a tight tracksuit. She is crouching on her haunches, much like the cat, and chewing gum. Her eyes are framed with thick eyeliner. Her expression is somewhere between curious and bored, I can't figure out which.

"You here to see Aunty?"

"Is she the fortune-teller?"

"Uh-huh," she drawls, without nodding. "This way."

Getting to her feet, she walks to the side of the temple, where there is a tiny courtyard. Dust motes dance in the cool air. She holds a diamanté-studded mobile phone, a small gold charm swinging like a pendulum from the end of it. She looks back at me and motions toward an older woman. The fortune-teller is nothing like I imagined. Perhaps I was expecting a bearded Lao Tzu in flowing silken pajamas. My fortune-teller is wearing jeans and is squatting on a stool. Her nut-brown face is pinched into an irritated frown.

"Don't worry," the woman in the tracksuit says to me. "She's just in a bad mood. I'll translate for you. Her English is terrible, so just ask me what it is you want to know." Her gaze wanders down to my left hand, clutching the handle of my purse. Those dark-rimmed eyes move back to mine. "Married?"

"Yes."

"Okay, well, money, health, whatever. Just tell me what you wanna know and I'll ask her. You get it?"

I know exactly what I want to ask, but the question is stuck in my throat. We stare at each other for a few moments, and I wonder if I should make my exit.

"Sure," I mumble.

I am passed a plastic stool to perch on while the fortune-teller looks into my face. Her hair is dyed black, with a thick margin of silver growing back near her skull. She peers at me as though inspecting for defects, her face a few inches from mine. Nervously I look down at her feet. Her sandals have gold straps, fake Gucci logos stitched lazily to the sides. She puts her hand on my jaw, the pads of her fingers leathery against my skin.

"What is this type of fortune-telling?"

"*Sang Mien,*" my translator replies. "Face reading."

The fortune-teller takes hold of my shoulder to bring me closer. I feel my cheeks flush, as if she can see my thoughts, my deepest desires and worst regrets.

"Oh," I say.

"Okay, she's saying she is ready," says the young woman with a yawn. She scrapes her stool across the tiles to be closer. Her aunt barks out a sentence, and she translates.

"Your face is very square," she begins.

I nod; my face can be described euphemistically as "broad," that much I know.

"Means you are practical. Shape of your eyes shows not so optimistic, but having . . . intuition, a little bit of creativity. Strong jaw, so you have determination and can be stubborn. But you are generous . . ."

There is a short silence. The fortune-teller cuts her eyes at her niece, who seems to be searching the air for something.

"I don't know what the word is. Sort of like not doing anything that is too out of the ordinary, not making too much trouble for anyone. Make sense?"

I nod. Conforming, I think to myself. She is right about that part too. Not like Mama.

The inspection continues. She tells me my ears show that I am a fast learner but can be shy. Then she peers at my nose. I feel a blush warm my cheeks. My maiden name is Raven, so Beak Face was a running joke.

"Nose shows you are independent, can be own boss."

I wish the teasing girls at school had known that.

"And Aunty says something like nose shape means you are working to help people."

"Uh-huh." I'm not sure my current occupation, if you can even call it that, is a help to others. A "trailing spouse" is how it is described. Trailing behind the breadwinner. Puts me in mind of the guy tagging along behind the elephant at the zoo. And you know what he does all day . . . Pete has always been the ambitious one, so we've moved where he has needed to be, where the casinos have needed him to be. Before this move I have worked as a waitress in cafés, pubs, restaurants, and hotel bars. Just enough of a job to avoid being unemployed and bored, but nothing fancy. I guess you could say it is helping people. They call it the "service industry," but it's not true service. Not like doctors and firemen and volunteers in Africa. I'm good at it, I guess, not only because I love food but because I grew up learning how to attend to someone else's needs. It's in my blood. Or my nose, it would seem.

I adjust my position on the stool, the bones in my backside starting to ache, as the fortune-teller leans forward to take one of my hands. She reviews the lines on my palm, her eyes focused and her breath damp and warm against my skin.

"Aunty says you have a love. I guess it's your husband, right? Only one, she says."

I nod again. That wasn't a difficult guess; we've been married long enough for the rose-gold wedding band on my left hand to practically mold to the finger, the skin underneath milk-pale and indented.

"Pretty good man, but there is a bit of sadness. For him and for you. Carrying it around here." My translator points toward her chest, I presume at her heart.

I nod slowly.

"You will have a good, healthy life. No problem with money. You'll stay in Macau for some time, but not too long."

The older woman frowns, looks up at me and then back down at my hand. I swallow. The young woman puts her mobile phone into her pocket and leans forward. The volleying of Cantonese starts up again, the volume cranked up a notch. I lean in also, as if I might catch a word or two, but it is meaningless to me. The aunt shakes a finger at her niece.

"All right, all right." She rolls her eyes. "She does this. It's like one thing or maybe another thing totally opposite." She frowns. "She's talking about children."

I take a quick breath and hope they haven't heard me, wishing I could snatch my hand from the older woman's grip. But she is still staring down at my palm.

"Maybe there will be one . . ."

The pause seems to hang, the dust motes swirling and spinning around us.

"It's a faint line. She is saying something like one, or *not* one."

The fortune-teller is stroking the side of my pinkie emphatically, as if to illustrate her point. I look back and forth between the two women.

"Go figure." The younger woman shrugs.

"I don't understand," I say hesitantly.

"Yeah, she's saying it as if it all makes sense, but she *doesn't* make sense. Then she says that the most important thing is don't worry. *Maybe* a baby is what she says."

I feel sad and seasick again. Telling me not to worry is ridiculous advice. I want to ask more; a thousand questions tumble over one another in my mind. I open my mouth, but the fortune-teller is speaking again. She has turned to face her niece. She drops my hand as the young woman shakes her head and waves her aunt's glare away. The aunt leans toward her and raises her voice.

"Excuse me . . ." I say, but they don't hear.

Now the aunt has her palm against her niece's knee, and she is pointing a finger at her. The young woman's face pales and she turns her cheek. More Cantonese, rough and choppy. I look from one to the other as their voices grow angrier and more urgent. I feel like I am watching something I shouldn't. As her aunt gets louder, the girl lifts her eyes to me. The pupils are dark and hard, like black beads, looking right into me.

"Can I ask . . ." I start.

"That's all—finished," she says too quickly, getting to her feet. The fortune-teller is still talking, but the young woman gives me a forced smile and ignores her.

I get the hint. I stand up slowly, my legs almost buckling, stiff from crouching and the cold. She doesn't reach out to help me up. I sway as I shuffle through the items in my bag, hunting for my wallet.

"One fifty?"

"Yeah." Then she adds, "That's not including tip."

"Uh, sure." I pass two Hong Kong hundred-dollar notes toward her. They are new and starchy. She takes them with both hands and pauses, staring at me with those dark eyes. Her aunt is still muttering, now shaking her head. My translator still doesn't turn around, keeping her glassy stare on me.

"Keep the change," I say.

"Thanks," she replies in a flat voice.

Heading through the temple, back out to the sweet smell of incense, I can feel my eyes watering, perhaps from the brightness of the light outside. My chest is tight too; I take in a big gulp of air.

Outside a crowd is still moving like one beast, the whole greater than the sum of its parts. The sun has split like a yolk through the white sky. As I head back to the main road, I avoid the bus stops and flag down a taxi. I say the only thing I know in Cantonese to the driver.

"Gee Jun Far Sing."

Remède de Délivrance—Rescue Remedy
Violet with Cream and
Bitter Black Currant Filling

Three days later, our couches finally arrive. A man rings our doorbell unannounced and stands there with two sweaty companions, two boxed couches, and a look as if to say, "So what?" He has them dragged in and unpacked, then taps on the sheet of paper where I should sign and is gone. Now I can sit in my living room and look out the window.

We live on the sixth floor of Gee Jun Far Sing, Supreme Flower City. The apartments are surprisingly spacious; our furniture barely fills ours up. There is a Super Flower City and a Grand Flower City and there will be a Prince Flower City, but our bright purple apartment building is Supreme. It is hard to ignore a forty-something-story purple building, rearing into the sky like a gawky exotic lily. On closer inspection it is not painted that color but tiled in tiny purple squares, like pixels. It turns out that almost all of the apartment buildings are clad the same way. I imagine the tiles are laid on in sheets, smoothed like wallpaper or icing on a wedding cake.

The view from the couches is of the residents' car park below us on the fourth floor, an empty block of land, and Nova City apartment block directly across from us. Nova City is an older building. It must have been white once, but now it is as gray as the sky on a pollution-filled day and striped with the dirty exhaust of leaking air-conditioning units. The empty block is supposed to become a park sometime soon, or so I have been told. Every week there are new rumors—it will become an underground car park, it is a station for a new light-rail system, they'll make it into another casino. Nothing happens. The block remains empty, tussocky, and worn.

The phone rings while I am gazing out at that lonely piece of land and doing what I do best. Waiting. My heart leaps out of my chest on the first ring. I try to breathe normally. *Just answer the phone, Grace.* My heart thunders on like a racehorse in the Grand National. I imagine my file in his hands, a folder with red and yellow stickers down one side that read G. Miller. I wait for the sound of his voice to reveal everything in the tone and pause, but the line is poor. I hear him clear his throat.

"Hi, Dr. Lee," I say.

I imagine him on the other end of the phone, on the other side of the world. Dr. Lee is younger than he looks, I think from all the smiling. The few wrinkles in his round face gather by his cheeks as though he has been dishing out good news for years. I think of him with his wide grin, armfuls of fleshy, giggling babies in rose pink and swallow blue booties. Although he is calling from an office in London, he is originally from Hong Kong, so he knows Macau, only a stone's throw away. He used to spend his summer holidays here.

Two years of crossed fingers and timely sex passed by before I even went to see him in that sea green office with the fake silk poppies in the reception area. There had already been a registered endocrinologist before him. My follicle-stimulating-hormone levels were high, and we knew what that meant. It was easier to talk about FSH than use the dreaded M word. Worse was when they mentioned "infertility." Casually, carelessly. It always made me feel sick.

"We'll try someone else. One more," I had said to Pete.

Dr. Lee gave us that smile of his, and we felt a new flickering of hope. There were junior Lees. That was a good sign, right? They smiled from the photos on his desk, sensitively turned away from clients but reflecting off the glass in the shelves behind him. A childless woman sees these things, she sees everything.

With his encouragement I tried acupuncture, yoga, gave up wheat, lost five kilos, and crossed my fingers on both hands before every test. The blue lines betrayed me every time; too many tears in that bathroom, falling into the white sink. I wished so hard for pregnancy. Then I just wished for a normal period. I wished and prayed, but nothing changed. There was just one more test. Even Pete whispered, "No more after this, love. Please."

He had put up with so much. The hormones, mood swings, tears. I wasn't going to argue with him, I was exhausted too. The last FSH test.

Now, looking out at Macau, I feel a desperate urge to put off whatever the doctor is going to say.

"Grace, I have the results back."

I can tell from his voice. Children in frames, their smiles reflected in the glass. Not mine.

"It wasn't what we were hoping for, I'm afraid. With the extra hormone support, the alternative therapies, I thought we might have a chance. But . . ."

This voice I have been waiting for becomes a strange hum against the bowl of my ear. I can't follow what he is saying, and it doesn't matter. All I hear is *Failure*. Premature ovarian failure. I am an old woman in my thirties.

*   *   *

When Pete comes home, I am still on the couch. The sky is dark, but the curtains are open. I hadn't called him, although I'd thought about it.

He squints at me while taking off his shoes. "Grace?"

I imagine what he is seeing. His wife, curled up, face old and tired. He sits down beside me and takes my hand. Leaning back, he lets out a sigh. We both stare at the television because it is the focal point of the room, but it is switched off. The black square is like the third person in our conversation.

After a long time he says, "We should talk about it. There could be things, things we could do . . ." His voice is strong and encouraging. His alpha male voice. This is the voice that makes men gravitate toward him like wolves to the leader of the pack. I guess it is why he makes such a good manager. Or perhaps it is some kind of pheromone. He never wears aftershave, so the natural smell of salt is always thick on him. That scent used to make me giddy. But not now.

I shake my head.

"Gracie, what did he say exactly?" He squeezes my fingers comfortingly, but he sounds patronizing.

I shake my head; I don't want to be coddled.

He says something else, but I don't hear him, although I do turn to look at him. The thick hair, loose and curly, made for a musician or an artist, not a businessman. It needs a cut as always, and I make a mental note of this. It has been so long since I have really looked at him, and I realize, through the fog of sadness, just how much we have drifted apart. He looks foreign to me somehow. The last few years of trying for a baby have had us walking more and more separate paths. I take in his dark eyebrows and the soft, sagging skin under his eyes betraying a lack of sleep. Two deep lines frame his lips, one on each cheek, like parentheses. He puts his head to one side and frowns. There is so much pity in his face that it makes me feel nauseous. What is there to say?

"I don't want to talk about it," I say dully.

A new talent. I go from waiting to sleeping. Pete gets someone to write a prescription for sleeping tablets, and I ingest them instead of meals. I take them at regular intervals, to keep from being awake. I do not want to be awake.

But a few days later I am wrenched from my sleep, covered in a greasy sweat. I have dreamed about Mama.

We were in a field of poppies, their fat and luscious red heads moving about in the breeze as we walked through them. Mama was a few feet from me and singing. I think she was singing. Maybe she was talking to the flowers. Her head was tilted toward them, and she had an openmouthed smile on her face. She tucked her hair behind her ear. The sun was warm, the breeze was cool, and her happy face seemed to say, "I love you, my Gracie," just the way she used to say it when she tucked me in at night. Like everything was all right with the world. But then there was a loud sound, like a crack of lightning, or a whip against dry earth, and a flock of birds flashed across the sky. We looked at each other, Mama's face turning pale and still. She looked lighter, not smaller but slightly transparent.

I think I saw her mouth the word *Sorry*. Dread filled my stomach. I stumbled toward her, my skirt catching on the poppies. Mama was still singing, but it was so quiet I could only see her painted red lips moving. She was fading away. I started to cry. As I caught her up in my arms and put my ear next to her mouth, my tears fell onto her neck and ran down to her blouse. Then I caught her whispering, "Summertime, and the livin' is easy . . ."

I sit up in bed and wish for the dream to leave me. Her face, her voice, even the smell of her favorite perfume are spinning around and around in my head, leaving me dizzy and breathless. I reach over to the bedside table and take another sleeping tablet. It won't work for a half hour at least, but being awake is too painful. My muscles ache, but my heart is worse. I wince at the sunlight coming in the window. Spring is coming, and the Year of the Golden Pig is almost gone. Now what? *Now what?*

It had been in those moments, all those times I was in the bathroom, waiting for those magical blue lines, I had started to think of Mama again. Now she is here with me in Macau, running into my dreams. Daughters never understand mothers until they become mothers, that's what a woman at work said to me once. Maybe she was right. Mama had come back into my thoughts as I sat in specialists' waiting rooms and stared at women with children in prams. I'd pushed her and her mysteries out of my memory for so long, but there she was again, dancing with my child hands in hers, making mud cakes, giggling, crying. Scenes from our past stringing themselves together like a crooked daisy chain. I couldn't stop thinking of her. Some days I'd imagine I saw her at the butcher's or getting onto a train. But I know one thing for sure: that woman was wrong about the understanding part. I will never understand Mama. I press my fingers to my temples and lean back into the pillow.

Pete has put a sandwich beside the bed, the crusts drying against the white plate. Underneath is a pad of writing paper. I can't help it. It's become a habit. I pick up the pad and look for a pen. I started writing notes to her when we began trying to become parents. Something about it calms me; makes me feel better. At least for a while. I guess some women have a journal; I have Mama. Ruby-red-haired Mama. Wild as a tomcat. The one person who knows the best and the worst of me. Never far from my mind.

Dearest Mama,

Do you remember that time the bird flew into the window when we were living in Borough? We were baking—meringues, tarts, something sweet and French. We were in the kitchen and we heard that sick-sounding thud and looked up, and you said, "Oh dear, sounds like an angel has fallen."

I thought for sure it was a real angel and tried to climb up onto the edge of the sink to see out. I think I expected to see a blond, curly-haired lady rubbing her bruised head and straightening her long, blue, glittering dress. You know, just like the angel on the top of the Christmas tree? But instead there was a tiny, frightened bird lying in the window box, on top of the soil.

Do you remember how we picked that bird up and put it in a cleaned-out ice cream container lined with a couple of socks? It lay on its side and stared up at us with one eye roving and blinking. You could see its little heart beating so fast and so hard I was terrified it would explode with shock. Then you took the box over to the bed and sat down next to it and started humming. Humming "Amazing Grace."

You unscrewed the top of a bottle of Rescue Remedy and put the dripper next to the bird's small orange beak. I was sure it wouldn't open its mouth, but it did, just a little bit. Some of the remedy got in, and some fell down its breast, onto the waxy feathers. You kept humming, and finally, after what seemed like such a long time but probably wasn't, it wriggled up and onto its feet. One eye looking at you and one eye looking at me. We took him up to the garden on the roof, do you remember? As soon as we got up there, he leapt out of the ice cream container and wobbled off into the sky. How quickly he remembered how to fly.

Mama, I don't know what to do or say or think or feel. All I can think about is other things. Like that bird. If I think about the real thing, it is as if I am drowning. It is as if I can't breathe. My heart

starts to jump about like that little bird's and I wish you were here. To
bake with me. To sing to me. To stroke my hair.

Your loving daughter,
Grace

Later that night, I am lying on the couch without the television on, staring out the window.

"Grace? You awake?" Pete asks. He has arrived home to find the apartment dark. I have forgotten to turn on the lights. He flicks the switch closest to the door while easing out of his shoes.

I give him a small smile; he looks so worried it is the least I can offer him. When he comes over, I reach up and touch his mouth with the tips of my fingers. It is the same mouth I kissed goodbye this morning, and yet how strange it feels. I lean into his face and kiss his lips again, like trying a new fruit.

He will never be a father.

When I pull away, he is staring at me, his frown softening.

He will never be a father and it is my fault.

I lean forward into him and kiss him so hard I can taste the iron in his blood. I must have knocked his gum, and I want to bite his lip. He makes a soft whine and struggles free to look at me again. I push him back into the sofa, the dark cushions swallowing up the contours of his face. He is blurry now, in the half dark, but I find his mouth and press my lips firm up against his so I can feel the shape of his teeth through them. I am sitting on him when I pull back for air. I can tell he is still staring at me, but he says nothing. The sound between us is of warm, short breaths and nothing else.

As I pull off his tie, it makes a whishing sound, whipping around and off his collar. He unbuttons his shirt while I wriggle back off him to take off his trousers. I pull my shirt up over my head, and he unzips my fly. When I unclip my bra, he grabs my arms for a moment; they are twisted behind my back. We are frozen, half undressed and both still wearing our socks. Pete's are short and dark, warm from being inside his shoes.

"I . . ." he starts, but doesn't finish. I can see from his face that he is aching to talk. A million unsaid things in his eyes. Silently, I beg him not to say anything now, and he doesn't.

I can feel him thick and hot against my underwear. In my head I try to remember my last period, when it was, wonder whether I might be ovulating. It is a habit. The thought falls away; it is no longer important. He lets go of my arms and drops his hands to my thighs. I pull down his boxer shorts and grasp hold of him. He lets out a moan, and his head goes back so I cannot see much of his face beyond his chin. I maneuver out of my pants and drop them on the floor. When I push myself down onto him too quickly, he sucks in air with surprise. He reaches up for my breasts, but I pin his arms by his sides. My nipples skim the hair on his chest as we move together. There is a dry pain, but I close my eyes so hard that I see stars, and that stops me from thinking much about anything. It feels raw and scorched and more wild than we really are. Pete cries out and comes loose from my hold. He grabs me like I am about to fall, pulls me tight and close to him. We make warm, wordless shouts into the dark. The shudder clashes our bodies together, and when it stops my face is buried so close to his neck I can smell the saltiness of his skin. How long has it been since we had sex for no reason at all? The thought is sad and angry all at once. He mumbles something into my hair, and I sink my teeth into his shoulder until he cries out. We fall apart from the grip breathless and panting.

Later, when he is asleep, I stare at his mouth hanging wide open and taking ugly, ragged breaths. I look at his face in the dark, the face of the man I married in Bali so long ago that I can barely remember the smaller details of the day. My eyes wander from his mouth down his stomach, over his legs and back again. No matter how many beers he guzzles or burgers he eats at his desk during short lunch breaks, his middle-aged body works just fine. It makes me feel so bitter. Bitter and broken inside. I lie in the dark, staring at him. The hair on his chest, the softness of his belly. Then I think of a tomato tart. Warm and sweet. The one that we fell in love over.

I had escaped from London and moved to Melbourne. The skies were bluer in Australia, and I felt like I could finally take full, deep breaths. All of my own. I'd found myself a lover who lived in Northcote, in a flat right behind the Coles supermarket. His name was Dan. He wasn't a great catch, but he was funny when he drank. To be fair, it didn't bother me all that much; I wasn't looking for the perfect man, just a half-decent kisser to be young and stupid with, and Dan was that.

One morning, when Dan was still asleep and I was nursing a hangover, I decided to get something to eat. I walked to Coles wearing Dan's tracksuit bottoms, a T-shirt, and a pair of old dark green flip-flops that I found behind the front door. The hangover made me ravenous but robbed me of my ability to make a decision. I don't know how long I spent wandering about the supermarket creating meals in my mind. Hot roast chicken and mayonnaise sandwiches. Pizzas on crispy bases. Big, heaving bowls of spaghetti Bolognese. Crunchy, cheesy nachos with sour cream. I did a full circle and ended back in the fruit and veg section. Next to the peaches were boxes filled with tomatoes still clinging to their vines. The ripe tomato smell was almost sexual. It filled my nostrils as I lifted up a box. There were some slightly rotten ones near the bottom of the box, but the rest were just perfect, thick with the perfume of their green vines, fat and red. Someone had hastily scrawled a sign: BOX FOR $5.

The scent pulled me back into memories of a tomato tart Mama had made one morning. I was about six, I think. It was still dark when I woke to the smell of roasting tomato and goat's cheese bubbling and bursting under the grill. Singing drew me toward the kitchen, where Mama was wearing a purple cable-knit sweater she had made and her pajama bottoms. They had mud up the backs of the legs, and she was wearing one red sock and one black.

"Miss Grace Raven!" she trilled, pulling the first glorious tomato tart out of the oven. It must have been five in the morning, but my mouth watered. The kitchen was warm, and Mama had a big smile on her face. When she'd put me to bed, she was simmering with a dark and stormy mood, so that smile held me still. I was waiting to see if it would last, making sure this wasn't a dream. She flitted about the kitchen like a summer fly, grinning and chatting. I followed her with my eyes, bare feet glued to the spot.

"Your mama has made a tomato tart for breakfast. A tart for the king and queen of this house. Which is you and me, darling girl. You and me!"

Her smile was somehow a little too bright, but I watched as she showed me how she had scored the puff pastry and brushed it with oil. She got me to smell the thyme pressed between her fingers and thumb, and told me how good garlic was for keeping away colds. She preached about food and sang and laughed and baked until the light started to come in the windows. Then we sat and ate hot tart without knives and forks. She kissed my cheeks and smelled like garlic. I remember the hot cheese dropping onto Mama's sweater and drying to a rubbery streak against the wool.

I carried that box of tomatoes all the way from Coles back to

Dan's house. I thought of Mama while I prepared the tomatoes and crushed raw garlic, the skin around my bitten nails stinging with the pungent juices. I was starving by the time it was in the oven and must have looked pretty frightful—hair a mess, mascara loaded in the corners of my eyes from the night before, the old T-shirt hanging off me decorated with gruesome splatters of tomato innards. I was half drunk on the viscous perfume of pastry rising and sunk deep in my memories when a man came into the kitchen from the lounge room without his shirt on and smelling of sleep. Drowsily, he tried to move to the fridge, but my tomato box with a few rotten specimens at the bottom was in the way. He looked even worse than I did.

"What the fuck . . ."

Thick, curly brown hair fell over his eyes, slightly crossed-over teeth stuck out of his lower jaw. The top teeth were nice though. Nice and white and even. I assumed he was Dan's flatmate.

"Sorry, I'll move that. Just tomatoes—I'm making a tart," I apologized. Britishly. I wished I had put on my bra, even if it did smell of smoke and beer.

"You're making a what?" He turned to face me properly and looked me up and down. His eyes settled for a moment on my feet.

"A, um, tart. A tomato tart. Sorry, that's why there's a box of . . ." I gestured feebly.

He cocked his head and laughed.

"Holy shit, that is a posh accent. A tart—like a pie or something, right?" He got to the fridge and yanked out a carton of orange juice. He checked the date on the top and frowned.

"Well, no, it's a tart. It's different from a pie."

I knew I sounded prissy. My accent is not posh. It's just English.

His nipples stood upright amid small circles of dark hair. The only hair on his entire chest, ringed around his nipples. Could he put some clothes on, for God's sake? He grinned at me with those teeth, so then I knew he had only been teasing. I'd forgotten that teasing was what Australian men do best. Like pulling a girl's pigtails in class.

"Okay," he said a little more gently. He leaned on the fridge door and drank straight from the carton. Juice clung to his upper lip before he licked it away. He turned toward the oven.

"Well, it does smell good."

"Thanks."

I could see him glancing at the mess I had made, red pulp covering the sink and knives and more than one chopping board. Hangovers are not conducive to being a tidy cook. My mess was even worse than Mama's.

"You can have some if you want."

He nodded.

"I'm Grace, by the way, with um . . ." I gestured toward Dan's room, as nonchalantly as possible. The door was slightly ajar, one naked cheek of his arse exposed where the duvet had slipped off.

Dan's flatmate looked where I'd gestured. "Oh, right." He seemed pretty unperturbed by the nakedness. I guessed he had seen it before. "I'm Pete. Actually, yeah, I'll have some if you're offering."

We sat at the table in the lounge room and watched the news. The tart was heaven, Mama would have been proud. The enormous sheets of it took up two whole shelves of the oven. We ate the lot between us before Dan even woke up. Pete sucked at his fingers and moaned that it was delicious. He told me he was a pit manager at the casino and he'd been to university with Dan. He hadn't finished his business degree because it wasn't very interesting and he liked his part-time job dealing cards better. That was when he moved in with Dan. Pete reckoned Dan was a good guy, but he "got pissed a bit too often for his own good," which was probably pretty accurate. Pete was going to move out in a few months, it was time; he and Dan had been flatting together for years now. I looked at his green-flecked eyes while he spoke in that low, strong voice, stared at the fringe of black lashes. We sat and ate and talked and watched the TV for a few hours. He told me my tart was the best *pie* he'd ever eaten. It felt easy, like being with family, if I'd ever had much of one other than Mama. And he pointed out that I was wearing his flip-flops.

Now, so many years later, Pete's naked body is stretched out on the bed, those handsome eyes closed. He is right next to me, but he feels so very far away. I go to the shower alone. When the tears start, they are hot and full. I stand under the stream and let the water flow over my eyelids and nose and splash onto my chest. Suddenly too tired to stand, I sit down and curl my knees toward my breasts. I imagine Mama coming in and seeing me like this. Whatever mood she was in, and there were some bad ones, she would give me a towel. Tell me to get up and come have toast. She'd put the kettle on and fill a hot-water bottle, slide it into a brown woolen cover. She'd make tea. I wait, the shower tiles leaving an imprint on my backside, but no one comes to wrap me in a towel; there is only the sound of water falling.

La Ville-Lumière—City of Light

Parisian Crêpe-Inspired Banana with Hazelnut Chocolate Ganache

Peace descends on the apartment after Pete leaves for work, a light and floating silence. Television news is switched off; taps have stopped running; shoes no longer clunk on the wooden floorboards. I lifted my head off the pillow once or twice to talk to him as he got ready, but as usual I didn't know where to start. He has tried to start conversations for weeks now, and I have buried myself in this bed to avoid them. Eventually he stopped trying. I risk opening one eye again. The sunlight is piercingly bright. Spring bright. I sigh and open my other eye with reluctance, squinting and blinking, and get to my feet. Standing at the window, I can see Pete's tiny figure walking to the office. It must be warmer now; he has his jacket slung over one shoulder, his attention firmly fixed on something in his hand. His phone, I bet. I urge him to turn around so I can wave. He looks up and I think he might turn and see me, might sense that I am standing at the window, hands pressed on either side of the frame. But he strides on.

The sun pours through the glass onto my skin; I can feel the small hairs on my arms standing up to greet it. *Good morning, sun.*

Good morning, morning. The clouds are fat and floaty, as if they have been plucked from the Sistine Chapel and slapped across the Macau sky. They rest against a sheet of bright blue, an unexpected pollution-free sky today. I lean my head against the pane and breathe in; perhaps the loveliness can be inhaled. I roll my forehead around to one side to look back at the island that is our bed. The sheets are tangled and need to be washed. There is a smell like warm dust and stale bread. I know I need to stop living like a hermit, but the effort of getting dressed and leaving the apartment seems too huge. I take a deep breath to give me resolve and search for my sports bra underneath strappy, lacy underwear I no longer wear.

The doorman looks up when I get out of the lift dressed in tracksuit bottoms, T-shirt, and runners, rumpled but awake and moving. I wonder if he is surprised to see me at this time. Or at all. His gaze follows me as I walk out the glass doors.

Despite the blue sky, the air smells of exhaust fumes and is filled with the noise of brakes and horns. The morning sounds of going to work and taking the kids to day care. Two destinations to which I will not be going. I long for a quiet English park or a sandy Australian beach as I walk past a woman still in her pajamas, slurping congee off a spoon. She looks up at me with a vacant, drowsy stare, then drops her head to concentrate on her meal. I'm relieved she is not interested in me. I can feel so self-conscious here. So pale and tall. Too foreign. Sometimes it feels like I've been growing more and more foreign over the years. Like I've been taking steps away from myself. First escaping to Australia, then back to London. Now here. China. I look at the shops on either side of me. None of them is open at this time; I made that mistake early on. They don't open till around ten, if not later, and they close late too. You can wander into a shop at ten at night and the shopkeeper will still come bounding out from a back room, wiping rice and soup from his lips, ready to serve you. But at this time of the morning, the corrugated-iron shutters are down, like tightly closed eyelids. SORRY, WE'RE SLEEPING, I imagine the sign in Chinese to read.

A few blocks away there is a school, a small playground in one corner. I try not to look, but I'm drawn to it. The playground is small, concrete and sad. It has a strange assortment of miniature plaster replicas of famous landmarks. There is an Eiffel Tower, a knee-high Sydney Harbour Bridge, and a lopsided London Bridge. Little pieces of my life, as if placed there just for me. I curl my fingers through the wire loops of the fence. The playground is empty, all the children now in class. Barren—no grass, no children, no squeals of laughter. I make myself walk on quickly, one foot in front of the other, trying not to cry.

I pass the bakery on the corner, the smells hitting me before I reach the shop itself. They are thick and sweet. Cars are double-parked down our street, locals dashing from the passenger doors to pick up their breakfast. A long queue snakes from the entrance. Inside there are piles of pork buns, slices of dark honey cake, rolls topped with pork floss, bread with ham laid on top and stuck fast with melted cheese. It is a different smell from bakeries back home. I tried a loaf of bread once, but the slices were thin and sugary.

A few blocks from the school I stop and take a long, slow breath. I am not crying. The moment has passed. I look around me; as if the urge or emotion might just be standing there, ready to surprise me. But there is nothing. Warm stillness. A breeze skates around the corner and lifts hair from my forehead. A taxi sails by; an old lady with a graying bob stares out at me. I realize I am only five blocks or so from Supreme Flower City. I can see it in the distance, iris purple, skewering that cornflower sky. In front of me, there is the building site for a new international school and a residential building in faded sage green. The sun is starting to heat up; I hear the sound of a drill making an effort. The construction site is not yet crawling with workers. There are a couple of men, but they are still rubbing their eyes, scratching their necks, and glancing around as if waiting for a supervisor to arrive.

One of the men notices me from where he is sitting up on a piece of scaffolding, swinging his legs. He is shirtless and smoking a cigarette. I know now that it is okay to stare here, but it still makes me feel nervous. Those dark eyes are unapologetic, as if asking, "What makes you so special?" Below him a dog, covered in mange, bits of rice soup stuck to his snout, gives me a canine grin, lips stretched back from his teeth and tongue hanging out to one side.

Mama might have gone to talk to the man. It wouldn't have bothered her that he was half naked or that he couldn't speak a word of English or that his dog looked like it was carrying a hundred different skin infections. She was a fund-raiser for Greenpeace once. She'd carry her sign-up sheets and clipboard wherever we went. She could talk for hours about harp seals or nuclear testing. She could describe a Japanese whale hunt in such gory detail it was as if she'd been standing on the deck of the ship herself. Her enthusiasm was electric—exhilarating and, under the wrong circumstances, slightly terrifying. Men signed up more often than women. It was Mama and not Greenpeace that did it. Especially in warmer weather, when she wore her hair loose and her skirts long. She looked as pretty as a fresh autumn leaf just fluttered to the ground. The kind that makes you think of days with cool breezes and walking hand in hand with someone you fancy.

I look back at the man on the scaffolding as he picks a piece of tobacco from his lips and spits on the ground below. His empty-eyed stare reminds me of Mad Martha. Mad Martha who used to wander outside my high school collecting soft-drink cans and muttering about Our Lord Jesus Christ. I don't think anyone knew her real name. The girls teased her, threw their cans over the fence for her to chase, laughed at her woolly hair and wobbling, glassy eyes. She spooked me, and I didn't go near where she usually was, until the day Jennifer Beasley came running up, an expression of urgency on her face.

"Your ma is down by the fence with Mad Martha," she said breathlessly, with all her fourteen-year-old lust for gossip. I knew before I got there it was going to be a scene. Girls were bunched up along the fence line—all high socks and giggles. I could hear Mama shouting. Something about being ashamed of yourselves and what would Gandhi do. I'm not sure my classmates knew who Gandhi was, but they were clearly amused. I peered over the shoulder of a girl with a blond spiral perm. Mama was holding Mad Martha in an awkward sideways hug. Her chin was thrust forward as she spoke. Poor Mad Martha looked bewildered, squinting out from Mama's armpit.

"If we all took an eye for an eye . . ." Mama declared.

Martha looked a little frightened, like Mama might be about to take one of hers.

"The whole world would end up blind!" Mama finished theatrically.

The crowd erupted in girlish laughter and twittering. Somebody actually applauded.

Perhaps Mama saw the red of my hair above the green-jersey-clad shoulders, because she called out, "Grace? Gracie, dear?"

But I had slunk back into the crowd. And then Mama was walking away, Mad Martha under her wing. The crowd cheered as another can went sailing over the fence and skittered near their feet.

"Mad Martha and her mate Barking Bertha," some girl with dark eyeliner joked. I caught Jennifer giving me a half-pitying, half-delighted, wide-eyed look. I ignored her. If it hadn't been hard enough to make friends before, with my secondhand uniform and chin full of bad skin, it was near impossible now. I would spend the rest of that year in the warm embrace of the library. Surrounded by piles of French cookbooks and out-of-date travel guides to far-flung places. Africa, Greenland, Australia, China.

The building site man breaks his stare and scratches his armpit. Perhaps I should head back home to bed. The air is humid and thick, and I feel worn out. Facing me is the courtyard of an apartment complex, three apartment blocks arranged around it in a U shape, all clad with green tiles that are chipped and graying with age. Most of the windows are covered in rusting metal grilles, off which damp clothes hang. I walk into the courtyard to look at the small businesses which occupy the ground floor, though most seem to have moved on some time ago. One looks like a travel agency, posters bleached and peeling against the glass. Another is a beauty therapist called Depil House. There is a blackboard outside advertising a sale on Havaianas flip-flops, a drawing of a single flip-flop carefully executed in lime green chalk. A barber must have worked here once, but the shop is closed up, the windows silty. A striped pole still rotates drunkenly.

There is only one piece of writing in English, and it catches my eye. It is handwritten at the bottom of a fresh sheet of white paper stuck to a window, topped first with Portuguese and then little black Chinese characters. SALE. SHOP WITH OVENS. GOOD PRICE. OR TO RENT. PHONE: 6688 3177.

I peer through the murky glass into what might have once been a café. Cane chairs are stacked against a wall. The floor is covered in white tiles with little black diamonds in the center of each group of four. They are filthy with a sticky-looking dust. At the back of the room is a counter, a Portuguese flag hanging behind it. The top right-hand corner has come unstuck, so it sags down from that side. I step away from the window and look back at the sign. SHOP WITH OVENS—there must be a kitchen back there, I think.

A sharp voice slices through my loose thoughts. Someone is yelling in Cantonese. I look up, and an old woman in floral pajamas is leaning out her window. Her face is twisted in disapproval. She jabs her finger in the air, shouting something in Cantonese. I can feel awkwardness creeping over me. Not knowing the language makes me feel clumsy and stupid.

"Sorry!" I call out in a strangled voice, raising my palm in an apologetic wave.

Taking a few steps backward, I stumble. My bum makes a thick, dull smack against the concrete.

"Shit." I don't look up in case the woman is smirking at my fall. I stand and brush the dirt off the seat of my pants. My face burns with embarrassment, and I move away from the shops. Just before I leave the courtyard, I turn one last time to look at the sign. It stares back at me, pale as a dove's wing on the dark, empty window. I put my head down and point my shoes toward home. A few steps on and I hear another voice. Laughing. I glance over my shoulder. Only then do I notice another woman leaning out on her balcony, in the block opposite the woman in her pajamas. She is calling back and pegging up shirts and trousers. She shakes out her wet clothes, grunting and nodding to her friend across the way. I realize then that they are just talking to each other, nothing to do with me at all.

Somewhere inside there comes the sound of Mama's voice, laughing. "Oh, Gracie, you need some courage, girl; some of your mama's shamelessness."

The shamelessness that was always getting us into trouble, her and me both. The shamelessness that had us packing for Paris to make our fortunes or holding midnight picnics in Kensington

Gardens. The less I had of that the better. Or so I had always thought. I chew on the inside of my lip as I walk home. Wishing my cheeks weren't now as red as my hair.

"It won't take long."

There is an almost imperceptible pleading in his voice as he lays a fresh shirt on the bed. I look up from my book.

"It's a work thing. It'll look weird if I'm there alone."

Again, I imagine him adding.

"They want to meet you, Grace."

Unemployed, infertile, waitress—wife. Yes, I am sure they do. I reply: "I don't know. I don't have anything to wear." It's at least partly true. I don't buy clothes for going out to cocktail parties, probably on purpose.

He takes a black dress from the wardrobe, runs his hand over it as if I were in it already. Down the side where my thigh would be. I haven't worn it since the Christmas before last; I don't even know if it will fit.

"How 'bout this?"

I turn back to my book and shrug, but feel his eyes on me.

When he goes into the shower, I stand up and touch the dress, lying next to his shirt on the bed. It's cool, with a wet kind of sheen like a seal. I take off my clothes and slip it over my head. It fits. I run my hand through my hair and think of Mama again. Now, she had some party clothes. Her wardrobe was always filled with the brightest rainbow of silks and satins. I prefer blacks and neutrals; they go with everything. I draw in a deep breath.

"I'll go," I say. Not loud enough for Pete to hear over the watery roar of the shower, but loud enough to convince myself.

* * *

I find myself hiding in a candlelit corner as far as possible from the DJ, bar, and crowds. I can see Pete over some heads, a little gathering around him, faces thrown back in laughter or leaning in as he whispers some story. Every time the waiter with the cheese platter comes by I take two or three cracker loads at a time. I give him a polite smile, hoping he can guess I once did his job and I know his feet hurt like pins are being driven through the heels. The expensive cheeses are salty and soft against the crispness of the crackers, and I realize how hungry I am. How little I have been eating these past weeks. Perhaps the waiter can sense this too; he begins to make a beeline for me each time he comes from the kitchen with a new plate. Goat, blue, Brie. Soothingly thick and creamy in my throat. I am grateful to be ignored in this nook of the room; no one notices my feasting. They are all concentrating on saying the right things, laughing at the right times, and smiling broadly to show how interesting everything is. These banal scenes are replicated all over the room.

A slender, gentle-faced Chinese woman breaks out of the circle around Pete. She glides my way. My stomach twists as I brush crumbs from the skin of the dress. I angle my body away from her and look out the window with what I hope is a casual glance.

"Grace? Grace, 'ello, I am Celine. I just met your 'usband, Pete. He said you would be standing somewhere 'ere." A slender hand extends into my view. The woman has such an unnervingly beautiful French accent that I am unable to resist turning to stare at her. The sound of it gives me a little jolt, like remembering something from long ago. I blink and forget to speak in return. She smiles warmly. Celine, which rhymes with *serene*, reintroduces herself with that voice as smooth as double cream. I shake her soft hand. Her round face, the color of moonlight, is pointed at the chin, making her look as innocent as a child. She chatters easily, as if she doesn't expect me to contribute much, explaining that her family is from China but she grew up in Paris. She is here with her husband and is working as a French teacher because, well, she is French.

"Pourquoi pas?" Why not? She says with a shrug and a laugh.

I find myself smiling back at her. She has that teacher's way of noticing a wounded stray and tucking her under her wing. I feel myself surrendering to being looked after.

"Now, you must meet Léon."

She takes my elbow and gently guides me out of the air-conditioning and onto the balcony. We are seventeen stories up in the restaurant of a brand-new and shiny casino; it's like being on top of a Christmas tree. The view from here is striking—Macau peninsula lies just beyond the water, its reflection shimmering in the dark. The lurid lights seem so much lovelier at night. Even the bridge is sparkling with the headlights of taxis streaming across it to Taipa.

A tall man leans forward on the railing, holding a big glass of wine. He seems to be having the same thoughts I am, a smile on his face as he gazes out at the city with eyes shaped like almonds, dark brows. His hair is thick and silvery, brushing the top of his collar. His full lips press against the glass as he takes a mouthful. He turns slightly and looks toward us, eyes softening with tenderness and smile stretching, displaying pearly teeth. My chest tightens, and I suddenly feel too drunk. A little dizzy at least.

"Léon! You have to meet Grace. Grace, this is my 'usband, Léon."

"Hi," I murmur.

He leans forward and kisses my left cheek, then the right.

"Good evening, lovely to meet you," he says with genuine warmth. He sounds just like the Paris I remember. City of love and mysteries. It makes me catch my breath.

I watch Celine's hair blowing in the breeze as she talks about her students. Her eyes light up when she describes one earnest child with terrible pronunciation; her laughter has the silvery sound of a flute. I want to know if they have children, but my throat thickens and I can't say anything. I look at the two of them against that glittering view. She is wearing a white silk shirt and he a blue linen one. It makes me think of laundry ads for detergents that make whites whiter and colors brighter. Such demanding, needy fabrics, silk and linen. But they look effortless, leaning into each other in a comfortable way that makes me feel a little sad. They look like the couple smiling out from the photo frame before you slide your own photo inside. The couple you wish you were.

Celine excuses herself to fetch more wine, and I look up to see Léon smiling at me.

"I'm so sorry, you must forgive my English, it is not very good." His accent is as thick as butter, but each of the words is clear. I wish I had learned more French, but I have never been good with languages. I think it takes an extrovert.

"Oh no, not at all. Your English is very good. My French is quite terrible; don't apologize."

"Well, you are kind. I find it hard sometimes, you know? People find it difficult to understand what I mean." He sighs and laughs. As he leans back on the railing, I notice a little crooked square of stubble he must have missed when shaving. I have a ridiculous urge to put my finger there to see what it feels like. "You like the food, *non*?"

"Sorry?"

"The catering. You like it? I saw you eating the cheeses."

My dress feels tight around the waist. I beg my face not to turn crimson. "Oh. Yes. I do like the food. It's very good."

"This is my restaurant, where I work. I am the chef here."

"I didn't know. I . . . I used to be a waitress." I don't know why I offer up this information. It seems to rush out of me. I change the subject. "The Pont-l'Évêque was very nice. It's from Normandy, isn't it?"

"*Oui*. Yes, it is." Léon raises his eyebrows and smiles. "Ah, a woman who knows food." Then he frowns. "I wish Celine would eat more. She is too small. Like a sparrow. I worry." Léon releases a puff of air from between his full lips disapprovingly. It must be a French version of "tut-tut."

"Oh, well . . ." I fumble for something appropriate to say. Inside my chest I feel my heart lift, and a proper smile almost reaches my face. Almost.

Pete and I head home that night in the wet air, silence drawn out between us. He makes little grunts every now and then, as if he is agreeing with himself. Must be thinking about something to do with work. We get home, and he puts on the BBC and takes off his shoes. I go into the bathroom to remove my makeup. There is the murmuring of English reporters in the background when I climb into bed with nothing on and put an extra pillow under my head. I reach under my bedside table for the pile of cookbooks I have stacked there. I am reading *Rick Stein's French Odyssey* when Pete comes in from the lounge room. He goes to the bathroom to brush his teeth.

"So you had a good time tonight?" he calls out.

"It was okay."

"Told you it would be."

"Mmm . . ."

He pulls off his shirt and tie, dumping them onto the chair by the end of the bed. He looks at me, or the book cover, I'm not sure which. He puts on fresh boxer shorts. The orange striped ones he likes to wear to bed. He lies on his back looking at the ceiling, places a palm against my thigh. The dehumidifier strums away, while I learn the secrets of good onion soup. Clear and brown, smelling of the streets and corners of Paris. What a lot of onions. I think about going to the Taipa market tomorrow.

"Night then, love," Pete says. He sounds cool, distant, his hand sliding off my leg.

A little while later I say good night to Rick Stein, closing his book. My mind is full of recipes and French food. My stomach is full of cheese. I turn off my lamp and roll over, facing the dark hump of bedsheets that is Pete asleep. I put my hand on his thick shoulder, feeling the warmth of him through the sheet, before turning over.

Dearest Mama,

I've been dreaming about French food. Remember the cheeses? The breads? How we imagined opening our own bistro? You and me serving baguettes and soup du jour. A terrace in the sun, white plates and silver cutlery. Dogs drinking out of saucers, high heels tucked under wrought-iron tables. The thoughts seem to scroll along with "Summertime." Playing in my head, round and round like a licorice-colored record. You know, from Porgy and Bess?

I've been thinking about Paris, Mama.

I remembered how I knew this song. I mean, the first time I ever heard it. When I woke up in the hotel and you weren't there. The night was black and cold. I was just tall enough to reach the light switch, although I had to jump to flick it on. I thought you might be in the corner or behind the wardrobe, playing a trick on me. I checked under the bed, but there was only a sticky throat lozenge covered in lint. I sat down on the bed for a while, pulling up a piece of the quilt, sticking it in my mouth and chewing. Then I put on my boots all by myself and my winter coat over the top of my nightgown, and crept out of the room and down the stairs. The porter was snoring in his chair.

Outside the night air was icy, and the tops of my legs got covered in goose pimples.

"Mama, Mama, Mama, where are you, Mama?" beating a little chant in my head. Right or left? The wind bit at my ears and blew around my thighs. My heart was racing in my chest. I turned left. No one was on the street; it was as quiet as a church and slick with the rain that had fallen that afternoon.

Not too far away, I could hear loud music coming out of a dark café. A trumpet! Bah bah baaaaaaahhhhh, it sang. It was warm near the doors, and there were a few people standing outside laughing. I moved closer, rubbing my hands together. They were smoking long, thin cigarettes and talking above my head. I stood near the glass of the windows and listened to the crooning of my favorite instrument. I loved that it sounded so pretty and so strong at the same time. I had tried playing it once in music class. It didn't sound like this—proud, pure notes streaming out from the golden tubes. All my sounds had been like farts—loud, rude, and brief. Listening to that trumpet, I suddenly felt too cold. I pressed myself against the window, fighting lonely tears. If I'd known a prayer, I would have said one. Instead there were just two words on my lips. Please, Mama.

As if by the magic of wishing it to be so, I saw you then, through the warped glass, dancing by the stage in your silky peach dress. Your cheeks were red, your skin shining. "Mama, Mama, Mama! It's Gracie!" I called to you, sure that you would see me.

People were looking at me now, through the fug of their smoke. A woman bent toward me. She wore a red jacket and tall black shoes. She was speaking, but I didn't understand her French. I felt like I was stuck at the bottom of a well. She tried to pull my arm away from the window, turn me to her, but I shook loose. As soon as she let go, I started running. Back to the hotel, hot blood and fear pumping through me. I was crying when I flew past the dusty lobby, my boots heavy on the stairs. I slammed the door behind me and locked it from the inside. I leaned back against it for a time, dazed, my chest heaving. Then I climbed into bed with my boots and coat still on and pulled the quilt over my head. Sticking my cold hands down between my knees to make them warm, I fell asleep.

I don't know when you came home. Late in the morning when I woke up, my coat was on the floor, folded on top of my boots, and you were at the window, tapping your fingers against the sill. The makeup was washed off your face, save a few clumps of mascara under your right eye. You were wearing a robe, wet hair twisted in a towel, red-painted toenails peeking out from the bottom. You had a little white patisserie box tied with a ribbon on your lap, and you smelled like sugar.

"Oh good, you're awake. Today we really have to go to the zoo, Gracie. I don't know how long it has been since we saw animals. Do you remember?"

I shook my head.

"Well, it's polar bear weather, don't you think?" You jumped onto the bed, squashing one of my feet as you landed. You tickled and cuddled as I bit my lip. Maybe I had dreamed it all.

"You left me . . ."

"Oh no, sweetie."

"Yes, you left me. Last night." I started to cry the same hot tears from the night before, like they'd been waiting behind my eyes.

"Shh, shh, shh . . . Hey, don't you cry now," you said. "Have this. It'll make everything better. Mama's promise." A wink as you handed me the box. Inside, the prettiest cake I'd ever seen, button-round. A macaron, *you told me.*

We went to the zoo that day, didn't we, Mama? Stayed out too late, until the sun went down and I got a chill. We never talked about the bar. The jazz bar playing music from Porgy and Bess, *where you were singing and dancing in that peach-colored dress. How you had* left me in a hotel room around the corner, until you came home in the morning.

So many mysteries, Mama, always so many.

Your loving daughter,
Grace

La Poudre à Canon—Gunpowder

Gunpowder Green Tea with Sweet Mandarin Buttercream

Pete has been busy with work. Late nights and dark circles ringing his eyes. A couple of evenings he falls asleep on the couch in front of the television so I have to wake him and guide him to bed. I have run out of sleeping pills, so I spend most nights listening to him sleep with my eyes wide open in the darkness. These are the long nights when I can't stop thinking of children. Skipping, dancing, running in after school for a warm snack. Pink babes in my arms. The smell of freshly washed hair. Feeding a small one from my own breast. This last thought is the worst; it makes my whole chest ache as if my heart is made of river stone. I cry in the bathroom with the door shut so Pete doesn't wake up. My mind races like a cat chasing its tail. Like there is no end. I wish for sleep over and over, chewing on the bedsheet like I did when I was a kid. When it finally comes, I dream my way through the mornings till midday, half the day blissfully disappeared.

During the afternoons the only thing that seems to hold my interest is baking. I go through my recipe books. Soft-centered biscuits, cakes slathered with icing, cupcakes piled up in pyramids on round plates. Pete doesn't say anything, although every morning he takes out the rubbish bags filled with stale muffins and half-eaten banana loaves. The only thoughts that seem to distract me from babies are those memories of Paris. A gray cold, tall men, black coffee, sweet pastries, and Mama laughing, with her hair and scarf streaming behind her. The smell of chocolate and bread.

On a warm Thursday night before sliding into Chinese New Year, we go to the Old Taipa Tavern. It's an English-style pub, popular with the expats, sitting on one side of a village square next to a Chinese temple. Adults talk and drink cold beer out of sweating glasses while their kids ride their bikes around and around on the concrete. The older boys buy "throw-downs" from the local shop, tiny paper packets of dynamite or gunpowder, something explosive, which fit neatly in a small palm and make a loud snap when thrown against the ground. They lay them down where the younger ones will ride over them, frightening the color out of their cheeks when they pop, making them burst into tears.

Pete and I sit outside, although the sun is fading, and I order my standard sausages and mash. Pete chews on his lower lip and can't decide. His face is dark and drawn when he finally places his order. A burger.

"Everything okay?" I ask as our waitress heads off to attend to a table of loud Aussie blokes calling for "another bucket of cold ones."

"Yeah, fine." Pete slugs down a big gulp of beer.

I watch a small man with sagging trousers lock the big red doors to the Chinese temple. His face is lined and serious, a single long hair sprouting from a dark mole on the side of his chin. He sees me watching him and blinks like a cat. He hops on a bicycle, rides away.

"Work is a mess."

I turn back to Pete. He is picking at the label on his bottle.

"The building work is shit. Everything needs to be done twice. I'm signing off on stuff I'd never approve back home. But there are deadlines, so what am I supposed to do?"

Pete has been involved with start-up casinos before. He has never shied away from a work challenge. In fact he's always seemed to relish them. That was why we moved to London before coming to Macau. Well, that and some half-baked idea that it would make me happier; that maybe I'd find some kind of peace and we'd have ourselves a neat little four-person family. Us, book-ending a small son and a daughter.

"Worst of all, half my team can't understand a bloody word I say."

I imagine him surrounded by Chinese, staring at him blankly, just as the man locking the temple had stared at me. Pete is used to being the captain of his ship.

"I don't know," he sighs. "It isn't what I expected." Then he pauses. "I mean, what are we going to do next, Gracie?"

I realize he is talking about more than his job, and I look down at my lap.

"Are you even here? Can I talk to my wife, please?"

He reaches over and lifts my chin. It's not so tender. His eyes flash with frustration and longing, his hand firm against my face.

"Pete . . ." I start, but nothing more comes out.

One of the guys at the table next to us looks over, his eyes curious across the top of his beer glass.

Pete says, "We haven't talked about it . . . I mean, a donor egg . . . other options . . ."

I twist my face away from his grip and speak through gritted teeth. "No! I can't do it, Pete. We talked about it before the test results, remember? I don't want to do it. I don't want to talk about it. I'm tired. My body is tired. I've had enough."

Pete lowers his voice. "Can't we at least talk about stuff? Jesus, Grace, it's not easy for me either, you know. All this and work as well. You don't understand. You don't *try* to understand."

I look up at him now. It feels like a slap. As if I have not been trying at anything. As if breathing and eating and sleeping weren't effort enough.

He looks deep into me, searching one eye and then the other as if hunting for something he's lost.

"I don't *try*?" My tone is cool and prim. I can't help it.

"That's not what I meant. Sorry," he says, the edge still in his voice. "It's just . . . Shit. I don't know what to do. What are we supposed to do now?" His voice is so low it is almost a whisper. He shakes his head sadly.

"I don't know," I say simply, strongly. It is a hard and clear statement, sitting between us like a piece of glass.

He sits back. We look at each other in silence. I have no energy for an argument. There are new lines on his face, like he has been lying against a wrinkled pillow too long, and I wonder when we got so old. I can see the loss and the sadness in his eyes. And I have to turn away.

"Sausage and mash? Cheeseburger?"

Our waitress has a white smile and skin the color of honey. Her name badge says SOPHIA. We both look up at her and nod like children. She brings cutlery, and I order a lemon, lime, and bitters. Pete cuts the burger into bits, chewing each piece slowly. The Aussies at the table next to us start to sing out of tune, some old AC/DC track. Then they cheer their own performance. They refer to each other by nicknames and last names—Fazza, Ballo, Smithy.

The light around us blushes into a rich apricot. In the courtyard a young girl on a bike yelps with such happiness she sounds like a tropical bird. Her long curls fly behind her as she races past her older brother, who whoops and tells her to go faster, faster. Her father quickly intervenes, scooping her up off the seat before she speeds and wobbles into a big crash. The bike tumbles sideways without her on it, and she laughs and throws her arms up in the air.

"I won! I won!"

"Time for bed, you," he tells her and laughs.

Pete looks down into his food, and we both pretend not to have noticed. I move the mash around with my fork.

The next morning Pete is gone when I wake up, the clock glowing 9:49. I add up the numbers like a bill. That's eleven cents change, round to ten, there you go, sir. I shake my head and sit up. The sheet is tangled around my waist, the legs of my pajama pants twisted around my legs. The pillow has been tossed to the floor, and my hair is thick and damp against my neck. Heat rises from me as from a road in summer, ebbing, ebbing, ebbing. I breathe out slowly, calming the quick skipping of my heart. The cool air from an open window finds me, caresses my temples as I let my head fall back to the mattress. *Hot flush.* The words get caught in my dry throat as I whisper them to myself. My body sending me a road sign—this is the direction now.

It has been a few days since I left the apartment, other than to fetch flour and sugar and royal icing mix. I have an impulse to walk to the gourmet supermarket, my mind already starting to wander the aisles. Maybe we can have an antipasti plate for dinner with cold wine in big glasses. I'll buy smoked salmon and ham cut from the bone, olives and cheese. Perhaps I can be a good stay-at-home wife after all.

I change into loose pants and throw on one of Pete's T-shirts. Beneath the sharp lemon scent of laundry powder, it smells like him. I tie my hair back into a ponytail and avoid looking at myself in the mirror, in case I give up on the idea altogether and go back to bed instead. The supermarket is several blocks away, and with the weather starting to warm up, it is not the most comfortable hike. When I finally get there, I am coated in a light sweat and my eyes are watering from the white sunlight. I curse myself for not wearing sunglasses; not only is it brighter out here than in the cave of my bedroom, but on the way I see one of Pete's colleagues waving at me from across the street. Sometimes I forget how small Macau is, all the expatriates practically living on top of one another. I wave and smile politely, relieved that he does not cross over to talk to me, and quickly enter the supermarket, where the air-conditioning chills the sweat on my skin.

"Grace?"

I squint toward the deep, rolling voice, my eyes still adjusting to the dim light. I make out only that it is a man, and he is tall. He comes closer and smiles.

"Hello? Oh good, I thought it was you. How are you?"

It is Léon.

I am sure I smell terrible, but he starts to lean in, so I just smile as best I can. He gives me a light kiss on each cheek, as soft as a bird's wing.

"Hi, Léon. I'm well, and you?" My voice is ever so slightly too high.

"*Bien, très bien,* very well. I haven't seen you since the party. What have you been doing?"

"Ah, this and that, you know. Not much." Hiding, hibernating, wishing the world away. He smiles at me so warmly, as if we are the greatest of friends, old mates. I feel like fading into the walls, wishing he would go back to his shopping. Instead he asks me what I am planning to make, and his eyes grow wide.

"Antipasti? This is a great idea! Will you let me help you?"

"Oh, sure."

"I have suggestions," he says firmly and takes my elbow.

He helps me find the salmon and recommends cheeses. I buy an herbed chèvre just because he seems so enamored of it. The same with a jar of stuffed green olives; they may not be fashionable, he whispers conspiratorially, but they are still the best. In the air-conditioned silence, he walks beside me, scanning the shelves. I find myself giving him pieces of information about myself I would never normally divulge. I, Grace Miller, chatter like a schoolgirl. There is something about him that sets my tongue loose. I am sure I look surprised while I talk; it's like listening to someone else. I tell him about going to Paris with Mama. The spontaneous holidays. The cafés, the pastries, the cups of dark coffee a young girl probably shouldn't drink. He listens and smiles and fills my shopping basket. He laughs hard when I tell him about the time I accidentally tipped a tray of glasses filled with red wine on a customer in a cream wool sweater, and I feel my heart race strangely in my chest.

In less than twenty minutes my basket is piled high and heavy. *Pata negra,* marinated eggplant, sun-dried tomatoes. Too much food to eat, let alone carry.

"Sorry," I apologize. "I've interrupted your shopping and here you are, having helped me with all mine."

Léon lifts the basket from my arms and passes it to the girl behind the counter, who glances at us as she scans the items.

"It is no problem. So good to meet another—what do you say, 'foodie'? And I was just buying jam." He holds up a single jar of raspberry jam the color of rubies. It is the same jam Mama would buy for us when we stayed in France, the texture runny, little lumps of berries soft on the tongue, tiny seeds sticking between teeth. "My daughter, she eats it every day. She is, how would you say it in English, an addict for jam?"

"Oh, of course," I reply, nodding. He has a daughter.

I try to refuse his offer to drive me home, but he calmly insists.

"You have too many things," he says simply. He plucks the shopping bags from my hands and puts them on the backseat. I get into the front seat and rest my hands in my lap.

"Okay, so where do we go?"

"Supreme Flower City, please."

"The purple one?"

"Yes. Please."

We drive in silence through the Taipa streets, lined with tall apartment buildings. Down the middle of our street a team of contractors is hanging up red and gold decorations. They are mostly depictions of rats, dancing and leaping in Chinese pajamas.

"You have just one daughter?" I ask.

"I have two." He looks over his shoulder to change lanes. "Lila and Joy."

"They're pretty names."

"*Oui.* Pretty girls too." He grins broadly. "And you?"

"Me? Oh, no. No kids." Saying it aloud makes me feel filled with sand. You would think I'd be used to it by now. But he seems not to hear my answer, watching the road as we swing into a roundabout. Either that or he knows not to ask anything further. I hold my breath until the right amount of time has passed.

"Just here, thanks," I say, pointing to the side of the road opposite the entrance to our block. After pulling over he hops out of his seat, leaving the engine running, and reaches for my bags in the back.

"You don't have to . . ." I protest, but he carries them to the door, the car still running and keys in the ignition. Inside, the doorman watches us from behind his desk with a blank kind of stare.

"Thank you so much, Léon."

"*Sans problème.* It's my pleasure. Enjoy your antipasti." He smiles easily and waves as he jogs across the road to his car. I watch him leave and feel my pulse return to normal.

When I open our front door, the television is blaring, which gives me a fright. Pete is sitting on the sofa, wearing only a business shirt, tie, and boxers. I drop a bag on the floor. He looks over, unconcerned.

"Hey, the tennis is on. Thought I'd come home for lunch." His head whips back to the screen. "That was out! Are you blind?"

I drag the bags to the kitchen and struggle to lift them onto the bench. A plastic container full of sun-dried tomatoes has split, and oil and tomatoes are all over the place. It is a mess but the smell is mouthwatering.

"Where were you?" Pete calls out.

"At the supermarket. I got us some antipasti for dinner."

"Ah."

"Léon was there."

"Ah."

"You know, Celine's husband, the French guy? The chef?"

"Huh?"

"Léon. He helped me do the shopping."

"Ah . . . Goddammit, he's going to lose. What is *wrong* with this guy?"

I rip open a packet of buffalo mozzarella, ivory spheres floating in a milky womb. I drain the liquid and cut a thick, creamy slice. Placing one of my runaway tomatoes on top, I stand at the kitchen counter and eat, the yellow oil running down my chin. It tastes rich and full. Like summer and sunshine. I lick my fingers.

I think of Léon and his two girls. What were their names? Lila and Joy. I wonder what they look like. Do they have Celine's slender gracefulness? Léon's full lips and thick brows? Do they have his sky-colored eyes? I think of them with inky ringlets and pretty silk dresses sitting at an old pine kitchen table covered in a red tartan cloth. Their tiny feet don't touch the floor, and they swing their legs with anticipation. Léon makes them toast, spreading it with thick layers of soft, salted French butter. One of them begs for jam. He smiles, full of love, and adds scoops of glistening raspberry preserve. He plants kisses on their high, pale foreheads as they grin up at him.

Pete walks into the kitchen. "Did I tell you about brunch on Sunday?"

I straighten up, feeling oddly guilty. The oil of the tomatoes coats my throat.

He crosses to the sink and fills a glass with water. "We've been invited to brunch on Sunday, at Aurora. At Crown."

My heart seems to hang suspended, mid-beat. I cough to clear my throat. "Oh? Okay, that sounds good. I love the *macarons* there."

"What?" Pete asks. "Those meringue things? Macaroons?"

"Maca*rons*. They're French," I add. "They're my favorite."

His gaze floats to the ceiling, thinking. He reaches down and pulls at one leg of his boxer shorts, which has crept up by his groin. I shake the thoughts of Léon and his girls out of my mind as if Pete might see them.

"I think the desserts have been cut. Too much effort. Or money. Who knows?" He shrugs.

"But what about Léon?" I whisper.

"Huh? What about him?"

"Well, it's his restaurant—is he disappointed?"

Pete snorts and shakes his head. "Don't reckon he would be if it's saved them some costs. I heard the price is reduced now too, lots more meat and Chinese dishes. Really good value."

"Oh, right."

"And they'll still have a small dessert menu in the evening, but it'll mostly be cheaper, outsourced stuff." Pete drains the glass and puts it on the counter. He kisses my cheek. "Don't worry about dinner for me tonight. I've got a late meeting with the builders. I'll grab a sandwich or something."

I nod dumbly as he leaves the kitchen and then look at the bags of shopping littered around me. I spot a grease-stained paper bag by the sink, balled up, smelling of chips and cheap oil. I watch Pete putting on his shoes, still twisting to watch the tennis, his mouth hanging slack. I lean against the counter and contemplate my antipasti plate. For one.

Une Petite Flamme—A Tiny Flame

Espresso with Dark Chocolate Ganache, Topped with a Square of Gold Leaf

Aurora's Sunday brunch buffet is world-class, desserts or no desserts. Your mouth starts to water the moment you enter and spot the seafood bar on your right—lobsters the color of blood oranges reclining on hillocks of shaved ice, oysters split open, their salty innards on show. Around the corner is an area devoted to cheese, huge rounds of fragrant, fresh Parmesan and a soft cheese with a gray-white rind, oozing and pungent. Behind the cheeses is a magnificent honeycomb hung on a metal frame and dripping down a silver gutter into a small bowl. The entire place smells like heaven—copper pots of hot, fresh bread being carried to tables, aged ham sliced from the bone, the chocolatier dipping soft pralines. It is an adult's Willy Wonka world, so far removed from the men crouched on street corners slurping congee and the aunties dragging stacks of flattened cardboard boxes to be exchanged for a few extra coins.

Pete takes me by the hand as I dawdle past the landscape of food; fresh, hot, sweet, sour, and salty. "Come on, we're late."

We arrive at a table with one couple already seated and two empty chairs. The couple is deep in conversation.

"Pete! Hey!" exclaims the man, catching sight of us. He has a strong Canadian accent. Thick brown hair springs enthusiastically from his forehead, and his jaw is wide and square. His face is a healthy caramel color; he looks like he should be hiking in fresh air somewhere else. "You must be Grace." He reaches out to pump my hand.

"This is Paul," Pete explains. "Paul works on the construction side of the project."

"That's me," Paul agrees and, putting his large paw on the shoulder of the woman next to him, says, "This is Linda. My wife."

Linda looks up, her pink mouth curved in a polite smile, and leaps to greet us. She is wearing a short floral dress, and her blond hair is pulled back in a ponytail. "Hi, hi!" she chirps.

Pete leans in to kiss her hello. She kisses him on each cheek.

"Nice to meet you, Linda. This is Grace, my wife; she hasn't met a lot of women here yet, so it's great that we can get together like this."

I cringe as he says this, feeling like some sort of charity case. "Nice to meet you both," I mumble. I stretch my lips in a smile, hoping it looks sincere.

"So good to meet someone new." Linda beams at me and then adds wryly, "This place is like a small country town."

I take a pat of cool, homemade butter from the small silver dish in front of me. Rock salt, placed on top of each round, sweats a salty dew. The butter softens against the warm flesh of the bread roll, spreading easily.

Pete and Paul talk of work permits and foreign labor. Their heads are close together across the table, apart from when Pete recalls something funny and Paul leans back and roars with laughter, clapping his wide hand against his knee.

I chew the hot, sweet bread slowly.

"So . . ." Linda leans in toward me. "You're not working?"

"No," I reply. "Well, not yet, I guess. I was working in London, up until Pete got the job offer and we decided it was too good to pass up."

"Oh, I know what that's like. When Paul got his offer and told me about the five percent income tax here I said, 'Honey, you've just got to take that job!' It can really get your whole family ahead, you know?" She flutters lashes that seem impossibly thick. I wonder if she has fake ones glued in among her real ones. I stare a little too long.

The conversation is interrupted as our waiter takes a drinks order. He has glossy black hair and smooth skin, a soft, kind voice. "What can I get for you, ladies?"

Beers for the boys, champagne for Linda, and a cup of hot black coffee for me.

"Strong, please," I add.

As he leaves Linda drops her voice and pats my knee. "They just don't get it, do they?"

"Sorry?"

"Coffee. They just don't do good coffee. I mean, sure, boil some water, drop in a tea bag, but coffee . . . It's killing me, living without my morning joe. *China.*" She shakes her head and rolls her eyes, pale and blue. "It's not easy to live here, especially when you're a *'tai tai'* like us. I get so damn bored." She pushes back a hair that has escaped the ponytail and grins at me. I nod, and she keeps talking, not seeming to notice that I'm not saying much. I get distracted looking over her shoulder at the buffet, the smells drifting toward me. I catch pieces of what she says.

"I cannot stand a badly ironed shirt. Isn't that the least you should expect from, you know, them?"

"Ballet and swimming lessons on the same afternoon! Can you imagine? That is just poor planning."

"There's only one place to buy your handbags. Don't worry, sweetie, I'll show you."

"So I said, 'You've just got to let her go!'"

I wish I were better at making girlfriends. Or at least understanding other women. Sometimes it feels like they are speaking another language. I can't keep up with Linda's conversation, and when I do I grow so bored I start to think about recipes and growing rosemary on our windowsill. Her mouth is perfectly pink, the liner blended expertly into the lipstick. I reach into my handbag for some Chap Stick.

"Hello." Léon takes me by surprise. He is dressed in his chef whites. He leans over to kiss Linda, who gives a pleased grin as he brushes each of her cheeks with his lips.

"How are you?" I ask, standing.

Pete's eyes drift over to us from across the table but then quickly move back to Paul, who is talking animatedly, gesturing with his large hands about some new concrete construction technology.

"I am fine," he says. "Happy that we are busy today and everyone seems to be satisfied. A relief."

"Yes, I'm sure it is. The restaurant deserves to be full, though, the food is divine."

He nods graciously, then quickly surveys the room. When the waitresses or other chefs see him looking their way, they smile.

"I heard that you're not serving desserts anymore?"

His face falls ever so slightly, but he masks his disappointment quickly. "No, I'm afraid not. Other than the chocolates and some catering we do, no. I am told they are . . . not financially viable." He gives a resigned shrug. "It is a pity. My pastry chefs are excellent."

"It *is* a pity," I agree. "The desserts were so good. Especially the *macarons*. I have heard they are hard to make."

"Ah yes, the *macarons*." He nods. "Well, I haven't given up hope. One day Macau will be ready for *macarons*. Maybe not with my brunch here, but one day."

Linda drums her nails against my shoulder. "Gracie dear, I'm *starving*. We're all heading to the buffet." She takes a sip of champagne before walking past us with a simpering smile, looking at Léon rather than me.

"I should get back to the kitchen," Léon says. "I hope you enjoy your meal. Make sure to let me know how you like it." He steps away politely, then turns back. "If you ever want to learn to make *macarons*, I am happy to share the recipe with 'the foodie.' They're not so hard when you know how."

"Thanks," I say with a smile.

Heading to the buffet, I see Linda, Pete, and Paul huddled together by the ham. The thick flesh glistens with a honey glaze, its skin studded with cloves, like neat freckles. It is so large it could feed a family for a week. Linda laughs at something Pete has said. Paul reaches over to him and gives him a couple of good-natured back slaps. Standing together like that, they look like old friends, maybe even siblings. Paul, then Linda, then Pete. A little row. I pause for a moment with my plate loose in my hands. Our waiter comes to stand beside me, tray full of dirty dishes, forks, and knives. We both look over to them like farmers watching cows, separated by fence and species.

"The turkey is good today," he whispers.

Later that night a boom thunders through the apartment while I am sitting on the toilet. The throaty rumble of an explosion. It is the fastest piss I have ever taken. Up and wiped, fumbling with my jeans, I sprint into the lounge room.

"Did you hear that?"

Pete is motionless on the couch. He lifts his head sleepily.

I do up my fly and the top button of my jeans, rushing to the window. In the distance there is smoke and light. I squint to make it out better. I put my hands on the glass.

"What is it? Are we safe?"

Pete saunters over, yawning. He puts his hand on my shoulder and gives it a squeeze. "Reckon we'll be fine."

Thinking of bombs or earthquakes, I push him away from the glass, but he just laughs as he stumbles back a couple of paces.

"It's just fireworks."

"What?"

"Fireworks. For Chinese New Year."

As he explains, plumes of green sparks flash across the sky and twinkle slowly toward the ground. A few seconds later the noise travels to us, booms and rumbles like an angry dragon. Steadying himself, Pete pats me on the back.

"You okay?"

"Yeah. I didn't realize. . . . A new year . . ."

"Yup. The Year of the Rat." He walks into the kitchen still talking, raising his voice over the noise. "I think it goes on for a week. You can actually go and let them off yourself, by the water. They're huge things, apparently. Even the little kids let off these enormous rockets . . ."

He comes back with a cold beer in his hand, a Tsingtao, the condensation sweating down the side of the bottle. He lifts it to his lips and sucks at the neck. I notice his unshaven chin, dark against the pale, hairless cleft in his throat. He looks back at me, his eyes green tonight, flinted with gold. I realize we haven't had sex since that day Dr. Lee called.

"We should go down there, check it out—if you want to." He shrugs.

I watch a red rocket explode into sparkling splinters. When

I turn back to Pete, I can see the reflection of the rocket's light splashed across his cheeks and forehead.

"Hello? Wanna go? Gracie?" He sounds exasperated. I hate it that he cannot wait for me to think for a minute and then reply. He's impatient these days. When we first married, he would put his head to one side and watch me while I made a decision, his gaze roaming over my hair and eyes and lips. He never shook his keys or told me to hurry up. It was a gift, the patience he once had for me.

"Sure, let's go then."

The fireworks area is cordoned off from the street with tall tarpaulins, which block it from view. It is on the side of the road closest to the water, facing Macau peninsula. There must be a site on the other side too, as fireworks are erupting sporadically in front of the pointed needle that is the Macau Tower. On our way in, there is a warning notice that reads: PLEASE BE CAREFUL WHEN ENTERING THIS AREA. ALL CHILDREN MUST BE SUPERVISED. NO ANIMALS ALLOWED. PLEASE REFRAIN FROM SMOKING. Smoking would be unnecessary, as the air is thick with gunpowder and fumes. Pete rubs my back distractedly, staring at the mayhem. Adults and children have the same look on their faces—round eyes, mouths split wide open in laughter. The delight is almost palpable. A few Filipino maids and nannies sit off to the side jiggling babies and covering their small ears. They seem to be the only grim ones in sight. They look worn down, from the inside out. One of them catches my eye and attempts a polite smile. I nod back at her.

"Did you see that?" Pete cries.

Above us a huge shower of golden light crackles and slaps against the night sky. Pete whoops and cheers, and people nearby turn to give him the thumbs-up, laughing.

"This is awesome," he sighs, suddenly sounding like an adolescent. "Wait here while I find out where to buy some rockets."

Before I can reply, he has disappeared into the fog. I lean back against the metal scaffolding holding up the tarp and cross my arms over my chest. Kids scurry in front of me, reaching up to grasp their parents' fingers or dragging them forcibly by the elbow. I spot a young woman standing off to the side, leaning as I am against a pole. Her face is set in the sulk of a teenager, but her makeup is thick and dark. She wears a deep purple sweatshirt with a high neck, studded all over with printed gold stars. She catches me staring and glares back, unnerving me. She looks a little familiar.

"There's a bunch of work people here," says Pete breathlessly on his return. "Paul and Linda are just over there." He points and coughs.

"This smoke is pretty thick . . ."

"C'mon." He slips his finger through the belt loop of my jeans, pulling my hip sideways. His voice croons, like when we were first dating, hair falling into his eyes.

The woman leaning against the pole looks away from us then, chin pointed into the sky. I see her hands move in the deep pockets of her sweatshirt. They crawl over her stomach.

"All right."

Pete walks ahead, skipping through a few paces to get us there quickly. Linda and Paul must have been there awhile. Linda has a smearing of soot brushed across her blond hair and looks jazzed on whatever is in the expensive silver hip flask in her hand. She is wearing a summer dress and heels, which are getting sooty from their points up. Pete drags over a large paper bag, the tails of rockets sticking out. A grin is slung close up to one ear and all the way around to the other. Linda gives me a wink as if I am part of the gang; then she turns toward Pete, placing a slender hand on his shoulder as he pulls the rockets from the bag, giggling like a girl skipping class.

I stand back from the group and watch. Before long the crowd weaves between me and them, jostling us farther and farther apart, like the tide pulling back from the shore. Linda's whoops become less loud; she faces the peninsula, watching the bright plumes. Paul has his hands on his hips and feet wide apart. He rocks back on his heels to see up into the sky. Pete's face glows as he lights the rockets, illuminated by the spark. His tongue hides in the corner of his mouth, and hair curls wildly from his forehead. He looks like a boy. Like the guy I fell in love with.

I am standing with my back against the tarpaulin. The noises aren't distinct now; the bangs and pops and whirs could be any of the rockets, laughter belonging to all the groups, huddled around their fun. The sounds become thick and murky, as though I am holding my head underwater. Somehow, in all the noise, my thoughts still. It feels as if I might be invisible, standing here alone in this sea of people laughing and cheering, among the smoke and the bangs.

"What are we supposed to do now?" Pete's question from the other night floats through my mind. *Yes, what now?*

Above me the night sky is pale and quivering with smoke, a temporary quiet, spits and sparkles silenced. A break between sessions. The guts of rockets and burned ends of matchsticks litter the ground. The crowd moves and sighs as one great big animal, heaving, swirling around me like water around a stone rooted deep in the bed of a river. Out of it I hear my name. It gets louder, like a song, over and over.

"Gracie! Gracie! Grace!"

The air has turned cold. I warm my arms with a brisk rub. Above me a final, rogue rocket soars and erupts in the gray sky. It glitters sapphire blue and bright. The crowd looks up, mouths in silent circles. Something deep inside me dislodges. Tears off, falls away. I feel a kind of unpeeling. It happens in under a second, and then I know that my mind is made up. It is so bold it is probably stupid. It's more like Mama than me. A little bit of Mama's shamelessness and courage. The kind that was always getting us into trouble.

My arms drop back down to my sides, warmed now, as Pete shuffles toward me, pushing through the throng. He has black soot on his wide hands and across his shirt. He keeps looking back up to the sky, distracted, checking to see if a rocket is going off.

"There you are," he murmurs. "I was wondering where you'd got to."

Un Bon Début—A Good Start
Coconut with Passion Fruit–Spiked Buttercream Filling

I have already programmed in the number, all I need to do is press one button.

"Hello . . . I'm calling about the shop?"

The man who answers the phone is not speaking English. He is yelling, but not at me, perhaps at the small child who is letting out the great dramatic sobs that I can hear from my end of the phone. It sounds like Portuguese. Now he turns his attention back to me. "Eh?"

"I was wondering about the shop. Is this a bad time?"

Now there is a woman speaking in the background. The man clucks his tongue and says something conspiratorial to me, which I wish I could understand. Then neither of us says anything and we both listen to the woman. She is loud but firm. The child whimpers. The woman says something soft, soothing. There is quiet. A mother's touch. The man and I remain quiet for a few more moments.

"English-a?" says the man, in what sounds like a tone of distrust.

"Yes. I'm English. I speak English," I stammer.

"Okay," he says. "You come tomorrow to the shop? I bring my friend. He speaks the English."

"Oh, right. Sure. I can do that."

"Two o'clock, no problem, okay?"

"Okay, yes. No problem. Um, my name's Grace."

"Okay, Grace." He hangs up.

Pete drops his bag and coat onto a chair by the dining table and shakes his head, his mouth a thin line. He flips on a light, which makes me realize I am sitting in the dark. I sip from a glass of wine.

"Bad day?"

"Bloody nightmare." He sighs.

He's come home irritated every night this week, normally making a beeline for the computer to check his sports betting and zone out. He wriggles out of his leather work shoes; they fall with heavy percussion against the floorboards. He pulls at his tie so that the knot hangs around the third button of his shirt—defeated. Then he comes over, sits next to me, and looks out the window. He glances at my hand, which is propping me up, as if he might pick it up and hold it or kiss it. Instead he turns his head to stare back out at the night sky.

"Everything okay at work?"

"It's not even worth going into. It's just a mess." He shrugs.

I imagine what he does not tell me. The mass of problems and glitches that bloom during the opening of a new casino. The deadlines that have been missed, the poor performers who continue to drag the team down, the unrealistic expectations of the investors and the board. Pete has been through all this before, but his shoulders still droop with disappointment, as though he had hoped for something different. He pulls his hand over his face, rubbing, as if he is trying to wipe off the day.

"Wine?" I offer.

"Yeah, thanks. That would be great."

I refill my glass and pour one for him. It's only my second glass, but I can already feel the effects, my legs soft and leaden and my head lighter. Dutch courage.

He sits up on the sill, leaning against the opposite corner. We watch people walking back and forth on the pedestrian crossing below. The view is always so dynamic, people moving and going places. This place does not sleep for a moment. Some days it makes me feel like I am the only person in the world inside an apartment, doing nothing. It makes me feel like a sad princess in her tower.

Tonight there are a lot of children walking about with their parents and nannies and grandparents. I've become used to seeing little ones up at midnight or even later. I imagine Mama's shocked voice whispering in my ear as a child walks home from a restaurant with his parents, being tugged along by the arm. "My God!" she would have said. "It's well past his bedtime!" Forgetting that I had been awake at that time often—baking cakes, making volcanoes out of flour, building with LEGOs, drawing pictures of whales.

"I think it's a lantern festival or something. The end of Chinese New Year," Pete explains, as though he can read my thoughts.

"So we're well and truly in the Year of the Rat then . . ." I say.

He nods before leaning his head against the glass.

I think back to last week's fireworks and the bangs that splintered through my thoughts like lightning. "Is that why there are so many kids out?"

"Yeah, I reckon." He traces his finger around the rim of his wineglass.

He must be right, as a few of the children are bouncing inflatable toys containing battery-powered lights. Below us a brother and sister are skipping. He has a blue toy in the shape of a hammer, which he grasps by the handle, and she holds an enormous Hello Kitty head tied to a thin plastic stick. She swings it up and over her shoulder, like it's a fishing line she's casting. After a few swings, she connects with her brother's head and he spins around to face her. Soon enough the blue hammer thuds against her forehead. She lets out a round-mouthed wail. We can't hear it from where we are, but her face is red and aghast.

"Ha!" Pete snorts. "Did you see that?"

"I think Junior is going to get into trouble."

He raises his eyebrows in agreement. I can see the effect of the wine, moving down over his face as he slumps back against the window. He starts to relax. There is something in the moment that is suspended, the two of us sitting up here looking down at the world below. As if it were a dreamland, a movie; as if we were above it all like puppeteers.

"Pete, I have an idea," I say slowly.

"Mmm?" He is still looking out beyond the glass.

"I want to open a café."

"Yeah?" he murmurs.

"I thought I could use, you know . . . the money."

He turns to look at me.

I am being vague so I don't have to say things out loud. It is money we put aside for in vitro fertilization. But you need healthy eggs for that, and we both know that hope has dissolved.

He studies my face, and I wonder what he sees.

"I want to sell sandwiches, coffee . . . *macarons* . . ."

"Right. *Macarons*." His voice has tightened up, the words squeezed as if wrung out.

"Maybe it sounds crazy . . ."

"Sure does," he answers too quickly.

"You won't have to have anything to do with it, Pete." I drop my voice almost to a whisper in the hope of pacifying him. "It'll be my thing. I'll manage it, I'll run it."

He takes a gulp of his wine but is still not looking at me. I know he is listening, but he looks out the window and doesn't meet my gaze. His chin is lifted so he has to look down his nose at the scene below.

"Pete." I plead a little, reaching out for his hand. "I need . . ."

He turns his face toward me slightly. "It's a big responsibility." His voice is clipped. He looks down at the glass in his hands and starts to roll it back and forth between his palms.

"It's a lot of money. I know. But it'll be a business. It'll be an investment. I'll *make* money." I can hear a little nervous quiver in my voice, so I pause and swallow. "We should use the money for something useful, right?"

He raises his eyebrows. "You sound like you've made up your mind."

I know he wants to talk about the end of our dream. Of having our own child. But I cannot.

"Well . . ." My mind hovers above my argument, as if looking down upon it. I try to muster strength, conviction. "I know we could use the money for other things. But, this . . . this is what I want to use it for."

We sit in silence for a few moments, looking at each other. I feel uncomfortable, like this is a kind of standoff, as we try to figure each other out. The distance between us suddenly seems vast.

"It's not a good idea, Grace," he says firmly. Unreasonably.

"Maybe," I reply. "But I need something. Something that is mine." There is that calmness in my mind again, thick and cool. "Maybe it's not a good idea, or maybe it is a good idea. I know I have to try."

He gives a strange kind of half laugh. "You've barely been able to get out of bed. Now you want to run a business?"

I stare at him in disbelief. I have moved all the way to China for his career. I have had faith in him and his abilities.

"Why are you even asking me?" he continues. "Like I said, it sounds like you've made up your mind already."

I raise my chin. "Well, actually, I didn't."

"Didn't what?"

"I didn't ask," I say, and my eyes lock with his. My voice sounds so soft, but feels so strong rushing out of my throat, it is a surprise even to me.

Pete's eyes widen. "Right then. You have it all sorted." He stands, angry, throwing back the last of the wine in the glass. He looks down at me before turning to go into the kitchen. "I won't get in your way then. I'll leave you to it."

I can hear him putting his glass into the sink, the base hitting the metal with a loud clang. I feel queasy from the confrontation. Pete always manages our money and has the last word on our decisions, a fact that has never bothered me. Until now. Now it needs to be different. Beneath the churning of my stomach, something deep within is firm and quiet with knowing, unconcerned whether the business fails or not; I have to try.

Pete walks through the lounge room without looking at me, goes into the study. I hear him sink into his chair and make out the beeps and whirs of the computer firing up. The jingle of the home page of a sports betting site. The chair wheels creak against the floorboards as he pulls himself closer to the screen. I take a few deep breaths, navigating back to that sweet, deep calmness. I turn to the darkness of the window, watching the steady stream of customers in and out of the stores and the silky, luminous lanterns swaying from the lampposts studding the middle of the road. Out there, in the night, is the land destined to be a park. I can just make out the shape of a single tree, like a lonely exclamation mark.

Dearest Mama,

They have planted one tree. I think it must be a trial, starting with one tree and seeing how it goes from there. Perhaps they are not optimistic. Perhaps they think the land is not going to nurture such a thing. Perhaps that is what they hope for. What I love is that they have planted it in the middle of the whole block. Not to one side where it could lean wearily against the fencing, fatigued by its solitude. Not in one of the corners. But smack bang in the middle, as if to say, Well, there you go. Try surviving right there. *I do get the impression they would prefer it didn't. I get the impression that they would much prefer it if the whole one-tree experiment was a bloody failure they could report to the government and happily get on with icing the block over with concrete and turning it into a car park.*

But it's been about a week now and it is still standing. This morning I just about waved hello. I did smile, I admit. A real out-loud kind of smile. I'm surprised my face didn't split in two with the shock. In the daylight the shadows of the clouds crawl over the empty block and up and over the tree. The land is suddenly three-dimensional. I imagine the shadows having to pick up their skirts like old dames as they navigate over the inconvenient tree. I hear them cursing and complaining, as they lift up their rusty knees and heavy petticoats. I love the idea of the tree being such a nuisance to everyone. Those who planted her, the shadows that have to step over her. Sometimes I think I am in love with this tree more than with my husband. It makes me feel bold. And resolute.

Your loving daughter,
Grace

The pastry kitchen is colder than I had imagined but smells delicious, as sweet and crisp as the bite of an apple. The walls are covered in white tiles, and almost everything is made of stainless steel. There are quite a few Chinese chefs in the kitchen, busy at work. They don't look rushed at all, carefully executing their tasks. One chef is releasing praline balls from their molds and then dipping them in a bowl of melted chocolate. It looks like a silken soup, and my mouth waters. He drops each ball in with a large fork and slowly stirs it around. When it comes up again, it has the satin sheen of the warm chocolate. He rolls it, the fork providing a cradle against a marble bench top until it is cool. The fork leaves no crease or mark on the finished product, a perfect sphere. There is such slow art to it; I feel hypnotized.

"Grace!"

I turn to see Léon, wiping his hands against his apron. He gives me a wide, white smile.

"So good to see you. Welcome to our kitchen." A few stray beads of sweat hang delicately on his upper lip, and he blows out a dramatic puff of air. "Pardon. I have been in the bakery; it is very hot in there. I'm a little . . . what do you say? Overcooked." He laughs.

"No problem. Thanks for having me." My gaze falls, briefly, to the floor, in order to avoid looking at his lips, rosy with the heat. I notice my shoes are dusty with sugar or flour or both.

"No, no, no. It is my pleasure. It is so nice to have someone interested. Maybe Macau is ready for the *macaron* after all."

"Well, I love them. I hope the rest of Macau does too. I used to eat them in Paris." With Mama.

"I'm sure your café will be a success. You know, the most important ingredient in this kind of business is passion." He lifts his eyes to mine for a quick moment before his gaze shifts. The words *your café*, along with his brief stare, make me feel slightly electric. Then I remember all the forms and red tape I'm plowing through, fortunately with the help of the Portuguese-speaking previous owner of the shop. English is not an official language in Macau, and I don't have any connections here to get things done, so I feel like a spare part most of the time.. I hardly expect success; I'm hoping just to get the place open. I need to show Pete I can at least do that much.

Léon begins to move around his kitchen. He is gentle but clear with the staff, leaving a sense of direction and purpose in his wake. He accepts two bowls from a chef: one full of what looks like flour and another with egg whites.

"Here we are, this is where we start."

I come around to watch him from a better angle, facing him and the bowls from the other side of the marble bench.

"This is ground almond, sugar, and what I think you call 'icing sugar.' Oh, and cream of tartar, the little acid to make it rise," he says, patting the top of one bowl. "This other bowl, of course, has the egg whites. And now we need to fold them together."

Léon explains that the "folding" of the *macaron* ingredients is very important, gesturing with his hands that the mixture can be too flat and runny or too rough if not mixed properly. He takes both bowls over to a shiny white mixer, adding the dry ingredients to the wet slowly.

I peer into the mixing bowl. Baking always fills me with such hopeful expectation; Léon can sense it too.

"You enjoy this, *non*?" He laughs.

"Yes, I love it." I notice that I am suddenly standing with my palms pressed together and raised close to my chin. Self-conscious, I move them behind my back and try to keep them there, fingers knotted together.

"Okay, looks good." Léon switches off the mixer. "It needs to look like whipped cream. Thick, but not too stiff. The mixture must . . . ah . . ." He struggles to explain it, so instead shows me. He puts his finger into the bowl and presses lightly. As he lifts his finger up, the mixture clings on and then reluctantly lets go, remaining to stand tall like the top of a mountain.

"The mixture must stand in peaks," I finish for him.

"Aha, yes, that's it. Once it does this, then it is okay and ready. Today we are going to make passion fruit *macaron,* so we need to add a little color before we put it onto the trays."

He reaches for a bottle filled with a radiant yellow liquid. He squeezes a few drops into the bowl, and as he mixes it through carefully, the snowy contents become bright, practically neon.

He notices my frown.

"Not to worry, the cooking makes it a bit browner. It's the almond, you see."

"Oh, okay."

Back at the bench, a chef has prepared a plastic piping bag and a tray covered in a silicone sheet. Léon spoons dollops of creamy mixture into the bag and then starts to push out tiny rounds from the nozzle onto the tray.

"These are *petits macarons.* You can make them bigger if you wish. These ones, they are a good size for our parties; the guests can have just a taste. Sometimes we get some catering requests for *macarons* . . . not as often as I would like." He starts to fill up the tray with rows, sunshiny as the centers of daisies.

"Thank you for showing me this," I say. "It's very generous of you." I am leaning on the edge of the cool bench.

He pauses to shrug and smile. "It's my pleasure. I'm glad you are opening a café. You know, I love the way people are about *macarons,* cakes, these kinds of things. Sweets, I guess. It's in their faces. How they look. They make people happy, you know?"

I think of a cake Mama made me for my eighth birthday. It was a clock tower, like Big Ben, laid flat against a tinfoil-covered chopping board. It was smothered in a buttery, cream-colored icing that was as thick and soft as a cloud. Smarties and jelly beans covered the face, and the numbers on the clock face were made with twists of licorice. Running up the side, there was a little mouse with a plump marzipan body and licorice tail. Mama sang "Hickory Dickory Dock" and planted kisses under my chin and tickled me till I squealed.

"Yes, I know what you mean."

Léon bangs the tray on the marble top. The yellow buttons spread a little but stay separate from one another.

"Okay, come now, we go to the ovens."

The ovens are in the next room, stacked like shelves, at least ten or twelve in two tall columns.

"They need to be inside for about eight minutes. The oven is preheated to three fifty. You must make sure it is very dry. No steam at all."

We stand close together staring into the heat. The warmth is dry and pleasant and the silence between us comfortable as we watch the *macarons* slowly rise. Around us the staff is busy: rolling dough through a machine, chatting and mixing, laughing and pounding. But the jumpy, sharp sounds of Cantonese, which normally interrupt my thoughts, fade into the background as I stare at the tray. I can feel Léon's breath beside me. We are joined in the holy communion of this miracle: sugar and egg white and almond coming together.

The tops of the *macarons* become rounded and shiny, like buttons or bottle tops. Léon explains that we need to cook the undersides for a few minutes and then they must sit for a day or so. When they are done, he takes the cooked *macarons* from the oven. Back in the main kitchen, he talks me through the art of ganache, the soft, silky center of the *macaron*. He is not going to make the ganache for the shells we have just baked as they are too hot from cooking, so instead he mimes the process, gesturing while explaining what he adds, how he mixes it, what is important. He looks to the ceiling, searching for the appropriate words. He is so concerned that I get it right. As if it is his duty as a friend, as a chef, as a Frenchman. Finally he asks one of the chefs to help him in another room. I wait for a few minutes, watching as someone carefully peels ripe pears.

Léon returns with a glass plate—a traffic light of *macarons* down each side. He places it in front of me. "Voilà. *Macarons.* These ones I made yesterday for a party tonight, so they should be delicious."

He is right, of course; they are perfect. The first one I taste is dark chocolate with a center that is firmer than I had expected but that melts on my tongue in seconds. The second one is raspberry, the ganache retaining the roughness and texture of the fruit. The almond paste is stronger in this one, nuttier; blended together with the raspberry, it tastes of autumn. The last *macaron* is passion fruit. I know the shells are unflavored, but it tastes as though the entire sweet—the shells, the ganache, the scent—is alive with the zest of passion fruit before it even enters my mouth. Then, acidic on the tongue and rounding off a heavy sweetness. The perfume of the passion fruit *macaron* is like a bunch of lilies, assaulting and exotic. I close my eyes for a second, savoring each one.

"So, what do you think?" He is close enough for me to notice that the color of his eyes matches the cornflower blue initials stitched delicately onto his white chef's shirt.

"Wonderful. Really lovely." I smile at him, feeling drunk on the taste of divine *macarons*. He grins and looks down at the empty plate. I swallow with some effort and feel my heart run through a few beats.

"Good, that's what I was hoping for." He smiles.

Dearest Mama,

I might be a wanton harlot.

I knew that would make you laugh. But it could be true. I can't stop thinking about a man who is married. And I am married. We are both married but not to each other, which means such thoughts are wicked, aren't they?

Mama, he has an accent that brings to mind a sweet and smoky caramel melting in your mouth. I feel so ridiculous even thinking about him. Léon. Léon. Léon. It's got that soft, floating ending that could go on and on. And, I don't know how to explain but, he looks like Paris.

Mama, do you remember the front desk manager at that hotel? You know—that god-awful place that smelled of wet dogs and old carpet. How we ate sandwiches in our room that night and watched French television while you stroked my hair? It was so ghastly that place, Mama; I can't believe we stayed there. Even though it had a pizza-slice view of the Eiffel Tower. You always were too much of a romantic.

But that front desk manager, maybe he was the first love of my life. Antoine. Beautiful, soft, sweet Antoine. Do you remember? With the coffee brown eyes? Maybe you don't remember. He excused us that last night when we couldn't quite pay the bill. Must have taken pity on us two red-haired English girls. He was so kind to us, and he even held my hand for a second when he kissed us goodbye and I thought I was going to faint or wet my pants or something equally dreadful and embarrassing. Léon and Antoine. French men. Their souls have been crafted from the same rainbow.

Mama, I am married to a good man, and I must stop thinking such thoughts.

Your loving daughter,
Grace

P.S. Mama, he is a chef.

Raiponce—Rapunzel
Bergamot and Cardamom with White Chocolate Ganache

Grace Miller owns a café. My signature is on the papers; I put it there, it is done. It all happened so much quicker than I expected, and I have that strange smarting feeling, like the one you get when someone pulls out your tooth or rips off a Band-Aid really fast. Is it shock? I wanted this, didn't I? Some days it is hard to remember. Here I am with a café. Or here I am, I should say, with a big dusty mess that used to be a Portuguese restaurant and somehow has to become a café in the next couple of weeks. I need a glass of wine.

Outside the window a thick mist swims between the apartment blocks. It fills your throat and settles on your skin like a sweat, strange and disconcerting. I watch it drift milkily in the spaces between and around things. Inside, the microwave clock reads 17:38, in a sickly lime green. Pete has become accustomed to twenty-four-hour clocks after working in casinos for so long. Twenty to six. The lease papers are a thick bundle inside a white envelope on the kitchen bench. My name is typewritten in daunting black letters. Is it too early to be drinking? I pour myself a glass of the chardonnay Pete has left on the bench. Its warm, small bubbles prickle down my throat. I stroll through the apartment with my glass in hand, looking at each of the rooms. They could all do with a tidying-up, but I can't be bothered. My muscles ache; hell, even my bones ache.

Today the builders came to remove a wall in the café so there is an easy view from the front counter to the kitchen. My ears still thunder with the echo of the jackhammers, cracking through old plaster and wood. The floors are now covered in gray muck, stepped through and kicked about. My shirtless builders left a different color from when they arrived, sweat turning the floury plaster dust on their bodies to a sticky ash. It is days like these I wish I could speak Chinese. The team leader, the one whose number Paul gave me after I rang him to ask for any contacts he might have, speaks English perfectly, but he is hardly ever around. Cantonese would be best, but even Mandarin would do. It feels like a disability, speaking only English. I have tried to encourage the builders to wear earplugs or hard hats, miming hopelessly with my hands, but I was met with confused glares and shrugs. I imagine that when I am not watching they smirk at me behind their drooping cigarettes. I quickly came to realize it was best for us all if I just got out of the way. So now I only watch, and then come home to my empty apartment, ears ringing. Tonight Pete has sent me a text message to let me know he is going out for dinner and then to karaoke with his workmates. Bonding over off-key singing and drinking green tea with whiskey. I'm a little relieved that he doesn't invite me to join him.

I settle in our study, turning the chair to face the window. The glass is freckled with rain, and there is a smudge where one of us has leaned against it, looking out to the street below. My head is still full of floor plans, wallpapers, light shades, and napkin colors. Soon, too soon, I have to decide about the espresso machine and the walls. Perhaps the cheaper espresso machine will have to do, although the one I really want is silver and topped with a bronze eagle, like the hood of an expensive car. Deliciously Italian-looking but out of my price range. I bite my lip. I wonder if Pete will be right about this venture; a ridiculous expense that will come to nothing. It seems that waitressing all your life and opening a café are two such different things, I feel exhausted just thinking about it.

We've been lazy about unpacking our boxes since the move. I notice there is a box untouched by the desk, still sealed with wide brown tape. I slice off the tape and open the box. The papers inside are a complete muddle. Pete's, I assume; old reports and project plans and a flotsam of boring corporate debris. But as I start thumbing through, my fingers connect with the stiff edges of a bundle of photos. They're old; they still have those rounded corners, the colors bled to oranges and ambers, the focus soft and hazy.

The first shot is of me, standing in front of our apartment block in Islington. I'm wearing my waitress uniform, from the first real job I ever had. And I look embarrassed. It's not hard to imagine Mama behind the camera, proud and giggling. The next one I'm in France, teenage and sullen, on a bridge, again being forced to pose. The weather is grim and the sky slate gray. Yet another wild, last-minute trip. I sink down into the reading chair, flicking through the pile. They are all pictures of me. Me and a chocolate cake with candles, eyes wide and dreamy; me sitting on a picnic blanket, squinting up at the camera; me and the Houses of Parliament. Here I am skinny and frightened in my high school uniform and then, years later, sulking at the kitchen table with my hair cropped short. I take a big sip of the chardonnay and lean my head back against the chair. The wine crawls through the rivers and inlets of my blood.

The last pictures are of Mama and me together. She has a terrifically bad hairdo in one, with two distinct layers, short on top, long underneath. Luckily for her she had wonderful, glossy hair that looked pretty in just about any kind of cut. She's smiling so wide in that photo, a toddler-size me pressed back against her legs. I think I'm dressed as a fairy—I have wings made from coat hangers and kitchen foil. I don't look very happy about it; probably not the girlie, gauzy number I had been hoping for. But Mama—Mama looks like she just built the Eiffel Tower.

Mama's not smiling in all the pictures, though. Sometimes she looks off into the distance, or seems to be gazing through the camera. She has that faraway look she used to get, like she's hovering between this world and another. These are the photos I stare and stare at. Bringing them up close to my face, reviewing every line in her forehead, the way her mouth is hanging, the tension in her shoulders. I am looking for something in her face that I cannot find, a clue or a sign. When my vision starts to get fuzzy, I put down the photos and stare out the window.

The light is fading quickly now, turning mauve. The lights in the apartments opposite ours flicker on, one by one. Across from us a dark-haired woman washes dishes, a long, thick braid over her shoulder. Her head faces down toward the sink, and she doesn't lift it, working quickly through pots and woks and bowls and tongs. The braid hangs like a snake down her front and swings into her armpit as she moves. Then she glances up and leans forward toward the window. Her face looks small and pale. She reaches her hand between the security bars. I imagine her, like a girl in a fairy tale, tying her hair to a rail and climbing out and down between the silvery bars. She empties her palm, which was probably full of crumbs or scraps, before plunging it back into the sink.

I place my empty glass on the floor and lean back. My bones sink into the softness and I close my eyes.

*　　*　　*

I am wearing a dress with a print of elephants linked, tails to trunks, along the hem. I run my finger along the edge, imagining them trumpeting and stomping their feet. Mama has my other hand, and she is squeezing it tight. I'm pulled along, my feet lifting up and skidding along the ground. I look from her long legs to my short ones, feet tucked into new black boots with shiny buttons. I love these boots; they remind me of Little Orphan Annie, just like in the movie when she sings "It's the Hard Knock Life" and jumps on the bed. That is the very best part of the whole movie. To be honest, they pinch my skin a bit, the boots, but I don't tell Mama because they cost her a fortune.

Mama's red handbag is tucked into her side, under her arm, which is bent like a wing. She clears her throat, pauses, and clears her throat again. I look up to see if she is going to say something, but she doesn't; just keeps her chin stuck out and round eyes looking forward. Now we are on a high street, walking past a corner store and then a post office and a bank and a charity shop. I turn my head to see the mannequins, half dressed in coats and hats, a gray-haired woman wriggling on trousers and skirts. I giggle at the pale statues, lower halves exposed to the street. They have smooth, neutral rude bits, not like rude bits at all, and staring, painted eyes. The gray-haired lady catches my grin and shoots me a disapproving look. Mama tugs on my hand again to scoot me along. Finally, she stops. She swallows and licks her lips and brushes hairs from her coat that aren't really there. Her hand twitches in mine.

"Where are we, Mama?"

She looks at me, like she forgot I was attached to one of her hands. As she crouches down, her hair falls across her forehead. She lines up her eyes with mine. Underneath hers are dark smudges from not getting enough sleep, but she has put makeup over the top.

"Just wait out here for a minute, okay? This is really important. Mama won't be long. Afterward you can have a doughnut."

She smiles then, and pinches my cheek. This is going to be a good day. I think of the crackle of chocolate as I bite through to the soft guts of the doughnut, and sugar on my lips. I'm going to eat right around the edge, the whole wheel of it, until I get to the hole. Only that tiny little belly button in the middle will be left.

"Can it be a chocolate doughnut?"

She nods, pats the top of my hair. "Sure. Be good, okay? I won't be long."

We're outside a bakery, warm, sweet smells drifting from the interior. I take in a sniff of flour and hot butter, soft sugar. The bottom half of the window is painted, so I can't really see inside, except for the tops of heads and the light on the ceiling. Minutes go by that feel like hours; I brush the ground and sit down. Gravel gets stuck on my tights, and when I tug at it, the tar sticks and makes a hole. I put my finger against it so I can feel the cold, bumpy skin underneath. Mama is going to have a fit.

Noises come from the shop now, a woman screaming and yelling and carrying on. It sounds like Mama, and my heart stops like it is frozen. A man with a moustache comes out shaking his head slowly, gathering his coat around him. The bag he carries away in one fist smells like a hot mince pie. Something inside the shop must have fallen down, because there is a clattering sound. I stay as still as possible. Pretty soon after that Mama comes out. Her face is gray and tight.

"Come on, Grace, let's go."

She breathes in, puffing her chest out, and takes my hand. She glances down at my dusty tights.

"What about my doughnut?" I whisper. It's a stupid thing to ask, but I am so hungry my tummy is hurting.

"What?"

"My doughnut . . ."

I brace myself as she brushes me down. Her hand is hard and efficient.

A man in a white apron rushes out of the shop. He starts to plead with Mama.

"Hell, you've got to give me a few seconds to get used to the idea." His cheeks are red like apples; he smells like hot sugar. "You can't come waltzing in with that kind of news right in the middle of a shift." He shakes his head. "Why d'you always have to be so bloody crazy, so—" He stops speaking as his gaze drops to take me in. He sucks in a good long look at my face, and his mouth falls open. His eyes are soft, as blue as painted china. I notice his hands are covered in flour, but underneath they are wide and square with nails cut short and neat. "Is this . . ." He is still staring at me with his eyes as round as saucers.

The way he is staring makes me nervous, so I stop looking at his face and notice a tattoo peeking out from beneath his sleeve. It is a baby bluebird carrying a pink ribbon. I always wished for ballet shoes with pink ribbon like that. My feet are really sore and swollen in my boots and I want to cry, but Mama is so mad I keep it inside. Instead I will ask one last time. Just in case she forgot and it is sitting on the counter. Mama doesn't like to buy something and then forget it; it would be a waste of money. I imagine the lonely paper bag, darkening with grease, waiting to be remembered. I tug at the hem of her pretty coat.

"The doughnut, Mama?"

Mama looks down at me with a look like I will stay quiet if I know what is good for me.

"Forget the bloody doughnut," she hisses through her glossy red lips, turning away.

"Hey! Hey, wait . . ." croaks the baker, his hands hanging limply at his sides, face as fallen as a half-cooked sponge cake.

I am half dragged and half carried back down the street. Past the charity shop with the partially clad mannequins and the bank and the post office. The man is still yelling for Mama to stop, but he doesn't move to follow us. I twist back to see his face before we are too far away and it is white and sad, but he just stands there, like a statue. Before long he and my doughnut and the bakery are small and in the distance, and we are across a park and around a corner and back at a train station.

I am woken by a metallic jingling. Pete is struggling to get in, his keys rattling as he tries to force one into the lock. I imagine him swearing on the other side of the door. I think about getting up to help him, but the wine running through my veins keeps me rooted dumbly to the spot, legs curled up into the chair and blinking to see in the darkness. I guess it is late; my feet are cold. I scrunch up tighter to conserve warmth. Pete gets the door unlocked and swings it forward. He staggers like a drunken sailor in the bright square of light. From here he is only a silhouette. I wait for him to call to me, but he stays there, huffing out air. When he closes the door, the room is once again in a deep, velvety darkness.

He moves into the bathroom, his footsteps heavy and deliberate. I can't see him from where I am lying, but I can hear the tap being turned on and water being splashed. There is the whipping sound of a belt coming off and grunting as shoes thud to the tiled floor. Awake now, I stretch, my toes pressed out and back arched like a cat's. I walk past the bathroom, but the door is closed. I put on one of his old T-shirts and climb into bed, grateful for the soft sheets. My head is thumping, perhaps from the wine, perhaps from being hunched up in the chair. I lay a hand over my forehead but don't will the headache to stop, knowing I will fall asleep soon anyway, with one foot still in the world of my past.

Someone comes into the room, and it takes a second or two to remember it is Pete. When I open an eye, I can see him standing at the end of the bed, the light from a window casting him in and out of shadow. He is naked, facing me. He sways a little on his feet. The sour smell of alcohol reaches my nostrils across the cool night air. Just before I fall asleep I realize he is searching for my face in the dark.

On Sunday, Pete offers to help me in the café. I'm surprised; he's been so wary of the whole idea. Perhaps he is just curious. He helps me clean up, stealing glances at the kitchen, around the walls, light fixtures, and window frames. He is soon covered from head to toe in plaster dust; it settles in his thick head of hair like snow, turning it a dirty gray. He leans forward and tries to shake it out.

"This stuff is unbelievable," he grumbles.

I shrug and pass him a heavy box of teacups.

"Where d'you want these?"

"Just somewhere out the back; I'll sort them later. No point getting them out now with all the—"

"Dust," he finishes for me, standing with hands on hips. His mouth is a thin, grim line.

"Yeah." I can't help but smile when I turn away from him.

I lean forward onto a chair; all of my muscles are singing with use. My whole body feels electric, as if all the currents have been switched on. I bounce from leg to leg, surveying the front room and figuring out what needs to be done next.

Pete comes up behind me and drops a hand onto my shoulder companionably. "Oven looks good back there."

"Yeah, isn't it a monster?"

Outside, an old lady with a hunched back pauses to peer in

through the film of dust on the front windows. I wonder how old she is—perhaps eighty?—and I wave. She stares back at me.

"Reckon it's time we cleaned up. When are the guys coming to put up the wallpaper?" Pete gathers the muscle across my shoulder blades with his palm. He gives a couple of absentminded, meaty squeezes. The old lady behind the glass doesn't return my wave but hobbles on.

"Uh, four o'clock, I think they said."

"Which means six," Pete murmurs sarcastically. "All right, brooms in the back?"

We tackle the front room from left to right. The dust makes us cough and splutter. I can taste it bitter in my saliva even after I throw back a can of Coke. It falls into Pete's eyes as he works. He mutters and swears, gray dust raining down from his curls. The sun starts to slip away from the sky as we brush up the ashy piles and then begin mopping. I catch him watching me as I refill the buckets of hot, soapy water. My hair is damp with sweat, my sleeves covered in suds. The lemony smell of detergent fills the room as the last splashes of sunlight hit the freshly washed tiles.

"One more mop?" I ask.

He nods an okay.

When we are finished, we sit against opposite walls and look across at each other. We're too exhausted to make conversation and instead watch the sun leave us and darkness come in. The heat of the day is still thick and moist in the air, our hard work stretched out shiny in front of us. The glossy tiles remind me of black-and-white-striped boiled sweets. I hadn't expected them to be so beautiful underneath all that grime.

A noise lifts our heads toward the door. A man peeks in; a full beard frames his chin, white teeth line up in a wide grin. "Is Lillian around?" he asks with a rumbling laugh in his voice.

"Hey, Paul." Pete struggles to his feet. He wipes his palm on his jeans, then shakes Paul's large hand.

"I was just passing by. Hey, this place is looking awesome," Paul exclaims, gazing around as I get up. "Tiles look great."

"You think so? Taken a bit of work but . . ." I shrug shyly.

"Yeah. And the sign looks good too."

Pete cocks his head and looks at me.

"Oh," I breathe softly. "They must have hung it when we were out the back. That's what the racket was."

The three of us walk outside and stand on the pavement. Paul crosses his arms over his broad chest and rocks back on his heels. Pete has his hands on his hips, chin to the sky. It hangs from a brass-colored pole. My sign. Without a breeze it is static, as if poised for our inspection. I can't breathe for a few seconds while I look at it. Pete lifts his head higher and squints to read it, and Paul grunts approvingly.

"You didn't tell me," Pete says softly, turning to look at me with a crease between his eyes.

They've done a good job; it is securely fastened, brass screws twisted firmly in place. The paint is fresh and bright. It matches our squeaky-clean tiles—sharp, contrasting black against white. Dark cerise poppies punctuate the *i*'s in the curling, black script. It is exactly as I wanted it.

LILLIAN'S.

"Perfect," I sigh, just loud enough for my ears alone. My voice is as high and light as a girl's.

Dearest Mama,

Tomorrow I open Lillian's.

Pete says I probably should have made a bigger deal of marketing it if I was really serious, but I am so nervous about the whole thing I feel ill. I put an ad in the International Ladies' Club newsletter, but I was late so it probably won't come out till next week. Thank goodness. Sometimes I think I don't want anyone to even notice the café. I just want to get through this first day and not be sick all over my shoes.

I have stocked up the coffee. There are grinds all ready to go in the machine. Oh, maybe they should be fresh; I can change them tomorrow. I have made three types of macarons, *and they're all good except the Chocolat Amer, which is such a shame 'cause it tastes so divine, but they all came out looking like hats that had been sat on. I have some cakes. And some muffins. The muffins will just need warming in the oven and they'll be as good as new. I have to make cream-cheese icing for the carrot ones, but I can do that in the morning. I'll get up in time. Well, if I ever get to sleep.*

Mama, what if no one comes? It's a possibility. I haven't said that to Pete because he'd just say, "Well, you should have thought about that earlier, Grace," all frown between the eyes. He looked at me last night over steak and veggies, and I could see right through to his thoughts, I swear. He was thinking, Does she really want to make a go of this? I know I've been spending money like crazy, and he wonders if this is just a money pit. He probably doubts if it will make any profit at all. I don't like to talk about it because I wonder too.

Linda was at the supermarket today. She let out this laugh when she saw me. "Oh goodness, I didn't recognize you!" Well, Mama, that was not really a surprise because I was wearing tatty old overalls with my hair pulled back, and I was dusty and greasy and smelling like old towels. I've stopped wearing makeup these last few weeks, and the wrinkles and freckles are popping out on my face, scaring me each time I look in the mirror. It is not worth looking pretty when you are setting up a café, let me tell you. I sometimes wish Macau wasn't the size of a bloody Post-it note so you wouldn't wind up bumping into someone you know every time you go to the supermarket.

Okay, Mama. You need to wish me luck. I feel like there are kangaroos in my stomach. I have to lie down now and go to sleep, and when I wake up it will be the day I open Lillian's . . .

Your loving daughter,
Grace

L'Espoir—Hope

Provençal Lavender with a Sweet Fig Buttercream

The sun slides down into the horizon, orange and sticky, like a lozenge. The chairs are stacked on the tables, the benches cleaned. Food is in the refrigerator, lists left out for tomorrow, tiles mopped. I take a chair off a table and put it on the floor, ease my tired bones down onto it and stare out the window at the mango-colored light.

Well. It wasn't too bad.

Given that there wasn't much promotion, I had more customers than I'd expected. Sure, there were moments I wished for more customers for the money's sake, but I put on a brave smile for the curious faces that bobbed past the window but didn't come in. Maybe they will tomorrow. Maybe the next day. The takings from the till fit in my pocket. Two hundred patacas and some loose change. I won't even calculate what kind of hourly rate that is. I've probably made more in tips some nights.

Paul came in during the morning and had a coffee with a workmate over plans they had to spread across two tables. Latte and a cappuccino, thanks. Linda dropped by with her kids after school, and they tore chocolate brownies apart, half in their mouths, half on the floor. She said she would come back later in the week with some girlfriends, show them the new place. She *luuurved* the decor. "So chic, Gracie!" Celine called to ask if I could cater for a parents' "French for fun" evening she was hosting next week. Some sandwiches, *macarons,* nothing too fancy. Considering her husband is a chef himself, I know the order is a gift. Then there were three Chinese schoolgirls, a *macaron* each and lots of giggling. Folders covered in doodles and colored stickers. Socks pulled up to their knees. The woman who needed a glass of water after her morning jog but who said she worked for the *Macau Daily Times* and looked around with approval in her eyes. Another woman, quiet, had tea by the window. That was it.

I have packed up the food that won't keep and put it in a large bag. I'll take it home; see if we can't eat some of it for dinner. Or if Pete knows someone who wants it. Perhaps even the stray cats around Old Taipa Tavern.

So there wasn't a fanfare; weren't a hundred eager customers queuing out the door. I feel tired, but in a good way. *Purposefully tired.* A warm feeling settles on me. I think they call it optimism.

Un Peu de Bonté—A Little Kindness
Watermelon with Cream Filling

The second day the café is open. *My* café is open. I am yanked from my dreams, body clock terrified I might oversleep, but it is only five in the morning. Lillian's doesn't open until ten, so I have five whole hours stretched in front of me. Pete snores softly on his side of the bed, facedown, with the sheet draped soap-opera style across his backside. I know I will wake him if I get up now. I feel like I did as a kid on Christmas morning, desperate for Mama to rise. I tick off items on a list in my mind: open doors, chairs down, signboard out front, *macarons* from the chiller, call Ah Chun about the dripping tap. A little thrill goes through me.

Sliding out of bed as silently as possible, I flick through clothes in the wardrobe. Nothing I own suits this new chapter in my life. Woolen coats hang next to yoga pants. And I refuse to wear a white shirt with black trousers; I'm not a waitress anymore. Skirt with a blouse? I check the time again on the clock radio next to Pete's heavy head. His mouth is wide open on the pillow. I change as quietly as possible, but when I turn around he is holding on to a pillow lengthwise like a lover, propped up with his head on his free hand. He stares at me unblinking.

"Hi."

"Sorry, did I wake you?"

He shrugs.

"I had to get up. Loads on my mind."

"Mmm-hmm." He is still sleepy.

I start pulling out the contents of my dresser. Armfuls of clothes pile up at the end of the bed. Surely I must have two half-decent things to put together.

"What did you wear yesterday?"

"That dress. The long charcoal gray one, with the belt. And sandals."

"Oh yeah. Couldn't you wear that again?"

"It's not a suit, Pete; women can't just wear the same thing every day like that," I say snippily. Certainly not in a kitchen with ovens cranking, I think to myself, rifling through the piles.

Pete rises to stand beside me. He still has creases from the pillow across his left cheek, and hair stands up to attention on that side of his head. "What about this with the pants?" He holds up a bright sleeveless top with a high neck and nods toward a discarded pair of black trousers. It is the top I bought on our honeymoon. To wear to the posh buffet dinners the five-star resort put on every night. We hardly ever got out of bed before midday, so dressing up for dinner felt like the beginning of the day. It reminds me of mojitos and mosquitoes.

"Yeah, okay," I reply softly. Actually, it will be perfect, I think with some surprise.

"Maybe I'll drop by for lunch today." Pete yawns. He turns toward the shower, his bare bum white and radiant against his tanned legs.

When I get to Lillian's, there is a woman standing outside, moving impatiently from one gold-sandaled foot to the other. I squint to see if she is real. Long limbs flow from cropped and cuffed white shorts as if she has wandered, lost, from a photo shoot on a yacht. Her tanned arms cradle a dog that is the color and texture of cappuccino froth. I can see she is squinting back at me, even though she is wearing large sunglasses, because her forehead is drawn down and her mouth is straight across in a line.

"Are you the owner?" she calls out.

My heart seems to lift. I wait until I am closer before answering; raising my voice always makes me feel nervous. Her hair falls neatly to her shoulders, the blond of a dessert wine. She looks around thirty-five and smells strongly of ginger lily, bold and tropical. A high-end retail store sprays a similar perfume in all their shops. It is not cheap.

"Yes, that's me."

"Oh good. I'm dying for a coffee."

I swing my watch up, as the face has moved to the underside of my wrist. It is a quarter past seven.

"I'm so sorry, but we don't open till ten." I can feel my cheeks warm. This being-the-owner gig is going to take some getting used to.

She leans forward to look at my watch with me. Her dog growls, scrambling like it is treading water. It bares a few small, pointed teeth at me, curling an upper lip, revealing gums as dark and shiny as licorice.

"Damn," she says, with the sharp spike of an Australian accent, then pleads, "Can't you open a bit earlier today?"

I think of my list and shake my head, blushing with apology. "It's only our second day. Maybe next week I'll start opening a bit earlier. Or you're welcome to come back after ten?"

She changes position to better handle the wriggling dog. "Never mind," she replies flatly. "That'll teach me for being myself in front of *those* ladies."

"Sorry?"

She pushes her sunglasses off her face onto the top of her head and rolls her eyes, which are a dark chocolate color, like American brownies. She hesitates a moment and looks squarely into my face as if deciding whether to explain. Then she sighs. "I can't go to Aurora for a coffee because some of the Ladies' Club meet there." Her voice is warm, not what I was expecting. "They don't approve of me swearing with their kids in earshot. I'm not sure if that's the whole story. They don't approve of me in general, is the feeling I get. Seems I wasn't a hit at the last barbecue."

I think of Linda and can't help but laugh. This glamorous creature with the mouth of a sailor.

"Yeah, it's funny all right," she says grimly. "What a bunch of snobs. They were all washing their own dishes and changing nappies not so long ago, now they act like the Prada mafia. I've been dying to tell them all to go fuck themselves, but Don says I should probably try and restrain myself." She wrestles with the dog and a large handbag to remove a mobile phone, which is buzzing. "It's my husband, Don," she says to me, putting the phone to her ear. "I'll be back!" She gives me a grin; her dog offers me another toothy growl.

The clip-clop of her shoes echoes in the quiet morning as she strides away. She reminds me of Mama. All mouth, no forethought. I am sure she had more than a few sets of eyes on her at the Ladies' Club barbecue. Men with gold bands on their left hands, no doubt. Guys must line up at her door, round the corner, and down the street.

Later, Pete rings and cancels lunch. Work is too busy for him to race over from Macau peninsula to Taipa and then back to the office within a lunch hour. Behind his voice I can hear the sound of his fingers tap-dancing over the keyboard. He forgets to say goodbye as he hangs up. I put the phone down and look across the café floor. It is empty. I imagine a customer tally etched on the wall in chalk and mentally rub out a line. Meaningful and meaningless tasks have been exhausted, and I am left standing behind the counter, limp and useless. The sun pours through the windows and reflects glossily off the clean floor tiles.

I take a sandwich from the counter fridge and move to a nearby table so I can leap up if required. The bread, a baguette, is fresh and slightly chewy from the cold. The filling is cranberry, Brie, and pine nuts. The salty, oily pine nuts are my favorite part. Keeping a close eye on the window in front, I watch as an old lady sidles up to the glass. It's the same woman I waved to just a few days ago. Now she's wearing practical thick cotton slacks, dark gray in color, and a short-sleeved navy blouse. She blinks at me with dark eyes. Small flowers blossom across her shirt, the collar sitting up attentively, in Mandarin style. I marvel at her frog clasps, twisted cotton in dark blue, sewn in delicate figures-of-eight.

She shuffles closer, leaning on a cane. As she moves it punctuates her slow steps. She leans in until her nose is almost touching the glass and I can see her wrinkled face. It is framed by short gray hair in a bob, held back with a headband, which makes her look girlish. She spots me, my mouth full of baguette, and gives a shy grin. I jump up and brush my hands against my apron. The chime on the door makes an angelic tinkling. Then she wobbles up to the counter fridge, hovering over the *macarons*, oohing and nodding. It makes me laugh.

"*Macarons,*" I explain with a smile.

She grins broadly but doesn't reply. She points at the muffins and then the cakes and then the rolls. I start to wonder if she is mute, but she begins to talk in Cantonese. I can't tell whether she's speaking to me or to herself. She rests against the counter, holding an English menu, not yet translated, to her face.

"Sorry . . ." I murmur, but she continues to hold it close as though it might become legible through some kind of osmosis. Then she shrugs and orders simply.

"*Cha?*" Tea. A word I know.

"*Cha.* Sure. *Cha.*" I nod idiotically. I gesture to the tables, and she plods to a seat at the very front of Lil's. She settles down into the chair, rests her cane against the tabletop, and folds her hands neatly in her lap.

I stare at the rack of herbal infusions and caffeinated teas, then look back to her. She smiles again, the soft purple of her aging lips spread wide across her brown face. There are dark streaks of youthful black among the silvery strands of hair. She turns back to the window, closing her eyes, and sunbathes her eyelids. I open a box that is a deep blue with white clouds printed across the corners. "Calm"—a soothing blend of chamomile, lavender, and mint.

When I deliver the tray—teapot and cup, a *macaron* resting on the saucer—she points to her thin chest and says, "Yok Lan."

"Yok Lan," I repeat.

She nods happily. I look over her tray, wondering if she is asking for something. Sugar perhaps. I fetch a bowl of white sugar cubes and place it next to her.

She grins and points to herself again, index finger pressed to her clavicle. "Yok Lan."

"Yok Lan," I say again, and she nods. Then she points at me and raises her eyebrows, which are mere wisps of graying hair in the center, fading to baldness by the outer corners of her eyes. "Oh, *you* are Yok Lan." I point at her. Yes, she nods. "I am Grace."

Her soft cheeks fall and pouch with confusion.

"Grace," I repeat, finger to chest.

95

"Grrr-ace-ah."

"That's me, Grace."

"Grrrrace-ah. Graça!" she repeats enthusiastically, the Portuguese version of my name rolling easily from her mouth. "Graça, Grr-ace. *Hai-a.*"

She pats my hand, and I leave her to her tea. She turns back to the sunshine. I slink behind the counter to finish my sandwich, watching her. Later, when I am in the kitchen, I hear the bell on the door chime. When I come out she has gone, tea drunk and *macaron* finished. She has left some money on her table, not enough to cover the bill, but perhaps as much as she would pay in a local diner. It doesn't bother me.

Yok Lan is my only customer for the day, but when I clean and lock up that evening, humming "Amazing Grace," it feels as if Lillian's has been consecrated.

And then, over the rest of the week, customers start to come in. A trickle at first, then a drizzle, then a stream.

Rêve d'un Ange—Dream of an Angel
White Chocolate with Hints
of Lemon Rind and Cinnamon

How it gets to be April I have no idea. Time might fly when you're having fun, but it's like a fighter jet when you are running a café in a little patch of China. Lillian's is even busier than I had hoped, but I'm exhausted from trying to do everything myself. Exhilarated, but exhausted. I crawl into bed each night around eight o'clock and leap out again around five-thirty in the morning, head full of *macaron* recipes and lists, lists, lists. Pete and I have become ships passing in the night. I see him only in the morning half-light when I tiptoe around his sleeping figure. A mouth wide open in snores, a foot kicked out of the sheets. Back of his neck, curve of his toes.

I am managing the workload, just keeping a handle on things, as it were. But that isn't to last. I am serving when it starts to fray at the hems, unraveling, as if in slow motion.

There is a line at the counter, a large, shiny-headed man tapping his foot against the tiles, arms crossed in front of his chest. His suit jacket strains against his girth, tie hanging from a meaty neck. In front of him, one of my regular mums orders a long black and a "fluffy," steamed milk in a small glass, for her son, who tugs at her hand. His knees are smeared green with chlorophyll, and above them his school uniform shorts are swiped across with a rust-colored stain I assume to be Marmite. Behind the thickset man is Yok Lan, who gives me a consoling little wave.

I put the two drinks on a tray and gently push it toward my customer. She is distracted by her boy, swinging dangerously from her arm.

"Oh, I wanted it takeaway," she says, apologetically.

I pour the long black into a cardboard cup and make a new fluffy. Although I am getting used to more customers, the queue still makes me nervous. The milk frother sings with steam as she moves to the side and the gentleman behind her comes to the front. He puts fleshy, wet palms on the counter and scowls at me. He orders a latte and a roast beef sandwich while I pour the steamed milk into a paper cup for the boy and quickly make the man's latte. Both are passed across. Then the man's mobile phone goes off, the *Star Wars* theme piercing the air. The mum jumps, the boy yelps as she treads on his foot. Then he falls back against the man; the man drops the latte onto his shirt. The stain soaks through to his skin, dark hairs sticking to the wet, pale blue fabric. The boy starts to cry as the man starts to yell. Yok Lan hobbles backward and, fortunately, out of the way.

All I manage to say is: "Oh."

Then I am dashing around to the front of the counter, checking first on the boy, whose tears are falling full and fast. His face has crumpled into itself, mouth twisted upside down. His mum begins to berate the man, who is yelling at me for not worrying about him first. He slams his cup against the counter, which breaks off the handle and splashes the last of the coffee onto my back. Now he is swearing, and the smell of hot coffee floods my nostrils. The woman gathers her son into her arms and marches out the door. The man too is gone by the time I straighten up, pieces of the cup in the palm of my hand. Latte on the floor, fluffy and long black left on the counter, and none of them paid for.

Yok Lan clucks her tongue and pats my arm.

A tall blond woman comes rushing in. Long white dress, gold sandals.

"I saw it all from outside. Are you okay?" Her eyes are round with concern.

It is the woman from my second day, this time without her dog. Yok Lan looks up at her and smiles.

She reaches for napkins and presses them against my back.

"What an animal," she mutters, taking the broken pieces from my hand and putting them into the bin by the espresso machine. She looks at Yok Lan and back to me.

"Can I get you a coffee?" I offer wearily.

"How about I wait till you're cleaned up and the rush is over," she says. Then she adds kindly, "Maybe we can have one together?"

"Okay." I am so tired my tongue feels thick and swollen in my mouth.

Half an hour later the chaos has subsided. The last of the lunchtime customers leave, the mess is mopped from the tiles, the afternoon light settles in, pale and still. Yok Lan sits facing the window, the steam of her tea floating up toward the collar of her shirt. She closes her eyes and leans back into her chair with a sigh. The blond woman looks at me over the top of a magazine. I make a cappuccino for her and a cup of tea for myself, pile some *macarons* onto a plate. They won't be sold at this time anyway.

"Sorry about all that," I say.

"All what?"

"The ruckus. Maybe it's a British thing . . ." I give a small laugh. "I'm not very good at confrontation, you see."

"Oh, that's okay," she says sympathetically.

"And I'm just so tired," I confess. I offer a *macaron* to Yok Lan at the other table, and she accepts eagerly. She places it gently on the edge of her saucer.

"Well," says the blond woman, "I don't think it's just a British thing. I'm hopeless at it too. Although I'm normally the one *causing* the ruckus." Her brown eyes have fine wrinkles radiating from the outer edges. She is older than I'd first thought, perhaps in her forties. She looks like one of the confident, cool girls from school, all grown up. Yet she seems slightly awkward. "I always say the wrong thing," she explains with a shrug. "I'm Marjory, by the way."

"Nice to meet you, Marjory. I'm Grace."

My tea is only half finished when my phone rings. I get up to answer it. Pete needs my passport number to file some kind of paperwork with the government. I am reading the numbers to him when Marjory comes to the counter. I finally hang up and apologize again. She smiles and leaves some money against the till. I try to give her change, but she waves it away.

"Hey, I'll see you tomorrow. Sorry I didn't come back earlier. The place is great." She gives me a shy smile.

"Thanks," I say.

"Take care of yourself, Grace. Don't work too hard," she says warmly, then she is walking out the door.

At home, after Lillian's has been cleaned and the door locked on the end of a long day, Pete gives me a considering look. I am slumped on the lounge, swollen feet soaking in a laundry bucket full of hot salted water. He starts at my feet and finishes at the top of my hair, the very ends sticking up in places they shouldn't. He moves his head from side to side and releases a sigh. I know he is going to give me a hard-edged little truth even before it leaves his mouth. This is Pete's way.

"Grace," he starts, "you need help. You need to hire someone."

There is a small electric pulse of pride, knowing that this beat-up feeling is due to the café becoming something of a success. Hey, this waitress is running a café, I think defiantly, giving him a quick, slightly smug glance.

But although he is right about getting help, it makes me feel strange. I'm used to doing it all myself. My way. I look up at the ceiling, or perhaps the heavens. *Mama, dear Mama.* I am so tired I ache in every single muscle. Especially the ones holding up my eyelids. I look back at Pete, standing tall, his long arms crossed in front of him. Steam drifts up from the bucket.

"You might be right," I say reluctantly.

Léon, with his contacts in the restaurant business, helps to line up several interviews for me; cousins and friends of people who work for him at Aurora. I'm grateful. I barely have time to stick an ad in the paper. And to be completely honest, I'm jittery about sharing Lil's. It makes me feel a bit vulnerable, somehow. Like letting someone wear your favorite pair of shoes.

The law here ensures that only Macau citizens are employed as dealers in the casinos, the need for which is immense. The salaries are so good there is barely anyone left over to be employed in cafés, bars, and restaurants. They'd have to have a burning desire to work in hospitality—and there aren't many with that burning desire at the best of times. Léon suggests I interview someone from the Philippines who can speak English with me. Everyone from the Philippines seems to know just about every other Filipino in town, he tells me; it is a wide net of connections. Léon assures me that finding someone will be an absolute cinch, but

I'm not convinced. I can't imagine finding someone with the same commitment to Lillian's; someone who will treat *macarons* as if they are semiprecious stones.

"It couldn't have been worse," I complain, phone pressed to my ear.

"What happened?"

"Well, the first one . . ."

"Cristina?"

"Yeah, that's the one. She was terrible. Turned up half an hour late, was obviously desperate for the job, proceeded to coo her way through the interview. Everything was 'wonderful, ma'am' and 'for you, no problem, ma'am.'" I don't want to be ungrateful for the help, but the interview had made me feel so uncomfortable.

Léon tries to stifle a little snort of laughter. "You didn't like her because she was desperate for a job? Grace, they're all desperate for a job. They're supporting their families back home on the salaries they can make here. You cannot blame them."

I lift my eyes toward the ceiling and nod reluctantly, as if he can see me through the phone. "Maybe she was desperate for the job or maybe she was just guilty because she was so late. Anyway, it made me feel . . . strange."

"Okay, okay. So what about the second one, then?"

"Worse. Couldn't speak a word of English," I say. "I ask her a bunch of questions, figure she's really interested, and that we totally understand one another. Her eyes are lit up and she's nodding . . ."

"Sounds good."

"Until I stopped asking yes-or-no questions."

"Pardon?"

"But kept getting yes-or-no answers."

"Ah, I see. Well . . ." Léon laughs again.

"It's a waste of time, I'm afraid. There's one left, and I'm thinking I should just cancel. Thank you for everything you—"

"Grace." Léon's voice is calm and low, almost a purr. I pause and feel myself leaning into the sound of it.

Before he can continue, I interrupt. "Okay, don't tell me. I'm being ridiculous. I'll meet this last girl." I give a resigned sigh.

"There you go. Rilla, right? My people here say she will be the best."

"Okay, okay," I mumble, realizing Léon and his accent could convince me of almost anything.

"Good." I can tell he is smiling. "Have fun . . ."

Five minutes before Rilla is due for her interview, I sit at one of the tables looking down the street for her. My chin is propped up in my hands, and I can feel the slight scowl across my face. I resent having to close Lillian's for half a day to interview people. All the cups and saucers are stacked and unused, the *macarons* resting in the chiller—it feels fruitless, and I miss my work; my real work. The Japanese green tea I made has settled cold in the bottom of my mug when I see a young boy walking up the street, heading toward the café. Young boys don't come to the café alone, as a general rule, so I sit up a bit and watch. He gives a shy smile and waves. I instinctively look behind me, to the wall, and then back again. He wears long shorts and a long-sleeved white T-shirt, which hangs loosely to midthigh. His shoulders are curved forward, the fingers of one hand grasping onto the bottom of his sleeve. His hair is thick and dark and shiny, cut blunt above his ears. Then he stops and knocks sharply on the window. He smiles at me again, and I realize there is a prettiness in his face.

"Sorry," I mouth, while shaking my head. I point to the Closed sign on the door. I give a weak, apologetic smile.

He looks at me, clearly confused, and says something that I can't hear through the glass.

I shake my head again. He holds up a few sheets of paper, which look like a document. I shake my head more vigorously and lift my hand. I hate being sold anything, as I'm always too polite to refuse.

"No, no, no. We're shut. Sorry."

He looks even more bewildered and leans into the crack between the closed doors. He says something again, in English. It sounds like "Sir."

I walk over to the door.

"Ma'am?" he says in a high voice. "Ma'am, Sir Léon sent me. You are Ma'am . . . Grace?"

As I come closer to the doors, I can see his eyes through the small gap, ringed with short but thick lashes. They are like the lashes of a little child. His skin is smooth and flushed.

"Yes, I am Grace," I say, opening the door a sliver.

"Oh, good. I am Rilla."

As he says this, I hear the gentle pitch in his voice, and all the other observations tumble into place. I am a fool. For the first time today—perhaps for the first time this week—I laugh. It creeps up on me, tickling in my chest, and then I let it go, loud and free. I swing the door wide, so she can come in.

Rilla enters and stands in front of me, her shoulders back and face lifted. Only now she is inside the café, standing in the light, can I see my mistake and I'm laughing so hard she joins in, cautiously, not sure what is so funny. Her round eyes sparkle with her smile. I ask her to sit down and go to make a fresh pot of tea, still chuckling as I walk into the kitchen, trying to cover my mouth with my hand. When I come back with two cups, Rilla is sitting up straight, her young face bright. Her résumé is on the table between us.

"Sorry about that," I say, grinning at her.

"No problem," she replies. She looks around Lillian's. "This is a really nice place, ma'am."

"Thank you, Rilla. It's taken a bit of work."

"Oh yes. I remember it was Portuguese café. Dirty and many old mens. You know . . ." She screws up her face and makes a motion with her hand toward her mouth. Then she looks up at me quickly and retracts her hand into her sleeve.

"Smoking?"

"Yes, always smoking. Not a very nice place. But now . . . very nice," she murmurs.

I think back to the heavy, stale smell clinging to every tile, wall, and piece of furniture. She is right about the smoking clientele. I feel as though I have scrubbed every past puff from the very fittings and floors.

"Well, now we are a nonsmoking café."

"Oh really, ma'am?" she says, sounding surprised. Almost all restaurants and cafés here and certainly all casinos allow smoking. Most places are clogged thick with it.

"Yup. No smoking around here. Only *macarons*. And coffee, of course. Sometimes screaming babies and kids too, I have to warn you."

"That is no problem," she says easily. She takes a sip of her tea and leans back into her seat. She is now looking around the café with interest. She seems to be taking in every light fixture and every table with wonder. She looks comfortable in this place. Happy.

"You've made it look pretty. And it feels safe," she says quietly, as if to herself. She pulls down her sleeve over the thumb of her left hand absentmindedly.

"Yeah, it's a safe neighborhood. I like it here."

I look down at my notepad and list of questions. There are eight questions, written neatly under the title "Interview Questions," with a space at the bottom for comments and a score. When I lift my head toward Rilla, she has two hands around her cup and is staring into the bottom of it, a gentle smile across her face. It is not a cold day, but she looks warmed by the tea. Tea has that effect on people; I love watching it bring comfort. She is so small, the cup seems almost to dwarf her, her soft, full cheeks and round, dark eyes childlike behind it. Taking a breath, I ask her only one question on my list. Number eight. *Trust my instincts, right, Mama?*

"Rilla, when could you start?"

Her eyes flick up toward me eagerly, and her face lifts. "As soon as you like, ma'am. Tomorrow?"

"Tomorrow," I repeat firmly. I lean over to shake her hand as if to seal the deal, her tiny hand in my big one. Then we both smile together.

By the time Rilla has worked three days at Lillian's, I've finally started sleeping at night, rather than lying awake, eyes wide and dry, mind churning over the chores to be done. I have told her that she is a godsend, but I'm not sure she understands what I mean. She smiles, as she always does, and carries on cleaning dishes, humming and scrubbing away. She works so quickly I don't have time to give her instructions. Before I ask for the storeroom to be swept out, it is mopped sparkling clean; before I ask her to wipe down the milk frother, she has all the machine's moving parts soaking in a bucket. She doesn't say much, but when she does it is normally "No problem, ma'am," her standard reply to any request. I try to encourage her to call me Grace, like everyone else, but this results in being called Ma'am Grace or Miss Grace. The address feels so foreign. Sometimes I don't realize she's talking to me. Earlier, I was staring off into the distance, hands plunged deep into the lukewarm, sudsy water, wondering whether to clean the tiny slice of window above the sink. The view outside is distorted by thick splatterings of grease and sticky dust.

"Ma'am? Miss Grace?"

"Oh, sorry. I was off in my own little world." I try to brush the hair out of my face with the back of my arm but instead succeed in dragging dishwater across my forehead.

Rilla laughs and dabs me with a clean tea towel. She pushes back the stray hair, tucking it behind my ear. Her touch is casual, almost sisterly.

"There is a man to see you. Out front."

"Pete?"

I pluck off my gloves and wipe the dampness from my hands on the front of my apron. He has come in a few times but doesn't stay long, always neck-deep in work and phone calls. I don't tell him, but I almost prefer it that way, to have Lillian's all to myself, my place.

"No. Another man. Ummm . . ." Rilla puts her head to one side, searching for the right words. "Tall with black shirt. Ummm, gray hair?"

"Oh, okay."

Finally someone has come to help fix the dripping air conditioner in the toilet.

The man has his back to me as I walk out of the kitchen. He leans on the counter, one elbow behind him, propping him up.

"Hello, can I help you?"

As he turns around, I see it is Léon, his face lit up in a smile. He is holding a bottle, its neck tied with a fat yellow bow.

"Grace!" he exclaims. The way he says my name always unravels me a little, the rolling *r*, the softness in his voice. He takes hold of one of my hands while I frantically consider my wilted appearance. Wet hair, flushed face, apron wrapped around my middle. "I'm so sorry I didn't come sooner. Aurora has been so busy. People are talking about this place, you know. Now I can see it for myself. Well, it is"—he shakes his head—"marvelous."

I feel myself blush. I'm tongue-tied.

"Oh well . . . thank you. It's all thanks to you, Léon. Your teaching, the *macarons*." I nod to the counter fridge. "And of course, now Rilla."

"Oh no, no. It's *your* hard work. This"—he makes a gesture to encircle the room—"it is not an easy undertaking. You should take credit. It looks superb."

"Well, it's not perfect. But thank you. We're getting there." I'm proud of Lillian's, whether I admit it out loud or not. "And now you're here, you need to try the *macarons*. As we say, 'the proof of the pudding is in the eating.'"

"Ah, you are right. What do you recommend?" He gives me a blue-eyed wink, like a partner in crime. A fellow baker.

"I recommend them all, of course," I reply with a grin. "Take a seat and I'll bring one of each."

"Perfect. Shall we have coffee and you can give me the guided tour?"

I look up at Rilla. She is drying a cup and nods to me.

"Sure."

He leaves the champagne, with its showy bow, on the counter and takes a seat at one of the tables. I notice the other customers lifting their eyes in his direction, women glancing at him over their coffee cups. That magnetism, like the type that first drew me to Pete. I take off my apron and try to smooth my hair while crouched down by the counter fridge. I choose a selection of *macarons* and wonder if the odd feeling in my stomach is hunger. Or a twinge of desire, perhaps unease. Probably both.

* * *

Marjory has become my regular morning institution. Rilla seems to like her. She says things like "Bloody glorious day outside," which make Rilla laugh. Marjory has one of those white, winning grins paired with a salt-of-the-earth quality—exactly the opposite of what you would expect from her polished appearance. I often find myself staring at her careful beauty and bubbling confidence, wishing I could be bolder, more put together. When I am in the kitchen putting on a batch of *macaron* shells, I can hear her voice from the front of the café, telling some joke or lovingly complaining about her husband, Don. I always come out to personally make her coffee just the way she likes it. A cappuccino with low-fat milk and "no faff." That means no cinnamon, no chocolate; just the steamed milk swirled into a leaf pattern. She allows herself to have one *macaron* with her coffee, daily, and gives me her frank opinion on some of my trials and new flavors.

"No good, Grace" or "Yup, awesome" seem to be the two standard responses. I tend to agree with her; my ideas do seem to be hit-or-miss. But I'm getting better with practice. I've been spending my evenings online, studying Parisian patisserie menus—Mulot, Hermé, Ladurée, Lenôtre—while Pete dozes in front of the television.

Today Marjory sits in her usual place as I wipe down the tables. A three-year-old boy has showered floors and tables and windowsills with sugar. It is crunchy underfoot. Fortunately, both mother and boy have left, his howls and whoops fading into the distance. I had watched while she let him slurp down half of her latte and he'd become tightly wound with the caffeine hit. Wiping the table next to Marjory, I offer an apology.

"So sorry about that. Wasn't sure whether I should ask them to leave or not. But in retrospect . . ." I roll my eyes toward the ceiling.

Marjory just nods, unusually quiet. She seems strangely rigid in her chair. I come in closer to brush a few crystal grains from her tabletop and notice that tears are making wet tracks through her bronzer and dripping off the edge of her jaw. She is still wearing her sunglasses, and her features are frozen in smooth composure. Then she pats at her cheek, smudging her blush, bronzer, and foundation. The white napkin becomes muddy and soggy, and she twists it in her fist.

"Do you . . ." I start, and then pause. I look around furtively, noticing that all the other customers have left, a little break in the morning tide. I pull out the chair opposite hers at the table. The legs clatter across the tiles. "Do you want to talk about it?"

Her chin is tilted toward her lap, and she pats at her cheeks again with the napkin. "There's nothing to say," she says and sighs.

I stay seated opposite her.

Then her breathing gets ragged, her mouth squeezed shut and turned down at the edges. She gasps for breath through her nose before a low cry escapes her. "It's Bianca."

"Bianca?"

"My dog," she explains. Her sunglasses make it impossible to see her eyes. I let go of my dishcloth, placing it on top of the table, lean toward her a little.

"She died. We had to . . . you see . . . we had to put her down." She brushes absently at the dark pools her tears are making against her skirt, then shakes her head. "Shit. Sorry. This isn't your problem."

"Hey, hey, it's okay."

"I shouldn't be crying in here. Sorry."

"It's okay, it's okay . . ." I put my hand on her shoulder, and she lifts her head.

"It's not that simple," she stammers.

I press my hand against her shoulder, trying to reassure her. I don't know what to say.

She lets out a deep breath and finally takes off her glasses. Mascara is smeared under her eyes like war paint. When she catches me looking at her face, she twists her napkin into a point, rolling it slowly under each of her eyes. It doesn't make any difference. Her painted face is undone.

"Why am I crying about this? I didn't even like her. God, that sounds awful. I sound like an awful person."

"Hey, it's okay. It's going to be okay," I say gently, feeling unhelpful. It has been so long since I have had a friend, I don't quite know how to comfort her.

"I mean, really, she was a nightmare from the beginning, and now . . . it turns out she had a brain tumor. That's probably why she was always so aggressive. Nothing they could do, nothing."

"Oh. I'm so sorry."

She gives me a watery smile. "It's okay. I'm surprised I'm so upset. You know, last week I was secretly hoping there would be some reason we would have to give her back. Or . . . something. She was an absolute monster at times. It sounds so horrible to say out loud." She gives a wry kind of laugh.

I let go of her shoulder and put my hands in my lap. "Well, she did seem like a bit of a handful. I mean, you shouldn't feel bad, you know. It wasn't—"

"My fault? Yeah, I know. I know that logically. Rationally." She shakes her head. "It's just that I got up this morning, still sleepy, and put food in her bowl and then remembered . . . and then . . . I didn't think I would feel like this."

"I think it's normal to feel sad," I say.

"No. I mean, yes, I do feel sad. But I didn't think I would feel so . . . lost?" She seems to look through me for a moment. "I used to be a dancer, you know. Oh hell, don't tell any of the ladies that, they already look at me like I'm some kind of hooker." She lowers her voice, picks at her napkin with her nail. "It wasn't like that.

Sure, we were a bit Moulin Rouge, you know, but classy, not strippers or anything. It was the best time, Grace. Seeing the world, getting drunk, suitcases full of gorgeous dresses. I had the best life I knew of, better than the other girls from school, ending up with quiet lives and boring husbands. Yuck. But I was getting too old for it in the end. That's when I met Don. Then being a wife was really nice for a while, but now, I don't know, I just feel . . ."

Part of me wants to offer her words. Descriptions that come to me so easily. *Empty. Confused. Directionless.*

As her voice trails off, she stares out at nothing. Then she sits up and looks a little embarrassed. "Hey, thank you. For listening. I guess I'm a bit stunned. Now I see Bianca was kind of . . . filling my days . . ."

We sit in silence for a few minutes. Marjory sniffles and I wish I had something helpful or useful to say. I know what it is to feel lost. To have your dreams dissolve in seconds. Things that were supposed to be a certain way suddenly turning out completely different. Why can't I think of anything to say? I glance around Lillian's. Rilla is in the kitchen washing up; I can hear her, the sloshes and knocks of plates hitting one another in the soapy water. I love that sound, the stillness of the front of the café, the busyness in the kitchen. I realize with a jolt that I am thanking God for this place. That I no longer feel quite so lost.

"It's going to be okay. It *will* be okay," I say again with conviction. I want to say more, but I can't think how to say it. I hope Marjory feels some reassurance from me. She gives me a weak smile.

"Do you want a cup of tea? Chamomile? Or maybe a cappuccino?"

She nods. "A cup of tea would be great."

We smile at each other, our eyes meeting across the table. She reaches out and pats my hand, and we both look down together—

her golden, manicured hand lying on top of my pale, damp one with the short nails lined with almond flour.

"Thanks, Grace."

"No problem," I reply softly.

I get up and take out a cup and saucer.

We seem to have won over several customers who now always choose Lillian's for their morning coffee or afternoon sugar buzz. Each has quirky habits I try to memorize. Some I learn the hard way, making mistakes, getting things wrong. Occasionally, just after I've mastered the customer's order, she will change her mind. Other customers let me know their preferences from the first time they come, cutting straight to the quick, not mincing words. Gigi falls into this category, ordering her coffee as if she's made the request every morning of her life.

She wears black trousers and a white shirt, the unmistakable uniform of a table games dealer, sans waistcoat, which the casinos don't allow to be taken home. She can't be much older than nineteen or twenty, although I find it difficult to tell with Chinese women. Their skin is always so taut and creamy; it's hard not to be envious. The ponytail on her head is high and tight, and a dark fringe brushes her forehead. I imagine her on the other side of the green felt, sullen and bored. She pushes her fringe to one side to give me a strangely curious and angry look. She seems familiar.

"Hi, I'd like a cappuccino. Chocolate on top," she says very quickly while I stare, trying to figure out how I know her.

"Sure. Take a seat; I'll bring it to you. Magazines are in the stand on the left if you'd like something to read." As I point she turns her chin and looks in the direction of my finger. When she turns back, I give her a smile.

"Thanks," she replies curtly. No smile.

She moves from one foot to the other, staying at the counter. She holds her bag in front of her stomach protectively, as though it might be snatched from her at any moment. I wait a few moments for her to say something.

"Anything else?" I ask finally.

"Um, which is the best one?"

"Sorry?"

"Of these . . . things."

"Oh, *macarons*." I move toward the shelf on which their round bodies are lined up primly. "Well, it depends, I guess. I like caramel flavors; some people prefer a lighter taste, like rose, at least to start with. The chocolate-flavored ones are lovely, of course . . ." I am rambling; it is like choosing a favorite child, practically impossible.

"What's this one then?" She points at my newest creation, a pale, creamy white with soft flecks of yellow, like glints of gold in white marble.

"*Rêve d'un Ange*. It means 'dream of an angel.'" She tilts her head, interested, and I shrug. "Hopelessly romantic name, I know. Couldn't help myself."

"What's in it?" she asks, lowering her voice.

"It's my white chocolate *macaron*. Ganache, that's a kind of chocolate cream, sandwiched in the middle. I've added a little lemon rind and cinnamon. Most people can hardly taste those flavors though. It's one of my newest. Would you like to try it?"

She has been leaning in towards the counter, peering at it closely, her dark eyes wide. Now she straightens up briskly. "Yeah."

She takes a seat at a table near the window. I expect to see her grab a fashion magazine, chatter to friends on the phone. But she doesn't. She props her elbow on the table and rests her head upon it. Then she picks up the menu and reads it carefully, over and over. When I deliver her order, she looks down at the plate bearing the single *macaron* and then up to me.

"Thanks. I'm Gigi." The words rush out as if unplanned.

"Hi, Gigi. I'm Grace."

"You came to see my aunty," she says, her eyes tracing over my face with a long, serious look. It's then I remember her in the tracksuit, chewing gum, fiddling with a mobile phone.

"At the temple . . ." I reply slowly. It is my translator from the fortune-telling. She has that same darting, curious look.

Silence falls between us. Despite her youth there is something in her eyes that seems to suggest wariness, mistrust. That she has seen more than she should, that she has been dealt some bad hands. Something passes between us, and I can't tell what it is.

"I just help out there. It's not my real job," she says.

"Oh, okay."

"She's my mother's sister," she adds and then looks embarrassed, as if she has said too much. I change the subject, glancing down at her uniform.

"So then you're a croupier—I mean, a dealer?"

"Was." She turns her head back to her *macaron* and away from me. It's too awkward to ask her anything more.

"Well, good to see you here." I smile and move off to the counter. When I look back, she is staring down at her stomach, arms crossed over it. There is a soft weight there. I wonder . . . The question sinks my heart like a stone. I brush it out of my mind with thoughts of chocolate ganache, dark, sweet, buttery, and as smooth as paint. Two women come to order coffees. I recognize them as friends of Linda's. They lift their tortoiseshell sunglasses onto their heads and chat about their latest shopping trip in Zhuhai.

Dearest Mama,

What happened that day Mrs. Spencer told you I was never going to be any good at maths? You always made it the best story. I miss it. You have to tell it to me again.

All I really remember is the part where you rose to your feet and said something like "What exactly did you just say about my daughter, Pamela?"

Imagine—Mrs. Spencer having a first name. Pamela. Then she faltered and put her hand to her throat, touching those pearls of hers and not able to get any words out for a minute.

And you said, "Well?" with both eyebrows raised.

I can almost see her, pursing her lips and gathering up every ounce of courage she had from the soles of her small feet, right up to the pointy tips of her cropped hair.

"Well, Ms. Raven"—with a disapproving buzz on the Ms.—"Grace lacks conviction. She lacks action. If she would actually participate in class, rather than huddling down in the back, maybe she would learn something."

That's when she stood up too. A moment of great bravery for Mrs. Spencer, I thought, because she barely came up to your chest, and she knew that before she left the seat of her chair. It was going to give you an advantage right away, towering over her with a face full of fury. Then the best part—you pausing, leaning down, coming in close to her face. Close to that horrendous breath of hers; her mouth smelled like dead fish stapled to a wall for three weeks and allowed to rot. Whispering, "Seems you don't know a thing about my Grace, Pamela. She is full of conviction, as it happens. She just saves it up. For. Things. That. Matter."

That was the end of that, wasn't it? You turned around and never went back for a parent-teacher meeting again. I'd give you the notices and you'd tear them up in front of me, the two of us giggling like a pair of parrots.

So, Mama, you'd like this—it turns out that, contrary to popular belief, a lily-livered waitress can open her own café. She can make it work. And she can make a profit, even if it is a small one . . . for now.

Your loving daughter,

Grace

Coeur Curatif—Healing Heart
Vanilla with Raspberry Markings
and Raspberry Gel Insertion

Gigi, who has been coming to the café and staying for hours, is pregnant.

I can't pretend that she's not. Even Rilla notices.

In a rare chatty moment, Rilla murmurs to me, "Should she be drinking *so* much coffee?"

We both know what she means, but I don't answer her. Pretend not to hear her and keep stocking the fridge with milk. Rude, I know, but I don't want to talk about it. I cannot help the ache in my chest, looking at the swelling in Gigi's front, growing day by day. She covers it with long T-shirts and big handbags, sweatshirts if she can, but the weather is heating up and stepping into summer. It's there. Whether or not either of us prefers it wasn't. Noticing it always makes me feel heavy, as if I have swallowed stones.

Gigi's face is normally hunched over the classifieds section of the newspaper, probably searching for jobs. Usually she's scowling underneath her makeup and dark eyeliner. Except, of course, when she examines the *macarons* in their case. Then her face softens, a strange melting, like butter in a pan.

Her favorite is the same as mine. *L'Arrivée*. That smoky, caramel sweetness, tempered with the sharpness of rock salt, the filling sticky and toffee-like. I watch her pick up crumbs with her
finger and lick them off. She never wastes a single piece.

Week after week she is here, circling ads with a bright purple
marker decorated with tiny cartoon mice and drinking her coffees. She must go to interviews but not get the jobs. I assume
she is a Macau citizen, the most-sought-after employee in this
tight labor market. Is it her attitude? Her lack of experience? Or
the obvious bulge? I try not to think about it, or I begin to feel
that little pinch of pity. One day I suggested she should try an
herbal tea. Lightly, trying not to sound patronizing or judgmental.
Maternal. She glared at me sharply, then asked again for a cappuccino, please.

But today Gigi has not been in. In fact, it's been eerily quiet.
Rilla cleans the milk frother and looks distractedly out the front
window. There is a stillness in the air; even the sky seems to slump
limply.

"It's an odd day," I mumble, to myself mainly. Rilla nods in
agreement, her small, dark eyebrows bunched together.

There have been so few customers today, although Yok Lan
came in for a couple of hours in the morning for a cup of tea
and three of her favorite pink *macarons*. It was the most she'd
ever ordered or eaten; Rilla and I exchanged curious looks. She
sat close to the counter and smiled at us over the rim of her cup,
happy to watch us work. She is a goddess of peace, that woman;
I swear even angry dogs or stormy seas would calm when she is
about.

Rilla and I are running out of chores to busy ourselves with. I
have refilled all the saltshakers, carefully lining the bottoms with
grains of rice to absorb moisture from the humid air. She has
folded an entire box of napkins, stacking them in neat triangles,

ready for use. We have scrubbed all the oven trays and cleaned the windows. Rilla finishes with the milk frother and starts to rearrange the magazine shelf.

I place my hands on the front of the counter, leaning my weight against them. Beside me the unsold *macarons* are lined up in orderly rows in their glass case. I notice I am biting my lip, knowing I will have to discard some of these beauties if they don't sell today. Rilla has refused to take any home, although she will gather up unsold sandwiches. I don't know why; perhaps she thinks the *macarons* are too exotic and expensive for her, or that I might disapprove? I guess I might treat them with *too* much reverence.

"Okay, Rilla. It's time we gave you a proper full-blown tasting session," I tell her, throwing my tea towel over my left shoulder.

"Pardon me, ma'am?" she asks, looking up.

"A tasting. You and I are going to have a tasting."

"Oh," she breathes and smiles wide.

After selecting the *macarons*, I come over to the table where she is sitting with her back poker-straight in anticipation. Her eyes are round under her short glossy fringe. I put napkins in front of us and fill teacups with the steaming hot green tea she likes to drink.

"Here we go. You ready?"

She nods, and I have to laugh at her earnest face, mouth almost turned to a frown.

"All right. We'll start with *Une Petite Flamme.* It's our espresso *macaron.* Go on, try it."

She looks down at her plate. "This one? With the gold?"

"Yup, go on."

She puts it against her tongue like she's taking communion.

"Good?"

She nods quickly.

Then I place a purple one on her plate.

Rilla lifts it up. "This one has the jam inside, right?"

"Yes; it's *Remède de Délivrance*. Black currant filling, in the middle of the cream."

She closes her eyes while she eats it slowly. So slowly I worry she will need to come up for air.

"What does that mean?" she asks when she has finally swallowed the last tiny mouthful.

"*Remède de Délivrance*? 'Rescue remedy.' It's violet-flavored."

"This one is so good, ma'am." She grins, and I grin back. Rilla's small hands wrap around a teacup, the mouth of it laced with gold filigree painting. Outside the world seems still, suspended.

"I'm sorry, Rilla; it's so quiet today I should have let you have the afternoon off. I should have let you go home ages ago."

"It's okay. Too many people in my house anyway." The boardinghouse where Rilla lives accommodates dozens of workers, mainly women sending money back to their homes in other countries. She doesn't speak about it much, except to say that it is a bit crowded. Pete and I have four bedrooms for the two of us, and she is jammed in like a sardine. She says she used to work in Dubai, living with her employers. She doesn't talk about that much either, but perhaps she had her own room. Here she can't even put posters on the wall in case they damage the paint.

"You don't like it there?"

"I like it. It's cheap, so more money to send home. It's fun sometimes, people always talking and singing." Rilla laughs.

It astounds me, her easy generosity. I notice it in her all the time, taking back food to share with her roommates, sending old magazines to her sisters and brothers, mailing money for a niece's new shoes or schoolbooks. Rilla reminds me of a gerbera. A bright, colorful bloom with a surprisingly strong, wiry stem underneath.

Sipping my tea, I realize that I envy Rilla's commitments to her family. In some ways, even though I have four bedrooms and she lives with strangers, she has what I always wanted. For her, sharing is an easy choice. She is part of something greater. Some, not one.

She tries a few more flavors, enraptured, and then stands, picking up the empty plate and her teacup.

"Thank you. So delicious." She smiles at me.

She goes into the kitchen, humming. It is soft and out of tune; I wonder if she even knows she is doing it. I look down at my teacup. Delicate, beautiful, with heavy bunches of purple grapes painted as if hanging from the rim. The saucer is a bold kind of mauve tartan. It's the set I always reach for. I think of Mama, of fetching her cups of tea and clearing her plate just as Rilla now does for me. How she would grin up at me as if I'd done the nicest thing and murmur, "Oh, thanks, love."

There is no breadth to my family, like there is to Rilla's. I wonder if it gives her a swollen, full feeling to have a big, interconnected family like that. A kind of completeness. Ours was such a small, tight circle. Two was enough. Sometimes too much. I sigh, and in my mind there is a drumbeat of one word: *Mama, Mama, Mama* . . .

When I carry my cup and saucer into the kitchen, Rilla is steaming and polishing cutlery. She is singing now, slipping and sliding out of tune. I had assumed she would be a good singer, her voice as light and soft as a bird's, as she seems so capable at everything. But, in fact, her voice is truly awful. It shakes me out of my daze and makes me laugh. When she looks up, catching my expression, she starts to sing even louder, and I join her, giggling at our two voices, crooning and keening like a couple of mournful wolves howling to the moon.

The door chimes interrupt us. We both come out of the kitchen as Gigi rushes into the café. She pushes her fringe to one side to give Rilla and me a wary gaze. She takes a cautious step back and looks around the café, lifting her chin to see into the kitchen.

"Hi," I say.

Her hands are closed in small, nervous fists.

"A coffee?" I ask.

She turns to survey me once again. Her sweatshirt glitters with tiny diamantés in letters that I can't quite make out.

"I'm looking for my grandmother."

"Yok Lan?" Rilla asks.

I shoot her a puzzled look. "Yok Lan is your grandmother?" I wonder, incredulous. You couldn't get two more different characters. Talk about generational divide.

Rilla nods and whispers to me, "I think so. She talks to her sometimes."

I am impressed that Rilla is so observant.

"She was in earlier, but she's gone now," I tell Gigi.

"Is everything okay?" Rilla asks quietly from the other side of the table. "Yok Lan, is she all right?" There is affection in her voice.

"We need to find her before she hears the news. Everyone we know is okay, but she might freak if she's not sitting down. You know, she's old." Gigi shrugs. "Anyway, I think I know where she is. It's her day for mah-jongg. She'll be at Mei's."

This is the most she has said to me for weeks. I have to think for a second before asking, "Sorry, what news?"

"*The* news," she says. Then, when she sees we have no idea what she is talking about, she adds, "You know. The earthquake in Sichuan. You didn't feel it even a little bit?"

"There was an earthquake?"

"It's been all over the TV. You should have a TV in here."

Most restaurants in Macau have televisions hung in the corners. It never ceases to amaze me that people here watch television even while they're dining out. They seem to ignore whomever they are eating with, staring blankly at the square screen. I know it is a cultural difference I will never appreciate and stubbornly refuse to put a TV in Lillian's.

Gigi gives us a dark-eyed stare. "It was massive."

Rilla and I look at each other. Earthquake. My mind turns the word over.

"I've got to go," she finishes.

When she has her hand on the door handle, she pauses for a second and puts her head down, thinking of something. She goes back over to the counter, picks up a napkin and a pen, and scribbles her name and number. "Hey, if you ever see my grandmother alone or sad or whatever . . . What I mean is, Ma is useless, so it's best if you call me if she ever needs help. I try to keep an eye on her but . . . Anyway, you know, she's old . . ." she says again. Her voice is quiet, the worry peppered through it, although she is trying to sound nonchalant.

I pick up the napkin and nod. "Yes, of course. We will."

She gives me the tiniest of polite smiles before leaving.

Rilla and I stay standing in her wake for a moment. Wordlessly we fetch our bags. Now is not the time to polish cutlery; we need to close and go home. Go and see what has happened.

Dearest Mama,

Sichuan peppercorns are one of the five spices in Chinese five-spice powder. Five spices representing the five flavors in Chinese cooking—sweet, sour, bitter, savory, and salty. Did you know that already? It seems like something you might know, something you would tell me in a whisper as I went off to sleep. I had always thought Sichuan peppercorns were bright pink, but it turns out that is another peppercorn altogether. Sichuan peppercorns are reddish-brown. Today is a bitter day. Not sweet at all. Maybe sour. The kind of day that leaves you without hunger, throat aching from the strain of tears kept from falling.

When Pete came home, he sat down on the couch next to me and we watched the news for an hour straight without moving or talking. He didn't take off his tie, his belt, or his shoes. We just sat there and watched and waited for more pictures and information. They say the quake has killed maybe as many as forty thousand, but each time the reporter came back on the screen thin-lipped and ashen-faced, the number seemed to be creeping up. I finally made beans on toast and Pete got into shorts and T-shirt, but we kept watching until we were rubbing our eyes. The same footage over and over again—unnaturally quiet and gray streets, buildings toppled over like they'd been made with a child's blocks. The dust as thick as snow; only a few people left walking about in it, stunned and aimless.

It's getting hot in Macau now, but I took a bath before bed. I couldn't stop thinking about all that dirt and mess, men and women with broken hearts coughing and crying among it all. The schools of children, crushed. I felt like my heart was going to snap in two. Pete was asleep when I got out of the bath. I put on pajamas and climbed into bed, the ends of my hair still wet and leaving damp patches on the pillow.

Your loving daughter,
Grace

The day after the earthquake Lillian's is packed to the rafters. It is so crowded that those who can't find their own tables join strangers and start to talk. It is as if the catastrophe has brought out the community-minded side of people. Conversations are hushed, and customers linger over their coffees. Children are sent to the corner to play with our basket of toys, mutely constructing castles or ships out of LEGOs; even they must sense the need for regrouping and rebuilding. Rilla and I move quickly, trying to keep up with the rush but maintaining an aura of calm. Everyone is understanding, even when orders are mixed up or delayed. Rilla has brought in a Red Cross donation box, which we place on the counter in front of the biscotti jar. Coins plunk to the bottom all day like raindrops on a tin roof. By late afternoon we are both worn-out, and I take two chairs back to the kitchen. I motion Rilla to join me.

"We have got to take a break. Aren't you hungry?" I whisper.

She nods gratefully and holds up two chocolate muffins from the fridge counter. They are the last two left, and although they are popular with paying customers, I nod quickly; we need sustenance. We sit in silence, eating hurriedly and washing the dark chunks down with cold milk. Perched on our chairs like this, we must look like teenagers home from school, the kind of afternoon scene I always wished for. Rilla lets out a sigh, and I smile at her; she has chocolate smudging her chin. Just as I finish, the bell on the door chimes and Rilla's face falls around her mouthful. I shake my head at her.

"No way, I'll get this one. Stay there."

"Thanks, Grace," she mumbles through her muffin. I pause for a moment, notice she has not called me ma'am.

Gigi stands at the counter wearing a dark sweater that hangs down to her hips. She has green lace-up boots over black leggings. Her makeup is thicker than paint, kohl ringing her almond eyes like bruises and eyelashes gluey with mascara. Her hair is pulled back off her face.

"Hey," she says firmly, drawing herself up to her full height.

"Hey, Gigi. Your hair looks nice, the bangs . . ."

"Oh yeah, I pinned it back. I like to mix it up," she says, lifting her chin.

"It looks pretty."

"Thanks." She seems surprised by the compliment; her expression softens and her cheeks flush. It's as if her cool façade has slipped a little. I suddenly see something of Yok Lan's gentleness in her features.

"What can I get for you today?" I ask, wiping my hands on my apron.

Her eyes fall on the fridge counter, pretty bare now. She takes in the sight of a cake with thick frosting, covered in edible silver stars. I call it Princess Cake, and little girls love it. One of my regular mums says it is magic; it keeps her daughter quiet for at least twenty minutes.

"A slice of that. Please. And an espresso."

"Sure, I'll bring them out."

She gives me a cautious smile. Something feels different between us. Maybe it's because of the tragedy of the earthquake that we all feel closer to one another. Or maybe it's because I've learned that Yok Lan is her grandmother and with this information it feels as though we know each other better. Whatever the cause, Gigi is more relaxed with me today.

"Hey, how is Yok Lan?" I ask.

Rilla comes to stand next to me and silently extracts an espresso cup from the shelf. She must have heard the order from the kitchen.

"Pau Pau? Oh, she's fine. She was with her friends, playing mah-jongg. They had forgotten the time. Ma had a fit."

The espresso machine rumbles into action, dark liquid spurting from the metallic spout, depositing a thick caramel-colored cream on top. Rilla finds a saucer and looks up, concerned. I realize that Yok Lan must be one of her favorite customers.

"Your mum was cross?" I ask, plating up the Princess Cake, a generous wedge with lots of icing.

Gigi shrugs, her sweater falling off one shoulder, exposing a white bra strap, which has worn to a soft, gray color.

"Ma doesn't like Pau Pau playing mah-jongg. Reckons it's as

bad as gambling. Doesn't want her to get involved with it. You should have seen her face when I first said I was going to be a dealer. Well, she couldn't stop me, but she wasn't happy about it. Didn't complain about the salary, though."

She rescues her sweater, sliding it back up and over her shoulder. Her mouth snaps shut as if she has said too much, and she turns to find her favorite table. I follow behind with coffee and cake on a tray.

Before she leaves she comes up to pay her bill and spots the Red Cross box on the counter. She retrieves her purse and drops in a generous handful of coins, patting the top of it as if sending her best wishes. Her face is unarranged, fallen soft and young, despite the thick layer of makeup. When she glances up, she gives me a careful, thoughtful look.

"You should bake something for this."

"What do you mean?"

"Maybe a muffin with a red cross on the top. You know, donate some of the profits to the cause. People would like that."

I thank her, hesitantly. I'm not sure I want business advice from this girl. When she shrugs I notice a pearl of icing stuck in the knitted track in her sweater. A kind of maternal instinct draws me to lean over and brush it off, but she turns too quickly. Rilla stands beside me, and we both watch her leave. Rilla is drying a cup slowly, pushing the tea towel through the curved handle. After Gigi turns down the street and is no longer in view, Rilla continues to gaze out of the window.

"It's a good idea, the muffin," she says tentatively.

I nod. Grudgingly, I admit to myself that it is.

The next day Rilla and I are hunkered down, peering through the glass of the oven door. Marjory has become such a regular feature she is sipping her morning coffee in the doorway of the kitchen, watching us. She is wearing a silky blouse and shorts with sandals. Beside me, Rilla pushes her hair back, and I notice she is chewing her lip. Inside the oven the *macarons* slowly swell and harden.

I ask Rilla what she thinks.

"I don't know," she murmurs. "I guess it might work." She steals a glance at me, looking for reassurance.

"They look pretty good to me," says Marjory, lips suspended over her coffee cup. The tray is dotted with the top halves of *macarons,* white with two thin raspberry-colored stripes forming a cross. Rilla suggested we try Gigi's idea with a *macaron.*

"It was a great idea," I say, and touch her shoulder.

"Well, it was Gigi really . . ." Rilla begins. But suddenly she squeals, straightens up, and covers her mouth, which makes me jump and wheel around, one hand pressing against my heart.

"Shit!" Marjory yelps with a laugh, coffee splashing onto her sandals.

"Yok Lan!" Rilla screams, having fallen into a giggling fit. None of us had heard the jangle of the door chime.

Yok Lan stands harmlessly next to Marjory, looking into the oven window and pushing her glasses up against her nose. Her face is wrinkled in a squint; her hair pushed to one side as if she has just woken up. She looks surprised as we giggle but joins in, looking from Rilla to me and back again, trying to figure out what all the fuss is about. It is the first time we have seen her since the day of the earthquake, and she looks the same as ever, her kind, round, nut-colored face smiling and serene. I can't help but grin just at the sight of her.

"Good God, you scared the life out of me!" screeches Marjory.

Rilla wraps her arm around Yok Lan, and I notice that they are about the same size. She puts her young, dark head close to the old woman's, and Yok Lan leans into her. She pats Rilla's hand, resting on her thin arm, and Rilla guides her to a seat, telling her that she will make her a cup of tea. Marjory, smiling, heads to the bathroom to rinse off her sandals.

I stay in the kitchen staring at the *macarons,* trying to think of a good name for them. I've already decided that we will donate fifty percent of the profits to the Chinese Red Cross, although Pete will no doubt think I have no business sense at all. I've decided not to tell him, save us both the aggravation of fighting about it. Every night I am haunted by images of the aftermath of the earthquake. There are faces that look like Yok Lan's. Faces that look like Gigi's. Children wandering lost without parents, parents without children, deep, gruesome wounds, and even more severe heartbreak. Rilla passes me the daily papers when they are delivered, begging me with a grim expression not to look at the pictures. I move back from the heat and sit up near the sink, thumbing through a French dictionary, the cover bald and worn in my hands. I scroll through some words in my mind—relief, aid, support. *Aide, appui, soulagement. Coeur* floats into my mind like a balloon let loose. *Coeur curatif.* Healing heart. I wonder if the French is correct and make a mental note to call Léon to check. *Coeur curatif.*

A few days later, when the *Coeur Curatif macarons* have completely sold out, a small woman with dark hair stands beside the café door. But I am distracted, thinking of Léon's order. He came in yesterday and loved the new *macarons* and the charitable component so much he asked me to supply dozens for a brunch special at Aurora this coming weekend. I told him he was welcome to take the idea for himself if he wanted to make them; he has been so generous to Lillian's after all, it's the least we can do. But his face fell as he explained they have sold off most of the pastry kitchen equipment to make more room for a Chinese noodle kitchen. So I happily agreed to the order and offered him a discount. Now I want to produce *macarons* that will make him proud. They have to be perfect. It's a huge order for us; it will take us some late nights to fill. For now I am busying myself with other things while I carefully think through the extra ingredients we need to buy.

I notice the dark-haired woman as I clean the windows, even though she has tucked herself nearly out of view. She looks down at her feet and pushes a stone with her toe. Her arms are crossed and wrapped around the front of her as if she is giving herself a hug. Although it is warm, she is wearing a dark green hooded sweatshirt, long hair tucked down into the neck of it. I don't recognize her.

"Rilla?" I call out.

"Yes?"

"I think there might be someone to see you."

Rilla comes up behind me and looks out across the road. "Ma'am?"

"Not there." I turn her gently to face left and point to the woman, who suddenly looks up. When she sees us, she freezes. Dark hair frames her round face; her eyes are as dark as soot. She is older than I imagined from her slight frame, maybe in her early twenties, about Rilla's age.

"Yes, okay. Can I . . . ?" Rilla asks. There is a strange resolve in her voice I have never heard before. Her mouth is set in a grim line.

"Of course." I continue to rub the glass fiercely, using a balled-up piece of newspaper. This was Rilla's tip, to use newspaper on glass, and she was absolutely right, it works like a charm. When I step back, the glass glistens in the warm afternoon light.

Rilla has taken the woman across the road and is now leaning toward her, holding her arm gently. Rilla's lips are moving quickly, her face concerned but gentle. The woman has her hands pushed into her sweatshirt pockets, pressed into fists, the outlines of which I can see taut against the fabric. Rilla takes both of the woman's shoulders in her small palms and looks into her eyes. The woman nods and then falls softly toward Rilla, who catches her in an embrace. She rocks her from side to side like a baby, her eyes closed and mouth making the shape of a shush. When Rilla opens her eyes, she looks toward me at the window, newspaper limp in one hand and staring at them both. A flush of embarrassment sweeps over my face. I turn too quickly, almost tripping on a chair leg. I put down the newspaper and glass cleaner on an empty table and walk into the kitchen. Dishes that Rilla was cleaning are floating among the suds in the sink. I put on a pair of gold-colored rubber gloves and plunge my hands deep into the water.

Le Dragon Rouge—Red Dragon
Dragon Fruit Filled with
Lemongrass-Spiked Buttercream

Y ou're being ripped off," Gigi says bluntly when she pays her bill with a pile of coins.

"Ripped off?" I repeat, scooping up the change.

"The delivery guys who come in here with your flour, sugar, all that stuff? They were talking about it. You're being charged almost double for some of those things."

I look up at her quickly.

"I'm not joking," she says defensively.

"They . . . talk about it?" I say slowly, closing the register.

"Yeah. I've seen them come in before, and just this last time, they were chatting about the supplier. I know him. Well, I know who he is."

I must look baffled because she carries on, her voice angry. "My grandmother, she had a restaurant. My family have always had restaurants. Well, till Ma ran it into the ground. Now she's in real estate like every other greedy . . ." She shakes her head. "Anyway, that guy, he's a crook. He rips off the *gweilos*, the expats. You should be getting your stuff from Red Dragon. They're much better *and* cheaper."

133

I lean my hands against the counter and take a long breath. "Seriously? I mean, they're really doing that? Charging double?" I can feel my face start to burn. I ask the question, but I know that Gigi is not lying; my instincts are singing with the truth of it. I had thought the price was high but didn't know what to expect here. I had trusted him. Now I am angry. All those extra supplies for the Aurora order, the cost. More money could have been going to the Red Cross. I feel so naïve, trusting Mr. Teng to give us a good deal. What a snake.

Gigi gives me a hurt look. "I'm not lying." She picks up her wallet and turns to leave. "Whatever," she adds coolly.

I step from behind the counter and catch her by the elbow before she is out the door. She swings around to face me, that round belly almost touching mine. I have that feeling again, like stones in the pit of my stomach. It takes me a second to shake it off. My problems are not her fault.

"Hey, hey, wait. Sorry." I suck in a deep breath. "I do believe you. I just feel like an idiot, that's all."

She shrugs.

"I didn't use another supplier because Mr. Teng speaks English and . . . I don't speak Cantonese," I explain.

"I can see that," she replies archly. She doesn't move, but one hand is on the door.

"Well, maybe I need someone who does." I sigh.

We look at each other like boxers in the ring. Staring and not saying anything. Each waiting for the other to make her move. I have to be the grown-up here, I say to myself. She blinks at me with those brooding, almond-shaped eyes.

And so I hire Gigi as a part-time employee of Lillian's. Her probation period is three months. We'll see how she goes.

Cirque—Circus

Lime with Chocolate Ganache, Dusted with Blood-Orange Sugar

The season has plunged, without warning, headfirst into summer; the air is suddenly lemonade-sticky and cloying. Feet slide sweatily in sandals, trousers cling wetly to the backs of legs. The air-conditioning in the café helps, but when the ovens are cranking, the kitchen turns into a blistering nightmare. I can no longer wear my hair down; rather I pile it up on my head like a half-fallen bird's nest. The only person the heat doesn't seem to bother is Rilla; she still wears long-sleeved tops that she tugs down over her hands.

I have made us both frozen treats from bananas dipped in chocolate then chilled in our freezer. We wait until the customers from the early-morning rush have left before sitting by the window, positioned directly under the air-conditioning unit. I let out a hot sigh; Rilla blows air up to her forehead. The bananas are hard and creamy, slivers of frozen chocolate sliding onto the table and floor. Rilla glances at the mess, pieces of her hair stuck fast to her forehead.

"Don't worry about that; we need a break. What a morning."

She raises her eyebrows in agreement. I know she is relieved that Gigi is starting this afternoon. I suspect she is a bit nervous about how it will all work out, she and I having found a kind of rhythm. But she's hot and tired too, and the extra pair of hands will make a difference.

Beyond the window a gaggle of schoolgirls saunter by in their uniforms—white T-shirts and maroon polyester trousers. They wear their hair in ponytails, long fringes dangling coyly over their faces. Giggling ensues.

"This weather is unbelievable. Not like home." I shake my head. Pete has a golf tournament with some suppliers this afternoon. He will come home the color of beetroot and cursing. Lazily, I put my feet up on the seat of a chair.

"Australia?" Rilla asks.

"No, London," I reply, realizing with surprise that I still consider it my home.

"Do you miss it?"

The question gives me pause. When I first moved to Macau, after living back in London for a few years, I did long for things I didn't know I would miss. Ridiculous, seemingly inconsequential things. Marmite on toast, the anonymity of riding the Tube, warm pubs. The weekend magazine inserts in the *Guardian*—oh, how I craved those. I even missed that horrible gray London sky. I remember back to those first months in China. How I had forgotten things. Misplaced keys and socks and papers. I had cried instead of laughing when I watched an episode of *Little Britain*; put eggshells into a cake mix and the eggs in the rubbish. And then, of course, I missed Mama most of all, her laughter over a cup of tea, the taste of her special blackberry syrup with pancakes. Homesickness really is like that—a kind of sickness, an irritating cough or rash you have to ignore until you forget about it, get used to it, or both.

I see it in my customers, suffering so transparently; I wonder if they realize how obvious they are. Their long faces over teapots and empty, crumb-laden plates. They stay too long and talk too much, relishing a familiar accent or an English menu. Personal details spilling out over orders or payments, then forced laughs, awkward smiles. If you ask them how they are, as I have now learned not to, there is always a polite lie, slick as rain on the road. *Oh, Macau is wonderful, such a great opportunity. To have a maid—imagine! All my friends back home are so jealous. And we're going to Phuket for the weekend, you know.* Just before they swoon and grin, you can catch the pause, if you're observant. Not a long pause, but enough. That pocket of truth, dark and silent. I hate this enduring need to make out that your life is perfectly blissful. I think this is why I have always been shy; I never learned this code. The oily lies and half-truths leave me feeling uncomfortable and queasy.

"I did," I say softly. I now know that what I really miss is what I thought would be my future, rather than my past. Children, baking cakes, making a family.

Rilla smiles. She settles back against her chair and starts to hum, breaking off the last pieces of banana from the stick with her teeth. Her skin is clear and bright; she is beautiful in these quiet moments. Content. If Pete and I have to leave Macau, we can always return to Australia or England. Hell, we could probably go to Canada, Europe, almost anywhere, with our passports. I wonder, grimly, about Rilla's limited options.

"Yok Lan!" she sings through an icy mouthful.

The old lady comes in leaning on her granddaughter's arm. Gigi is early. She wears a pair of leggings and an oversize shirt, freshly ironed I notice. Her hair is tied off her face neatly. She lifts her eyes to me a little shyly, lashes thick with mascara. Rilla leaps up to make a pot of Yok Lan's favorite tea.

"You two want some frozen chocolate bananas?" I offer.

Gigi translates to her grandmother, who shakes her head. "Pau Pau won't, but I will." She sinks into a chair, and I can see she is getting heavier week by week. She takes Yok Lan's cane, puts it out of the way, then lifts a menu from the table and fans her with it. It is a small gesture but filled with love. Yok Lan smiles and closes her eyes, cheeks falling into soft, doughy folds.

"Can you ask Yok Lan if she wants me to make it iced tea today?" calls Rilla from the counter.

"No, she has it hot no matter what the weather is," Gigi replies for her, shrugging. She mutters to me with a raised eyebrow, "She's just old school. You know, traditional."

Yok Lan smiles at her granddaughter.

"Um, we have something for you," Gigi says to me awkwardly.

Rilla brings a cup, a teapot, and a plate with a medley of *macarons* on it to the table. She hands Gigi her frozen treat, and Gigi takes it, plunging her other hand into a bag at her feet. She huffs a little as she bends forward.

"Pau Pau . . . ?" She finishes her question in Cantonese.

Yok Lan sits up and nods. She looks to me with sparkling eyes and takes a birdlike sip of her tea.

Gigi passes me a thin plastic sleeve, a piece of paper sandwiched inside. "Pau Pau found this and wanted you to have it," she explains.

The paper is soft and worn, about seven inches square. It is a print of children in bright shorts and shirts, dancing and whirling red fizzing rings. The girls have long dark plaits like ropes down their backs and the boys half-sphere cap-like haircuts lifted up in the pretend breeze. They wear their shoes with high white socks. A narrow slice of moon hangs in the sky. Down the left-hand side is a faded red border with black Chinese characters, at the bottom a notice in English: YICK LOONG FIREWORKS CO. I feel Rilla's breath near my shoulder, leaning over to see what it is.

"It's an old poster. The company used to be famous. Their factory was right here in Taipa; friends of hers used to hand-roll the crackers. She thought you might like to hang it in the café? But only if you want to," she adds quickly.

Yok Lan looks at me, her cheeks lifted in a smile. She watches for my response.

"It's brilliant," I declare. I am already thinking of where I can put it. Perhaps frame it with a green mat and get Pete to help me with the right hook. I step out of my chair and walk with it around Lillian's. The light falls nicely on one wall, but perhaps the glare will fade it. I hold it at arm's length, pressing it up against the walls. Yok Lan is grinning in delight, palms pressed together. She chatters gleefully in Cantonese. Gigi gets to her feet to join me. She pulls her ponytail closer to her scalp and presses her lips together in assessment.

"Maybe here?" she suggests, leaning over a table. I put my head to one side and look at the short wall, near the counter. It is bright enough, but the sunlight won't fade the print.

"We'll have to move the table . . ." Rilla points, pouring Yok Lan tea from the pot with the other hand.

"Here, I'll do it." Gigi energetically leans across the tabletop to grasp its sides. Her shirt sags in front of her as she lets out a breath. Yok Lan looks up sharply. She bursts out in Cantonese, scared, warning, reaching for her cane.

Gigi lets go of the sides of the table and stands back, bright red with embarrassment. "I can do it, Pau Pau!"

Rilla puts a hand on Yok Lan's shoulder to calm her. Gigi's cheeks are flushed. The urge to ask a million questions tugs at me, but not one will sit still in my mind. Rilla is looking at me, but I can't stop staring at Gigi, catching Rilla's pointed gaze from the corner of my eye. All four of us remain in our places, the air hanging heavy and silent.

Finally, Rilla says, "Hey, who would like a *macaron*? We have a new one . . . Grace, what is it called?" She clears her throat deliberately.

I find my voice and reply. *"Le Dragon Rouge."*

"And it's dragon fruit . . ."

"With a lemongrass-spiked filling."

"It's fruity and creamy at the same time." Rilla nods at me. "It's so good."

Gigi glances at Rilla and then back at me. She lowers her head and whispers, "I'm okay to do things, you know. I can work."

Her face is so earnest, so free from her usual anger; I almost want to wrap my arms around her. But there is something deeper and resilient in her too, which keeps me from reaching over.

I nod and put my hand on her slender shoulder. "I know. It's okay."

I can hear Rilla chatting with Yok Lan about the different *macarons* on the plate, pointing out each one and describing it, even though the old woman cannot understand a word of her English. Yok Lan watches Rilla's finger move over the white plate, one vivid circle at a time.

Gigi looks at me directly. Her face is determined. "So where do I start? You want this table moved? I can do it."

I shake my head slowly. "No, not till I have the poster framed and we can make sure it's the right spot. Besides, there are more important things for you to do. I need you to help me tell Mr. Teng where he can go shove his supplies."

"Where he can *shove* them?"

"Yeah."

She gives a small laugh and replies, wryly, "Now *that* I am good at."

* * *

I hear it from the kitchen; quickly putting down the dirty plates I have just carried in, I rush to the doorway.

"This is ridiculous!" a customer bellows, leaning a large and unhealthy gut against the counter. "You can't serve cold coffee. You'll have to get me a new one. But now I'm late, aren't I?" He slams his cup down on the counter. He had ignored Rilla when she brought it to his table, conducting a noisy business call on his phone, meaty arm resting across the tabletop. She found a place for it and set it down gently, but by the time he finished his call and noticed it, it was indeed stone cold.

Rilla grabs at the ends of her long sleeves and looks down at the tiles. I wait for her to look up and address him squarely. She normally dissolves the tension of these situations with her peaceful smile, but something has her undone.

"Well?" he demands.

She remains mute.

Gigi looks up from her tub of dishes. She flashes me a violent glare. "What an asshole," she hisses.

I call out, "We'll get you a new coffee in a takeaway cup, sir. Won't be a moment."

As I come out of the kitchen, he straightens up and runs his eyes over me. His gaze hovers for a few long seconds on my breasts before drifting back up to my eyes.

I give him a cocktail-sweet smile. "Take a seat and we'll bring it over to you. Just a minute, that's all."

"Right." His breath is warm and sour, stale coffee clinging to his tonsils. He looks pointedly at Rilla, who has not moved, grunting as he lowers himself into a chair. He makes another call, the inconvenienced expression falling easily from his fleshy face. I move around Rilla to fetch a takeaway cup.

"You okay?" I whisper.

She nods and takes the paper cup from me, filling the espresso machine with grinds and placing the cup under the spout. Her hands shake. I pat her shoulder and feel her angle her body ever so slightly into the cup of my palm. She looks up at me, an apology in her eyes. "I . . . it was just that guy. I'm sorry." She shakes her head like she wants to dislodge something from it.

Gigi has come out of the kitchen, water dripping from the cloth in her hands. Her face is dark. "That rude bastard. I'm going to go talk to him."

"Dammit, Gigi, you're dripping all over the floor. Go back there and we'll handle it. It's okay," I tell her.

Gigi shrugs angrily and turns around.

Rilla murmurs, "Sorry, Grace."

"Hey, it's fine. Don't you worry," I whisper.

Rilla delivers the coffee, holding the cup up for the man to eyeball. He glares at her and lifts his head reluctantly in acknowledgment. Tucking papers and business magazines under a flabby wing, he leaves Lil's, still bellowing into his phone.

Rilla sighs as the bell above the door chimes his exit. A quiet peace settles over the café. When she returns to the counter, she quickly changes the subject.

"Aren't you going to the circus tonight?"

"Oh. Yes, you're right, I am."

I had forgotten. Before she'd gone away for a long weekend break with Don, Marjory had won four tickets to Cirque du Soleil at a charity auction and asked me to go with her. She had held them up casually, but her face was tinged with a strange hopefulness. It takes a woman who doesn't make friends easily to recognize another; Marjory had that look, and I knew it. Besides, Pete and I had spent only about five minutes together in the last month. I look around Lillian's—the tables need wiping, the cash register has to be balanced, and the espresso machines must be cleaned out. The dishes can dry on the rack overnight, but there is a lot still to be done. Rilla spies me chewing on my lip and staring at the dirty tabletops.

"Don't stick around, Grace, we can close up."

"No, no, Marjory won't mind, I can go another day . . ."

"No, let us do it. You should go. I know how to do it all, it will be okay." She touches my back lightly and goes into the kitchen.

I can hear Gigi complaining about stupid men and how some guys think they are the Kings of Everyone and what she would like to say to That Big Fatso. I take a cloth to the tables, sticky with crumbs of *macarons.* I tap the side of my trousers, underneath my apron. The familiar bulge of my mobile phone meets my fingertips. I could call Marjory now, see if we could postpone, do it some other time. Rilla's light laugh comes from the kitchen. Turning back, I can see her framed in the small window to the kitchen.

I finish the last of the tables and lean into the kitchen. "Rilla?"

She glances up at me, gloves deep in the sink.

"I will get you two to close up, if that's okay."

She nods and smiles.

"Thank you."

I walk home briskly, breathing in the cooling dusk air. I love the circus—cotton candy, clowns with painted faces, music too loud, colors too bright. Reminds me of Mama. But I had forgotten all about it until Rilla mentioned it. The day has been a blur of broken cups, supplies to unpack and stack, dishes covered in buttercream and ganache. Gigi has been a saving grace; she seems comfortable managing contractors, anyone who needs bossing about. She also loves the *macarons;* I can see it in her young face. She asks me a hundred questions about how they are made, where the recipes come from, what they are like in Paris. She and Rilla are starting to form their own little partnership, each doing what she does best. There are still a thousand chores, we are still busy. By the time I leave each day I am coated in a salty film from the roots of my hair to the soles of my aching feet. Lillian's is swallowing up not only all my time but also all my thoughts. My head is an overstuffed suitcase of recipes, appointments, to-do lists, timetables, a date with Don and Marjory to go to the circus . . . The last thing to go in often seems to be the first to fall out.

When I rush through the front door like a whirling dervish, Pete is sitting on the couch, flicking through a magazine. He is wearing jeans, ready to leave. His face, dimly lit, doesn't give any clues to his mood.

"Sorry, sorry, busy day—*mad*. I won't be long," I sing out, heading to the bedroom and the wardrobe. On the walk home I'd worked out what to wear tonight, so I only have to squeeze myself into a pair of jeans and throw on a white linen blouse. I give a small thanks to the heavens that the blouse is already ironed. The night air breathes through the linen to my skin, keeping me cool. I curse as deodorant seeps through the cloth, leaving a small stain under each arm, but there isn't time to change. I find my silver earrings; dig out silver sandals from the back of the wardrobe. I hop into the living room, still slipping on the sandals. I figure it's taken me about eight minutes to get ready. Nearly the same amount of time it takes to make a smooth ganache for the center of a *macaron*.

"Okay, I'm ready." I smile at my husband.

As he looks up, I can see there is no resentment in his face, just weariness. His cheeks are ashen, left eye bloodshot; he has obviously been rubbing it. He looks frayed around the edges.

"Oh good, love. You look nice. Different," he murmurs.

"Thanks—it's probably the jeans, they are getting really tight. I've been eating my version of Hermé's *Ispahan macaron* all week, trying to get it right. It's a curse."

"Eating what?"

"*Ispahan.* It's a rose *macaron,* with raspberry insertion . . . that berry jelly in the middle. It doesn't matter."

The clock distracts me. We have eleven minutes to find a taxi and get to the Venetian Macao, where a theater has been custom-built for the show. Linda and her book club friends have been clucking about it for weeks. "It's a marvel," I had heard her gush, while claiming to know the choreographer personally. I wonder what the costumes are like. I have seen the poster of a girl with a long tangerine silk scarf floating behind her trapeze while she sails across a black and starry sky. Sparkling and citrus-colored, she looks like a confection.

As Pete and I ride down in the elevator, I catch a glimpse of my milky reflection in the unwashed mirrored wall and realize I have no makeup on. I lean forward for a closer inspection. I look terrible. Skin floury white and eyebrows unshaped. Pete reaches for my hand. His is cool and as smooth as stone in my warm, damp palm.

"No makeup, huh?"

"That's why I look different. Shit." I curse. "Why didn't you tell me?"

He squeezes my hand. "I don't know. I guess I like it. You look natural."

Pete is so quiet I have to listen closely. He looks down at me, his freshly washed hair falling silkily over his forehead, and smiles.

"Damn, I don't have time to go back upstairs, do I?"

"No, stay here. I . . . Grace, it looks kind of nice, you know?" he says somewhat shyly.

I am not convinced. My eyelashes are pale; my lips are a washed-out pinkish gray without lipstick. I notice the circles under my eyes, new wrinkles spreading from the corners. I lift my head resolutely and hope that Marjory won't look too much like a movie star tonight, although that is like wishing for the Pope to be a little less Catholic.

Don is not what I expected. I guess I thought someone like Marjory would have a picture-perfect husband. All white teeth and hair and muscles. Don isn't even as tall as Marjory, who stands, column-like, beside him, her hand gripping his firmly. She wears a white minidress and gleaming golden sandals. Gold earrings swing from her ears. She looks as good as Mama used to look when she dressed up for an evening out. All legs and smile. Men walking past us do double takes, and I know it's not for me. She's been to Boracay for a few days, and her skin glows as if she captured the sun in every pore. She catches my elbow and whispers, "So glad you came. Don and I are so excited to get to know you and Pete a little better." My eyes drift over the crowd of heads, stopping at the silver hair among the throng. Léon passes a glass of champagne to his wife, Celine. Diamonds sparkle in her ears, dimples punctuate her cheeks as she smiles. His hand rests against her bare shoulder while she takes the glass from him. I stare too long; he must feel my gaze as his eyes lift to meet mine. Blue, sparkling in the artificial light. He raises his hand and smiles. I do the same, my cheeks feeling warm.

Marjory introduces me to Don, who grins and shakes my hand vigorously. He must be a good ten years older than she is. He is short, bald, and has a face like a turtle. Big eyes and a wide smile.

"I've heard so much about you, Grace," he says warmly. "Marjory says Lillian's is the best café in Macau."

"Oh, well . . ." Pride flushes through me, although I look at the ground modestly.

"It's true," says Marjory.

Pete stands awkwardly to one side. There is a strange pause, and I realize I need to introduce him. Normally it is the other way around.

"This is Pete, my husband. He's working with the Marvella Resort project."

Pete shakes hands, and Don gives him a jovial slap on the arm. He may be older, but he has the energy of a younger man. Sprightly, despite a little flab around the middle. His eyes crinkle up at the corners.

"Pete Miller! I've heard all about you. Good to have another Aussie bloke around, getting things done."

Marjory gives her husband a smile and puts her other hand against his arm. "Babe, we're going to miss the first half if we don't get in there."

She releases Don's hand, and she and I walk toward the entrance together, while Don and Pete follow behind, chatting about the project. As our tickets are checked, Marjory leans in toward me. "I feel like I've been away for weeks. You have to tell me how it's going with Gigi. And how is Rilla getting along with her? I want to hear *everything*."

Dearest Mama,

How you would have loved tonight. So strange and beautiful, Mama. My heart still races in my chest, my thoughts crashing into each other. My skin burns, and I cannot sleep.

Out of the velvety darkness of the theater came a circus show like no other. A dream. A vibrant fantasy. Like one of your stories, Mama. Characters flying through the air, bodies electric and magical, fire seeming to flow directly from throats, illusions and visions.

The way the performers use their bodies, Mama. The music runs through them, rushes through them, as if it owns their physical beings. Passion, strength, and music coursing through veins and muscles, they move as if they have given themselves over to a power greater than any of us, as if they are surrendered to life force itself. Leaping, rolling, diving, hair flung back, eyes wide, and faces upturned with abandon. It was almost too much to watch. It seemed somehow too personal. Bodies embraced and thrown, the smell of sweat and greasepaint, faces in concentration and ecstasy. I felt my breath catch in my throat and my heart quicken. I longed to be there with them, moving as one, feeling hands on me, catching and tossing me into the dark. Feeling the knots of muscles under those costumes against my body, against my skin; breath in my hair and hot against my neck.

Then the world went quiet. The stage black as night. A man and a woman appeared as if in the moonlight, the lights against their bodies making them look like snow. Gray and silver and blue and white. They held each other on a pedestal shaped like a floating iceberg, moving together as though in a kind of trance. Languidly lifting and sliding over each other like water. They made a single being, holding each other with their faces pressed close together like Klimt lovers. Each breath tangled with the other's, fitting into each other's bodies like a jigsaw. The man's face was ethereal and silver, strong and perfect, as if carved from marble. I could almost feel the shape of his cheekbone against mine, his cool, thick fingers on my flushed skin. A sweet shiver rippled over my body. The thought of him against me, pressing into me. My breath caught in my throat.

Pete leaned over as if to say something. He reached for my hand, perhaps looking at me in the dark. But I could not turn to him. My eyes were fixed on that stage, on the being that seemed made of ice. My body quivered with that wonderful feeling. Desire. My skin tingling. The thought of a touch that could make me shiver all over, cool my burning skin and make me feel like I was melting.

Your loving daughter,
Grace

La Fièvre—Fever

Rose with Dark Chocolate and Hot Ginger Ganache

igi disagrees with Rilla about the placement of the *maca-rons*. She leans over the counter, clucking in disapproval.

"You can't go putting *this macaron* with *that macaron*," she says, exasperated. Her fingers tap on the glass, pointing out *Rêves d'un Ange* and *Coeurs Curatifs* lying next to each other like casual lovers. I glance over Rilla's shoulder as I spoon froth onto the top of a cappuccino. They are both white, and would look better separated. Marjory doesn't look up from her magazine and coffee, but I hear her stifle a knowing laugh, so I can tell she is listening.

Rilla's face falls, wounded. She gives me a quick look, hoping I'll rescue her. I shrug; this is not my battle.

"Well . . ." Rilla stammers, pulling herself up to her full height, which is still tiny. "Well, thank you. But that's your opinion."

Gigi flicks her eyes skyward and shakes her head. Her eyelids are painted with fashionable charcoal gray; a red, oversize watch swings from her slender wrist. "Yeah, okay. Whatever." She sighs dramatically.

Rilla looks back to me, biting her lip. I give her a reassuring wink. She smiles, flushed with new confidence. When the door chimes, they both turn toward it.

"'Ello!" The voice carries across the café as Léon strides to the counter, carrying a bag in his left hand. There is laughter glittering behind his eyes, a broad smile on his face. Rilla offers him a polite hello, but Gigi stands back, staring suspiciously.

"Hi, Léon, how are you?"

"I am well, Grace, and you?" He leans forward to kiss my cheeks, his warm breath whispering across my earlobes.

"Fine." I falter slightly and clear my throat.

Rilla takes the cappuccino from my hands and delivers it to the customer waiting at a table by the window. I can see Marjory lifting her head, glancing between Léon and me.

"Léon, this is Gigi."

Gigi looks at me and then gives Léon her hand. He takes it and shakes it lightly. She gives him a wary stare.

"Hello, and congratulations," Léon says, beaming. I wonder how he can tell instantly that Gigi is pregnant; she hides it pretty well. I am always aware of it, the taut barrel of her stomach against the grain of her clothes, but that may be because of my own history. Gigi looks up at him, surprised, and slumps her shoulders so her shirt pools forward. She mumbles something under her breath, her almond-colored cheeks turning pink.

"Do you know if it is a girl or boy?" he adds.

She looks up quickly, eyes growing dark. Her embarrassment shifts to haughtiness. "No idea." She turns on her heel and walks back into the kitchen with a coffee for herself.

"I don't know if so much caffeine is good for the baby," I murmur.

"Ah, don't worry. Celine, she had everything when she was pregnant, even wine. In France we don't make so much fuss." He shakes his head with delight. "She reminds me of someone, that girl. Such spirit."

"Spirit? She's a wildcat. Sorry about that, she can be a little . . . impolite." I laugh.

"Oh no," he replies, voice as soft as butter against hot toast. "It is passion. People like this, they will be the successful ones. She will be okay. After all, she is still young."

To that I have to nod.

"Tell me, how is business?" He leans on the counter.

"Actually, it's great. Making a profit now, would you believe it?"

"Ah, you are a natural for this industry. It must be in your blood."

I nod, realizing how accurate he is. *The man. The bakery. Mama.* It sends a strange sensation down the back of my shoulder blades, tingling at the base of my spine.

"Can I get you an espresso? On the house, of course."

"*Oui.* With pleasure. I also want to buy a box of these." He points to the white *macarons,* red crosses in the centers. "They're still my favorites, and if I bring some home tonight I'll be 'in the good books,' as you say. Are you still raising a bit of money? Such a marvelous idea."

Rilla is back and takes a white takeaway box from the shelves behind the counter.

"We are, a pretty steady little donation each week. It's not much, but it's something. And the idea came from Rilla and that wildcat back there." I put fresh coffee grinds into the machine. The smell is rich, intoxicating.

"Ah, well, you see, I knew she was the kind to have talent."

Hot water presses through the grinds, squealing with the effort, a dark stream bursting forth into the small cup. Léon turns back, and I catch a flash of his eyes. They are that duck egg blue of an autumn sky before it rains. The whites are clear and bright, the lashes pied, dark and gray. Looking into them makes me feel a bit dizzy.

"I have a present for you," he says gently.

I push his coffee toward him and then, remembering my manners, come out from behind the counter myself, wiping my hands against the stripes of my apron.

He lifts a long-handled fork with three thin prongs from his bag. It has an aura of danger about it, like a devil's trident.

"What is it?"

He laughs at my bewildered expression. "In French we say *fourchette à tremper.*" The words roll from his tongue like sweet marbles. He holds it gently in both hands and presents it to me. "I thought you might use it, if you are making chocolates to put onto cakes or something like that."

"A chocolate fork?" I remember the chef in the kitchen of Aurora, dipping pralines in the dark chocolate lava, rolling them against the pale flesh of marble. The memory makes my mouth water.

Léon's eyes are smiling at me. "Yes, a chocolate fork. I'm sure you know how to use it. Anyway, it can take some practice, but . . ." He shrugs in the way only a Frenchman can, curling his bottom lip almost petulantly.

A chocolate fork. What a gift.

"Thank you, Léon. This is so thoughtful." I take it with both hands and then lean closer to give him a kiss on each cheek. The rough hair of his jaw brushes against my lips. He smells of hot baked bread and cinnamon.

Over his shoulder I see the top of the door open and then close against the chimes. They jangle like champagne glasses knocking together at a wedding.

"Pete!" I call out, a little too brightly.

My husband looks from Léon to me and back again. His gaze drifts slowly to the fork in my hands. A key ring is looped over his index finger.

"What are you doing here?" I ask with a smile.

"Thought you might like a ride home." There is a frown between his eyes. He catches sight of Rilla, who gives a small wave. "Hey, Rilla."

"Hi, Pete," she sings back.

Gigi peeks out from the kitchen; she has not yet met Pete, but she quickly retreats with her cup in her hands. Pete comes to Lil's every now and then, but he's not what I'd call a regular. I know we've grown distant; it's as if our lives are moons orbiting different planets. Pete belongs to Mars, Grace to Venus. But he is here now, and it feels strangely awkward to have him in my territory, the slice of Macau that is all mine. Pete looks back at Léon, his gaze cool. An energy zaps among Pete, Léon, and me that I can't even understand, let alone explain. It's as though Pete can read my mind, my heart, those little teenage waves of lust.

Léon clears his throat and steps forward to greet him. He shakes Pete's hand with a broad smile, his other hand grasping Pete's shoulder. Perhaps he doesn't notice when Pete leans away from him.

"Long time no see." Léon grins.

"Yeah, yeah. It's Léon, right?" Pete anglicizes his name, stretching out the *e,* the *n* thick at the end. I see Léon's face drop just a little.

"Léon, yes," he replies, gently correcting Pete's pronunciation.

"Uh-huh. How've you been?" Pete smiles with closed lips and a slight lift of his chin. The frown is still knitted in his forehead.

"I am really well. Business is good. Perhaps not as good as Lillian's, but I can't complain."

Pete looks around the café. Marjory gives him a smile, which he returns.

"It does a pretty good trade, huh?" he admits. There is a confused mixture of pride and shame in his voice. It looks to me like he wants to say something more, but then his gaze drops to the floor.

Léon speaks instead, his voice light and unaffected. Perhaps he is the only one of us not noticing the obvious. "Well, I should get going. Thanks for the coffee. And the *macarons*." He lifts the box of *Coeurs Curatifs,* which Rilla has tied with a ribbon.

"My pleasure. Thank you for the chocolate fork."

"No problem," he replies graciously and turns without kissing me goodbye.

When he leaves, the café seems quiet, the large, bright presence of him emptied from the room. I eye the door through which he left as darkness creeps into the early-evening sky. The register closes with its signature ring. I look back to Pete, who is staring at me.

"I've just got to tidy up, get ready for tomorrow . . ." I say quickly, moving back around the counter and untucking my tea towel.

"Sure." He nods. "I'll have a chat with Marjory. I've been meaning to get Don's number to catch up for a beer."

"Okay."

"Okay," he returns.

It takes him a moment to turn and me a moment to start clearing out the counter fridge.

Later that night I wake up on the couch. My foot has fallen drowsily to the floor, and I make a short sound between a grunt and a moan. It is dark beyond the open curtain, and I'm covered in sweat, my hair stuck to my forehead. The television is blaring, pictures of people jumping up and down with bright flags. It takes me a few seconds to rearrange the details into a lucid ensemble. I am in the living room, Pete is dozing on the couch, opposite; we had been watching a documentary about the upcoming Beijing Olympics. There have been protests and arrests, violence in Tibet, people evacuated as their homes are replaced with stadiums. I rub my eyes and look over at Pete. He is stretched out, full-length, and snoring loudly.

I wobble to the kitchen. My head is heavy and fuzzy, like a watermelon on my neck. I pray that I am not getting sick; I don't have the time. I drink a glass of water in big, urgent mouthfuls. When I put it down, I misjudge the angle. The glass skates along the countertop before falling to the floor and shattering. The pieces fly apart, making pretty, dangerous shards all over the floor.

"Shit."

I crouch down, my legs feeling a little shaky, and start to pick up the fragments. A tiny diamond of glass presses into my fingertip and makes me curse again. Being crouched like that, my head thundering, and feeling the shock of the cut, which is now leaving tiny tears of blood on the floor, seems to hurtle me back into memories. The dark kitchen could be any kitchen. Here and now or then and there.

I try to focus on picking up the last slivers, but I am distracted by a foggy kind of remembering.

"Mama?"

There she is in the corner. Sitting on the floor. Knees bent up toward her chest.

"Hey, Mama?"

Her eyes are red-rimmed and wild-looking.

"Gracie," she whispers, as if someone might be listening.

"What are you doing?"

She's got her satin dress pulled on over a pair of jeans. She stares at me, bewildered and lost. Her eyes make two brown pools in her face. I squint to see her better in the dim light. The dress has a tear down one armpit, like she tried to tug it on too fast.

"Mama, what are you doing in here?"

"Oh. Oh well . . ." She glances to either side of her, not letting go of her knees. "I was just . . . looking for something I guess," she says, and I can hear the tremor in her voice.

"What were you . . . ?"

"Come here, Gracie girl. Come sit beside your mama." She pats the floor beside her, as if I am still a child, not an awkward, leggy teenager, and gives a tremulous smile.

"I've got an exam in the morning."

"Come on, darling. Just a little minute. Please?" Her voice is so raw and pleading, her eyes searching for mine. I walk over and lower myself onto the floor. The tiles are hard and icy under me.

"There, there . . ." she soothes, as if I need it. Her eyes light up as she pats my knee. "You know, darling, I was just thinking we could get you those riding lessons you were wanting. We might even be able to get you a pony of your own." Her cheeks are flushed beneath those wide, feverish eyes.

"I don't want riding lessons."

"Sure you do. You haven't stopped talking about them."

"That was when I was eight, Mama."

"No . . ." she starts and then stares at me. Legs too long. Acne on my chin. Breasts not quite grown in. Her gaze is drawn out and strange. It makes me feel uncomfortable.

"I'm sixteen, Mama. I'm going to university in a few years."

She keeps staring. "No, Gracie," she says.

"Yes, I'm going to study geography. You remember."

Now her face grows dark and she starts whispering urgently. "No, no, Gracie. You can't do that. You're too young; you need to stay here."

"But you said . . ."

Mama can't be interrupted. She carries on whispering frantically. "You can't go, darling. You're much too young."

"I'm sixteen, Mama."

"And besides, I need you here. You can see how it is."

I look around the darkened kitchen. There's nothing here but the two of us and a floor that needs sweeping.

Her voice grows more desperate. "You won't go, will you, Gracie?" She takes my face in her palm and turns it toward her. "You won't leave, will you, Gracie?"

"Mama . . ."

"You can't leave your mama, Gracie. We need each other, my girl. You need to stay with me here."

"I want . . ." Even in the poor light I can see the tears welling in her eyes, and her expression is so despairing I fall quiet. I look at the worn lipstick on her lips and the hollows of her cheeks. She has grown skinny in the last month; it makes her look older.

"Say you won't leave."

"Mama . . ."

"Promise me, Grace. Promise me you won't leave."

I take a deep breath and feel a heaviness on my shoulders.

"Gracie?"

"I promise. I promise . . ."

She lets go of my face and pats my knee. We sit in silence, staring out across the floor.

"Did you have lunch today?"

"Oh, I expect so," she says absently.

"What did you have?"

"I'm not sure, darling. I was out. I had a million things to do. I found this blue bird's egg, did I show you? It's incredible. Nature's art, Gracie."

"I saw it."

"It's beautiful."

"Yeah, it's pretty."

She smiles and takes my hand. She holds it to her cheek, kisses it and sighs. Her cheekbone is as hard and pale as a chess piece under my fingers.

"How about I make us some quiche?" I offer.

She nods. "That would be lovely, darling."

I stand up and then help Mama up too. I look across the countertop to the bag of onions.

I shake my head.

The kitchen of my childhood dissolves and becomes the kitchen in our apartment in Gee Jun Far Sing. My hand is full of broken glass. I shake it over the bin and let the pieces fall to the bottom. I pour myself a fresh glass of water and head to the bedroom, passing Pete's dark, sleeping figure on the way. I fall into bed and put my head onto the pillow. Sleep comes quickly and with it hot and feverish dreams.

I am flying across a tenebrous sky, peppered with blinking stars. The wind draws its long, cool fingers through my hair.

I sigh, my mouth in a light smile, my eyes wide and wet. There is someone above me—no, he cradles me gently, like you might embrace a lover.

"Are you happy, Grace?" he murmurs. His voice runs right through me. Beyond the sphere of us there is silence, deep and still. I breathe him close, the scent of him, a sliver of his bare chest against my skin. It smells familiar. He smells of baking bread. I breathe it in deeply, let it fill me.

Suddenly we are arching upward, higher and higher as the air becomes lace-thin. Suspended for an instant before tumbling towards the ground in tight spirals. He holds me closer, and I melt into him, letting him control me and, at the same time, keep me safe. Soon enough we are back to flying through the air in long, wide ovals. I feel light-headed and hot, like I have been kissed slowly and deeply. I glance up and see that he is grasping bright orange silk ribbons in his free hand, his other muscled arm still wrapped firmly around my waist.

"So?" he whispers again. That voice. Silkier than a touch. A touch I want on my body, my breasts. A hot shiver ripples over me. I close my eyes and let the moving air stream over the lids. *Touch me. Touch me,* I beg silently.

"Are you happy?"

"Mmm . . ." I moan. There is a pulsing in the core of me, that part that makes me a woman, desperate for him to put his lips against me. *Please.*

Léon's lips move to my ear as if he might say something, but instead he starts to kiss my neck. I hear my breath tumble out of me in a groan. His mouth is warm and wet as he breathes and kisses and whispers into the bowl of my ear. His full lips graze my cheeks. I yearn hungrily to feel him with my own mouth; I struggle to turn toward him.

"Careful," he warns, but he is smiling at me, teeth ivory-pale. I reach for him, desperate, finally tasting his mouth with mine. It feels like I am pouring myself into him, into this kiss, drowning and disappearing into him. My body aches to be part of his, to feel him as part of me.

Gravity is tugging at me. Léon has only one arm around my waist. He is kissing down my neck, my body throbbing with the need to have my mouth against his once more. I want him. I want him to be mine. I bite my lip as I feel the heat and shape of him against my inner thigh and taste the salt of my own blood full of lust.

"Please . . ." This time I beg out loud, my voice thickened with wanting, husky and raw. As I draw myself closer to him, I slip down against him. He catches me, his arm now tight and pressed up underneath my breasts.

"Careful," he warns, this time a growl that makes me thirst for him even more.

But we are unbalanced, and I am falling from his grasp. I cry out, desperate for the heat and scent of his body.

"Grace!" He calls as he reaches to clasp my wrist.

Suddenly there is a rush of noise, like listening to the heart of a seashell. The sounds of a wave against a pebbled shore. Out of the darkness there comes a wall of faces with open mouths. I squint, focusing. It is a theater of people, watching me swinging from Léon's hand. Their eyes and mouths and faces sharpen out of the darkness. A Chinese lady turns to her friend, whispering, tutting. Her face zaps into focus as she raises an arched pencil line of an eyebrow. Léon's grip pinches, and I yelp. Then the woman is gone, disappearing into darkness. I am flooded with fear. My heart beats loudly in my ears. I beg him with my eyes, *Don't let me go!*

"Grace!" he calls from above, his accent rich and purring, his voice desperate in a way that makes me ache with need. I am falling.

Falling.

Falling.

Falling.

"Hey, hey, hey," someone coos.

I gasp for air.

"Hey, Gracie. It's okay. Darling?"

Pete holds on to me as I wrestle and twist. He is behind me, trying to cling on to my forearms, keep them down against my chest.

"No!" My voice is breathless and twisted.

"You just had a bad dream. It's okay . . ."

It's as though my body is electric, alive and zinging with long-ing. I am panting. *Léon!* my body seems to call, while I find my breath. The heaviness of my head slowly comes back to my atten-tion, the weight and the steady thrum against my skull.

I stop thrashing and surrender to the mattress.

"What was all that about?" Pete whispers, uncurling himself from me. Blood rushes through me as if I have run a mile. I am still reeling with the spinning and tumbling of my dream, the room swinging about me in dizzying loops. *Léon.* Ribbons. Fall-ing. *Léon.* River-blue eyes.

"Huh?"

"I've never seen you like that. Are you all right?"

I pull off the covers and lie on my back, naked and gasping for air. Fever rises off me, pulsing in waves. The room slows, and then settles to a comforting stillness.

I turn my heavy head to look at Pete, his brow furrowed in a frown, his eyes serious.

"I think I might be getting sick," I answer simply. Then I swal-low and turn away, my body still shivering with want, knowing that Pete's face was not the one I had hoped to see.

Brise d'Été—Summer Breeze
Yuzu with Dark Cherry Filling

The air is thick and gluey with heat. It feels as though I've just stepped out of a scorching bath, steam clinging to the hairs on my skin. I have to blink to stop the world from slipping sideways. My head thumps with a steady drumbeat. This morning I woke up somewhere in between being completely awake and completely asleep, a place in which Mama hovered over me singing and spinning. *Paris, Paris, Paris,* she was begging. *We'll move to Paris, Gracie. You don't need to go, we'll move to Paris.* The only way to shake her out of my mind was to force myself into a cold shower and then stumble out of the house.

I pass a Chinese health store and a tea shop before reaching the pharmacy. Normally I move so fast I don't even notice my surroundings, rushing to get flour or sugar, to bank the daily takings, to drop off a cushion cover, splattered with coffee, at the dry cleaner's. Today I can barely walk faster than Yok Lan, each step an effort that leaves me breathless. There are no bottles of vitamins in the health store, no bright posters with happy faces. Instead there are dried shark fins, the color of skin hardened to a callus, yellowy and transparent; bottles of puckered mushrooms; herbs; the smell of fish. By the front step is a miniature shrine, red with gold writing. Incense sticks stand in an old cup, burned down to their yellow stubs. A woman inside fans herself with a magazine, staring at me blankly through the window. Her face hangs limp, bored or wearied by the heat.

At the tea shop, the aunties behind the counter are engaged in an animated conversation. They wear maroon aprons, leaning over the brass tops of the big tea containers, shaking their heads and sucking their teeth, gossiping. It doesn't matter that I can't hear or understand them, the postures and gestures of women judging other women are universal. *No, she is not a good mother. You are right, she has become fat. What about her husband, does he not see it? My God, what a busybody she is. Who can manage such a mother-in-law?* They seem full of energy, even if it is for slander and lopsided truths. I wonder if their tea would fix my cold but decide to use the more traditional route and head toward the pharmacy.

It is reassuringly light inside, and a man with thinning hair stands behind the counter in a snow-white coat. His hands are folded together; the few strands of his hair raked neatly from one side to the other like the sand of a meticulously maintained Zen garden. He does not smile at me; he is too busy nodding and listening to another customer. His face is awash with confusion as he concentrates on her moving mouth. She is as small as a child, but her body is that of a woman, hidden under a large hooded sweatshirt. She must be sweltering in it. Dark hair is flung out from the neck, satiny and long. She whispers urgently to the pharmacist, leaning toward him as though she might grab his lapels in her hands. Her voice rises and quivers, but I cannot hear what she is saying. Moving closer, focusing, I recognize her: the worry written in the lines in her forehead, the beautiful hair. It is the woman who stood outside Lillian's talking to Rilla. The pharmacist drums his fingers impatiently against the glass counter. Time is money. His pinkie finger has a nail longer than mine, yellowed at the tip.

"Excuse me," I interrupt. "Can I help?"

She jumps when I put my hand gently against her arm.

"Rilla works with me; I've seen you at the café," I murmur in explanation.

Her eyes grow wide with understanding, and she nods. "I . . . we need some cream, for burns," she says with a pronounced Filipino accent. I have no doubt she is a maid or helper, taking care of a house and someone else's children. She must have touched a hot pan, or perhaps it was one of those wild and unruly kids who come to Lil's with their mums, swinging from tabletops, sprinting around chairs, roaring with a sugar rush. I feel a wave of pity for her. The pharmacist hears our English and motions to his young daughter, who sits on a stool sucking a lollipop. She skips up and removes the lolly from her mouth.

"Cream, for burn, hot, ouch . . ." I act out for the girl behind the counter, speaking loudly. She nods and explains to her father, who fetches a cream from the third shelf behind him. Printed red and orange flames lick the bottom of the tube, so we know we've been understood. The woman reaches into a coin purse. Her hair covers it for the most part, but I can see she has dozens of notes folded into tiny squares secreted inside. It doesn't look like a few bills an employer would give her for an errand. She carefully extracts one note and hands it to the girl.

"I'm Grace." I smile at Rilla's friend and offer her my hand. She doesn't take it.

She bites on her lip and doesn't meet my eyes as she mumbles, "Ma'am. Jocelyn."

"Nice to meet you, Jocelyn," I reply.

She nods and exits with small, quick steps, eyes fixed on the pavement.

"How 'bout you, ladeeee?" sings the girl behind the counter. She talks through the lollipop wedged into one cheek. She looks like a squirrel, her cheek taut and round.

"Cold. Flu."

She bugles a translation to her father in Cantonese, and he places the medication on the counter. I look at it for a few grateful seconds. If it works, I can be back at Lil's in a couple of days. I worry about Rilla and Gigi managing without me. Of course they will be fine, Marjory will probably keep a watchful eye on the place too, but it leaves me feeling surprisingly empty and sick in my stomach. Lillian's, my baby.

Eventually, after a few blurry days, the fever lifts. The first morning without it I sit up cautiously, worried it might be teasing me, lurking in a corner. But it doesn't come back. Pete has already left for work, the mattress indented where he lay, sheets wrinkled. My nose runs and my throat still burns, but there is no fever and Mama has not disturbed my dreams. I get up and have a cool shower, lathering soap to a velvety mousse and sighing happily in between hacking coughs.

Rilla squeals when I come in, Marjory claps, and even Gigi cracks a grin. Yok Lan looks up at me with the softest, gentlest smile. Her face looks tired, but I am so happy to see her, radiating serenity. I put my hand on her shoulder, and she spontaneously lifts it and kisses my palm sweetly.

"You don't think you're here to work, do you?" warns Marjory, wagging a manicured finger. Gigi stands beside her, leaning on the back of her chair, a fashion magazine open between them. The model is wearing purple tights and sits awkwardly on a stool. Her mouth is open, red lips glossy and moist.

"I'd love to," I reply, "but I'm not quite there yet."

Rilla rushes over from behind the till. She throws her arms around me in a tight hug.

"We missed you, Grace," she gushes. "Everyone has been asking about you. Tea?"

I nod gratefully. As she goes to fill a pot, I call after her, trying not to sound nervous. "Everything okay? Any problems?"

Marjory pats a chair beside her. She whispers as I sit down, "They've done a wonderful job, Grace. Run off their feet, but coping so well. You'd be proud."

"Nothing gone wrong," Rilla replies as she returns. She has placed a *Thé pour Deux macaron* on my saucer. The filling is infused with Earl Grey, a sweet contrast to the smooth chocolate. I notice the perfect, unblemished roundness, the frill or "feet" on each shell.

"I made them," Gigi interrupts, as if reading my thoughts. Her hands rest on her stomach, unself-conscious now. It is tight and swollen against the cloth of her singlet. She wears shorts and black boots, hair piled in a messy bun on the top of her head. Her right arm is loaded with noisy bracelets.

I take a bite, the elegant pink-gray shells crumbling to give way to the soft center.

"Well, it's good," I tell her, winking at Rilla, who grins. "Great job, both of you."

After my tea I stand with Rilla behind the till, and she talks me through the business of the last few days. Details that wouldn't mean much to most people bring a smile to my face. Léon coming in to buy another dozen box of *macarons* for his team meeting. A mixed selection, although he admitted that *Cirque* is his current favorite. A teapot has broken; one of the faux-pearl-handled teaspoons has gone missing. Mrs. Thompson, we say in unison. She wears pearls every day, even in summer, and is prone to thieving, despite having more money than the rest of my customers put together. I'm not concerned; I can buy some more from the supplier next month. We need more cream, more almond flour. Gigi spilled half a bag of sugar when they were cooking *macarons,* Rilla confesses nervously. I reassure her it is no problem; we'll add sugar to the list. She goes into the kitchen to see if there is anything else we need to buy. She hums to herself as she goes through the door, dark hair swinging.

"Yoo-hoo, Gracie!" I turn to see Linda waving at me from the corner.

I give her a weak smile.

"How're you feeling, love?"

"Better, thanks, Linda."

"Good to see you back," she says kindly.

Linda's book club meets at Lillian's every fortnight. She and three of her friends spend a couple of hours here before their kids need picking up from school. I can't figure out whether they actually read the books they bring in. They definitely don't discuss them. Linda pulls out a pen and paper at the beginning of each meeting, presumably to take notes, but the paper goes back into her bag blank when the two hours is up. The other women are slender, with long, well-coiffed hair and big-rimmed sunglasses. They wear sleeveless dresses and high-heeled shoes. One used to be a department store catalog model, Pete has told me; he knows her husband from work. Another is married to a pilot; I overhear her talking about a house in Boracay, the prettiest resort beach in the Philippines. I appreciate the business, despite their loud laughter and chatter, which can make the place feel crowded even when it is close to empty.

Linda comes up to pay her bill. She looks over my shoulder quickly before saying, "Gracie, dear, I've been meaning to ask you—where did you find your girl?"

"Pardon?"

"Your *girl,*" she repeats.

"Oh, you mean Rilla? Léon helped me find her. She's such a huge help."

Linda purses her lips together and finds change in her wallet for her last latte.

"Linda, the kids will be out in a minute," one of the ladies calls to her from the door. The other two are talking about a new ring a husband has bought. How many carats? Made where? How much?

Linda passes me two twenty-pataca bills. I return some change in coins.

"There in a second!" she sings out brightly. She leans in toward me and drops her voice. "Just be careful, dear."

"Sorry?"

"Of *the help*," she says. "They're not always what they seem, you know. And they all know each other. All cousins and whatnot."

I open my mouth to reply, but nothing comes out. I can feel my face start to redden.

"Elsie over there, she had things stolen. More than once. Thinks her maid had, you know, sticky fingers." Linda holds up her palm and wiggles her fingers to demonstrate.

I assume Elsie is one of the women in the gaggle. The two ladies talking about the ring have started laughing about something. Cackling like parrots. Now they are discussing Japanese hair straightening. The one by the door sighs and rolls her eyes.

"Linda?"

"I . . ." I start to reply.

"Look, don't say anything to anyone. *Very* embarrassing for Elsie. But just be smart, okay? Not too friendly. You're a sweetie and they can take advantage of that. You know what I mean." She raises her eyebrows and gives me a meaningful look. Then she straightens up and smiles. She takes the change instead of leaving a tip. Her handbag has fasteners that make a loud snap. "Coming!" she coos to her friends, pulling her sunglasses over her eyes. "You take care of that cold, Gracie. There's a nasty bug going around. All the kids got it too."

"Yes, well . . . I will. Thanks."

Their laughter and gossip and the sound of their shoes against the pavement drift away, and the cicadas, invisible in the long grass and debris of the nearby construction site, soon feel confident enough to resume singing their summer song.

"Hey, it's quiet in here." Rilla smiles as she comes through the kitchen door. She holds a dishcloth in her hands, heat rising off it. She passes it from one hand to the other.

"Yeah," I murmur.

"You feeling okay, Grace?" she asks, peering at my pink cheeks.

"Oh, yes, I'm fine. Thanks, Rilla."

She sets to work wiping down the table the women have left: sticky coffee rings, discarded napkins embossed with lipstick prints, and torn-open paper packets of artificial sugar.

Days later Rilla is shopping for food coloring, so it is just Gigi and I together, figuring out a new *macaron* recipe. The kitchen seems a little smaller with her in it, especially now that she is so round her belly enters the room well before she does. She is still trying to wear her regular clothes but failing more often than succeeding. One day she reached to grab my *macaron* notebook on the top of the fridge and her shirt rode up. The zipper of her short shorts was completely undone, gaping to reveal lime green, lacy underwear. She had fashioned a kind of belt out of ribbon and they were holding on, but only just.

She caught me staring and rolled her eyes. "Don't even say anything. I know it looks dumb, but you should see what they would have me wear otherwise."

I assumed *they* meant her mother and grandmother.

"Soooooo ugly. Seriously . . ." she drawled.

I could sympathize, I guess, on this point. There didn't seem to be many fashionable options available to expectant mothers in Macau. A lot of the women wore big smocks, which floated down to midcalf, waddling about like Tweedledee or Tweedledum. But since the shorts incident, Gigi has started wearing bigger clothes, mainly oversize T-shirts and leggings. She has bought a pair of sandals just like Marjory's favorites, so the combination is still hip. Personally, I like the T-shirt slogans with incongruous English translations:

LOVES MAKES PEACE FOR WORLD AROUND. MAKE HAPPY TIME! TOMORROW IS SUNSHINE, WEAR A SMILE, DANCE TO THE BEAT OF THE HEART.

And my all-time favorite: I GOT JOYFUL LAST NIGHT, WHAT ABOUT YOU?

It was so ironic seeing Gigi, bloated with pregnancy, in that T-shirt. Her English is near perfect, so I'm sure she could guess what the slogan implied.

We are trying to make a yuzu-citrus-basil *macaron*. I have been inspired by Ladurée's seasonal flavors, having read somewhere that they created a citrus-basil *macaron* for an article in *Vogue*. Or was it French *Elle*? Either way, it was *très chic*. I am trying to be *très chic* too, but for now that means I'm caked in a strange herbal-smelling ganache and shiny with sweat.

"Grace, that smells totally gross," Gigi tells me.

"I know, it's not the best, is it? I can't get it right. Do you eat basil?"

She screws up her face.

"It's an herb. An Italian one. And I don't think the bloody thing likes Macau." I hold up a limp leaf. The color has turned an ominous dark gray-green.

"Yeah, well, neither do I. It's too hot with this enormous

bump," she complains, dipping her finger in my ganache and pulling a disgusted face, her pretty nose scrunched up. Well, that won't sell, I think.

"I think I'll give up on this," I tell her. "How do you fancy making some dark cherry ganache with me, and we can fill these little yuzu shells with that instead? They can be a temporary special: a *macaron de saison*." I scrape the offending basil mixture into the bin.

"Whatever you want." Her brightening eyes betray her.

"That's the enthusiasm I was looking for," I reply, smiling. "What shall we call them then? It has to be French."

We surrender to a thoughtful silence. Outside the cicadas are playing their noisy summer symphony. I imagine them boldly serenading one another from old tires, forgotten woodpiles, discarded plastic noodle bowls.

"Something about summer . . ." she mumbles.

After conferring with my worn, flour-dusted French-English dictionary, we agree on *Brise d'Été*. Gigi offers to write a Chinese translation of the description on the notice board. I think of Yok Lan coming in and reading the beautiful Chinese characters. I wonder if she will recognize the handwriting, the particular slope of each shape, as her granddaughter's. We stand back, shoulder to shoulder, and look at it together. I catch the corners of Gigi's mouth lifting, her arms crossed over her huge belly.

"So do I get to eat one of these things, or am I just your blackboard slave?" she teases, not looking at me.

"Yeah, yeah, all right. But you have to make me a cup of tea first. Tea slave too, you know."

She grins down at her feet, perhaps thinking I do not notice.

We sit down at my favorite corner table, where I can spot customers if they approach, although I'm not expecting a big rush today. Marjory, who lives in the same apartment block as many of the expat mums, told me it is sports day at the School of the Nations, so most of the parents will be cheering their kids on. It is a swelteringly hot day; I instinctively worry about sunburn and heatstroke. I remember Mama marking me with zinc, like an Indian princess from an old Western film, when we went to Brighton in the summer.

Gigi takes a seat opposite me and serves me a cup of tea before pouring one for herself. I am older than she; she does it without thinking. I take a sip. Black Ceylon with mandarin peel, one of my favorites. Gigi puts an entire *macaron* in her mouth, sinks her teeth down on it, and leans back in her chair with a sigh.

"Oh, man . . ." she croaks through her mouthful. And then, when her mouth is empty, "*Brise d'Été* . . . well. Holy. That is good."

I can't help but laugh. "Here's to *Brise d'Été*. And summer." I raise my teacup, and she lifts hers to make a porcelain clink. She looks happier today. A little lighter, as if being in the empty café gives her some kind of relief.

She looks at me. "Grace, why don't you have kids?"

The question slaps me like the cold of the ocean. I almost wince. My throat tightens with that remembered sadness and the familiar feeling of my heart falling. I wish she hadn't asked that question. I glance at her belly and feel a kind of keening in my own stomach.

"It's complicated."

She frowns and plows on innocently. "You didn't want them, right? Marjory said she didn't ever want them. They tie you down, don't they?" Her face is soft, showing her youth, even through the makeup. There is a look like fear in her eyes, round as an owl's.

"No. No . . ." I sigh. "It's not that. We did want them."

She puts her cup down and looks at me again, curious. "When?"

"When did we want them?"

"Yeah, did you change your mind or something?" She speaks

gently, as though she's realized that maybe she shouldn't have asked.

"No, we didn't change our minds. I'm not sure when we started wanting them. A long time ago it feels like. We were living in London."

"But not now?"

"Yes, we want them now. I mean, I guess so."

I haven't talked about it with Pete for so long. Our conversations move around it like a split in a stream. It is not that we want to avoid confrontation or argument; we seem to bicker all the time. Last night we fought about whether we should buy a new can opener. He thought our current one was useless and I thought he was being defeatist. Somehow it became something worth arguing about, the stupid can opener. I was so mad the heat practically rose off my skin, and I seethed all night lying beside his dark, snoring shape. Talking about kids just makes us sad. We can always buy a new can opener.

I look up at Gigi and correct myself. "I don't *guess*. I *know* we want kids. We really want kids."

She stares up at me, waiting for me to finish. The words seem just out of reach.

"But we can't have kids ourselves. It's not physically possible for us. Well, for me. I can't have kids." My voice falls flat and lifeless between us. Like the hope that ran out between Pete and me.

"I thought maybe you just didn't want them," she whispers carefully.

"No, we do. I just can't." I sigh. I haven't said it out loud to anyone else but Pete. I thought I would cry if I did. I certainly didn't think I would be telling a young pregnant woman over *macarons*. I find myself saying more.

"I don't have . . . eggs. Not anymore. It turns out we left it too late and I ran out too early. I guess you could say our timing was off." I take a breath through my nostrils and let it out, counting slowly. She looks at me, and I can tell she is really listening. Her eyes soften, and she seems to stare into my depths. Like she somehow knows what it feels like inside. It is the first time I can remember her looking me directly in the eye.

"That's shit," she declares.

I nod. It *is* shit. Who knew that the dark, tangled knot of hurt and disappointment could be explained so simply?

Gigi sits with me, letting silence fall between us. There is jack-hammering in the distance and a car horn blaring. It is a beautiful, clear day. The clouds are moving slowly through the sky. We sip our tea.

"Grace?"

"Hmmm?"

"I'm sorry about that. The baby stuff."

"Yeah. Me too, hon. Me too . . ."

She looks down at her hands and then up to the table. The plate in front of us is covered in sunshine-colored *macarons*. They remind me of a bunch of daisies.

Gigi lifts up the plate and holds it out. *"Macaron?"*

We eat a whole plate of *macarons* together, chat and drink more tea. She even pulls my hand over to her stomach and lets me feel a few kicks. The tears don't come, the cicadas keep singing. Some weight is lifted from me, I can feel it leaving.

At the end of the month we have made a good profit, even on the days I was away ill. I stand at the counter doing the quick and dirty calculations and feel like laughing out loud it makes me so proud. Rilla is in the kitchen, and Yok Lan is sipping tea in her usual spot. Gigi is standing beside Marjory chatting as the late-afternoon sun streams in the windows. Their conversation drifts over to me. They are talking about the places Marjory has been. Gigi's kohled eyes are wide.

"Even Paris?"

Marjory nods. "Even Paris. You know, Paris is the home of *macarons*. I'd never tried one outside France until I came here." She lifts her eyes to me. "Grace, have you been?"

I smile. "*Mais, bien sûr*. Ladurée, Pierre Hermé, the best pastry chefs are in Paris."

"Who are they?" Gigi pipes up, curious.

"They are the rock stars of the *macaron* world," I explain with a wink.

I think of me and Mama lifting *macarons* from a white box as if they were jewels. Colors like precious stones—ruby red, soft turquoise blue, pale as a pearl. Letting the flavors rest on our tongues, closing our eyes to the decadent sweetness. Of course we would have no money to pay hotel bills later, but she bought Ladurée *macarons* for breakfast. For a child, no less.

"Paris has the most beautiful cafés . . ." Marjory sighs.

I think then of Pete. Last week he asked me out for dinner to a nearby French restaurant. A strange look crossed his face when I said I was too tired, we had such a big order of *macarons* to fill the next morning. He looked older all of a sudden, and sad.

Gigi's voice is tinted with awe. "You've been everywhere," she says to Marjory.

"We've moved a lot, yeah. But you've traveled, haven't you?"

"Not really. Hong Kong, of course. Guangzhou. And Taipei, we had a school trip there once. I had to sell balloons in San Malo for six months to save up for it. That's it," she concludes. Her hands move automatically to her stomach, resting against the curvature.

"Everywhere can start to look the same," Marjory observes wistfully. She takes a sip of her cappuccino and puts her *L'Espoir* to her lips. She pauses before taking a bite. "There are the same things. Wealth, poverty, happiness, suffering. It's easy to think you are better than other people because you are always leaving. You aren't going to be caught in their nine-to-five. The humdrum. You always have the promise of someplace new."

Gigi looks down to her hands, bangles sparkling against her wrist. "Must be amazing."

"It is. For a while. Then you start to feel a bit . . . jealous? They are permanent." Her voice fades to a whisper. "They, at least, belong somewhere." She bites into her *macaron* and looks vacantly around Lillian's.

That's true, I think.

They sit in silence for a few moments, until Rilla's voice, singing, skims out from the kitchen. It slides painfully off-key, slicing through the still air. Marjory coughs on her mouthful, Yok Lan chuckles, Gigi lets out an enormous guffaw.

"Shit, she's awful," says Gigi, with characteristic tactlessness.

Rilla comes out, gloved hands dripping onto the tiles, and we cover our grins with our hands.

"What are you laughing about?" she says, a baffled look on her round face.

We all erupt in giggles. I look at the four women—Gigi, Rilla, Marjory, and Yok Lan—and smile.

Dearest Mama,

Sometimes I wonder what would have happened if I had chosen something different. Married someone else. Gone to a different country. Played a different hand.

Would I be Marjory? Skipping from place to place like a stone across water. Unpacking and repacking every few years. Not making friends in case ties have to be quickly broken. Feeling like a spare part. Would I be perfect on the outside and dislocated on the inside?

Or would I be Rilla? She seems happy enough, but it's hard to know. Does she wonder, like I did working in restaurants all those years, whether there is more? Something with more meaning? Something she could call her own?

Maybe I could have been Gigi? Young and shattered, trying to pretend everything is okay. She's pregnant, Mama. She's not as young as she looks, so I shouldn't be shocked. Early twenties? But she looks fifteen; so slight . . . If I had made her choices, I'd be a mother by now. I could have had a baby at her age, I guess. I was too busy taking the pill and worrying about other things. Not knowing this clock inside was always ticking, ticking, ticking. She will never have to know what it is like to have the precious possibility of motherhood snatched from her. But I think her life is not always so sweet. It is there in her face behind the boldness and arrogance; things unsaid, dreams dashed. She sometimes looks lost and lonely, like a mouse that woke up and found itself in a cage.

But even with all I do not know about her life and her burdens, I cannot help but think she will get to be Yok Lan one day. Gazing up at a grandchild taller than she is, who puts a hand against her shoulder and whispers kindnesses into her ear. She will have that. Someone to care whether she is playing mah-jongg when she shouldn't be. Someone to notice her.

Could I have been one of these women, Mama?

Or could I have been you? A head full of red hair, stories of crickets and lollipops and flying fish. Singing at two in the morning, dancing as if drunk in the afternoon. Was it a choice I made, not to be like you were? Could I have been you? I think of you so alive your fingers and toes are glowing with it. Your eyes are sparkling and hair flying. You were never halfway anything, Mama. Always so full up.

I guess all there is, is what there is. I am who I am. There's no changing things now.

Your loving daughter,
Grace

Saison Orageuse—Storm Season
Lemon and Ginger with
Brown Buttercream Filling

Typhoon season descends upon Macau. One moment the skies are as blue as cornflowers and the sun the color of honey falling on the pavements, the next a storm spins through, all gray and blustering. Today we have the postcard version, sunny and clear. Marjory tells me the skies are so heartbreakingly blue because all the factories have closed in China for the Olympics. They've also stopped granting visas into the mainland, to discourage protesters from entering. No more Zhuhai shopping trips for the expat ladies. Lillian's is consequently chock-full of bored women. Waiting through the long, hot days for the next storm makes everyone feverish. It has tempers and morals worn paperthin. At least everyone feels at home, I try to think optimistically; Lillian's is like a big, messy family room most days.

Today even Marjory is left without a seat. When I return from doing some shopping, she is standing behind the counter with her cup. Gigi and Rilla are laughing loudly as she bobs up and down gracefully. Her toes point and her knees glide in and out of an almost ninety-degree angle. Gigi mimics her but groans with one hand to her belly and the other on the countertop.

"What are you all doing?"

They look up and grin.

"Marjory is trying to *kill* me!" Gigi complains, but the smile remains.

"This girl never does any exercise. Did you know that?" Marjory tuts.

"What do you call them again?" Rilla asks.

"Pliés. They'll be good for her in labor; she needs to get fit and strong."

"Oh, she's too lazy!"

Gigi swats Rilla with a tea towel. Rilla takes the shopping bags from my hands, and the two of them head into the kitchen to unpack them. The air-conditioning of the café cools the sweat beading along my hairline. I tie on an apron and give Marjory a refill.

"You're going to the Ladies' Club tennis event next week?" she asks.

"Huh? Oh, that."

I have a pile of flyers about it next to the counter fridge. We both glance over at them. Linda and her book club ladies have been asking me every week, and I've been successfully avoiding giving a straight answer. I find it harder to dodge when Marjory asks.

She gives me a hopeful smile and then laughs. "Grace, you've got to go 'cause I've got to go. Don is making me; trying to woo some people at work, I think. If you don't go, I'll be stuck with those snobs, trying not to end up with a mouthful of my own foot."

Marjory has a way of putting things; I have to laugh. Gigi isn't the only one not doing any exercise; I have eaten so many *macarons* my flesh rises up and over the waistline of my trousers like soft bread dough. Besides, Pete wants us to go, and it wouldn't hurt to do him one favor, especially considering the distance that's only grown between us as Lillian's has become successful. We've not done anything together in a long time.

"C'mon . . ."

"All right. But you owe me." I point a wet cloth at her, and she grins.

The noises of Rilla and Gigi bickering and laughing comes out of the kitchen. They are becoming more and more like a pair of mismatched sisters.

Marjory leans on the counter. "They sound like they're having fun in there."

"Yup. They seem to hate and love each other in equal amounts." I mop up some loose grains of sugar and coffee.

Marjory asks softly, "Do you ever feel like you're on the outside looking in?" Her face is serious, like it's a question she's been thinking about for some time.

"What do you mean?"

"I don't know. Living in Macau. We're never going to be locals, never going to be Chinese. But look at Rilla; even she fits in more than we do."

As if she senses she is being talked about, we can hear Rilla start humming and Gigi yelling at her to shut up or her ears will bleed. We look at each other and laugh.

Marjory lifts her cup to her lips and then puts it down again. She speaks pensively. "I never wanted kids, you know. I didn't even really want a husband . . ."

My stomach gives that familiar little lurch, but not like it used to. Marjory blushes, as if she is embarrassed to be talking about such personal things. "Don's girls think I am a wicked stepmother, but I'm used to girls hating my guts, so it actually doesn't bother me too much."

"No?"

She shakes her head. "It's the ex-wife telling tales, and I just have to suck it up. I figure they might grow out of it. Anyway, I love Don, and he is enough for me. But sometimes I think: what next? I mean …" A deep wrinkle stretches across her tanned forehead. "Do you feel like you belong somewhere, Grace?"

I put down the cloth I am using to wipe the counter. I think of Pete first. His dark head, eyes full of unspoken talk. Mama; a flash of red hair. The cold of London and the bright sky of Australia. It's like a series of flash cards.

Marjory is still looking at me. Behind her, women sit sipping coffees and gossiping. Yok Lan is in one corner, dozing over a half-drunk cup of tea. A child drives a toy truck into a table leg.

"I belong here?" I reply, like it's a question, but I know it to be true.

She nods. I can see she is thinking, staring off into the distance, hands around her cup. I wonder if she thinks I mean Macau. Or maybe wherever Pete is. I can see her fondness for Don; when she speaks of him, the love radiates out of her. She may be a princess and he may be a frog, but she adores him, that much is clear. It makes me realize, with a twinge of guilt, how much I have been avoiding Pete. But what I mean is that I belong here. Right here. *In Lillian's.* This little square of café and kitchen. My tiny world.

A light storm has finally broken through the series of achingly hot, clear days. The forecast says it is a category three typhoon, but in Hong Kong it has been elevated to a six. Customers are sparse. I watch Filipino maids battle the wind to hold umbrellas over children's prams, their own heads bare. Tarpaulins billow from construction sites like ladies' head scarves. Wind seems to come from every direction, left and right, above and below. I wonder, hopefully, if the tennis event will be canceled tomorrow. Gigi leans over the *macaron* counter, resting her belly against the cool glass while I clean the coffee machine. She looks tired. She has finished mopping the floor.

"How'd the doctor's visit go on Monday?"

"Fine."

"Was she nice?"

"Sure." She shrugs. "She wasn't too bad, I guess. She says the baby is fine and I'm fine, no problems."

"Well, that's good."

"Yeah. She told me the due date is the twenty-ninth of October."

"Really?" I look up at Gigi, who seems unmoved. I try to count the weeks in my head. About nine weeks to go. The time has sped by so quickly. I must look dazed, because she laughs at me.

"It has to come out sometime, Grace," she says, raising her eyebrows.

"Good point," I concede.

"But I don't wanna think about *that* part too much," Gigi says, standing back from the counter now but holding herself up, her hands gripping the top. She is turning a foot in front of her in slow circles and gazing down at it. A look of frustration sweeps across her face.

"Do you know now if it's a girl or a boy?"

"Well, it's not a boy," she replies matter-of-factly.

"Oh?"

"I'm pretty sure it's a girl. Man, my feet are killing me," she grumbles. "They've swollen up about as big as yours with the heat and this stupid pregnancy."

"Gee, thanks," I say with mock hurt.

Gigi grins up at me without apology. I recognize now this is her way of connecting with me, pulling me in and teasing me as if I were an older sister. Her grin shows off her small incisors, hanging cheekily over her bottom lip. This smile makes her look so much younger. I bang the dirty coffee grains into the rubbish bin and wipe across my hairline, where I feel the itch of fresh sweat.

"How do you know it's a girl?"

"Pau Pau and Aunty, *they* think it's a girl. Mum doesn't give a shit either way." She pulls a chair out from one of the tables and lowers herself into it. "Pau Pau used some kind of old calendar to check. Some kind of Chinese thing."

"Oh, okay, well, a girl. Wow."

Gigi looks up at me and rolls her eyes, but she is smiling again. "Grace, seriously. It's either a boy or a girl, right? Fifty-fifty."

"Yeah, yeah, I know," I reply and roll my eyes back at her to show I don't care. But I can feel my heart skip a few beats inside my chest. Gigi is picking absentmindedly at something on the table in front of her. A bit of *macaron* or ganache or dried milk not cleaned off properly.

"Do you have any names in mind?"

"No. Well, not really. There's a Chinese name I like that matches my last name. It's cute, I guess. But I haven't thought of an English name."

"She will get to have both? I mean, on her passport or birth certificate?"

"She'll only have her Chinese name on her documents. But I'll give her an English name too. We all get one."

I move on to polishing the top of the counter, the metal gleaming up at me like a mirror. In its curved surface, my face is elongated, like the snout of a horse.

"Who gave you your English name? Your mum?"

"No, Pau Pau. She thought it was easy to say, and I think there was some famous singer called Gigi? I don't know."

I take out the trays of *macarons* and place them carefully on top of the shiny surface.

Gigi says, "I just want this thing out now. Frank, my boyfriend, he . . ." She trails off, then purses her lips. This is the first time she has mentioned her boyfriend. I assume he is the father of the baby she's carrying.

I prompt her. "He what?"

"Oh, nothing. He's just acting weird."

"Yeah?"

"He's kind of avoiding me. I mean, he's probably just busy. He's been promoted to supervisor, so he's doing a lot of shifts, I think. But then he's partying as well. I never see him." She pauses. "I was going to be promoted too, you know. But . . ."

"But?"

"I got pregnant. One of those skinny bitches, probably Crystal, she told the big boss and I didn't get the promotion. Then somehow they ended up not needing me anymore . . . you know what I mean."

I look up with a frown. "What? That's crazy; I didn't know that. If you deserved the promotion, you should have got it, Gigi," I say forcefully.

She gives me a wry look. "You don't get it, Grace. This isn't London." She puts a pink *macaron* in her mouth and closes her eyes for a brief second as the shell dissolves against the roof of her mouth and her tongue, making a quiet crack when it crumbles. "It doesn't matter anyway. I like it here better. I wish I could study how to make *macarons* as good as you."

I brush off the unexpected compliment. "Well, you're eating all our profits." I laugh and slap the top of her hand.

She grins, then looks into the distance, and her voice drops. "All I used to want to do was make money and have nice things. That's why Frank and everyone, they work in casinos. My mother, she thinks money is the only reason to do anything. She wouldn't let me study, I know that much. Especially anything to do with cooking. She thinks the restaurant business is a bad investment. You throw the money in and it never comes back out again."

I bite my tongue, thinking of Mama. Not being able to study myself. Feeling trapped. I look over at Gigi, her belly so heavy and eyes so dark.

She keeps talking, as though the *macaron* has loosened her tongue. "Did I ever tell you about the picture of the Louis Vuitton handbag I had on my wall next to my bed?"

"No."

"It was up there for two whole years," she says wistfully.

Those handbags cost an arm and a leg; they are treated like Fabergé eggs in this part of the world. No one would ever put her handbag on the floor by her feet. Some of the finer restaurants even offer tiny chairs to prop your precious cargo on.

"Did you ever get the bag?"

"Yup. Bought it with the bonus money the government gave us a few months ago. That and some savings." She takes a sip of her tea.

I raise my eyebrows. "Louis Vuitton? Well, good for you. All that work; you must love it." I have never seen it on the hooks in the kitchen. She and Rilla normally carry scuffed backpacks. Gigi has covered hers in fashionable pins and buttons.

"Where is it?" I ask.

"I don't use it. I was going to once, but I couldn't bring myself to take it outside. I unwrap it sometimes and look at it. It is gorgeous, but . . ." She sighs. "It didn't make me feel how I thought it would. I thought everything'd be perfect when I had that handbag."

She glances at her stomach and looks a little sad. She changes the subject. "Anyway, whatever. I need to call those suppliers about the almond flour. It's not as good, don't you think? If they are giving us the cheap stuff, I am going to give them hell."

She strides into the kitchen, and I follow her with my eyes

for a moment. Picking up one of the *macarons*, I place it lightly on my tongue. The crisp shell dissolves into soft sweetness. But there is something a little bitter about it. Not much, but a thicker taste, like marzipan. Most people wouldn't even notice. She might act like a careless teenager sometimes, but she sure does have the palate of a chef.

Apart from a few broken branches and ripped tarpaulins, the next morning seems to have amnesia about the storm the day before. The sun is bright and orange, and the air tastes like syrup. I am sapped of energy even before getting to the tennis courts; the wet heat leaves me lethargic and slow. Pete, on the other hand, is raring to go. He leans against the netting and stretches his hamstrings, one, then the other. He is always so competitive. This morning his body hums with a kind of animal scent, spicy and fierce. It makes me feel queasy and undone at the same time. I watch as others arrive, so clearly couples, even when they don't touch or kiss or hold hands. They glance at each other, carry each other's bags, speak the same abbreviated language, which never requires further explanation. Pete and I, on the other hand, could be strangers. We barely look at or talk to each other, let alone make love or lie close at night like we used to. I know it is a distance I have mapped out between us. I have turned away from him to immerse myself in work. Lillian's is a safer world, one that doesn't ache so much. Because when I do look into his face, the face I know too well, I can see anger and disappointment and then, deeper still, grief. That is the part I cannot bear.

"Hey, you two!" Marjory sings out as the door to the courts clangs shut. She is dressed all in white, topped with a navy blue visor.

She springs onto the court with the grace of an antelope, her long arms cradling a silver racquet. "Don will be down in a minute. It's us and another couple doing a round-robin kind of thing."

She starts bouncing a ball on her racquet without looking at it. She has an ease with anything physical, comfort in her own skin. I imagine her dancing onstage; she would have been a sight to behold.

Pete looks over from his stretch; his eyes squint in the glare of the sun. He gives Marjory a wave.

"You want some water?" she asks, spying the empty water bottles in my hands.

"Yes, please. This sun is a killer. I'm melting."

"Tell me about it. You better have put on sunscreen this morning or you'll be burned to a crisp in minutes."

I take in her long, tanned limbs and can't imagine her skin frying or even breaking out in a sweat. I already have widening dark circles staining my T-shirt, the taste of salt on my upper lip. I wish for the dark, cool quiet of Lillian's on a slow day. We fill up our bottles at the watercooler inside the clubhouse, and as we come back out, I see Celine and Léon on the court chatting with Don. Léon's silver hair shimmers in the light. Pete stands slightly apart from the group, staring down at his racquet and his shoes.

Don looks up. "Hey, ladies, we've got our work cut out for us. We're up against the French!"

"Bonjour!" trills Celine when she sees me.

She is wearing a light blue dress with white shoes. Léon introduces himself to Marjory and comes over. He kisses my cheeks, despite the wet sheen on my face. I blush and catch Pete looking at us. I'm relieved to notice that Don is sweating more than I am, wet streams trailing down his broad neck and sliding beneath his shirt. As he explains the program, Pete's gaze slides from Léon and me over to him.

"Right," Don says. "So it's Léon and Celine first, against you two. Then we play the winners, and whoever wins that match goes on to some other round. You should prepare yourself for a whipping. I'm going to tear up the court."

He proudly lifts a flabby arm; his biceps seems to have fallen to the underside, and we all laugh. Marjory swats him with her racquet and flashes a grin.

As we take our place on the court, Pete looks over at me. "You all right?"

"Yeah. It's just so damn hot." I wipe sweat from my brow.

"Hmmm." He looks across the net, and Léon waves. Pete doesn't return it, but gives a tight smile and lift of his head. "I didn't expect him to be here."

"Huh?" I ask, but before he has a chance to respond, Léon calls, "You are both ready?"

"Yes!" I call back.

"Bring it on," Pete mutters, his voice low.

The first points are fast. Léon and Celine are soon winning. Then I try to serve but botch it up. Watching Léon on the court is distracting; he is so calm and collected. When I finally sort out my serve, the ball heads back Pete's way. He smacks a perfect shot, outside the singles line but inside the doubles, and Léon grunts to reach it.

"Nice one!" shouts Marjory from the sideline.

I keep making awful shots and apologizing.

Léon just shakes his head and laughs lightly. "Hey, hey, not to worry. Just for fun."

Pete and I catch up, and soon we are slightly ahead. Pete is as focused as I have ever seen him, that dark expression on his face.

"Okay, so who is winning now?" Léon asks.

"We are," Pete replies quickly.

The sun lifts in the sky, swimmy and lurid, like orange cordial.

It's Celine's serve. The ball plonks neatly in the middle of the square, just where it should be. Léon gives her a high five. Finally, after we make some lucky shots, it is Pete's turn to serve.

"Don't wear yourself out, mate, you might have us to play next!" Don calls from the side of the court. We all laugh except Pete, who is staring across at Léon as he serves, hard and fast. Léon returns Pete's serve, slicing across the ball, adding some weighty topspin. It shoots over the net at high speed, and Pete scrambles to arrange himself, his body still leaning forward from his serve. As he pulls up, the ball connects with the brow above his left eye, and there is a sickening *thwock* from the contact of ball and bone. Pete slaps his hand to his face and keens like an animal before falling backward. His legs crumble beneath him, his feet slide to one side, and his body falls to the other. His racquet drops from his hand as he meets the ground; the thud seems to shudder through me as my hand flies up to my mouth.

"Pete!" Marjory screams from the side of the court and rushes toward us. We both crouch over him.

"Merde!" Léon curses and jogs around the net to join us. Celine lifts her hand to her eyes, to see beyond the glare of the sun. Don stands up from his chair.

Marjory looks into Pete's face, holding it between her hands and saying something to the effect of "Can you hear me? Are you okay?"

Léon, above, offers her a water bottle.

"Perhaps splash some water onto his face."

My mouth has fallen open, but I'm not saying anything.

Marjory gives me a sharp look. "Grace?"

The shock of seeing Pete's body so limp and crumpled has me winded.

"Is he all right?" I hear myself whisper.

Pete's eyes fly open and search around for a few seconds just as

Léon sloshes water onto his face. Pete makes a sound somewhere between a yelp and a gargle. He sees Marjory first, as she is leaning close, then me. Finally he sees Léon, now standing back, water bottle in hand.

"Pete, are you okay?"

Pete looks back at me. "Shit," he swears. I imagine the hot pain flooding into his senses. He wipes the water from his face.

"You're fine," Marjory says slowly, soothingly. "You were just hit with the ball."

Pete tries to sit up. I put my hand against his back, helping him. His face is twisted in pain. He looks up at Léon, his eyes full of fury.

"Should I get some ice?" Don calls out.

Marjory says, "Yes, that would be great. See if the clubhouse has an ice pack in the freezer."

"I'll go with you," Celine offers.

As they jog off together, Pete continues to stare at Léon. His gaze is hard.

"You fucker," he hisses.

"Pardon?" Léon leans forward, concern and confusion on his face.

"I said, *You. Fucker.*"

Léon turns to Marjory and me, as if for an explanation. We glance at each other.

"Bloody hell, Pete," I whisper, rubbing his back.

"It wasn't his fault," Marjory says gently.

"Like hell it wasn't!" Pete growls. He winces and closes his eyes.

Léon stands up straighter. The tone of Pete's voice and the look on his face do not need any interpretation now.

Pete's eyes spring back open. "He walloped that ball right at my face! If that wasn't enough, now he's dumped water all over me!"

190

"Pete, I don't think . . ." I raise my voice now, hoping to reason with him. Or just shut him up.

"French prick. You did that on purpose and you know it. First Grace and now this," he spits.

Marjory stares at me but says nothing. Léon doesn't even look at me. I feel like I am being pulled into a sink that is being drained of water. Sucked down and down. I can feel my stomach lurch.

Léon's confusion has been replaced with a cool mask. "I'm very sorry, but you are mistaken, Pete. I did not hit you on purpose," he says.

"Ha!" Pete cries.

"Why would I hit you deliberately? That's . . . that's absurd."

Marjory looks at me again, caught in the middle of this unexpected conflict.

"I don't know *why* you would hit me. Shit! I don't know why you hit me, or why you insist on hitting on my wife. How should I know?" Pete is practically snarling now. "You French bastards are all the same."

Léon takes another step backward.

"Pete, I think maybe you have a concussion, I think, ah . . ." Marjory stumbles to a stop.

"What are you talking about?" I whisper to Pete urgently. I feel slightly nauseated.

"Oh God, here we go. You *know* what I am talking about, Grace!" He throws his hands up toward the sky. "He helps you at the supermarket, he makes *macarons* with you, he buys champagne, bloody chocolate forks . . ."

"What's going on?" Marjory mouths to me over Pete's head.

"You are *my* wife, Grace," he spits. "Or did you forget?" His eyes are accusing as they lock with mine.

I have that tumbling, guilty feeling again in my stomach and try not to look at Léon. Pete leans back against his palm and presses his weight into his legs, trying to stand up. He lets out a weak grunt. The raw emotion makes him look ugly.

"Hey, what are you doing? Sit down," I say, grabbing his shoulder. "Please, just sit down and take it easy."

"I'm not stupid!" he screams at Léon.

Léon draws himself up even straighter. He looks a little pale. "I have never . . . I would never . . . *hit on* your wife." He glances back over his shoulder as if checking for Celine, but she is still at the clubhouse. He picks up his tennis racquet and has turned to walk away when Pete leaps toward him. Pete's fist plunges into Léon's stomach, below his rib cage, and Léon doubles over. I hear Léon's soft bark as his breath escapes his chest. Marjory lets out a shrill cry, and that's when I notice Don has come up behind us. He grabs Pete's shoulders and yanks him backward. Léon looks up for a split second, and his blue eyes connect with mine.

Verre de Mer—Sea Glass
Pistachio with Buttercream Filling

The doctor recommends ordinary painkillers and a good spell with an ice pack and sends us on our way, the tension between us seething. We say nothing of the incident. I'm scared to open my mouth in case I say something too terrible, something I can't take back. I can't look at him. Pete tells me he will make a roast chicken, perhaps a touch of apology in his voice. I nod but say nothing, heading into the study to complete some online ordering for Lillian's. One of the specialty pastry goods suppliers in Hong Kong will now ship to Macau. I have been so excited about it but am filled only with guilt and confusion and anger as I scroll through the screens of Microplane zesters, tart molds, sugar thermometers, Mauviel beating bowls.

Pete pushes his dinner around his plate. Yorkshire puddings, glossy carrots, chunks of crispy-skinned potatoes. The smell is heady. We sit opposite each other at the dining table.

I clear my throat. "Nothing has happened, Pete. Léon is a friend."

Pete puts down his knife and fork and holds his hands together. He looks at his plate rather than at me.

"He's . . . he has helped me. With Lillian's. There's *nothing* going on."

I think of the chocolate fork, the blue of Léon's eyes, my dream. I swallow down a piece of chicken that seems to have swollen with my guilt.

"I see how you look at him," Pete says quietly.

I open my mouth to respond, but I can't think of an explanation. He is right. I can account for my actions but not my fantasies. My pause reveals my feelings; we both notice it.

"Nothing has happened between us," I repeat, holding on to the truth of each word, despite my face feeling warm. "Pete? Nothing."

Pete stares at me for a moment, then runs a hand through his hair. He pushes a potato around his plate with his fork. Then he puts the cutlery down slowly and exhales. His breath is long, as if he is breathing out the weight of the world. Then he leans on his elbows and puts his fists to his mouth.

"We have to talk. I'm sorry, Grace." The words seem to catch in his throat.

"Well, you shouldn't have hit him."

"It's not that."

"What then?"

He pauses.

"Gracie, I had . . . sex . . . with . . ."

The air seems to go still and hot.

"What? Who . . ."

"A prostitute. At the Lisboa."

Now I feel like I have been elbowed in the guts. "At the Lisboa," I echo. I reach for my wineglass, feel the smooth, cool weight of it against my palm.

Pete looks down. I stare at the top of his head and notice where his hair is thinning.

"At the Lisboa," I say again.

There are a few silvery hairs on his crown, new ones, or at least ones I hadn't noticed. I imagine this head above someone else, someone else having this same view.

"God." The word rushes out like a little prayer. I wonder if I will be sick.

"Grace, I . . ." His chin is lifted now so I can see his face, the lines and deep grooves. He looks different to me, foreign somehow. It is as if a mask has been stripped away. His face is a curiosity, like I am seeing it for the first time. The stray hairs between his eyebrows and above his nose, the creases of his neck, the wisps of hair by his collar which need trimming. He doesn't finish his sentence but looks at me with his mouth open, as if paused to say something further that got lost.

"When?" My voice sounds like it is coming from far away.

"March, it was in March. I got drunk . . . I . . ."

I think of the nights he came home late. Maybe drunk. I don't know. It suddenly feels as though I haven't really noticed him in a while. My husband. More like a flatmate. Have we really been living like this since March?

"Grace. It was a mistake. I don't know what I was thinking."

And then he says the very thing neither of us has had the guts to say. He brings up the subject that has hovered over us for months. He speaks slowly, tasting each bitter word as it comes out of his mouth.

"When you said . . . when the doctor said that we couldn't have . . ."

I think of Pete on our wedding day. The orange shirt. Bali heat. The look on his face. But then I imagine his head above someone else. His face, straining, looking down at another woman's body. My stomach aches, and it is hard to breathe. I observe it as if outside myself. The odd feeling, the mouthful of meal netted in my throat, my chest tight.

"Because we can't have children you had sex with a prostitute?"

"It wasn't like that. It's just that . . . Shit. We never talk about it, Grace. I mean, babies. The tests. We never talk about any of it."

"You want to *talk* about it?"

I stand up, unsure what to do next but unable to stay sitting. The tight feeling in my lungs starts to burn. I want to say the nastiest things; I want to spear him with something he will never forget. I want him to hurt.

"You want to talk about it, after you accuse me . . . *me* . . . of looking at a man the wrong way. After *you* sleep with another woman . . ."

"Grace . . ."

"A woman that you *paid* to have sex with you?"

"Shit. It wasn't—I mean, it was awful . . . I . . ." He is reaching for my hand across the table, but I step back, my chair sliding a few inches. I scream at him inside my head. How dare you? How could you? I will never forgive you! I feel like Mama, so hot and mad I could do anything. I can almost see her face in front of me, pale and ferocious.

"Please, Grace," he says, "don't go. We need . . . we need . . ."

"We need what? Huh? We need what, Pete?" The words come out growling. I can feel a stinging heat racing through my blood, through my veins. I feel like I have been injected with Mama. Red and wild. I want to say things I cannot retract. Things like, I shouldn't have married you. The things she said to me once: *I don't need you. I don't want you here. Perhaps you were a mistake.* I feel myself start to shake. His hand reaches for mine.

"Don't come near me! Don't you come near me!" My voice wobbles.

He looks up at me, silent, mouth hanging open uselessly. He implores me with his eyes, dark and sorrowful.

I want to scream those things Mama had said. The last terrible things that could never be erased. *Leave me! Leave me now and never come back! Don't you ever come back!* I can feel the tears bubbling up as if from the depths of my being.

"I don't want to talk to you; I don't want to even look at you."

I pick up my plate with a quivering hand and throw it against the wall. It shatters loudly. Gravy slides down the paint in a sticky brown stain. My heart pounds, as though trying to tear through my chest. I can't be in this room anymore. I push the chair aside and hear it clatter to the floor. I don't look back. I storm into the study and slam the door. I sit in front of the computer screen, panting, with tears running down my hot cheeks.

My hands shake as the sobs hurl themselves out of me. I breathe in and then out, in and then out. Slowly, slowly. The tightness in my chest subsides to a dull ache, like a headache from a hangover. I feel so exhausted. As though I've run a marathon.

Eventually I hear a rattle as Pete picks up his keys. He leaves, closing the door behind him quietly. I put my head down next to the keyboard and stare at the Tab key until it goes blurry.

Dearest Mama,

I am worn down. I feel like a piece of glass in the ocean. Starting out all bright and glittery, and now soft and green and tumbled and opaque; laid out on the sand. Is there a way back from here?

Did you wake up one day, Mama, and feel surprised by how your life was? I felt like that this morning. The sun shining through the windows of the spare room. Pete wasn't beside me. I reached out for him, but my hand fell on smooth, empty sheets, and it woke me up with a throat full of anger. I put my hand in front of my face, and I thought, Whose hand is this? Aren't you supposed to know the back of your hand like, well, the back of your hand? I don't know my hand at all, Mama. I don't know my hand or my leg or my face. I certainly don't know my heart.

I am a stranger to myself.

The only place I know myself is in Lillian's.

Your loving daughter,
Grace

Une Vie Tranquille—A Quiet Life

Pineapple with Butterscotch Ganache

The bell above the door chimes, pulling me up sharply from my thoughts. I am staring into the oven in a dull kind of stupor, watching *macarons* rise; the gentle forming of something new. My stomach twists into a knot when I hear a man's voice talking to Rilla. I know I shouldn't, but I lean a little toward the sound of it. Rilla's head pokes around the kitchen door, and she speaks quietly.

"Grace? It's Léon. He wants to see you."

I wonder if she notices my eyes widen, whether she can hear my heartbeat thrumming in the cage of my chest. She doesn't say anything, just moves to the sink with cups and saucers. I run my fingers through my hair.

He is wearing a black leather jacket and jeans. He gives me a careful smile. Heat rises from my neck and crawls up my chin to my cheeks.

"Hi, Léon, how are you?"

"I am fine," he replies calmly. He leans over the counter to place a kiss on each of my cheeks, and I bump against him. The teapot rattles on the bench.

"Can I get you anything?" The percussion of my heart increases its tempo.

"Oh no. I mean . . . I wanted to talk to you."

I gesture toward a table and untie my apron.

"Rilla?" I call out.

"Yes?"

"Would you mind getting us some coffees and a couple of *macarons*?"

She comes out of the kitchen, and her eyes dart between Léon and me.

"Of course, Grace."

Léon gives a little forced smile. "I'm sorry; I don't mean to interrupt you during your work. I just thought it would be best to talk. About . . . well, you know."

I nod. I know.

He settles into his seat, then looks around the café for a few moments, as if checking to see who is here. The whistling of the milk steamer pierces the awkward silence.

"Léon, I'm so sorry about the other day . . ."

"Here you go."

Rilla places an espresso in front of Léon and a cappuccino in front of me, and sets a plate of yellow *macarons* between us. Pineapple and butterscotch—*Une Vie Tranquille.* She smiles, then goes back to the kitchen.

I start to speak again, but Léon puts up his hand.

"Grace, please. If I can, I want to explain."

"Okay."

"Perhaps there are things that have been a bit, er, lost in translation. I don't know. Your husband was very upset. Obviously he thinks there is something going on between us."

"Léon, Pete . . . he . . ."

Pete and I have hardly spoken for days. We speak only of toast, dropping off dry cleaning, picking up milk from the store. I can barely look at him without filling with anger and a searing bitterness. I don't tell him when I will be late home or what is happening at Lil's. The silence is a kind of poison, slowly seeping.

Léon sighs and leans toward me. He smells of aftershave and, as always, bread.

"Grace, I need to be very clear. You are a remarkable woman."

I feel my face flush.

"Everything you have done here, with so little experience. I mean, you have a gift for cooking, for this industry. I respect that." He gestures toward the counter where Rilla is humming and restocking *macarons*. "Your staff . . . they seem to really like you, you seem very close. I think you must be a very good leader. Like a mother to them."

I want to reach out and touch his hand, but he has moved both hands into his lap.

"I am very impressed by you, by all of this. But Grace . . ." His eyes flash, the color of a cloudless sky. "I am not interested in you. I didn't mean to give you, or Pete, any wrong message." He pauses. "I'm sorry."

I nod and will myself to look calm. To look at least a little bit normal. My throat feels strangled as I pick up my cup. My face is burning now, cheeks probably fire-engine red. I take a sip, even though the coffee is too hot and scalds my tongue.

"Of course. There is nothing to be sorry about." I force a smile. "There is nothing going on between us; it's . . . it's crazy." I put my cup down, and it clatters against the saucer.

Léon sighs and pats the top of my hand. "I am so glad you can see this misunderstanding."

I hear myself laugh. It comes out tight and too high. "Yes, yes. God, you didn't think . . . ?"

He laughs too, low and relieved. "Celine thought that maybe you thought . . . Anyway, you and I understand each other. We are just a couple of foodies, right?"

"Exactly."

He picks up a *macaron* and eats it slowly. I do the same.

"Maybe, sometimes . . ." He shrugs. "Well, Celine says I flirt. For attention, like a little boy, she says." He shakes his head, unconvinced. "I think it is ridiculous. I am pleasant to everyone, you know?"

I nod. It's as though he is talking to himself. He's still not looking at me. He has stirred his sugar into his coffee, and now he is just stirring. The black liquid moves around and around in the cup.

"I like people. I like women. So? I like food and drink and cards too, I mean, this is *living life*." He puts the spoon down and lifts the cup to his lips. "Anyway, as you say, it's crazy. *You* and *me*?" He snorts again as though to emphasize the ridiculousness of it. "Right?"

"Right." I laugh with him, although my chest feels tight and my cheeks are burning and I want to throw my cup against the wall. I remember the gravy sliding down the wall behind Pete's head. The adrenaline pulsing through me. I sip my coffee as carefully, calmly as possible. How stupid I have been.

That afternoon Gigi is late. Her hair is a mess. She grins at Rilla and me behind the counter.

"Well, I sorted *them* out."

Rilla looks up. "Who?"

"Cheating suppliers." She slings her bag onto the hook on the kitchen door. There is a little sweat stain around the neck of her shirt. "They said they couldn't tell the difference with the almond flour. Idiots or liars. We certainly won't be taking any more of that cheap shit."

Rilla laughs. She doesn't have the same culinary interest in *macarons* that Gigi and I do, but she loves it when Gigi swears.

Which she does more and more now, especially when she is excited. Marjory seems to be a bad influence.

"Don't swear in here, Gigi," I say tersely.

Gigi looks around the café. It's pretty quiet. One guy on his mobile phone sitting in the corner. The lull before the after-school rush.

"There's no one here." She waves her hand around Lillian's. "So are we making something new today? I've got an idea that is going to blow your brains out, it is so good."

"A new *macaron*?" Rilla asks, polishing cutlery with a tea towel.

"Oh yeah, my friend. It is a beauty! Grace, we're going to need some more lemons for zest."

A boiling feeling rises in my chest.

Strands of hair fall around Gigi's face, loose from her sagging ponytail. She reaches behind her back to tie on an apron. It is strained, these days, around that bulb of her stomach.

"If it doesn't blow your mind, I'm the fucking queen." She grins, her dark almond eyes glinting.

I give her a sharp look. "Gigi, I'll ask you not to swear no matter *who* is in the café."

Rilla and Gigi glance at each other.

"And try and be on time? It's a quarter past and neither of us has had a break yet."

Gigi crosses her arms. "What's up with you?"

"I *own* the place, if you hadn't noticed. Pay your wages? You're late." I'm on a roll now; there is a strange kind of poison in my voice. Something pushes me to add, "And you look like a tramp."

"A what?" whispers Rilla to Gigi.

"She's saying I look like shit," Gigi replies clearly. Her face is drawn now, sullen, but her back is straight.

"Are you deaf? No swearing." Now I have raised my voice to a level where the customer has looked up from his phone call.

I straighten. I am not their sister, their schoolteacher, or their mother. I am their boss. Why does it seem like no one ever listens to me? I lower my voice and hiss, "Yes, you look like shit and yes, again, you are late. Try and take this a bit more seriously, Gigi. Act like a grown-up, okay?"

Rilla moves, wide-eyed, toward the cutlery drawer and away from us both.

Gigi narrows her eyes. "Take it a bit more seriously?"

"Yes."

The door chimes, and I notice our customer has left. Coins lie in a saucer on the table. Lillian's is empty. The sunlight has that hazy look of early afternoon. Oily and swirling.

Gigi breathes in slowly and lifts her head. Her mouth is pinched tight. She arches one black eyebrow. "Right. Well, I will try and do that, *Grace*." She bangs the kitchen door as she opens it, a thick and painful slap of her palm against the wood. Mama's voice seems to shudder around my head again. *Don't come back!*

As the door swings closed, I call out, "Good, glad to hear it, *Gigi*," and even I can hear the spite in my voice.

That night I have the house to myself. Pete is working a night shift, which I know only because I overheard him talking about it on the phone to some shift manager. When I go to the kitchen to pour a glass of wine, there is a piece of paper folded into a little tent next to the olive oil. My name is written across the front. I unfold it.

> *Grace,*
>
> *It's been days since we spoke about it. The silence is killing me.*
>
> *I promise you it was only one time and that it will never, ever happen again. I am so sorry, Grace. I was lost and angry and I didn't*

know what to do. I was drunk and stupid. I don't know if you will believe me, but I know it will never happen again. I wish I could give you more than this. There is only faith and trust left, I guess. Not much, maybe just enough, I don't really know.

I want to talk. I think we both need to say some things. Actually we both need to say a lot. Probably about five years' worth of somethings. Don't you notice the not-talking? So much not-talking? I miss you, Gracie. I miss you so much.

Please talk to me,

Pete

I hold the paper loosely in my hand. The neighbors downstairs must be having a party. There is a steady, muffled beat rising from the floor. Then a squeal, some laughter, chairs being scraped across floorboards. I put my hand to my head. My forehead is throbbing as if keeping up with the rhythm. Aside from the headache, my whole body feels like it is on fire. Every pore is hot, alive and crawling with sweat. I know it is a hot flush, just another symptom of menopause, my body's mean little joke. I fold the letter back up and fan myself with it.

Faith and trust.

I shake my head.

All our wineglasses are dirty, along with a pathetic gathering of plates, saucepans, and cereal bowls to the side of the sink. I pick the bottle up by the neck and drink from it instead. Cold sauvignon blanc streams down my throat. My head is still full of thunder. Thumping, thumping, thumping.

Downstairs there is an eruption of laughter. A chorus of men, women, low and high, big guffaws, tinkling giggles, parroty cackles.

My fist slams against the kitchen bench. "Shut the hell up!"

* * *

The next day I fumble with the café keys in the pale, early-morning light. My head feels pinched from drinking too much wine the night before and tossing and turning instead of sleeping. Pete came home around three in the morning and crept into the spare room. I was having awful dreams of children being hit by cars, red-haired witches on broomsticks, falling off a trapeze. I'm so tired this morning my eyes hurt.

I'm carrying a bag of flour balanced against my hip and putting the keys back into my handbag when I see one of the back tables has two chairs down on the floor. I pause. We always stack the chairs onto the tabletops at night so we can mop the floor. I shake my heavy head and open the door to the kitchen.

The storeroom door is ajar.

The bag of flour feels heavy in my arms, and my chest is as tight as a drum. I put the bag down on the counter, trying to make as little noise as possible. My heart races. I press my hand hard against my chest. Don't be ridiculous, I scold myself. Why on earth would someone want to rob a *macaron* shop?

I lean toward the hinges of the door, listening for sounds, breathing, the shuffle of a shoe against concrete, but it is as quiet as a church. I peek in, but I cannot see anything; the storeroom is too dark. I look up at the ceiling briefly, again willing my heart to slow down and my mind to think with clarity. Moving toward the door handle, I grasp it gently and then pull it just a bit. Silence. A deep breath, then I yank the door open. The storeroom floods with light, and I take a step through the doorway, willing myself to have courage to face what is inside.

Two figures are on the floor, curled into each other. They are absolutely still, but when I look closer, I can see they are pulsing with the small in-and-out breaths of sleep. A blanket is thrown across them.

I recognize Rilla and feel my breath tumble out of me in relief.

Rilla must sense the light because she lets out a soft grizzle and moves her chin down to the top of the other person's head. I see now it is a small woman. Her face is hidden, but she has long dark hair spread out around her. Who is she? What are they doing here?

My relief quickly simmers into anger, coursing through me. I look down again at Rilla's figure. My mind races with a thousand questions, a thousand thoughts all fighting for space. What is she doing here? Has she been kicked out of her boardinghouse? Why didn't she tell me? And if she didn't tell me that, what else hasn't she told me? Could Linda be right? Have I been too trusting? How many weeks has it been since I've counted the money at the end of the day? I've been letting Rilla do everything: close up at night; deposit our earnings at the bank. I should have been watching more closely. Could she be taking advantage of me? Or Lillian's? Sleeping here with some stray woman? How could she do this? In Lillian's. *My* Lillian's.

"Rilla!" I hiss.

The two women start in fright. Rilla's eyes spring open and stare blankly into the light.

"Get up!"

Rilla blinks, dazed, as she looks around to see who is speaking. Then she recognizes the shadow in the doorway. Her eyes grow wide.

"Wake up."

The woman in her arms tries to bury her head in Rilla's shoulder, confused by the light and my voice. *Jocelyn.* I recognize her now, the small, humble shape of her, as if she wants to become wallpaper, invisible. She has a bruise across one of her cheeks and large dark eyes, her pupils almost black. Who knows what trouble she has got herself into? Jocelyn contracts into a ball on the floor, hugging her knees to her chin, as Rilla scrambles to her feet.

"Grace, I'm . . . we're so . . ." Rilla is wringing her hands.

"What the hell are you doing in here?" My voice is louder than I expected. I can't figure out what to ask first. I'm confused. I feel lied to; betrayed. I am suddenly and uncontrollably furious. Pete's confession still burns in my heart.

"I can explain . . . There is a good reason, I promise. It's complicated . . ."

"Goddammit, Rilla, you gave me the fright of my life! I thought there was a thief in here." I nearly roar.

I see her cringe with embarrassment, and she averts her face from my gaze.

"Don't look away from me."

"I'm sorry, Grace. So sorry, we just . . ." She looks over to Jocelyn, still on the floor.

"You just what? Thought my storeroom was a bloody hotel?" My body is shaking. I feel like I am in someone else's skin.

"No, no . . . We just needed somewhere to sleep." She is still avoiding my gaze.

"Look at me, *both* of you."

Rilla looks up, but Jocelyn doesn't. She seems to be swaying from side to side, her long hair falling over her face and shoulders like a dark curtain. Rilla's face, now turned to mine, has tears running down the cheeks. Her lips are pressed tightly together.

"Well, Rilla?"

"Jocelyn . . ." she starts and looks over to her companion. "Please, Grace," she begs.

Her eyes swim with tears.

The raw, angry feeling in my chest is thumping like a big dark heart next to mine. I'm rattled. Hurt. My head spins. First Pete and now Rilla. Haven't I dealt with enough? Can't I trust anyone? It feels like Mama has entered my bloodstream, full of heat and spit and fire. "Just get out. Both of you. Get out now!" Again I hear Mama. *Don't come back!* I clench my quivering fists.

Rilla's face clouds with fear, and Jocelyn springs up from the floor. They dart past me, and I follow them into the café and watch as they rush out the front door. I wait for a moment for Rilla to turn back and look at me, but she doesn't.

When they are gone, the whole café is bathed in a heavy silence. I watch them from the window, the two of them holding on to each other as if battling a strong wind, bumping into each other as they hurry away to the bus stop. I take a deep breath, gasping for air as if I am drowning.

I sink down into one of the chairs. My head throbs. What has happened? It all happened so fast I feel dizzy. It is as if I wasn't even present for the past few minutes. Like some strange force had taken control of me. Why hadn't I paused to wonder what was going on with Rilla? Jocelyn? Her voice echoes through me. *Please, Grace.* But wasn't I right to be angry? It is my café, isn't it? They had been taking advantage of me. Why didn't they tell me they needed a place to stay? Why doesn't anyone talk about anything? My thoughts crash and collide into one another.

I rub my temples with my fingers. I wish for arms around me. A hug, a whisper, a kiss against my hair. Someone to tell me it's going to be okay. That I did the right thing. *Oh, Mama.* I think of her kind touch. Then I think of waking up next to Pete in the mornings, like we used to. Warm sheets, the salty smell of sleep, his lips on my hair and his hands on my breasts.

I bury my face in my palms and let my shoulders heave with sobs.

Pardon—Forgiveness
Plum and Hibiscus with Chocolate Ganache

By Friday, Rilla has not been in for three days and Gigi is barely speaking to me. In fact she makes a point of using Cantonese almost exclusively. To customers, to Yok Lan, to herself in the kitchen. All without a shred of translation. She gives me sidelong glares full of things she is refusing to say. I try to call Rilla, but her phone is switched off or disconnected. I've never had the need to call her before now; she is always on time and never sick. One morning I think I see her across the street as I am carrying over Yok Lan's pot of tea, but when I look up there is no one there, only the wind leaning against the long grass.

Without Rilla the work weighs heavily on me; my limbs throb and sing with pain each night. I'm often in the kitchen, cooking almost mindlessly while Gigi serves. One day I hear Léon's velvety voice ordering a coffee and making small talk with her. She serves him with icy coolness as I hide away, not daring to come out for three whole hours in case he is still there. I can't bear to see him, on top of everything else. Now that everything seems so unraveled. I feel so worn out I catch myself looking toward the storeroom, wishing to rest on that floor like Rilla and Jocelyn, to curl up like a field mouse. It is so tempting. Just a short nap, put my head down and forget about everything.

If Pete and I had been talking, perhaps he might have asked me what was wrong. Instead we barely see each other. We cook our own little meals for one, head to bed at separate times, watch television or use the computer apart from one another. We sail around each other on a roiling sea of rage and regret.

Marjory catches me in the bathroom at Lil's, staring at my tired reflection in the mirror. She leans over me to wash her hands and glances up to my hair, perhaps thinking I was looking for gray strands, which there seem to be more of these days.

"I've been getting those for years," she says with a wink. "Why do you think I dye it?"

Her hair shimmers like gold, even in the dim light of the bathroom. I had assumed it was natural. Mama used to say a redhead never goes gray but often white all at once. Like magic. As a little girl, I'd always imagined waking up with a white-chocolate-colored mane. I wonder what happened to hers.

Marjory frowns at my long face. "Hey, I'm trying to cheer you up here."

"Sorry. It's been a rough week. Thank God we're closed tomorrow."

"The parade?"

I nod. Our street will be closed for the Olympic gold medalists' procession, and I am relieved. I need the break.

I splash cold water onto my face, hoping the chill will enliven me.

Marjory passes me a hand towel. "Gigi told me about Rilla. She hasn't come back?"

I shake my head.

"Shit."

"Yeah." I wipe the mascara from under my eyes, pat my face down slowly, makeup coming away with the towel.

"Did she tell you why she was sleeping here?"

"No. It all happened so fast." My voice comes out more jagged than I mean it to be. There is a lump of guilt at the bottom of my throat.

Marjory leans up against the wall with a frown. "It's too bad."

I remember the snippets of stories I've heard about maids stealing jewelry. Nannies running off with cash, thieving from kids' piggy banks. Drinking, lying, and worse. Gossip over lattes and cappuccinos. I don't think Rilla ever stole from me, but I feel like there's so much I don't know about her. I think of all those times I let her count what was in the register at the end of the day. What if she had been pocketing some of Lillian's earnings? Why would she be so afraid to come back unless she's guilty of something?

"I don't want any trouble here, Marj. If you know what kind of mess she's in, I'd rather not know."

Marjory is still frowning. "I don't think it's what you suspect—"

I cut her off. "Really, I just don't want to know. I have enough going on and this, Lillian's—" My throat catches. "It's the only safe place left."

Marjory puts her hand on my shoulder.

"Sorry," I mumble.

"Hey, it's okay. I'll shut up. Lil's is your place; you run it however you want. I'm worried about you, though. You look exhausted."

We both look at my reflection in the mirror, and I think of Gigi's comment the other day.

"Are you telling me I look like crap?"

Marjory grins. "Totally awful."

"Thanks."

"Anytime. That's what friends are for."

I can't help but laugh.

She puts her arm around me, pulls me into a sideways hug. "You and I need a Friday drink," she declares.

I couldn't agree more.

The night sky, punctuated with buildings and lights, glitters beyond the window. Marjory has been to the bathroom; her lips are freshly glossed and as shiny as a new car bonnet.

"Wow, I didn't know you liked champagne so much," she says, waggling the empty bottle at the waiter. She tilts her head sideways in what seems like admiration.

"It's nice and fizzy," I reply, my tongue thick in my mouth.

"That it is."

Our seats face the window, to suck in as much view as possible. The Crystal Club is on level thirty-something and turned back toward Macau peninsula like a dancer facing its partner. The lights swim against the glare on the window and the water between. The crowd is young and slender; girls wear skinny jeans and billowing shirts. They are tall reeds wavering in the warm night breeze. Some young man floats past me and winks. He is wearing a trilby and a waistcoat as if it is the 1930s.

"Macau looks pretty from here." Marjory sighs. She accepts a new bottle of champagne from the waiter, who bends over us in his black uniform and refills our glasses.

Macau *is* pretty from here. Bright and popping out of the darkness. The view reminds me of the party where I first met Léon. The memory is now curdled through with all the embarrassment of a teenage crush. It makes me cringe. Only a few floors down, at Aurora, and so many months ago. It seems like my life has changed so much since that night. Thoughts of Rilla and my tattered marriage rise to the surface, like the bubbles in the glasses. I know I would feel sad if I let myself, but it seems like too much effort.

The guy with the hat comes past again. He does a double take and gives me a sweet smile. He has soft charcoal eyes and caramel skin. A mole dots the middle of one cheek.

"How are you, ladies?" He leans on the back of the couch.

Marjory looks up at him and then at me. I stare at my glass and remember the champagne Pete and I had on our honeymoon. Our feet dug into warm sand, watching the sun drift down into the ocean. Pete's kisses tasting of pineapple, his laughter in my ear, his arm around my shoulder.

"Yeah, fine, how are you?" Marjory returns politely.

"Good. Gorgeous night," he says a little wistfully. "I'm Tom."

"I'm Marjory." She leans over and shakes his hand.

"And you are?" Tom leans down so I have to look at him.

"Oh. Grace."

"Hi, Grace." He grins and sits down on the low table in front of me. I wonder when he will ask for Marjory's phone number and go away. He is blocking my view. He says something to Marjory while a girl standing near the window catches my attention. She has a wide red belt around her tiny waist. She looks down into her drink and giggles with little snorts.

Marjory digs an elbow into my side. "Tom was asking if he could get us a drink," she says out of the side of her mouth.

"Uh-huh."

"I said we could use some snacks. We don't need more drinks, do we?"

"Yeah. Oh yeah."

A girl nearby pulls at her ponytail, making it tighter and higher on her head. She holds a silver purse between her lips while she does this and gives me a look out of the corner of her eye, sly and catlike. The confidence of a young woman, future unwritten. I stare back at her. I drink my champagne fast; it leaves a scalding of bubbles as it goes down. Marjory takes hold of my arm. I notice that Tom is not in front of me now, and I look back at the city. The lights are soft and swimming on the water.

"Hey. Earth to Grace. Are you all right?"

"Huh? Yes. I'm fine. Great night." I raise my glass to her with a wobbly smile.

"That guy could've burned holes in you with looking. You were away with the fairies."

"What?"

"Tom. The guy with the hat."

I look at her shiny lips, which have left tacky marks against her glass. "Sure. He was all over you."

Marjory looks into my face as if searching for something. "Seriously, Grace, you couldn't tell it was you he was after? He couldn't stop staring, especially at that hair of yours."

Tom comes back, and I look at him properly this time. He is taking me in and grinning. I can't seem to hold my focus on him; perhaps it is the champagne making my gaze slither sideways. I wonder what his hair is like underneath the hat.

He pours champagne for us and throws cashews in the air, catching them in his mouth. He talks, mainly to Marjory. I catch parts of the conversation. He's with Cirque. Yeah, he likes Macau. Well, we're not all hippies, you know, ha ha ha. The conversation goes on and on and up and down. He buys us some margaritas and says he is from Mexico. He asks me what I do. I tell him about Lillian's, and he leans forward, elbows on his knees. I can't think of anything more to say, but he is looking at me as if I am about to. Tom pulls a pack of cigarettes out of his pocket, and Marjory takes one. She is staring at me with a hard kind of face, her eyes like marbles behind the smoky puffs. I didn't know Marjory smoked. Then Tom buys us mojitos and watches me pick out the pieces of mint skating on the surface.

* * *

When my head falls against a soft, cool pillow, I hear myself giggling, as if from a great distance. There are hot breaths above my face. The room seems to be moving slowly, like the gentle rolls of a ship on the ocean. I laugh again, and there is Mama's voice.

"Where have you been?" It's cold and slicing.

I kick a shoe off my foot and onto the floor. "Out."

"With whom?"

"Out with friends, Mama."

"You're drunk."

If I could nod I would, but my head is like lead against the pillow. I hear that giggling again.

"Blind bloody drunk," she says bitterly. She is taking off my other shoe and throwing it toward my closet. She throws it hard, and it crashes against the wall. "Which friends?"

"Just friends." Why is she always so suspicious? It was just a couple of girls from the restaurant. I've never really had a proper night out with girls. We laughed a lot. Men bought us drinks. One of the girls got a feather boa from a tribe of women on a hens' night. I wore it around my neck all night like a showgirl.

"I needed you here, Grace."

"No you didn't." I can hear the slur in my voice. A feather is tickling against my lips.

"Yes I did. You can't just go out like that."

"Shit, I just . . ."

"Don't swear."

"Shit, Mama," I plead, then realize I have sworn again and giggle.

"Don't you talk to me like that. I'm your mother. Don't you talk to me like that!" Her voice is getting louder and louder.

"Okay, okay, stop freaking out."

"You can't just go out like that!" Now it's all high-pitched.

I roll onto my back, and the room seems to lurch along with

me. I put my hand over my forehead. "I'm twenty years old for chrissakes, Mama. I should be able to go out for a couple of drinks."

"You didn't even call me!"

I can hear that she is losing it. Her voice is loud and high and desperate, like she is falling off a cliff.

"Mama . . ."

"I needed you here!"

"Mama, calm down. It was just one night. I wasn't going to the moon. I was in a pub. A goddamn pub. In Islington."

I can hear the sobs coming out of the darkness. Normally I would comfort her. Tonight I am tired and drunk and angry. One of the girls is going on holiday to Lanzarote. She'd talked about lying on the beach with a book and a cocktail. I could practically smell the coconut oil. Feel the grains of sand against my back.

"What are you going to do when I'm not here?" I add nastily.

Mama pauses her sobbing. "What do you mean?"

"Like when I'm on holiday or whatever."

She starts to shiver; I can feel it against the bedspread.

"Where are you going?" It is an accusation.

"I dunno. Lanzarote. Greece. Maybe Australia." I have no plans at all; the destinations just leap up at me from my subconscious. Hot places. Faraway places. Places with sunshine and salty oceans.

"Australia?" Mama is almost hysterical now. I can tell she is hanging on to that cliff with one arm. "Australia?" She is practically yelling it.

"Chill, Mama." I'm regretting saying anything at all. It was the piña coladas. They set my tongue loose. She leaps off the bed. I can't quite see her in the darkness, but I can feel the force of her anger.

"If. You. Go. To. Australia . . ." she says slowly and with a tremor on each of the words, "Don't. Come. Back."

The giggles have left me now. I feel a little sick. I try to sit up, my head like a ten-ton weight on my neck.

"Mama . . ."

"You heard me, Grace Raven. If you don't care about me, if you don't want to be with me, then you go. Go and leave me."

"Mama!"

"Leave and do not come back!" She storms out. The heat of her fury seems to have charged up the whole room. The air prickles. I feel nauseated. Leaning over the side of the bed, I make out a flowerpot, the flowers long since dead. I grab for it just in time. My stomach heaves, and I empty three piña coladas into the desiccated soil.

When I wake up, I smell lemon. It is coming from the crisp white sheets. Everything is light and bright. I hear a moan and then realize it came from me. The sound of typing in another room pierces my brain. I roll over. There are satin cushions in soft coffee and chocolate colors in a pile beside me. Thoughts come together in my mind like sugar settling at the bottom of a glass.

"You awake?"

I twist around; Marjory leans on the doorframe. She is wearing a gray T-shirt and fleecy white tracksuit trousers. Her hair is pulled up on the top of her head. She has a strange look on her face.

"Um, yeah." I pull myself around and up so I am sitting. I am wearing a T-shirt with a painting of a gorgeous black woman singing jazz. She has bright red lips the color of a tomato. CHICAGO BLUES CLUB, I think it says. Reading upside down makes me feel queasy.

"Don's," Marjory explains simply. She sits on the end of the bed. I glance around and see that almost everything is white. White curtains, white bedspread; there are just a few colored cushions and a chic mocha-toned rug to relieve the blinding color scheme. My eyes hurt, so I close them. I remember looking into Tom's face and noticing that mole.

"What happened?" My eyes spring back open, and I feel so dizzy I have to hold on to the side of the bed.

"We got drunk," she replies. "Well, you got *really* drunk." She is looking down at her hands, which are resting on her knees.

"Did . . . anything, you know, *happen*?"

She turns to me and frowns.

"That guy? Tom?" I say slowly, my stomach feeling twisted.

"Oh. Right. No." She looks back down at her fingers. "Unless you count throwing up on his shoes."

"Oh."

"It's okay. He was okay about it. We came home after that. He still wanted me to give him your number. Had to tell him a million times you were married."

"Oh." Guilt laces through my relief.

"Grace," she says awkwardly, "what's going on? You and me, we're both private people; I know that. Maybe that's why we've become friends. But with what happened at the tennis, and Rilla, and then last night . . ." She looks up at me with a grim expression. "You're not yourself. Or at least you're not who I thought you were."

I put my head back against the wall. I wish it would stop aching. I close my eyes and place my hands over my forehead. They smell of tobacco and wine. My nose curls up involuntarily. Silence rolls out between us for a few minutes, until I open my eyes.

"Is it Rilla?" she asks.

"No. Well, yes, but no."

Marjory waits.

My throat is dry. "Pete slept with someone. One of those women from the Lisboa." The words hurt. I didn't expect them to hurt so much.

Marjory moves up the bed and puts her arm around my shoulder. "I'm sorry, Grace."

I nod. Then I start to cry. Again. Silently at first and then loud. Heavy and wet. It hurts my poor head even more, and that makes it worse. Crying and hurting, crying and hurting. Marjory whispers "shush, shush, shush," but I can't stop; her shoulder becomes wet with my tears.

She drives me home with my clothes from the night before in a bag. They are folded neatly with my shoes facing each other. I am wearing a pair of her tracksuit pants and her flip-flops. I have told her about the premature menopause, our hopes and dreams dashed, the silence, the slow growing apart. It all tumbled out faster than I thought possible, and she listened and said little. Now she pats my knee.

"It's going to be okay, you know," she says in a hushed voice.

"You think?" I look down at my feet; the nail on my big toe is broken. I must have done it last night. "Aren't you supposed to tell me to leave the cheating bastard?"

Marjory turns the car off and leans forward onto the steering wheel. The sun has started to set, and the colors are rich. Sunsets like these don't come often in Macau. We stare out at it and not at each other. Blues blush to apricots burn to rusty oranges. Great big smears of clouds ice the view.

"Nah. I'm not going to tell you that," she says.

"Why not?"

"He's a fool for what he's done. But he loves you, Grace."

I let out a snort. Strange way of showing it. The anger crawls up my insides like those champagne bubbles in the glass.

"He does, Grace. I know because I care too, so I can tell."

I turn to face her.

"Sleazy, no-good blokes came to watch us dance all the time. The kinds of guys who cheat on their wives, their girlfriends. Not once or twice but all the time, like the worst kind of habit. I've been pretty close to that seedy world, and I can tell you—yes, Pete screwed up. He made a mistake. But he's not one of those men." Her eyes are firmly set on the sunset, the warm colors reflected on her. "C'mon, Grace, he wouldn't have hit Léon if he didn't care about you."

"He was just jealous. He acted like a bloody Neanderthal."

"Exactly," she says. "He was jealous, because he could sense that you liked Léon and he couldn't bear to think of you loving someone else."

"Couldn't bear to think of me sleeping with another man, more like. But now . . ." I shake my head at the sky, urging myself not to cry. "Now I have to think of him with another woman."

Marjory puts her head to one side. "Maybe it wasn't thinking of you sleeping with Léon that got him so bloody mad. It was the thought of you sharing yourself with him."

"What do you mean?"

"Letting him in, Grace. To what makes you tick. The in-here part." She stares into my eyes and taps her collarbone.

The in-here part.

"Look, I'm no counselor. Hell, I'm far from perfect myself." She sighs. "Just . . . just think about it, hon."

A few moments of silence pass. We watch the clouds crawl by. I take a couple of long breaths. Marjory straightens up against the back of her seat.

"Come on," she says. "You need to get home and I need to do a DVD workout with Cindy Crawford."

She reaches over and squeezes my hand before I slide out of the passenger seat to stand on the curb.

"I'll see you tomorrow," she promises.

Waving as the car does a U-turn, I see her give me a sweet smile, lifting one palm from the wheel. The night is coming in and the light is disappearing. The sky turns inky and soft around the edges. I take a big mouthful of the cold air and step inside.

I stand like a shadow by the door. Pete is in the lounge room, the laptop propped up on a stack of books on the coffee table in front of him. He's wearing the reading glasses I bought him a year or so ago. Another sign that we are both getting older. He doesn't notice me for a few moments, flicking through the papers next to him while I stare at the curls on the back of his neck. It makes me remember cool summer nights in London, sitting in the beer garden of a local pub. Talking about the babies we would have. He wanted them to have my lips and my red hair, and I wanted them to have his hazel eyes, fringed with those long lashes. Those nights he'd reach over and squeeze one of my hands and tell me that he loved me—to the moon and back— and I would believe him. Those nights we decided on favorite names: Rose or maybe Eva; Dylan, Matthew, or Jack. *We were so happy then.*

He frowns at his papers, covered in graphs, black lines leaping up into peaks and falling into valleys. He sees me by the door when he looks over the top of his glasses at his screen. He breathes in sharply.

"You gave me a fright." He takes in the T-shirt and flip-flops. "You didn't come home. Are you okay?"

I'm not sure what to say, so I don't reply. I just keep looking at him. I feel as if there are birds trapped in my chest, beating their small wings to get out.

"Grace?"

I put my bag down on the floor.

"Where have you been?"

I take a deep breath, urging the racing feeling to leave my body. I don't know why it is so hard to talk to my own husband.

"I was at Marjory's. I stayed over." I sound like a teenager.

"Okay."

We stare at each other like strangers. I come closer to the couch, sit down a few feet away from him, and speak softly. "I was just thinking about the Approach Tavern. The pub. Do you remember?"

"Of course I remember." I can see his face relax.

"The tables out front, you know? And those great nachos."

"London Pride on tap."

"Yeah."

He pushes the coffee table away from us and sighs.

"I'm still angry at you, Pete."

"That's more than fair." His voice is thick with remorse.

"I feel sick when I think about you being with someone else. I can barely think about it."

"I'm so sorry, Gracie. I can't tell you how sorry I am."

When he looks into my face, I realize how long it's been since I have really seen him. The color of his eyes, the curve of his lips. He has not shaved today; stubble shadows his chin. His eyes are wide, and from all the years we have known each other I know he is telling the truth.

I take a deep breath. "Was it . . . safe? I mean . . ."

He frowns and nods, understanding that I am asking if he

used a condom. He opens his mouth to say something further, but I hold up my hand.

"No. Don't tell me. Don't tell me any details. I can't bear it."

He waits, and when I look up at him again he speaks like the words are sticking in his throat. "It makes me feel sick. I wasn't going to tell you. I didn't want it to be real, that I had done something like that."

I nod.

"I can't explain it. It sounds so stupid, but it was like a kind of madness. Not being able to have a family with you, us not talking ..."

I understand the madness part. That Mama wildness that has had me tumbling in love with Frenchmen and screaming bloody murder at poor Rilla. I put my hand out by him on the couch. He sees it and glances up to me as if asking my permission. That little look makes my heart crack. Have I made him so unsure of me? I move closer and take his hand. When I exhale, it feels as though I have been holding my breath for an eternity.

"Gracie, it tore me in two knowing you wouldn't be able to have children. I wanted it, sure, but you dreamed and breathed it every day. I knew you wanted so much to be a mother. I could see that, and I couldn't fix it. But worse, even worse than all that, is what is happening with us ..."

"I know." It's so hard to say. I swallow. "I tried to lose myself in Lillian's. In ... daydreams. I didn't know what else ..." My voice quivers.

He leans his head toward mine, and our foreheads touch. We sit like that for a few minutes, a funny little triangular shape of space between us.

"I love you so much," he whispers.

"I know."

"I'm so sorry."

I sigh. "I know. I'm sorry too."

Dearest Mama,

Can two people make a family? Is it enough?

I guess we did it like that, didn't we, you and me? More than a pair.

I think it's time Pete and I try to make it this way too.

Your loving daughter,
Grace

Thé pour Deux — Tea for Two

Pink Earl Grey Infused with
Dark Chocolate Ganache

The calendar in the café kitchen is running out of days for September. Soon it will be Christmas and then a new year. The thought shivers over me oddly, as if I've been trying to keep time leashed, like a pet. I stare at the little black boxes and numbers across the page.

"Someone here to see you."

Gigi is standing in the doorway of the kitchen, arms crossed in front of her huge belly. She has started speaking to me again but makes it clear she is not happy about it.

"Thank you, I'll be there in a minute," I reply with a smile. She just glances away. I untie my ganache-splattered apron and wash my hands.

When I go into the café, Pete is at a table by the wall, a newspaper unfolded by his side. Instead of reading it, he is talking to Gigi, who now has a stack of plates and cups balanced in the crook of one arm and against her round stomach. She gestures with her other arm, telling a story. Pete smiles up at her. I stand for a minute and watch them, Gigi shaking her head and rolling her eyes. On the table are two plates, a baguette lying on each one, and behind him the windows frame a gray sky. Seeing him here makes me feel a bit giddy, like when we first started dating.

"Hey," I interrupt.

Pete leans back; his smile softens.

"Do you want me to make you guys a coffee?" Gigi asks in a clipped voice. She looks at Pete more than at me.

"Thanks, that would be great."

"I'll have a green tea, if that's okay," Pete adds.

Gigi nods. "Nice to meet you."

"Yeah, you too, Gigi."

As she walks back to the kitchen with the dishes, Pete raises his eyebrows. "She's a character. Smart too."

"You're right; she's a character. Does my head in sometimes, but she's good. She's a big help with the suppliers and our local customers."

Pete looks around the café, and I can see he is really taking it all in. Soaking it up. I wonder what he thinks. I want to ask him, but it feels like too much, too soon. I realize I know Léon's opinion about Lillian's but not Pete's.

"Where's Rilla?" he asks.

A knot forms in my stomach, and I give the simplest explanation. The one that leaves me feeling the least guilty. "We had a kind of argument."

"Oh."

Gigi, who is now behind the counter at the coffee machine, shoots me one of her mutinous glances. I wonder if she can hear me. Yet again I wish for Rilla's face. Her smile and kindness. I turn back to Pete. "So, green tea?"

"Yeah, I've been drinking it at work." He shrugs. "I quite like it."

He takes off his tie and lays it across the newspaper to his side. After unbuttoning his top button, he clears his throat and says, "I thought . . . I thought we could have lunch?"

I look around the quiet café. Yok Lan is in the corner by the window, nibbling a *macaron*. She sees me and grins, lifting her hand in a wave. I smile in return.

"It's not so busy. Okay."

Pete smiles and leans forward as if to whisper to me. The move is so intimate it's as though I can feel the heat of his skin before he touches me. "You have something—look, I know this sounds cheesy, but you have something in your hair," he says quietly.

"Ah," I breathe.

He reaches toward me and smooths down a piece of my hair by my forehead, then sits back and cocks his head to one side, making sure it is fixed. Gigi arrives with a tray and puts down my coffee and Pete's tea. She looks at the two of us, then at the baguettes, before going to talk to her grandmother.

"Just suds," Pete explains, taking a sip of his hot tea. "Just soap suds. In your hair."

I nod from behind my cup. This feels like a date; even my palms are sweaty.

"How's your day been?" I ask.

"My day? Fine." He pauses, his sandwich at his mouth. "No, actually it's been bad. Sorry, I'm used to saying it's been fine, but it's been really rough." He bites down into the sandwich while I spread a napkin over my lap.

"What's up?"

"Economy," he says simply.

"What about it?"

"It's not good. Things are changing, and fast. Too fast," he says, between mouthfuls.

"What do you think is going to happen here?"

He shakes his head slowly in response. "I'm not sure. Not sure at all." He sighs.

We talk about it while eating our sandwiches. The share prices for all the casinos are down, the government wants to restrict visitors from certain provinces, construction is behind schedule, and lenders are getting fractious. Pete keeps shaking his head. The industry is in a state of turmoil. They've been used to reliable profits and gleeful shareholders. The old saying about creating casinos in Macau was "Build it, and they will come." Now things aren't so certain. Pete drinks his tea, sip by slow sip.

When Yok Lan stands up to leave, she comes to put her hand on my shoulder and smile down at me. Her face is round and content, eyes half-closed like those of a meditating Buddha.

I introduce her to Pete. "This is Yok Lan. She's Gigi's grandmother."

Pete says something in Cantonese. She leaves with a smile and a nod of her head.

"What did you say?"

"I said nice to meet you and see you later."

I find myself staring at him in surprise, but he doesn't notice; his attention is on his sandwich.

"These are really good, Grace." The look on his face reminds me of a younger Pete. Pete with a mouthful of tomato tart.

"Thanks," I whisper.

"It's a great café. Truly."

I glance up at him and smile shyly. We sit together in silence as we finish eating. It is easy, gentle, not awkward.

He doesn't kiss me when he says goodbye but puts his hand on my shoulder, like Yok Lan had. He squeezes it softly. A kind of warmth floods my body and, although I know our problems are far from mended, it feels like they could be, one day. There is apology and love in his touch; my body recognizes it.

"Have a good day."

"You too," I reply, still sitting. There is a stormy wind that sends the door chimes into a silvery cacophony when he opens the door. Once he is outside, the wind picks up his hair and whips it around his face. He screws up his nose and grins ruefully; Gigi laughs at him through the glass. He lifts his hand in a wave to me, and I return it.

That night the rain gives the windows a hammering. I shouldn't stand so close, but I'm so restless I am pacing. I keep ending up next to the windows trying to see out, feeling like a caged lion. Pete is in front of the television. The wind is so strong the trees down our street are bent into arches. It rumbles and roars ominously; I can feel it thumping violently when I press my palm against the glass. This is no regular typhoon.

"Hey . . . umm . . ."

"Yeah. I'll stand back," I reply before he can ask.

He knows I am worried about Lillian's, and I'm sure he is nervous about his own construction site. His eyes fix on mine, and he gives me a reassuring smile. The last storm hadn't inflicted too much damage, but this typhoon is much worse. There are motorcycles toppled from their parked positions and strewn along the sidewalks; the streets are empty of cars. It's eerie and January-cold.

The weather report comes on, and Pete turns up the volume. *"In Hong Kong over one hundred flights were either canceled or delayed today due to Typhoon Hagupit and amber rain warnings. Scaffolding damage and flash flooding have been among the worst consequences of the typhoon which swept through the region this afternoon . . ."*

There is a mournful howl which drowns out the television. In the bathroom a fan has started to spin, the wind streaming through it. I rush to shut it and weight the drawstring with a glass jar full of peppercorns. When I come back to the living room, Pete looks up at me again, concerned.

"You okay, love?"

I sit down next to him. "I can't stop thinking about Lil's."

"It'll be all right," he says hopefully.

There is the sound of a tree against a window, a tapping against glass or wood. Pete turns from me to look at the front door. His forehead is gathered in a frown.

"Was that the door?"

"Huh?"

"Is someone knocking at the door?"

"I'm not sure."

He gets up and opens the door. Someone is framed in the doorway, small and soaked, shivering.

"Oh my God. Come in, come in, quickly," Pete says.

When he moves out of the doorway, I can see a tiny face, white and wet. I breathe in quickly. "Rilla?"

Pete looks over to me. "Grace, grab a towel."

I stand for a moment staring at her; she is mutely looking down at our floorboards. She has a rain jacket, but instead of covering her, it is bunched up in her hands. She is holding on to it so tightly her knuckles are pale. She coughs, and her lips are purple against her skin.

"Grace?" Pete says again.

I hurry back with a towel, and Pete wraps Rilla in it as if she were a small child just out of the bath. He looks so huge beside her; his hand is a bear's paw against her back. He guides her to the couch and asks her to sit, which she does somewhat reluctantly. I go into the kitchen and pour a big mug of hot water, drop a tea bag into it. I can hear him saying something to her, but I don't hear her talking back.

"It's really dangerous," he is saying when I put the mug in front of her. She still avoids my gaze but nods gratefully at the teacup. "What were you doing out there?"

When she doesn't reply, he sits beside her and rubs her back with his palm, a deep wrinkle of concern between his eyebrows. I perch on the edge of the coffee table, watching her take bird-like sips of tea. She looks so cold and small I can feel tears prickling my eyes. Eventually she stops shaking, and her lips and cheeks regain their color. She lifts her head and gives me a quick look.

"Rilla, what's going on?" I whisper.

Her lips quiver above the rim of her cup. She mumbles a reply without lifting her head. "I'm sorry, ma'am, sir. I went to Lillian's, to check . . ."

"You went to Lillian's?"

"To see if everything is okay. Then the buses stopped running so I couldn't get home. I knew you lived nearby . . ." Her face is apologetic.

"Oh, Rilla," I breathe.

"There are some breaks, windows smashed. And . . . this."

From beneath the towel she draws out her rain jacket, folded like a package. She unfolds it. The café sign is in pieces. There is an unexpected ache in my chest, seeing it like that. Her name, splintered into bits. I inhale sharply, and Rilla looks up at me then. Her eyes are wide.

"It's okay, ma'am," she says, her gaze darting between Pete and me. "It can all be fixed. Just window breaks. Some water inside, but it will be okay. Macau is a safe place, no one looting or robbing." Her eyes are fringed with wet lashes, her forehead lined. Her solicitude makes me feel both guilty and grateful.

Rilla whispers to me again. "Ma'am? Grace? It will be okay."

I shake my head. "I'm more worried about you, out in a typhoon like this." I bite my lip. The wind is whistling and howling outside as I place my hand on her wet knee. "Rilla, I'm so sorry. I've been trying to call . . ." Pete stands, lifts the broken sign from my hands, and picks up Rilla's empty cup. He goes into the kitchen to refill it, leaving us alone with each other. How wrong I was to think she would steal from me, or take advantage of the friendship that had been growing between us. Shame blooms inside me, and my voice shakes.

"Rilla, please, will you come back to Lillian's? We need you so much."

"Oh."

"If you haven't already found another job . . . ?"

"No. I haven't found another job."

We sit in a little pocket of silence looking at each other, until she murmurs, "I think I should explain, Grace—about that morning."

I stiffen with embarrassment as she gazes at me, eyes serious. But then Pete is back with fresh cups of tea. I'm grateful for the interruption.

"Don't worry, you two," he says. "It will all be fine. You'll both be back making *macarons* in no time." He looks at Rilla. "But you're going to have to ride this typhoon out with us. There are towels in that spare bedroom there, and Grace will lend you some clothes, right, Grace?"

I nod, my hand still on Rilla's knee.

"Are you sure?" Rilla asks. "It would be okay?" She is looking at me.

"Of course," I say. "Please stay."

We are not the first to arrive at Lillian's the next morning. Marjory is sitting on the footpath with Gigi, whose round belly swamps the lower half of her body. Around them wet debris, pieces of windowsill, and broken glass glitters like diamonds. Rilla helps to lift Gigi to her feet. Gigi groans with the weight of her belly but grins widely at Rilla and holds her hand for longer than necessary, giving it a sisterly squeeze. She is wearing a gray maternity dress over black jeans. Her face is free from makeup, bar a thick coat of mascara on her lashes.

"You're back," Marjory says to Rilla, smiling. "We missed you."

"Hell, Grace. Lil's is a wreck," says Gigi with characteristic bluntness.

My gaze drifts over Lillian's while I try to remind myself that we have insurance to cover repairs. Still, dread fills my throat and chest. The post for the sign is bent, the empty chains swinging drunkenly in the light breeze. The front windows are smashed, although one has stayed stubbornly within its frame. The fractured glass is broken like a starburst. A piece of window frame hangs out from its moorings, leaves caught in the deep splinters. Even from outside I can see the floor is flooded, table legs soaked. One table has fallen on its side, a deep vein of a crack through its center, and all the chairs are against the west wall. The other tables have skated into one another and are huddled in a corner. As I step closer to the door, Rilla puts her hand on my back.

"Are you all right?"

I nod, grateful that she's here.

When I open the door, water floods out to greet me. A lost wind whistles through the café; the window in the kitchen must be broken too. I wonder about the state of the ovens, refrigerator, and storeroom. All the *macarons* we made. The almond flour. Glasses. Cutlery. The disconcerting smell of dampness fills the air. The others follow me in, and the four of us stand ankle-deep in water among the tables and chairs, staring around the walls. A dull sadness swells inside me.

Then there is a quick audible breath, and Gigi has her arm outstretched. "Look at that."

We all follow her pointing finger to the wall beside the counter. There, right near the espresso machine and the cash register, is the poster that Yok Lan gave me. Frame undamaged, glass intact, it hangs straight and proud on the wall. The children still dance among the spinning flames and sparks.

Un Petit Phénix — A Little Phoenix

Cinnamon with Dark Chili Chocolate Ganache

B y the end of October we will be able to remove the sandwich board at the door.

LILLIAN'S OPEN FOR TAKEAWAY COFFEE AND CAKE!

CAFÉ SOON TO REOPEN!

TYPHOON DAMAGE UNDER REPAIR!

Rilla added the exclamation marks; I think she fancies they
make it look cheerful. Gigi translated it into Chinese for us. The
takeaway trade has been surprisingly good, the regulars still dropping by and standing on the pavement to watch the repairs or
gossip about the latest social scandal. Who slept with whom and
who got drunk and fell asleep on the roundabout. Pete seems to
have sent the word out to every secretary and personal assistant in
town, as they have all been dashing over in company cars to pick
up coffees and cakes for work meetings, slipping boxed chocolates
into their handbags for themselves. But it's been a trying time,
with the place looking like London in the Blitz. I've been feeling
rattled, as if the typhoon thundered through me and overturned
everything inside too. My heart, my desires, my secrets, Mama.

Like I have to start from scratch. I have dreams of bombs dropping, of planes crashing through glass, even of my teeth falling out. Pete brings me glasses of water when I wake up in the early morning, shaking and covered in sweat.

Gigi and Rilla try to keep me steady, acting as though nothing is different. Deciding on cake flavors, bickering like bratty sisters, chuckling and singing in the kitchen. Rilla even rallied some friends to help us clean the floors and strip out the worst damage. They all have the same coffee-colored skin and generous smile as Rilla. They laugh and work with ease, calling Gigi and me "ma'am" and Rilla "Aunty Boss." She has been so supportive that my remorse over the way I treated her grows and grows. While I put together sandwiches and drinks for everyone, I watch her effortlessly direct the crew in her native language, like a woman who is used to both crisis and chaos. Despite everything—the wet and messy conditions, the extra hours, and the unspoken incident between us—her smile is brighter than ever. Her confidence has soared, radiating from her like a warm light.

Lillian's is slowly being reborn when Macau slinks into autumn, the winds cooler and nipping at bare ankles. On a morning when my nerves seem to have stopped jangling and the sky is fresh and clear, Marjory suggests creating a new *macaron,* to bring us some good fortune and "make lemonade out of lemons," as she puts it. Soon enough Gigi and Rilla are in the kitchen, dark heads huddled together, discussing flavors and names and concepts while I listen and try to guide the debate. Rilla is reciting a list of suggestions.

"Chocolate?"

"Boring."

"Strawberry?"

"Even worse."

"Lemon?"

"Ugh. I'm so sick of lemon. It's so . . . cupcake. We need something unique, more chic." Gigi looks at the ceiling thoughtfully. "Something like . . . salted plum."

Rilla bursts into laughter. "That sounds gross."

"You have no imagination. It's *Japanese*," Gigi retorts. Her face is more drawn these days, dark circles under her eyes. She is probably exhausted from sleepless nights, the pregnancy now impossible for her to ignore. She presses down on the top of her bump and arches backward. Heartburn.

I wade into the fray. "Salted plum might be a little out there, Sorry, Gi."

She gives me a withering look.

Pete pokes his head into the kitchen and looks to me.

"Hey." I smile.

"Hey. I've got the wallpaper guy here with the samples."

I leave the girls to their debate. Out in the café, Marjory is leaning over piles of tiny white mah-jongg tiles. Yok Lan sits opposite her and gives instructions in Cantonese. Marjory is trying her best to follow the tone of voice, hand gestures, and context, but mah-jongg is incredibly difficult to grasp, let alone in another language.

The wallpaper samples are beautiful, and this contractor speaks fluent English. He has worked with casinos all over Macau, so the quality is good. I can feel my chest relax, my shoulders loosen. I imagine the walls looking like those of a true Parisian café. Marjory comes up behind me and looks over my shoulder while I point to my final decision. Mint green with gold fleurs-de-lis; it looks like a pretty Indian sari. It will be striking with the black-

and-white tiled floor. Pete moves off to one side to start negotiations on price and delivery.

"Is that the wallpaper you've chosen?" Marjory asks.

I nod.

"I like it. You know, I think it's better than the old stuff."

"I think you're right," I say.

Rising voices can be heard coming from the kitchen, and Marjory turns her head to look toward the door.

"I'd ask those two what they think, but Gigi is in a mood to disagree with everything and everyone. Think I'll leave them to the *macaron* argument."

Marjory laughs. "Rilla keeps her in check."

"Rilla keeps us *all* in check," I agree. "She's been a lifesaver these last few weeks. Especially getting all her friends to help. We'd probably still be ankle-deep in water without them."

Marjory says, "They all look up to her, what with everything she has done for them and everything she has been through. She might be tiny, but she's a powerhouse."

"What do you mean, 'everything she has been through'?"

Marjory frowns. "She didn't talk to you about Jocelyn?"

My heart sinks a little. "She tried once, but I guess we never found the right time, and we've been so busy . . ." I know this is only half true.

Marjory looks down at her shoes, perhaps sensing my embarrassment. "Well, I'll let her explain. It's not my place to talk about someone's past."

I feel that familiar knot of shame at the base of my throat. "I was wrong to doubt her, wasn't I?"

Marjory tilts her head to one side and gives me a little smile. "It's your café, Grace. You need to do what you think is best. You own the wins and the losses. Besides, I reckon you had a fair bit on your mind at the time."

I can hear Pete discussing the job with the contractor. How many days? How much labor? We both look over at him, and he, obviously sensing our gaze, gives us a thumbs-up behind his back. Then he shakes the man's hand, and the contractor leaves, setting the new bell above the door ringing. I'm getting used to this new relationship between us. Not fixed, but not completely broken either. We are being kind to each other again. We are being friends.

Pete comes toward us. "Well, he says he can get it done in two days. Ten percent off if you'll make lunch for him and another bloke." Pete shows me the quote. I smile.

"No kidding. I'll give them coffees and breakfasts too for that price." I give his arm a gentle squeeze in thanks.

Something crashes in the kitchen, and all of us, including Yok Lan, look up. The door swings open, and Gigi storms out. Her weight is the only thing slowing her down. Rilla follows. I look to Yok Lan, but she just shrugs and goes back to reading her Chinese newspaper.

"What was that?"

Rilla sighs and holds out her hand. In her palm is a mobile phone in pieces. Pieces of the plastic studded with diamanté stickers. I turn to head after Gigi, but Rilla grips my arm to hold me back.

"Just let her go. It's that boyfriend. He called and they had another fight."

We all watch Gigi waddling down the street as fast as she can.

"That guy sounds like a loser," Marjory says, shaking her head.

"Oh, he is a loser. A no-good daddy," Rilla agrees.

"Poor Gigi."

"She hasn't got long now," I murmur.

The air stills and returns to calm. The scent of cool breeze and almond flour drifts around us.

Rilla takes a breath and smiles. "Well, we came up with a new *macaron*." Her dark eyes are shining in her small, round face.

"You finally agreed?"

"Oh yeah," she says. "It's a good one too."

Un Petit Phénix is born as Lillian's is resurrected, even more beautiful than before, with new wallpaper, new windows, and repaired chairs. It is a cinnamon *macaron,* pressed together with dark chili chocolate ganache. The result is surprisingly delicious—spicy, sweet, lingering long in your mouth, like a bowl of Aztec hot chocolate. It tastes best with a shot of the blackest coffee.

The following week I wake up too early, dreams of Mama and Paris still clotted thick in my dozy mind. Pete has moved back into the master bedroom but sleeps close to the edge of the bed, respectfully distant. I reach out to put my hand against his back as if to steady myself. It moves with his breath, in and out, like cool waves against a shore. I shut my eyes, willing myself to drift back to sleep, but there is a pulsing, pulling ache in the lower part of my belly. I lay a hand on it. Lights travel across the ceiling, a sign of cars already driving on the roads. I wish to hear the sound of a bird, celebrating a new day. Instead there are just car horns and roller doors screaming open in their tracks.

I get up to go the bathroom; perhaps something I ate hasn't agreed with me. Pete groans and stirs in the bedroom.

There is a shift between my legs; I tentatively spread them to look down into the toilet bowl. A stain spreads. Blood meets the water, curling like paint dropped from a brush. I stare down at it, blinking sleep from my eyes. The water slowly turns pink and then red.

Pete calls, "Are you all right in there?"

At the back of the cupboard is an old box of tampons, four

left. I insert one and stand at the sink. The doctor said I still might have a period or two with my condition. Not so many as to get my hopes up. Just the body's last-ditch efforts, the final few words at a retirement party. My reflection stares back at me, my vision suddenly clear and sharp. I look older without makeup, two or three silvery strands in my red hair, face pale and drawn. There is dry skin on my cheeks, lines radiating from my eyes. I breathe out a sigh of surrender. It leaves my body in a long, warm stream of air.

"Gracie?" Pete opens the door.

The evidence is still in the toilet bowl, and he sees it. He looks back to me.

"The doctor said it can happen," I say softly.

He takes my hand and squeezes it. His eyes are sad.

I pull him in closer, lean into his chest, which smells of sleep and freshly cut timber. He wraps his arms around me. It is a relief to be in his embrace, like all the pieces of myself are slowly coming together, and I don't feel as rattled as I have since the typhoon. It feels like I can breathe again. I put my lips near his neck and sigh.

"I missed you," I whisper, just realizing it myself. He glances down at me and then back over to the toilet, his face falling a little.

"It's okay," I say. And I actually mean it.

It is the lull of the afternoon, when the mothers have left to pick up their kids from school. The sinking sun at this time of the year fills the café with a golden light. The new wallpaper is bright and regal, the tabletops polished to a high gloss. The phone rings.

Rilla answers while I sweep the tiles. She presses the receiver to her ear and looks up at me with a frown. She repeats something a few times and then listens in silence.

I pick up a napkin that has sailed to the floor, still folded neatly in a triangle.

Rilla says something fast and then hangs up. She lets out a loud whoop.

"Yee-ha!"

"Are you okay?" I shake my head at her as she sings a few lines in Tagalog. It's a song I've never heard before. *Something, some-thing, baby, baby.*

"Yes, I'm okay!" she cries. "That was Yok Lan—well, it was a nurse translating for Yok Lan."

I look up sharply, my thoughts moving to Gigi, who is having her day off.

"Gigi just had her baby!" Rilla laughs.

"What?" I drop the broom.

"There was a nurse who could speak English. Yok Lan told her to say that Gigi wanted Rilla and Grace to know she'd had her baby. A long labor, but everything is okay." Rilla is grinning so proudly you would think it was news from her own sister.

"Well." I pause, wordless.

"It's a *girl,* Grace, it's a girl." She sings some more lines and grabs both my hands. The joy is contagious. I start to laugh.

"You are nuts!" I say, giggling.

"A girl!"

"A girl."

"She's seven pounds something, she said. Healthy as a little bear. Isn't it great?"

"It is." I smile.

"Gigi had a girl, Gigi had a girl!" she sings to me, swinging my hands from side to side.

I shake my head again. "Wow. Gigi had a girl."

It's a girl.
Our young Gigi has had a girl.
It's a girl.
No one will ever say that to me.
It's a girl.
But they said it once to Mama.

La Foi—Faith

Wild Strawberry Filled with Pink Grapefruit Buttercream

It is a Sunday morning, and Lil's is closed to customers. I put the final *macaron* in an eggcup and place it gingerly on the top of the cake as the bell over the door chimes an entrance. I know it is Pete letting himself in. I have started to know his walk, the sound of the fall of his feet. Things I hadn't noticed before but which became familiar to me during those long days of silence.

"Wow. This place looks amazing. How long did it take you?"

I come out of the kitchen and see his hair is still wet from a shower, face flushed from a morning jog.

I had planned on a few streamers, but once I got started I couldn't stop. You can barely see the walls for crepe paper, hung in strips, as if it is carnival time in Rio. Dozens of balloons bloom in bunches, and the tables are covered in luminous lipstick pink fabric I bought at Three Lamps.

"A little while. Do you think it's too . . . bright?"

Pete picks up a polka-dot balloon from the floor and fixes it to a cluster in the middle of a table. "I think it's wonderful. I think she'll love it."

I laugh. "Well, that'll be a first. Gigi doesn't get excited about much. It's not 'cool.' But maybe she'll like it, just a bit—that's all I was really after."

Pete puts his arm around me. He smells fresh, like the thick green skin of an apple. It is the scent of the conditioner he has used.

"What's that?" he exclaims. He is pointing at the top of the cake behind the kitchen counter.

"Oh, you'll have to see. Come have a look."

I had been inspired by a cake I saw in a bridal magazine. When I opened the pages and saw the photo, my heart almost skipped a beat. It is the amateur cake maker's equivalent of scaling Mount Everest. A soft blush-pink four-layer cake, the layers alternately square and round, completely covered in tiny *macarons*. Perched at the very top is a small porcelain dish cradling a single *macaron*. I had been studying the picture every day since Gigi had her baby, figuring out how to re-create it. It wasn't easy, but I've done it—finished the beautiful cake, with a pretty eggcup replacing the porcelain dish.

Pete walks around it like he is observing a museum exhibit. His hands are plunged deep in his pockets, as if to stop himself from touching it.

"This is amazing, Grace."

"You think?"

"Oh yeah, it's really . . . amazing," he repeats. He turns from the cake to me, his head slightly cocked. "You're good at this stuff, aren't you?" he says quietly.

I glance back at the cake, which has an air of French architecture. "Yes. I am good at it." I can't help but beam at him.

Pete pulls his hands from his pockets, and I notice that he's holding a red bag.

"What's in there?"

"Oh . . ." He shrugs. "Nothing really." He places it on the counter. "I got it a little while ago. Saw it in a shop." He pulls out a toy, soft and floppy in his hands—a small gray rhino with loose limbs, two beige horns, and weighted feet. It has a tiny stump of a tail and a straight smile, which makes it look sleepy. "Maybe it's better for a boy? I dunno, he's . . . cute?"

I hold the rhino in my hands and look at my husband. He has shaved, which he never does on the weekend. He rolls his lips over his teeth and presses them together.

"That's sweet. I think she'll like it," I say gently. Noticing how handsome he can be. That fresh face against a crisp blue collar.

Marjory, Don, and Rilla arrive together. Marjory carries a helium balloon with IT'S A GIRL! written in purple. Rilla has a clear plastic box with knitted booties inside.

The cries of her baby herald Gigi's arrival. Yok Lan trails behind her, moving slowly. Gigi holds the little one against her chest, looking tired and a bit dazed. My breath catches in my throat seeing them together like that. One plus one equals two. Our Gigi, now a mother.

She apologizes over the head of the sniffling baby. "Sorry we're late. She won't stop crying."

Inside, Yok Lan stands beneath a bunch of balloons and grins like a child. *"Ho leng,"* she exclaims, and Pete translates, "Very beautiful."

"Yeah, looks great, Grace," Gigi agrees.

"Here, everyone take a seat. I'll get teas and coffees," Pete says.

Rilla scoops up the baby and begins jiggling and shushing her softly while Don and Marjory talk to Gigi. I get a chance to look at Gigi properly; she is wearing a large, worn T-shirt, tracksuit bottoms, and purple flip-flops. Her hair is pulled back in a pony-tail, a little greasy at the roots. Her skin looks paler than usual, with light coffee-colored freckles on her cheeks. I realize she is not wearing her usual thick layer of foundation to cover them up.

Marjory gives Gigi a pair of earrings the same as her own;

small gold hoops. Gigi smiles and gives her a hug. After a few moments, the baby's cries subside and Pete has ferried all the cups to the table.

"Are there more people coming, Gi? Your friends?" I ask, looking out the window, half expecting to see a flock of dark-haired girls in bright socks and skimpy tops.

Gigi shakes her head. Her eyes are ringed with dark circles, and there is a small stain on the front of her T-shirt.

"What about your mum? Should we wait?"

"Ma's not coming," she says, too quickly.

Marjory catches my eye, but we say nothing. She puts her arm around Gigi's back and rubs her shoulder. Almost imperceptibly Gigi leans into the touch.

"Wanna hold, Grace?" Rilla asks.

I look at the baby properly now, a little nervously. I swallow down a few jitters and nod; Rilla places her in my arms. She is a tightly wrapped bundle in the crook of my arm. The muslin is soft, as is the weight of her. She has static tufts of black hair springing from her head as though she just stuck her little finger in a socket. Although the cries are quieter, she is still grizzling, eyes tightly closed. She is so small, her nose the size of a penny. I find myself staring at her tiny, frustrated face, transfixed. There's a strange falling sensation in my stomach. Her fingers grasp at the air as she whines and I bounce her gently up and down.

"Shh, shh, shh," I whisper into the tiny shell of her ear.

Rilla gives Gigi her present, whispering that she knitted the booties herself. She beams with pride when Gigi thanks her with a kiss on the cheek. "Thanks, Rilla."

"My pleasure, Mama Gi."

Pete has slid a finger into the baby's palm, and despite her upset she grips it. He holds it up to me and gives a wobbly, shy kind of smile. I kiss the top of his head and feel Gigi watching us.

"Shall I get the cake?" Pete asks me.

"Yes, please. Thank you."

I don't want to put the baby down. She smells sweet and clean, like new sheets or the air after rain. When Pete brings the cake back to the table, I watch Gigi's face. She glances over, does a double take, and then stares. Her face goes soft, the muscles holding her frown falling. Yok Lan is looking up too, not at the cake but at Gigi. She looks caught off-guard. She is younger with this expression, and without her makeup just a regular young woman. Yok Lan gives me a quick look, like she wants to say something. Her eyes come to rest on the baby, growing heavy now in my arms.

"Oh," breathes Gigi as if she might start to cry.

"It's a kind of orange sponge," I explain to the crowd around the table.

Don lets out an impressed whistle. "It's a beauty," he says.

"Gorgeous, love," says Marjory.

"So pretty, Grace," says Rilla.

Pete smiles proudly.

Gigi looks at me, then back to the cake. "Can I slice it?" she asks.

"Of course. It's for you, after all. You and . . ." The baby girl in question is blinking at me. Her eyes are dark and curious. She stares up at me, and I stare down at her. She lets out a sad, sleepy puff of air before resting her cheek against my chest. "What is her name?"

Gigi looks up from the cake; she has the knife in her hand, and her eyes are glazed and worn. I think I see the gloss of tears, but when she blinks it is gone like a trick of the light. She looks back and forth between Pete and me, and then back to the knife in her hand and the cake. "It's Faith. She's called Faith."

Faith. Now her face is still and calm; skin smooth and creamy. Her mouth is like a petite, pale pink confection, wet in the middle as she lets out small breaths. Gigi and Rilla are cutting the cake together, and Gigi has the *macaron* from the top in her fingers. Yok

Lan struggles out of her chair, leaning heavily on her cane. She hobbles over and sinks into a chair next to me with a quiet moan. She is still looking at the baby but rests her hand on my arm. It is cool but soft, her skin papery, like layers of mille-feuille; I can see through the age spots and lines to the pulsing of thick, dark veins. Pete comes to stand behind us, his breath warm against the top of my head. He looks down into Faith's face and sighs, as if he's been holding on to that breath for weeks, maybe years.

Yok Lan says something in Cantonese and pats my arm. Then she leans over to stroke Faith's forehead with the back of her index finger. She looks back up at my face and smiles a delicate smile. It is then I notice that her eyes and Faith's are exactly the same color, the color of oolong: clear, dark amber. The color of tea.

Dearest Mama,

It pulls at the strings of my heart to know that Pete will never be someone's daddy. He'd do a good job of it, Mama.

For such a long time I didn't notice there was a man missing in my life. I loved you and you loved me and we were a team, like Batman and Robin. There wasn't anything we couldn't do ourselves, was there? We could open too-tight jar lids or clear out a blocked sink. We didn't have a car so we never needed to change a tire, and if I wanted something from the top shelves of the kitchen, you never minded me scrambling up on the counters. We could reach or fix anything, couldn't we, Mama?

But I had always wanted a pet. A kitten or a puppy. You remember me begging? Do you remember what you would say to me?

"Oh, Gracie girl, a child is more than enough for your mama, more than enough."

You were right.

But what I really wanted more than a pet was a daddy. I just couldn't tell you that. I couldn't ask for that.

*It felt like a betrayal to want more, to want a father for myself.
You didn't know how much I wondered about him, how much I craved
to know. Was he tall? How did he take his tea? You loved me so much
it sometimes wrung the both of us right out. I couldn't make you feel
as though you weren't enough. I know you tried to make up for the bits
you thought I missed out on, taking the ferry across the Channel to
Paris that summer, feeling the salty wind through my hair. You said,
"Isn't this heaven?" and squeezed my cold hand with your warm one.
We went to rock concerts and football matches together, you taught me
how to ride a bike and make bacon butties for a hangover. I know you
did your best.*

*Families are all different shapes, aren't they? Today I watched
our odd little gang. All with different kinds of families, making up
different kinds of families. Rilla seems like she has a whole tribe of
people: cousins, friends, fellow Filipinos. Then there's Marjory and
Don, Pete and me. Pete will never be a dad, I will never be someone's
mama, but we do have each other, and for that I am now grateful. I
think Gigi is exhausted, coping with a little one on her own, without
a partner. She has a hollow kind of look in her eyes. Who knows
where Faith's daddy is? And Yok Lan looks around at us all, not
understanding a word but content as a cat in the sun. What a strange
little clan we make.*

I wish you were here to be part of it.

*Your loving daughter,
Grace*

The following Saturday, I am in bed, a deep sleep thick upon me,
when I hear something ringing. Reluctantly, I open my eyes.

"Gracie, sweetie? Wake up." Pete's voice is gentle.

"What . . . ?"

"It's your phone."

I reach for it. Pete is sitting up in bed, rubbing his eyes with the back of his free hand.

"Hello?"

"Wai?" is the only word I catch, and then a stream of Cantonese follows. It is a woman on the other end of the phone, I can make out that much, but she is speaking so fast I can't even pick out a word here and there. I am awake now, pressing my ear to the phone as if it will help me to understand.

"Hang on, hang on. Hang on a second. Slow down. Huh? Sorry, I . . ."

Pete puts his hand on my leg. "Who is it?"

"They're speaking Cantonese. I don't understand."

"Probably a wrong number."

"Mm sik teng ah," I wedge into the steady barrage of Chinese coming at me through the phone. I use this sentence often. *I don't understand what you are saying.* Or, literally, *I don't know how to hear you.*

"A wrong number, Grace," Pete says again.

The woman on the other end of the phone finally pauses, and in the background there is a siren, but it is very faint. Other than that, wherever she is, it is quiet. She says something else, and it is slower. There is only one thing I understand. It is "Gigi."

Pete is tugging on my pajama top, motioning for me to come back to sleep. He lies down and pulls the duvet over his shoulder.

"Sorry, what? What about . . ." I have my finger in my other ear now, trying to focus.

She speaks again, frustrated and sighing, before hanging up. I catch one last bit—Kiang Wu—before the line goes dead and rude beeping drums my ear. The hospital in Taipa village. I throw the covers off and scramble out of bed. Pete rolls over, and I tell him what I'd heard. We are dressed in three minutes and out the door in seven.

Prenez Ce Baiser—Take This Kiss
Honeycomb with Milk Chocolate Ganache

*Y*ok Lan is waiting for us in the lobby. Her soft hair sticks out at the back of her head like the ruffled feathers of a little bird. She stands up to greet us, seeming unsteady on her feet. When she smiles, I feel my breath fall out of me, a little slice of relief. It can't be that bad. She leans on me for support as she guides us into a hospital ward. She is talking to us earnestly, her gaze on the floor, watching each of her steps closely. I wish, not for the first time, that I could understand what she is saying. Something that can explain why we are in a hospital at three in the morning. Pete is leaning toward her voice, but he shrugs; he can't understand her either.

We round a corner into a ward on the ground floor. It has four beds, but only one is occupied. I steel myself as Pete takes my hand. His eyes are on the woman in the bed and Yok Lan, now sitting beside her. Her arms are bare, palms facing the ceiling. Medical bits and pieces hang from her; her mouth is open, slack and sagging to one side.

"Is that Gigi?" Pete asks.

"Yes," I whisper. She looks so small against the stark, white rectangle of bed. I can see the small rise of her tummy, the remaining evidence of her recent pregnancy. The rest of her looks like a twelve-year-old, small and vulnerable, stripped of her usual defiance and energy. Yok Lan tugs at the sheet tucked in at the bottom of the bed, and Pete goes around the other side to help pull it up and over Gigi's frame. Yok Lan smiles a thank-you and then sits back down and gazes at her granddaughter's pale face. Pete comes to sit next to me on the neighboring bed, and we watch them both. I feel as if I am watching a foreign movie, without the subtitles. Everything dreamlike and confused. I wonder where Faith is, the sweet smell of her still in my memory.

"What's happened?" Pete murmurs.

"I have no idea."

A few minutes later a woman strides into the ward. She is probably in her late forties but has the style of an older woman. Her hair is piled high, crispy with hair spray, and a designer handbag swings showily from her wrist. She is wearing a suit and pumps with a medium heel. And she is pushing a pram. All of this put together, and at three in the morning, renders me mute.

The woman starts to speak when she is only halfway into the room. Even without knowing what she is saying, it is not hard to recognize anger, and disgust. Each word sounds snapped off—sharp and broken. Her eyes are hard as she rants at Yok Lan, who is now standing. Pete and I stand up too; she is the kind of woman who makes you feel as though you ought to, if you know what is good for you.

When the tirade appears to be finished, Yok Lan responds, pointing at Gigi. The woman crosses her arms. She shrugs, but it is not nonchalant. She sees us, staring at me first and then Pete beside me.

"Who . . . ?" Pete starts.

A steady stream of Cantonese follows while she points at us, the pram, then Gigi. At last both women are quiet. The air seems to prickle as the whirring of machines and soft rubber-soled foot-steps in the corridor fill the awkward gap. The woman pushes the pram toward Yok Lan, almost striking her in the shin, and throws up her hands. She says one last thing, cool as ice in a glass, then leaves. The quick beat of her shoes on the linoleum echoes down the hallway. We turn back to Yok Lan. Her face has fallen, and she looks so tired.

"Mama," Yok Lan explains, pointing at Gigi. From the pram, Faith lets out a lusty wail.

It is a long night. As the sun starts to come up, Faith finally sleeps. We find formula in the pram, and Pete somehow manages to mime to a passing nurse what we need. A full bottle, burping, and tight swaddling later and we have silence. Yok Lan positions herself with her back against the wall. Pete and I watch her snore, her jaw slack but making such a noise.

Pete leans back into his chair, and I lean against him, relieved to have him close. We whisper to each other as the three of them sleep.

"Do you think she was in an accident?"

"I don't know. She doesn't look broken or bruised, does she?"

He shakes his head above me.

"She was angry."

"Who?"

"Her mother."

"Oh, yes. She was."

I remember Mama in one of her furies. The accusations, the threats. But with Mama it always came from fear. Please don't leave me, please keep loving me. Her heart was so fragile but so full. I knew she loved me.

"She seemed . . ." Pete pauses.

I think of the cool look in the woman's eyes as she shoved the pram toward Yok Lan. The spite toward her own mother hovering over Gigi. Something else too. Bitterness, jealousy . . .

"Hateful," I finish.

"I hope she's okay." He nods toward Gigi.

"Me too."

I glance at Faith, who is as still as a painted cherub. I search her head for the place where her skull has not hardened, watch the tiny pulsing beneath her hair. Feel the relief in me, knowing she is still breathing. She needs her mama to be okay too.

I yawn, and bury my head in Pete's sweatshirt. It smells of Mexican food. Must have been the last time he wore it. Guacamole and hot tortilla chips, brushed with oil. My body is aching and calling me to sleep, but my stomach is starting to grumble, ready for breakfast.

I wake up, and the bleach and steel smells hit me. I remember where I am; my head heavy with lack of sleep, my body feeling as though it is filled with wet sand. I look over to Gigi. Her hair is damp with sweat but her eyes are still closed. Pete wakes up just as a doctor and two nurses come into the ward. Yok Lan and I move back, out of the way. The doctor starts some checks, listening to Gigi's young heart, pressing down on her soft tummy. His shiny name badge reads DR. CHANG below some Chinese characters. The doctor gives short directions to the nurses and straightens up with a grunt. The nurse staring at us shakes her head and sends the other nurse back out of the room with a flick of the wrist. The doctor looks at Faith and then Pete and me.

"You are friends, or family?" he asks in perfect, clipped English.

"Friends," I reply.

Pete takes my hand and holds it between the two of his.

"I see." The doctor picks up a clipboard at the end of the bed.

"Dr. Chang? Excuse me, but what is wrong with her?"

He doesn't look up from his notes. "I can only talk to family."

Pete releases my hand and stands up. "We're good friends. We've been here all night."

The doctor looks from us to Yok Lan and back again. Then down at the pram. "I'm not allowed to say. It's hospital policy. You'll have to ask the grandmother."

Pete and I look at each other. "Yok Lan called us here. I'm Gigi's boss. We're worried," I add. "That's all."

The doctor finishes his notes and hangs the clipboard at the end of the bed. Gigi's toes peek out of the covers. The nails are painted black with silver sparkles. Somewhat reluctantly he pulls the sheet over them and sighs. "It's drugs. Pills. That's all I can say. She will be fine."

I must have questions in my eyes because he lowers his voice and adds, "Zhuhai. Parties across the border. Young people get themselves into trouble."

Pete shakes his head. "But, how . . ."

"Sorry, that's all I can tell you. You'll have to ask the family." He walks out of the ward.

Faith seems to sense the tension; she wakes up and begins to wail. I lift her from the pram. The nurse comes over, holding a cloth, which she puts on my shoulder. I pat Faith between her small shoulder blades, where her wings would be if she were an angel.

Yok Lan says something to the nurse, who then addresses me. "Miss Grace?"

"Yes?"

"The lady says, can you take Nok Tong? For the day? To . . . to . . ." She closes her eyes as if to imagine the word.

Pete leans in toward me. "Who is Nok Tong?" he whispers.

"Faith. Faith's Chinese name."

The nurse frowns and looks at us to help her. "Maybe to take her to . . . the kitchen?"

"Lillian's? It's a café," I explain.

Her eyes light up. "Yes; caff-ay. The lady says very sorry and she will come to see you to pick up baby. Later?"

I hesitate momentarily, thinking about the *macarons* I need to make today for sale the next two days.

"I can take some time off, Grace. It's okay," Pete says quickly, like he is reading my mind.

We tell the nurse that we would be happy to look after Faith, and she relays our words to Yok Lan, who comes to squeeze my hands in hers.

Pete bends over Faith and puts his finger near her clenched fist. The fist pops open, and she swiftly grasps his finger in a tight grip. He laughs. "Well, Miss Faith, it's your lucky day. Today you, me, and Gracie are going to make *macarons*."

He looks at me, his face covered with this new kind of smile. His exhaustion seems to fall away; his eyes are deep and soft. I give him the best smile I can manage in return and relish the sweet weight of Faith in my worn-out arms.

Later, when the day has slid into night, Pete lies back on the bed with me and looks up at the ceiling. Smells of baking and regurgitated baby formula cling to our clothes. Yok Lan came by late in the afternoon to pick up Faith, tying her onto her back with a long piece of cloth. She is much too old and fragile to be caring for an infant, but her face was full of resolve as she walked away with Faith's shock of black hair peeking out from the wrap. I can see where Gigi gets her determination.

"Well," Pete says.

"Well."

"We should have given Yok Lan that extra formula we bought."

"Oh. Didn't we?"

I can feel his head shaking no beside me.

Moments like these, staring up at the ceiling, make me realize how dusty and disorganized the apartment has become. There is a basket of clean laundry which has not been put away for at least a week stationed at the end of the bed. Perhaps I should ask Rilla if she knows anyone who could help me tidy, give them some extra wages. I am trying not to think of Gigi. Or Faith.

Pete rolls over to face me. "Hey you," he whispers.

I turn my head to look at him.

"You okay?" he asks gently.

"I'm okay," I sigh.

I shimmy in closer so that the smell of him is all around me and his arms are looped over themselves across my back. There are the scents of heat and flour and dirty coffee cups. His breath is on my neck, under my ear, rushing in and out like little secrets. We used to lie like this all the time, but I can't remember when we last did. These last few weeks have made me realize my own sins in the marriage. Neglect. Avoidance. Imagining someone else's lips against mine. Hoping for someone else's lips against mine. I put my cheek against my husband's to feel our skin together. There is memory in it. He gives me a light squeeze and presses his lips to my neck.

"You feel like home," I think out loud.

"So do you," he agrees, voice thick with knowing.

When I twist around to face him, he is ready for it. He rains light kisses on my face, then reaches my mouth, softly, softly. Inside me there is a great pull, like the water rushing back to the ocean after the wave has broken. It almost leaves me breathless. He leans back and lifts off my top, then unclasps my bra so my chest is laid bare. He bends down and drops a kiss above my left breast.

"That's your heart," he whispers.

That's when I start to cry quietly, looking at the crown of his wild hair, watching him plant kisses all over my breasts. He is careful with me, handling me lightly. Feelings tumble over and over one another, each one bringing on more tears. Pete soothes me while removing more of my clothing, but he doesn't try to stop my tears. Perhaps we both know it is time for crying. When he too is undressed and naked, he pulls me back into that warm grip and kisses the salty drops from my cheeks. He brushes the hair away from my forehead and cups my face in his hands. His palms cover my ears, and it sounds like the sea. It is the whirrings and movements of the blood in my veins, the beat of my heart. I am silent so I can hear it. The tears ebb.

When he enters me, it is smooth and sleek. He moves slowly at first until I pull him deeper and deeper, faster and faster. In the quiet, all I can hear is the sound of our breathing. I kiss his neck and his eyelids and any part of him that comes close to my lips. He fills me inside and in my heart too. That dark, gaping space that was aching, unnoticed. When it is done, he barely makes a sound, but I cry out. He falls onto me, his ear by my lips. The tremors pass and we are still lying together, body on body, skin against skin.

Even before Rilla calls out, I know Gigi is here. The tray needs rotating in the oven so that the *macarons* are cooked evenly. Instead I straighten up and pause. It has been several days since I saw her stretched out on that hospital bed. Perhaps it is a kind of maternal instinct; the feeling starts in the deep bowl of my stomach.

"Grace?" Rilla's voice is light and careful.

"I'm coming." I wipe my hands on my apron. "Would you mind turning the tray?"

Gigi is sitting at a table at the front, looking out the window. She has her hands clenched together in her lap. In the pram beside her, Faith is quiet. I cough as I approach, and she looks up quickly. Her skin looks scrubbed almost raw, so different from the old Gigi, who would have been painted smoothly in makeup, post-punk geisha princess.

"Hey."

"Hey," she murmurs.

She holds my gaze as I sit down.

Rilla brings over a pot of tea and smiles into the pram. When she puts her hand down into it, I imagine she is stroking Faith's soft cheek. I want to peek at her but feel the pull of Gigi's gaze. She needs me to concentrate on her.

"Sleeping," Rilla says softly.

Gigi nods and makes a face between a frown and a forced smile. Rilla leaves us, and we both take sips of our tea.

"Are you all right?" I ask her.

"Yeah." She sounds awkward. I allow the silence to settle. She lets out a little sigh as she drinks her tea, both hands wrapped around the cup.

"Thanks, Grace. For looking after Faith."

I place my hand lightly on top of her arm. She turns to face the window. "I really appreciate it," she says earnestly but doesn't look back at me. Down her face drips a full, clear tear. It falls along her cheek so slowly I watch it make its journey toward her chin. She bites down forcefully on her lower lip and blinks quickly. More tears follow, and I move a napkin toward her. She ignores it and stares resolutely out of the window.

"Frank has left." Her voice starts to wobble.

"Oh, Gigi."

She shakes her head slowly. "I know he would be a terrible father; I can see that now. Not that I'm much better . . . The pills

261

were his idea. A bit of fun, he said. I just wanted things to be like they had been, before everything. I was an idiot to take them. Now . . . now he's gone."

I nod, unsure what to say.

"He's gone back to the mainland somewhere. Too much . . . shame here. A baby out of marriage, me in the hospital, it looks so bad." She pauses. "I guess I understand." Her voice is soft, like it has floated off someplace. Not the defiance and spunk I am used to from her. She wipes her palm against her chin, drying up fallen tears.

"His family probably made him do it. Ma would have me do the same if she could. She'd love for me to be somewhere far away where I can't embarrass her anymore."

"I'm so sorry, Gi."

"It's okay. I mean, it's all a stupid mess. But it's probably better without him around to make it even worse."

I want to say something helpful. But the words are lost. She clears her throat and lifts her chin, and I remember that girl from the temple. The chin reminds me, but everything else about her seems so different now. She turns to me with her dark eyes wet and whispers. "I'm not sure how long we can stay at home for."

"What do you mean?"

"Ma wants me to go back to dealing cards, says casinos make more money than cafés and that I'm a loser for working here."

My heart sinks. "Oh, Gi."

Macarons and Lillian's seem to be the only things holding the poor girl together. She looks up at me and knows what I am thinking, gives a small nod as if she agrees.

"I think she's going to kick me out if I don't do what she says."

I remember the woman in the hospital. The careful hairdo, percussion of high heels, face full of bitterness.

"Where will you go?"

She shrugs and sighs, long and low. "I don't know that either. The worst bit is Pau Pau. She keeps sticking up for me. Drives Ma so mad she threatens to throw her out too. She's so old now; she needs me to take care of her. She's taken care of me long enough. Ma would do it too, I know she would. Ma and Pau Pau never really got along. She's just like Grandfather. He died a long time ago, but Ma seemed to pick up where he left off. Treating Pau Pau like a servant, looking down her nose at her."

I think about the strange nature of genetics. How life can deal out good people and bad people, just like that. Crazy people and sane people, all from the same deck. All in the same family. I reach out and take Gigi's hand. She gives me a worn but grateful shadow of a smile, yet her voice is frail. "This is not what I imagined for myself. Being a mother right now."

I don't know what to say. I squeeze her hand and hope that she can feel some empathy in it. I want to tell her everything will be okay, but I don't want to lie; I don't know if it is going to be okay.

"It's too hard, Gracie," she says very softly, as if she might split in two from admitting it.

Words are still stuck in my throat, and I can feel tears of my own threatening.

Faith whimpers in her sleep but doesn't wake.

"What are you going to do?" I ask gently.

Gigi looks up at me. Tears have dried on her flushed cheeks, but her eyes are still pink-rimmed. "I really don't know," she replies. We sit like that, staring at each other, for several long moments. I have the feeling the rhythm of our breath is matched. That perhaps she is breathing in as I breathe out and vice versa.

"We'll help you, Gigi. We'll help any way that we can, okay? You just tell us what we can do. Promise?"

She nods. "I promise, Grace." She pauses. "Thank you. Without this place, Lillian's . . ." She swallows and doesn't finish her sentence. It hangs between us.

I nod and whisper, "I know." Because I truly do.

I am sitting on the window ledge with a glass of wine when Pete comes home. He has his laptop bag in one hand, newspaper wedged under his arm. He does a double take when he sees me.

"You're home early."

"Rilla is closing up today.".

"Oh, right." He takes his shoes off and loosens his tie. He goes into the kitchen and comes back holding an empty glass.

"Mind if I join you?"

"Go ahead."

He wriggles himself back against the window. We lean into the corners and put our feet together. My toes are slender, my feet narrow, but they're not small. I have struggled to find shoes to fit me in China. I've always wished for dainty feet. Pete's feet are practically the same size as mine, but much broader. He takes a large swallow of his wine and sighs.

The view from up here is still fascinating, although we see it every day. The sun is fading, rather than setting, in the thick pollution. Kids are playing basketball in the apartment complex leisure area below us; I watch them miss shot after shot.

"Everything all right at Lillian's?"

"Sure. Everything's fine."

Pete nods. Encouraging.

"Gigi came in today," I start awkwardly, committing myself to talk with him. To share more, as we have promised each other we'd do from now on.

"Really? Is she all right?"

"Honestly? No. I'm so worried for her, Pete. Faith's father, Frank, has left, and her mum sounds truly awful. She's threatening to throw Gigi and Yok Lan out of the house if Gigi doesn't go back to dealing cards." I take a breath. "No wonder Gigi has been so full of anger." Pete drinks some wine and frowns. "She's got a talent for cooking, Pete, I know she does. Now that is going to be taken from her."

"It's not going to be easy for her. A baby and no father. No support. In this economic chaos . . ." His voice drifts off.

I nod; it will be hard in these times. It's hard enough already. "I wish I could make it different. Help her. Help Faith. Yok Lan. It's such a mess, and Gigi's a good girl, really. Tough but kind and . . . I don't . . ." I pause, drinking in his attention. His eyes are so dark in this dim light. "I don't know what to do for her," I finish. I can feel the tears, so close.

He says nothing for a moment. We both look back down at the basketball court.

"I think she will tell you what she needs, when she's ready to. Maybe there aren't many people listening to her at the moment. Maybe that's what she needs right now, just someone to listen."

As he says this, one of the boys puts his ball through the net. The kids yell, jumping around and hugging one another. The boy runs in small circles, shaking his fists in the air in victory.

"You might be right," I reply. I try to let my worries about Gigi and Faith and Yok Lan fall to the bottom of my mind. Settle, like sediment in my wineglass.

I look back to Pete. He arches his foot so his toes press against mine. His socks are shadowed with cool sweat. They leave my feet wet. I make a disgusted face, and he grins. We turn back to the basketball court to see the boys hang their heads. Mum has come to round them up. She is saying something in Cantonese that we cannot hear. She points her finger, and they all march off in that direction.

"Just be her friend, Grace," Pete says softly.

Les Soeurs—Sisters
Peppermint with Dark Chocolate Ganache

*L*ater that week, close to closing time, Rilla brings laughter into the kitchen when I need it the most. I am still worrying about Gigi when she interrupts my thoughts by turning up the radio and dancing with her mop. She wiggles her hips beneath her apron and taps her feet. I realize I must have been frowning when I break into laughter. She winks at me as if to say, "That's better," and I shake my head. Her dancing ability closely matches her singing skills. Neither is good, but they never fail to make me laugh. I am reminded of how lucky I am to have her in my life, every day, here at Lillian's with me. I flash her a grateful smile. When the phone rings, it startles both of us. Rilla turns down the radio as I leave the kitchen to answer it. Marjory's voice is breathless and rushed.

"Grace, it's me. Is Rilla there?"

Rilla comes out from the kitchen, and I meet her eyes.

"She's here. Are you okay?"

"We need to come by to pick her up. It's Jocelyn."

"Jocelyn?"

Rilla moves quickly to fetch her jacket and bag. I suddenly feel on edge as Marjory presses on.

266

"We need to pick her up from the refuge. We think her employers know where she is and we should move her just in case. Not good for her or the other women. It might be unnecessary but . . ." I can hear the sound of an engine shifting into a higher gear.

"Is she . . . ?" I start.

Marjory's voice gets louder as a car horn sounds. "I'll have to explain later. Sorry, we just need to get her somewhere safe. She won't come with me, but she'll trust Rilla. Is it okay for Rilla to leave early?"

"Yes, that's fine."

"Good. Grace, can we bring Jocelyn back to Lillian's? Just until we sort out somewhere for her to go?"

I nod and then realize she can't hear me. My heart is beating fast now.

"Grace?"

"Yes. Of course. Yes."

"Thanks. We'll see you soon, okay?"

"Okay."

The line goes dead, and I stare at Rilla putting on her jacket, hastily organizing herself to leave. I feel a bit lost.

"Is everything all right?" I ask.

Rilla just looks at me with an odd expression and shakes her head, before dashing off to use the bathroom.

Within a few minutes Marjory's white SUV brakes to a stop outside. The Lillian's sign is reflected in the car's dark windows, the orange, melting sunset a backdrop. Rilla races out and clambers into the front seat, purse in one hand, apron in the other. Then she holds the apron out to me, her hand shaking. Her face is pale and serious. When I take the apron from her, Marjory catches my eye from the driver's seat.

"Hopefully we won't be long. I'll explain when we get back,

I promise," she says, then accelerates away. My left hand is limp against my side, still holding Rilla's mauve apron. A tiny tornado whips up sand and dust from across the road, and I watch it blankly as it twists and dances toward me. It skids to a still pile of dust as it hits the curb. I reach into my pocket for my mobile and call Pete. I barely get two sentences out before he tells me he'll come straight over. I sit on the edge of the sidewalk and wait.

Pete and I are in the café by the time Marjory's car pulls up outside. The sun has slid away, to be replaced by a fingernail moon. The back door opens, and Rilla gets out, then helps Jocelyn from the car. Jocelyn starts when she sees Pete. Rilla puts her arm around her friend and ushers her into the kitchen. A cold breeze whips inside as Marjory comes in. Her pretty face is white and pinched. Pete asks if she'd like a coffee, and she nods. She sits opposite me and reaches for my hands.

"Oh, Grace." She lets out a big sigh. "Thank you. Thank you for not asking any questions before."

"It's okay," I murmur, confused.

"I think it was important to get there fast. You know, I didn't realize just how bad this kind of thing can be. I didn't believe it. Or want to. But now . . . now I know." She shakes her head.

When Pete brings over the coffee, Marjory wraps her long fingers around the cup. Pete takes a pot of hot water and cups into the kitchen. I can hear him offering tea to Rilla and Jocelyn but do not hear the replies. When he comes back, he sits beside Marjory and puts an arm around her shoulders. She leans into him gratefully.

"Rilla told me Jocelyn was in trouble, so I let her know about the Sisters of the Good Shepherd; they run a refuge. I heard about it at a charity auction."

"Good Shepherd?" I repeat.

"The sisters, the nuns, help women who are in trouble. I've been out there a few times since Jocelyn moved in, but she's been too scared to talk to me. When the sisters heard her employers might know where she was, they rang me to see if I could help. They need to protect the other women too." She puts her hand against her forehead.

Pete looks to me for clarification, but I'm as confused as he is.

"I'm so sorry," I say gently, "but I'm lost. What kind of trouble?"

Marjory looks at me, her head tilted to one side. "Rilla didn't tell you?"

I shake my head, feeling guilty. "No. We haven't talked much." Marjory takes a long, steadying breath. "Jocelyn came to Macau to be a domestic helper. These recruitment agents, if you can call them that, put her in a job with a family here. Then they told her she had to pay them a fee every month for the privilege."

Pete is nodding, so I look at him.

"*She* has to pay *them*?" I ask.

"It can work like that," he says wryly.

"That wasn't really the big problem." Marjory's voice is bitter. "It's her employers. A couple and an elderly father. Right away they took her passport and kept her from having a day off. They told her she was too slow. Treated her worse than you would a bad dog." She shudders. "She appealed to the agents, but they wouldn't help her. She's just a paycheck to them. They advised her to stay quiet and keep her head down, and reminded her that a maid here makes more than a lawyer back in the Philippines, and that if she wanted to be a good mum to her kids back home she would work harder." Marjory laughs cynically. "Work harder! As if she were lazy, as if it were her fault . . ." Her expression becomes hard. "So Jocelyn ran away. She has been staying at the refuge since that night she and Rilla stayed here."

269

My mind steps back over the last few months, and I see the two girls lying in my storeroom. Pete looks at me as I shake my head.

Marjory continues, "No one else could really tell how bad it was and what might be happening; they just thought she was a bit strange and quiet. Or they didn't want to know. But Rilla knew, because of what had happened to her in Dubai. Probably just from the look on Jocelyn's face. They became very close friends."

"Yes, Jocelyn would come meet Rilla here," I murmur, remembering her waiting for Rilla outside, hovering at the edge of the door, her long hair across her face.

"I guess in Rilla she had someone she could trust. But when Jocelyn stopped turning up for their meetings and Rilla wasn't getting any calls or text messages, she got really scared. She spoke to some of the other Filipinos in Macau about it, and they said they would all keep an eye out for Jocelyn. That was one lucky thing, having such a network everywhere. Guys in security at the banks, the shops, women in most of the apartments, walking with prams. You know what it's like.

"Finally someone saw her at San Miu, that Chinese supermarket. Said she had a cap pulled down on her head, so he couldn't see her face, but it was Jocelyn for sure. That made Rilla happy for a little while, knowing she'd been seen, that she seemed okay, but I think she just knew things were getting worse and worse. Anyway, Rilla got a text message a few months ago asking her to go to the car park outside the racetrack. It wasn't Jocelyn's number; it turned out she'd had to steal one of her employers' phones, but you can't blame her for that. They'd taken hers and were keeping her penned up in that bloody house."

Marjory guesses what I am thinking.

"That was the night you found them here. The night she ran away."

My throat is dry. "What had happened?"

Her eyes meet mine, and she pauses for a moment before she says grimly, "She'd been beaten with a frying pan."

My throat seizes up and my eyes smart. Through tears I can see Pete has his head in his hands.

"Oh God," he says.

"I didn't know," I plead, my voice distorted.

"Hey, hey . . ." Marjory shushes me. She leans over and pats my arm. "None of us knew, Grace. When Rilla first tried to ask for my help, I wanted to close my ears. I didn't want to get involved. I figured it was none of my business . . ."

"But it is," Pete says slowly.

"Yes," she sighs. "Yes, it is our business. These people come here to work for us—the expats and the wealthy locals. But no one stands up for them, looks out for them, so this is what can happen. This and even worse." She looks at me sharply. "Grace, it wasn't your fault. We didn't know, okay? But now we know, we can do something. We have to."

I nod and press my lips together. We can hear Rilla's comforting whispers coming from the kitchen.

"They can stay with us tonight," Pete says firmly.

Marjory turns her head to me. "Are you sure? I don't mind . . ."

"Yes," I say. "Please, let them stay with us."

"Okay." She sighs. "That's good. We can figure out a way to get this resolved. What these women need is an organization that will protect them, help them when things get ugly like this. Don has a lawyer friend who might be able to help file some kind of action and begin the paperwork to get Jocelyn a new passport if necessary. Don is calling around, seeing what needs to be done. Her bosses still have her passport, and they'll be trying to stop her from talking about what happened with them. Who knows what they're capable of?"

"It's okay," I say quickly. "We can look after her. We can look after them both. There's plenty of room."

Pete says to Marjory, "You need to go home to Don; you look exhausted. We'll take them back to our place and get them settled in."

Marjory gives him a grateful look, then stands up. Her makeup has faded, and I can see faint age lines by her eyes. She takes the sunglasses off her head and folds them in one hand. As she turns to go, something strikes me. It's a thought that feels like icy water down my back. My heart skips a beat.

"Marjory? You said something about Dubai . . ."

She turns.

"Did this happen to Rilla in Dubai?"

Marjory frowns. "Didn't you wonder about the long sleeves?" Her voice is soft but pointed. "Yes. It happened to her in Dubai. You need to talk to her, Grace. I've been learning more and more about what can happen to these women. It's not pretty, that's for sure." She sighs, then turns away again, promising to call early in the morning.

These days Lillian's seems full even before the customers arrive. It is a hive, a coven, a sisterhood of women. Women all packed into the hot, tiny kitchen; working, laughing, talking, and looking after one another.

After a few days and nights, Rilla moves back to her apartment, but Jocelyn continues to stay with Pete and me. She walks to and from Lillian's with me each day, barely saying a word and practically attaching herself to the kitchen sink when we get to the café. I tell her she doesn't need to work, but she just shakes her head. She sways from counter to sink to counter again in a graceful rhythm. She washes everything slowly, purposefully, cleaning the handles of the cups, gently wiping the crests on the bottoms of the saucers. The *macarons* are barely off the trays before she is rolling the metal sheets into the hot, soapy water. Occasionally she murmurs a tune. When I catch snippets of it, I realize she has a good voice, although the notes are so quiet they sound haunted.

Gigi too has grown quiet. Something I would have once thought was impossible. She comes in before our regulars are waiting at the counter for a morning coffee, or sneaking muffins into their little ones' mouths, too rushed at home to have fed them breakfast. She is not yet due back from maternity leave, but I can't keep her away. I'm sure Lillian's is a friendlier place to be than home. Her face still has that slightly erased look, her skin the color of white socks washed too many times, her freckles standing out on her blanched cheeks. The whole of Gigi seems to have been washed too many times—her voice subdued, her spirits flagging. She talks with me about *macarons,* all she seems to want to discuss. I assume she has managed to hold at bay her mother's threat to kick her out, although she doesn't like to talk about that either. Perhaps she is lying to her mother about where she spends her days; it wouldn't surprise me. The café and *macarons* seem to give her steel. She scribbles ideas and thoughts into a notebook she keeps tucked in her handbag, a tiny smile flashing across her face before it too quickly disappears.

After Gigi there is Rilla, rushing from the bus stop. She carries her head high, racing in to check that Jocelyn is safe. She helps her with the first load of dishes. There is a new strength in Rilla that is hard to explain, a sort of confidence. Marjory tells me Rilla has become known among the Filipinos for supporting girls who have been tricked by so-called recruitment agents or abused by bad employers. They've heard her story and have seen the cigarette burns on the insides of her arms. Since I asked she has started to tell me about what happened to her in Dubai: paid much less than promised, indebted to agents for mysterious fees, beaten into submission and silence. She considers herself lucky—some girls are forced into prostitution, and some girls never escape.

These days she sometimes pushes up her sleeves, and I see the scars for myself. Moons of smooth, red skin tattooed into her. If it weren't for her head held so high and the pride that radiates from her, they would make me cry. I apologize for the way I treated her and Jocelyn when I found them that morning, and she tells me not to think of it again. "You didn't know." I remember how cowed she had been by the businessman complaining about a cold coffee and think about how she would deal with him these days. *Look at her now.* It fills me with a motherly kind of pride. And somehow she seems to keep Jocelyn and Gigi just buoyant enough, like an emotional life raft.

Marjory is the last to join the gaggle, arriving in the afternoons, once the lunch rush is over. She settles in her usual seat and lingers over cappuccinos. She drags Jocelyn out from the kitchen to sit and talk with her, sliding a long arm around her shoulder and speaking in whispers. Marjory passes her tissues, and I see her sliding money into Jocelyn's pockets when Jocelyn refuses to accept it from her directly. Marjory's mornings are now spent at the Good Shepherd refuge. She talks rapturously about Sister Julietta, and I tease her about a woman with such good fashion sense hanging out with nuns.

"She does the most amazing work, Gracie," Marjory gushes. "We're working with a group in Hong Kong that might be able to bust some of the agents bringing these poor girls in for domestic work. Domestic work, my arse." A ferocious look crosses her face. "It's modern-day slavery and they know it."

She even shares her frustrations and stories with Yok Lan, who listens patiently, not understanding a single word. Marjory tells me that they are close to being able to send Jocelyn home to the Philippines, back to her children.

Gigi brings Faith in with her, swaddled in puffy jackets and woolen hats, the air now chilled with winter. She settles her in a corner by the counter where we can all watch her like a big pack of mamas. Faith blinks at us from her pram, round eyes like currants and cheeks rosy red from the cold. Sometimes she gurgles or stretches out unconsciously in her sleep, hands closed into fists above her soft, dark hair. I am transfixed by her pink mouth and pale skin, even when she is awake and crying the roof off the place. Her babyness seems fresh and hopeful against all the sadness and violence of the last few weeks. I lift her up to hold her close, breathe in the talc and baby scent of her, and tell her stories that Mama used to tell me. Fairies, queens, poisoned apples, princes and flying carpets. I can feel my heart filling up on love and hope when I am with her.

Yok Lan and I take it in turns to rock her pram and change her nappies. Gigi leaves us to it, passing warmed bottles of formula for her feeds and taking over the till when I tend to her. Part of me feels guilty for latching on to Faith while Gigi works, but she looks at me with relief; serving her regulars seems to make her more like herself, brings a little color to her face. It is like some kind of therapy for her that I can't explain. And maybe Faith is the same for me.

Dearest Mama,

There are some ugly people in this world, aren't there? People who will kick a person when she is down or throw her out on the street or wring out her dignity, her spirit, till there's nothing left. How do people get to be like this? So damn rotten inside. Did they learn to be this way? Were they born this way?

Every day I look at two mothers who have been beaten down

like they were no good at all to the world. They've been told that they're useless. Hopeless. Lashed with a tongue or a fist. The very same women who are working so hard I can barely get them to leave at the end of the day. And it's not just that. They're trying so hard to be good mothers, in the only way they know how. It's like they're swimming and swimming just to keep from drowning and never reaching a shore.

This is what you were doing, isn't it, Mama? Swimming and swimming, just to keep from drowning? I wish I could tell you to your face—I know how hard you tried. I see it now. I forgive everything else. Will you forgive me?

Your loving daughter,
Grace

Le Retour—Going Home
Tart Mango with Buttercream Filling

I pad through the house as quietly as I can, but the floorboards squeak in the cold. In the kitchen I drop two pieces of bread in the toaster and put the kettle on for tea. I don't want to wake Jocelyn, who is still sleeping. I notice she has dried and put away the dishes I left in the rack. As much as I beg her not to, tidying seems to be her nervous habit; she is always restlessly folding tea towels or organizing cupboards, her gaze falling into the spaces between objects. It's as if she hopes that by keeping her hands busy she will keep her mind from straying into dark memories. The kinds of memories I don't like to imagine. Only Rilla seems to know how to really comfort her. She is full of small kindnesses, as if Jocelyn is a younger sister. She brings her packed lunches with boiled eggs, smiling faces drawn on the shells, or puts little bouquets of wild daisies next to Jocelyn's sandwiches. At Lillian's she pats Jocelyn's back, whispers in Tagalog, and guides her to the bathroom to cry when she needs to.

My toast bounces on the springs, brown and hot. I reach to turn off the jug before it whistles, steam curling out of the spout. Behind me I hear a lazy yawn.

"You don't need to be up," I say softly.

Pete runs his hand through his hair. He is striped from head to toe in blue and red and green pajamas. His left cheek is lined with the creases of his pillow. He smiles lopsidedly.

"Thought I'd have an early breakfast with you," he whispers, glancing at Jocelyn's closed door.

"It's okay, she is still asleep."

I put two more pieces of bread in the toaster and offer him a slice of my toast, swiped with butter that has pooled in the pores of bread. He accepts it, and we eat leaning against the stovetop. I take a sip of my green tea, the liquid finding the corners of my body and warming them. I let out a yawn in symphony to his.

"I forgot to tell you," he says, swallowing a mouthful of toast. "They're closing some of the restaurants . . ."

There's an awkward pause.

"You're going to tell me it's Aurora, aren't you?"

He nods and slides an arm behind my back, giving my waist a squeeze. I let out a breath. It's been so long since I have thought of Léon, helped by the fact that he has stopped coming to Lillian's so regularly. Thinking of my old feelings for him makes me feel so ashamed. It's like he was some delirious fever that shivered over me and then subsided, leaving me stripped bare and embarrassed. I bite into my toast. Feeling Pete's warm arm around me calms me. His eyes shine green and gold in the early-morning light.

I lift my chin. "What will happen to Léon?"

Pete looks at me, into me, as if searching behind my eyes for something. I know what he is looking for, but he does not find it. His gaze softens, and he shakes his head, brushing crumbs from his fingers on the leg of his pajamas. Reaching for the kettle, he pours a cup of tea for himself.

"I don't know. I'm going to call him, find out what's going on. It's not my area, but . . . well, I probably owe him a phone call anyway." There is embarrassment in his voice too.

"Poor Celine," I say. Then I think of their girls.

"Yeah. I think they can move him on to another project somewhere else if he wants, but I don't know, the rumors are that he'll stay. He likes it here in Macau apparently. The casinos, the lifestyle."

My mind wanders back to the brunch we had in Aurora, the tables laden with food, the honey dripping and bread fresh and hot. I shake my head. Time feels strange and elastic, as if we were there just yesterday and also years ago. Back then there was no Lillian's; no Marjory, no Rilla, no Gigi, no Yok Lan in our lives. I assemble these people in my mind like pieces of a quilt. Sewn close so their edges line up beside one another. Memories duck and weave between the pieces, stitching them together. Gigi looking for Yok Lan after the earthquake, Rilla and Gigi humming and singing and laughing at Lil's.

Pete puts down his cup and stands in front of me. He takes both my hands in his and looks into my face. It is such a solemn gesture, and it feels like the room just got dimmer. I inhale quickly and hold my breath in my chest until it aches with the effort. His smile is a grim line across his face; he seems a little nervous.

"Grace, I'm not sure how long . . ."

I break away from his gaze to look down at the floor. My feet are cold, toes pale against the bright red polish on the nails. He looks down at them too, lining his own toes against the ends of mine and then pressing his forehead gently against my own.

"Grace . . ." he whispers but doesn't finish his sentence. His breath is warm against my face, and sweet from the smells of toast and sleep. He leans into me and then rocks back on his heels. He plants a soft kiss above my right eyebrow and frowns. "I know how much this place means to you now."

My throat feels like I have swallowed a handful of pebbles.

"When will we have to leave?" I say, in a voice so quiet I can barely hear myself.

The end of the year rushes by us in a strange blur as we prepare for Jocelyn's departure to the Philippines. She might have to come back to Macau if there is a trial, but the lawyer friend of Don's has warned us that often these kinds of cases fall apart at the seams. He's not convinced a Filipino maid is going to be believed in court. It's her word against her employers', and they will paint a picture of her as a lying, untrustworthy immigrant. It hurts to realize how easily that story could be swallowed. If I could come to doubt Rilla so easily, then who will believe Jocelyn? It makes us all furious that the employers may not be held accountable, but we try to focus on what is really important right now, which is getting Jocelyn home safe to her children.

Marjory says she has to be ready to leave at any time, so there is always a packed shoulder bag by the foot of her perfectly made bed. Christmas is upon us, but it is hard to have a normal kind of festive season when we all jump at the sound of a knock at the door or a ringing phone. I give Rilla, Marjory, Gigi, and Jocelyn little silver ornaments with their names engraved at the bottom; for Faith I have bought a soft, stuffed gold and white angel. On Christmas Day we have a bottle of champagne at Lil's with some truffle-centered chocolates I have made, and later Pete, Jocelyn, and I have a roast chicken dinner, but it is a quiet affair. One minute it is Christmas and the next minute it isn't, that is what it seems like. Jocelyn puts her ornament carefully into the side pocket of her bag, and I catch her checking it is still there every so often.

Finally, on the morning of New Year's Eve, Marjory arrives. She has Jocelyn's new passport and an envelope with plane tickets and cash inside. Rilla rushes over from her apartment to see her friend off.

"Have you got everything?" I ask, like a nervous mother.

Jocelyn nods and smiles, pats the side pocket of her bag. Rilla looks her in the eyes and gives her advice in Tagalog. She holds on to both her shoulders as she speaks. I imagine her advice: Don't talk to strangers, get straight on the bus when you get to Manila, keep your bag close, have you been to the toilet? Jocelyn smiles; we must look so concerned. Even Pete seems melancholy.

"I'm going to miss her," he mumbles to me, putting his arm around my waist.

"I know, me too."

We have seen photos of her children and heard stories about them. A little boy called Matthew and a girl named Teresa. Saints' names, as if she has known right from the beginning that they would need the extra protection. In the pictures they have her dark eyes and small face. Teresa likes drawing and stories about fairies. Matthew likes to climb trees. Jocelyn doesn't talk about their father and I don't ask, but he is not in any of the precious photos, edges worn and colors faded from rubbing.

"You'll be seeing those babies of yours soon," Marjory says, as if she can read my mind.

Jocelyn looks up. "I will be so happy to be with them." Her eyes are shining as she gazes around at us.

"You take care of them, Jocelyn. Don't let them out of your sight," Rilla warns.

"I won't."

"Give them hugs from all of us here. Squeeze them tight," Pete adds.

"Well . . ." Marjory catches my eye. I am trying not to cry. "We'd better get going, I guess."

"Shall we come to the airport with you?" Pete asks.

Marjory shakes her head. "The fewer people the better. I'll just nip in to make sure she's all right. We don't want to draw attention to her."

We all troop down to the street together. As Jocelyn climbs into the passenger seat of Marjory's car, her long hair falls down over her shoulder. I remember seeing that sheet of hair and the horrible black bruise. Now when she lifts her face, it is clear and shining, as if lit up from the inside. She is safe. She is going home. She mouths "Thank you" to us with one hand pressed against the car window. Rilla, Pete, and I stand together, waving.

Marjory starts the engine and toots the horn a couple of times before pulling away from the curb. We watch the car until we can no longer see it.

Rilla receives a text message from Jocelyn the next day. She is back home with her sister and her children, in her little town by the sea. Everyone is healthy. Matthew and Teresa look taller. They had fish and rice for dinner. Her sister took photos of everyone, and she is going to post us some copies. She ends her message with a smiley face. We all breathe a sigh of relief.

"I could kill the people that did that stuff to her," Gigi says with menace.

"We all could," I agree.

"God, the world is full of assholes," she adds.

Rilla looks at me as she enters the kitchen with a tray of dirty cups, but I don't scold Gigi for swearing. She is right. The world *is* full of assholes.

"Is anyone out front?"

"Just Linda and the book club," Rilla replies.

"Are they almost finished?"

"I think so. School's out in ten minutes."

"I'll go do up their bill."

Rilla looks at me, and I think she looks a bit relieved but I can't tell. She starts to sing along to a song on the transistor radio on the kitchen windowsill. She's recently began listening to country music, and somehow her voice sounds a little better crooning along to the lilting lyrics of heartbreak and the dog on the porch and the pickup truck that got a flat tire. Gigi doesn't love it—she rolls her eyes at me.

I print the receipt from the till as Linda heads to the counter. Her blond hair is unusually long, over her shoulders.

"Thanks, Gracie, the *macarons* were lovely today," she coos.

"My pleasure. Just yours or are you paying for everyone?"

"I'll get the lot. We're celebrating."

She pauses and waits for me to ask. I have a mind to just let the silence sit between us, but it seems rude.

"What are you celebrating?"

Her face brightens. "Paul got a job in Singapore. The new development there. It's a pretty big role."

"Oh, well, that's great."

"We'll be leaving in a few months."

"I'm very happy for you." I smile as I put her notes into the till and hand her some coins.

"It's going to be a big change from *here*." She raises her eyebrows. "Singapore is so different, you know?"

"I've never been," I admit.

"Oh, you have to go, Grace! It's marvelous. No rubbish on the streets. Great restaurants. No one spitting." She gives me a look of wonder. "It's so *civilized*. It's so *clean*."

"Right," I say bluntly. The door chimes, and over Linda's shoulder I see Marjory come in. She is wearing white trousers and a black shirt that hugs her body beautifully. Following her is the contrary version of her style—a nun in a brown-and-white habit, face free from makeup, eyes sparkling fresh and blue. This must be Sister Julietta. They both smile broadly at me.

Linda hasn't noticed my gaze sliding away from her. "You'll have to visit, Grace. It's marvelous," she repeats.

"Yes, I should go someday," I say, distracted.

Linda closes her bag and sighs, leans in a little. "I've been meaning to say, I'm glad to see you got rid of that other one. They can be trouble."

My attention snaps back to her. "Pardon?"

"The other girl, the one who's gone."

"Jocelyn?" My voice sounds tight.

"Was that her name? Well, if you ever want a spare pair of hands, I'm sure one of us girls could lend you a few hours. If you were ever in a jam, you know."

"Us girls?" My tone is caustic.

Linda's mouth hangs open for a second. Then she lowers her voice. "One of us *expat* girls, Gracie. I mean, we're very busy with kids and husbands and what have you, but we could always rustle up someone for a few hours if you got into a pickle."

I try to imagine Linda with her manicured hands in soapy water. She probably doesn't do her own dishes at home, let alone have the stamina to stand for hours over my tacky baking trays.

"Jocelyn was a wonder, actually, Linda. We miss her terribly. And we're fine. No need for help; Gigi and Rilla and I have it all under control."

Linda takes a step back, and her lips come together. Her eyes narrow a little, but she quickly forces a smile.

"Well . . ." she says.

"Linda George!" Marjory exclaims; her voice both icy and sweet.

Linda wheels around.

"Haven't seen you for ages. Don't you look great. Hair extensions?"

Linda stares at Marjory for a moment, taking in the white trousers, the superb dancer's body underneath that tight black top.

"Were you just leaving?" Marjory asks with a cool smile.

"Ah, yes . . ." Linda looks from Marjory to the nun and back again. It's like an equation she cannot figure out. Marjory, the nun, back to Marjory. They both blink back at her with no explanation or introduction.

"Just leaving, yes?" Marjory says again.

Linda nods dumbly. When she is halfway across the floor, she turns back to me and lifts her head. As if to show we are the best of friends, she raises her fingers and waggles them, gives me a big white-toothed smile. "See you, Gracie dear."

I take great pleasure in replying slowly and loudly so that everyone can hear: "Piss off, Linda."

Out of the corner of my eye, I watch Marjory's face break into a huge grin.

La Môme Piaf—The Little Sparrow

Pear and Chestnut with
Poire Williams–Spiked Buttercream

Early, when the sky is still dark, I am yanked from sleep. The cool January air wraps around me as I take a few deep breaths, figuring out where I am and waiting for my drumming heart to slow. In my dreams Faith was lying in our bed, her small, sweet weight curled between us. She was clutching Pete's finger. I sit up and place my hand against the cool sheets, but of course she is not there. Her face slips into my mind. Tufts of hair, sweet skin, dark oolong eyes filled with fresh tears. She has been in Lillian's every day for weeks now. I find myself looking out for her in the mornings, desperate for her to arrive with Gigi, to hold her and kiss her and smell the baby scent of her. Now she is in my dreams.

Pete has told me the Melbourne team needs him to come back to Australia. There is a hotel to be built there, and the construction in Macau is struggling to remain funded. It's an easy career decision for him, but he knows it is breaking my heart. He's given me more time than he can afford to, the job offer pending while he puts off giving a firm answer. But I know they won't wait long.

As much as I love my work, it doesn't provide for us like Pete's does, and I guess the argument is that I could make a café any-where. But could I? Pete's going to need my support, we're in a marriage after all, and soon I will have to decide what to do with Lillian's. That is the hardest part. That and knowing that soon I won't have these faces to keep me company every day. Marjory. Rilla. Gigi. Faith.

As I lie down again, I let out a sigh, which turns into a sob that catches in my throat. Pete sleeps on, unaware. His face is soft and beautiful when he is sleeping. Tears fill my eyes and spill down my cheeks. I put the side of my hand into my mouth and bite. The tears slowly stop, stray drops finding their way down my neck and onto the collar of my pajamas. I wish for Faith to be with us, the feeling making my chest ache.

I imagine Mama lying in bed, blankets up to her chin, won-dering where I was, whether I was safe. Could she tell I was being looked after? Did she trust that I knew how to look after myself, that I was old enough to survive on my own? Without her? Maybe I reasoned that she was too selfish and needy and wrapped up in herself to worry about me. But I have been wrong about this. She would have worried. I know that beyond all doubt now. Mama would have worried about me the way I do about Faith, her sweet face always interrupting my thoughts.

I imagine Mama in my empty bedroom, hand pressed against the sheets of my bed, walls still covered in posters, concert tickets collected in an old ice cream container on the dresser. Would she have sat down and held the pillow against her? Cried for me to come home? Back to England? I never guessed I would go home too late. I didn't plan it that way. Of course I expected we would see each other again, when I was ready and she had apologized for the things she had said. I just wasn't ready for so long. *And then.*

Dearest Mama,

They say the truth will set you free. Do you believe it? Perhaps it is time to see.

I know it won't bring you back.

Your loving daughter,
Grace

So it should be told—how I found out about Mama.

Pete and I came back from our two-person wedding in Bali. We were tanned and happy, still kissing one another every chance we got. The ends of my hair were split from salt and sun, as red and dry as autumn leaves. I was so delighted to be married I kept turning my ring round and round on my finger. I could make a new family now, I thought. London felt oceans, worlds, universes away, and I liked it that way. My past was too complicated to deal with, Mama too heavy a burden to carry, and the future seemed so sweet and full of love. I was making breakfast and Pete was in the living room watching television, calling out "I love you" in the ad breaks, when the phone rang. I took my time answering it. There was a delay and a buzz, and then a woman's voice came through.

"Grace Raven?"

I thought of my new married name, Miller, and cradled the phone under my ear while I reached for the toaster.

"Yes."

"Oh, it *is* you! I thought I heard an English accent, but it's so hard to tell. Lovey, you are a hard woman to track down."

English accent. Northern. I put the hot toast on a plate and paused, still.

"Sorry, who is it that's calling?"

"I had a real battle to find you, let me tell you!"

Manchester accent. She took off like a roller coaster making the downhill turn.

"I'm Fran. Fran Adamson. I'm a nurse at St. Bernard's. You know she *said* she had a daughter but I wasn't sure, and then it took so long to find you. Births, deaths, and marriages are hopeless. More hopeless than hospital admin. Which can be *hopeless*."

A nurse from Manchester, calling from a London hospital.

"Did I go to school with you, Fran?"

"Oh no, I doubt it." She laughed. "I'm quite a bit older than you. And I know, 'cause I have your birth certificate right here in the file."

"Pardon?"

"When you were born I was halfway through my O levels, dear."

"Sorry?"

"You are Lillian's daughter, aren't you?"

That caught me off-guard. I swallowed, then answered "Yes."

"I knew your mother. I was one of her nurses."

I didn't notice the past tense at first. It was a delayed reaction, like you see in the movies.

"Mama is sick?" I asked.

"Well, we don't like to say it quite like that, but she did have an illness. A mental illness. I thought you would know all this . . ."

"Know what? Sorry, but I should know what?"

She carried on, "I'm calling because you're next of kin. I have to notify you of her . . . passing."

I tried to hold on to the phone with both hands as I slid down to the kitchen floor.

"Are you still there?" Fran went on, unrattled, as if she said those words every day. Mama had been in St. Bernard's for months. Maybe eight months, she thought, but she couldn't be sure as she didn't have the admission records in front of her. The hospital records were "a right old mess" and, besides, she hadn't been working there when Mama was admitted; she only heard about it later. They said she'd come in soaking wet, wearing a nightgown and a pair of black opaque tights. It had been raining that day when the police picked her up, and they took her to St. Bernard's straightaway. A good thing, because sometimes they wind up in jail or aren't picked up at all, and that is no good. *They*. Who was she talking about?

I almost forgot where I was, listening to Fran's voice reciting these facts of my mother's life which I knew nothing about. "Bipolar disorder" they call it now, she says, flying through descriptions of medications with names like long tails. The floor seemed to dissolve. Fran said Mama talked about me during her good days. Said she had a daughter living in Australia but that we hadn't talked for a while. After she died Fran wondered if there truly was a daughter, but when she looked into it she found a birth certificate. The dentist I was registered with, Crystal, was a girl from school, and she had asked someone else where I was. I hadn't had a wide circle of friends at school, so it took a while to find someone who had my phone number.

There was a short pause in the stream of speech. I straightened up against the cupboards; Fran's voice became crisp.

"So, I needed to call you and tell you about your mother. You know, in the *official* capacity. Not that she had much, but there are a few things here. I don't know if you want them."

I remembered again about her dying. It was like I forgot and remembered in waves, coming and going from a shore.

"It . . . It was good of you to call." The words were wooden.

"Such a drama finding you," she reminded me. "People never moved in my day, now here you are in Australia. My son is in Boston of all places. We're all spread around these days, aren't we?"

I shook my head. Courage needed to be summoned from somewhere.

"Can you tell me about her . . . dying, Fran? I don't understand."

Fran paused for a moment. Or maybe it was the delay. I couldn't tell. She sighed, sounding a little wistful even. She told me Mama had died about three months earlier. They had been pleased with her progress; she was having a good spell. She wasn't so "wild," that's how Fran said it. They'd let her wander out a bit farther, do some shopping, that kind of thing. Fran said she liked getting a sweet something from the bakery or walking down to the park.

"One day she was out and hadn't come home on time. Supposed to have been back a couple of hours earlier. Anyway, we get a call from John, the ambulance bloke. Lovely fella, John. Says one of ours has been hit by a car."

My heart leapt into my throat. One of *theirs. My* mama.

Fran went on. Mama didn't suffer. The lady who'd been driving was pretty cut up about it. Such a tragedy. Didn't see Mama at all. Dusk, the turning light, it's tricky, she said. I imagined it. Conjured visions of the light becoming gray, a little rain on the road, the sound of a dog yapping in the distance and tires straining around a corner. The smell of dusk, dewy and green.

Fran kept talking, but my attention waned. She said there was a tape among Mama's personal items, a letter, a book and a sweater, that kind of thing; photos she kept in a wallet of a baby, a little girl, a teenager. You, I suppose, Fran said. She asked if I wanted these things of Mama's. Perhaps that's when Pete came in. He took one look at me and removed the phone from my hands.

"Shhh, I'm here. I'm here, love," he said, his voice sounding far away.

* * *

291

I get out of bed and go into the study. I have to crouch down under the desk to retrieve the box. Inside, one envelope sits on top of a pile of others with my handwriting. This one is so light. I open it up carefully. I have read the letter so many times the paper is thin, the folds almost worn through. I touch the looping letters with my fingertip.

My Gracie girl,

I'm afraid your mama has got herself into a bit of strife again. No surprise there, I guess. I seem to have a certain special skill for getting myself into trouble, don't I, my darling? But you don't have to worry this time. I'm in a good place. They're taking care of me here, and I feel much better already. It's probably something I should have done a long time ago, come here myself, but what's done is done. C'est la vie, non?

I've been thinking of you, Gracie. Wondering what it is like over there. Are there really kangaroos on the streets? Someone told me that once. I think they were pulling my leg. The thought kind of tickled me, though. I imagine you dodging kangaroos and wombats on your way to the supermarket. Carrying back bags full of mangoes, pineapples, and bananas, a huge white sunhat on your head. All Jackie O! Watch you don't burn over there, love. We Raven girls have sensitive skin, you know. Don't be like all those skinny little things sunbathing till they're orange, will you, Gracie?

Have you met any boys over there? Oh, I know, mamas aren't supposed to ask. I should have given you a sister to talk to, I guess. To whisper under the covers with, sharing secrets and stories. We used to talk like that. Do you remember, love? Before you were old enough to be interested in boys. You told me everything. We talked till you fell asleep midsentence. You made me laugh. Right in the middle of Lizzie's riding ribbons or Bill Ringwood bringing his trumpet to school or asking for a kitten for the hundredth time. And then snap, you'd be out like a light. You could snore pretty loud, my darling girl. Do you still snore? I guess you'd need a boy in your bed to tell you that. Ha! There I go again.

I bet you do have a love though. You never did know how beautiful you are. Men do notice, darling.

Well, maybe I'll come and visit you and see for myself. Come play with you and the kangaroos. I know I said some spiteful things before you left, Gracie girl, but you forgive your old mama, don't you? You know how I get sometimes. A little excited. I'm seeing a doctor here and he says it can happen. He's helping me understand it all. Makes me feel a bit better about being such a crazy thing. But I'll tell you all about it when I see you. I'll get myself better and I'll come find you and we'll make things right again, won't we, Gracie? I didn't mean what I said.

I can't wait to see you. I feel lopsided without you here. I want to hear all about your travels. Everyone you've met and everything you've eaten. Did I ever teach you how to make pavlova? It's an Australian meringue cake. You would like it. I know how you like your sweets. Just like your mama. I could show you how to make it just right. High and fluffy and full of sugar.

Talk soon, baby girl,

Your Mama
x x x (and many more)

I slip the letter back into its envelope. I have never stopped feeling guilty that I could not reply to Mama's letter. Her last letter.

When I couldn't get pregnant and I couldn't stop dreaming of her, thinking of her, that's when I started writing notes back. Wishing that she would read them somehow. Maybe call out from the heavens, whisper replies in my dreams. I wanted her with me so badly it made me sore. Perhaps these letters would make up for all the letters that went unwritten before, when *she* needed *me* and I didn't know it. A kind of confession, a way for us both to redeem ourselves from the past. Our private, one-sided conversation, secret even from Pete. Like so many things I had kept from him for so long. Feelings, memories, guilt, fears. Years of things unsaid.

Underneath Mama's letter are all those I have written her. I have tied them with a purple ribbon, which I run my fingers over slowly. The silk is cool against my warm skin. She loved the color purple. The envelope slides under the tie to rest with the other notes.

I think of her baking, cheeks flushed with the heat of the oven. Her smile. I think of her dancing in Kensington Gardens, not wearing enough clothes, getting a chill. Her long legs. I remember her dragging me out of bed to see the stars and telling me their stories. Each one a banished prince or ballerina, a wish flung up to the dark heavens, the spark of Father Sky's cigarette. I think of her flaming, curling hair and eyes that glittered too brightly. I think of her in bookshops, laughing too loudly in movie theaters, hugging me too tightly at the school gate. I think of my hand in hers. I think of her in Paris, giving me a *macaron* in a box as if its sweetness would make every single thing that wasn't right perfect. I let the tears fall from me; falling, falling, falling. I sit with my memories watching the lights of the casinos shimmer against night clouds.

When the sunlight creeps through the bedroom window and illuminates the dust floating in the warm morning air, I am sitting at the end of our bed with the box in my hands. It is a new year and the past should be buried. I want to start over. I want to love again. This growing apart has not been all Pete's fault; it is a two-person equation. I feel like I finally understand how family love is. Tangled, wounded, and wonderful. Imperfect. A forever love. I feel strangely light. Like the little *macaron* shells when they rise in the oven.

Pete groans as he sits up. His body has aged since we came back from that honeymoon, but it is still familiar. His skin smells the same. His eyes are the same green-gold I looked into when I said "I do" in Bali. He rubs his face, his mind no doubt still thick with dreams. He blinks at me staring at him from the bottom of the bed. I push the box of letters toward him across the waves and dips of duvet. He curls his fingers over the edge of it. Then I slowly start to explain. Years of things unsaid.

Later that week, with the sun barely awake, I stand at the back of Lillian's. I have called Gigi to help, although I am not really sure why. Perhaps because I know her mother is hard to love too. Or perhaps because I want to see Faith's sweet face when it is all over. Pete looks on as Gigi and I stand together. He stood next to me like this, above the tiny, public-issued gravestone in England. It was a paltry marker, nothing like Mama herself.

I had been so numb back then, looking at her grave, holding myself back from Pete and anyone else who might have wanted to get too close. I hadn't been ready to let go of her then.

"Is this the right thing to do?" Gigi looks concerned.

I am now digging in the tiny patch of dirt behind the kitchen, and the soil is full of glass and metal. There is a silvery shriek each time the spade cuts through the soil to something unexpected. Pete lines up pieces of Tsingtao bottles, twisted forks, and the warped spokes of a bicycle. His face is grim, as if he too is worried about me.

"I need to do this." My voice rises above the fresh earth and debris. They nod and carry on clearing whatever muck comes up next. Finally we have a hole almost one meter deep and half a meter wide, the shape of a squashed oval. Our three heads hang over it; Pete brushes dirt from his hands.

"What next?"

"Next we bring out the tape player," I instruct.

The tape player was not easy to find, as antiquated in these parts as a gramophone. Gigi hurries inside and in a minute is knocking on the frame of the kitchen window.

"The cord only reaches this far." She holds up the cassette player to illustrate. It just sits on the sill, threatening to topple backward.

"It's okay; that'll do."

Gigi comes out and hovers uncertainly by the door. I stare down at the empty gash in the earth.

Pete takes the spade from my hands and passes me the plastic bag. He props the spade up against the kitchen wall and puts his square hand against my lower back. *Go on,* it seems to say. The words take a moment to come, and then they leap forth, rushing over each other.

"Dearest Mama . . ." I cough to clear an invisible stranglehold on my throat. "This is my last letter."

I feel the weight of the bag in my hand and remember that Pete put it there.

"But today, we move on, you and I."

Finally the tape player crackles into life, and Edith Piaf's voice fills the small courtyard, brave and haunting. I hear Gigi breathe in quickly and realize the song is moving even to people who have never heard it before. That would have made Mama smile.

"I want you to know how sorry I am that I abandoned you. I didn't understand. How you were, what you were. I was young—I needed my freedom. I didn't know . . ." I pause. "I left you."

Pete grabs hold of my hand and squeezes it.

"But, Mama, I *never* forgot you. This place is for you. It is named for you and it is everything you would have wanted. Full of beautiful things. *Macarons,* tea, love, and wonderful people. I want you always to have a place here no matter where you are now. So I am leaving some of your things here. An anchor for you to come back to."

The singing on the tape grows louder and louder, and when I glance over at Gigi, she is crying quietly, tears falling onto the soil. I start to cry too.

"I loved you, Mama. I am your daughter and you will always be in me, with me, wherever I go. I forgive you for everything, and I hope you forgive me too."

As the music, full of whirs and clicks and imperfections, pours from the kitchen window, I translate the lyrics in my mind, closing my eyes for a moment, letting everything go dark and disappear behind my eyelids while I find my breath. Then I open my eyes and lift the plastic bag to let Mama's last few things fall into the earth. A book falls first, probably the last she ever read, the cover white and red. *Poem for the Day.* The pages are folded and ripped, and there's a tea stain like a bruise down the spine. Her sweater falls next, followed by a string of purple beads. I remember her singing jazz and dancing around the house, those beads jumping up and around her face as she sprang and skipped. There is a hairbrush and one sock. It is gray. Thick enough to keep a London winter from nipping at her toes. Finally an envelope sails down onto the top of the small heap. "Gracie" is written in loopy letters. I fish it out and slip it into my pocket. It is all that is left, and I will keep it. That and Edith, still singing. *I regret nothing,* she warbles.

Finally, Pete passes me the shoe box and I untie the ribbon. My own letters flutter down into the hole, white as doves' wings. *Rest in peace, Mama.*

Pete holds me while I cry. I wonder who I will be without the guilt and the sadness that have been weighing me down all these years. I miss her.

From somewhere outside of myself I feel that lightness again; it's as if I am being pulled from above by a string. The wind rakes its fingers through my hair and, when I look up, the clouds have parted. There is a vein of blue sky painted between the buildings above us. Pete lifts his head and sees it too. Gigi goes back inside. We can hear her rewind the tape and then hit Play again. Miss Piaf lets rip. I imagine the English as subtitles, scrolling across that Renaissance painting kind of sky. Speaking of no regrets, leaving the past behind. Then the tiny seed of something quite new. Piaf doesn't say what it is, but I know. Hope.

Pete places a kiss against my forehead and then lets me go. I take the spade and cover the small grave. With the last shovel of soil, there is now a lump in the earth. I put my fingers to my lips and then press them against the loose dirt.

"Bye, Mama. *Je ne regrette rien.*"

Later that evening, when the day is over and the café is closed, I am surrounded by women. I guess it is a wake, of sorts. The kind Mama would like. Women, gossip, sweet things, and laughter. There is a full moon in the dim sky and a bright peppering of stars; we sit together in candlelight staring out at it. We have eaten *macarons*, pieces of cake, drunk tea and told stories. Marjory has her hair over one shoulder and her fingers in Gigi's, twisting it like bread dough into a plait. Rilla is pouring Yok Lan some tea. Faith sleeps. Their faces shine golden in the flickering light.

"Your hair is getting long, Gi." Marjory smiles.

"I haven't been in to get it cut. I don't really care about it at the moment. It can grow as long as it likes." She shrugs.

"You're not supposed to cut it until sometime after Chinese

New Year, right?" Rilla asks as Yok Lan pats her hand in thanks. The old woman lifts the steaming cup to her lips and takes a sip.

"Yeah. Something like that. I should ask Pau Pau, she knows all the old traditions. I do know it's lucky to wear red underwear."

Marjory secures the end of Gigi's plait with a hair tie. "Yee-ha!" she says. "I like that one. I wonder if I have any saucy red knickers to wear on Chinese New Year?"

Rilla and Gigi laugh.

"I bet you do," Gigi says and smirks.

"Mama would have liked that too," I murmur.

They turn to me, their faces solemn now.

"Hey, it's okay," I assure them. "It's good. I feel as if she's around us, like I've set her free to go to heaven or wherever she needs to be. She's probably looking down on us."

Yok Lan looks at me as though she knows what I am saying. There is something in her dark eyes that warms and calms me right the way through to my bones. Her wrinkled face breaks into a smile, and she nods. *Good girl,* I imagine her saying.

Marjory gives me a hug.

Rilla passes me the plate of *macarons,* and I take the plum and hibiscus with chocolate ganache. *Pardon.* The shells crumble under my teeth, the chocolate melts into the roof of my mouth and against my tongue.

"What is this new year?" I ask Gigi.

"Like, which animal?"

"Yeah."

"Ah, this is the Year of the Rat, so next is the Year of the Ox."

"The Year of the Ox," Rilla repeats.

I look around at them all again. Their different and beautiful faces in this buttery candlelight. Young and old, different colors, different shapes. Faith is in a pram next to me. I lay my hand against her belly and feel it rise and fall with her breath.

"Hey, let's toast," I say, lifting my teacup by the handle. The faces turn to me, and there is a clink of china against china. Orange pekoe tea sloshes onto a tablecloth I have laid out, and Rilla laughs. I imagine Mama's face looking down on me and seeing me, really seeing me. All of my past without censorship, gazing right through to the core of me. She would be proud of this. I imagine her dark eyes, the flame red of her hair. It sends a shiver from the base of my spine up to the tips of the hairs on my head. Her smile.

"To the new Year of the Ox."

Their eyes are all on me.

I look down at the tea stain blooming across the white cloth. My voice catches. "I promise never to forget you. Never forget any of you. Yok Lan; Gigi; Marjory; you, Rilla . . . Faith." The last name comes out as soft as a whisper. Tears gather in my eyes, the contents of the table swimming in my view. "You have changed me."

Marjory laughs nervously. "You say that like you're about to die," she observes, her jovial voice tinged with doubt.

Only Gigi stares at me, cool and calm. Her face is as pale as if she has seen a ghost; the color has slid right off it. She places both her hands against the tablecloth. Navy blue polish is splashed across the top halves of her nails, grown out from painting long ago and since forgotten about. She inhales slowly and stares through me for a moment. Then she sighs, as if she has always known.

"She's not dying. She's leaving."

La Promesse—The Promise

Orange Pekoe Dusted with Gold and a Mascarpone Filling with Rose Gel Insert

Over the next few days Marjory is almost always at Lillian's and Gigi and Rilla work every day, early till late. I wonder if they are trying to spend as much time as possible here, worried it may soon be gone from their lives. I am anxious too. What to do with the very thing that saved me from despair, gave me hope? *My baby.* Who can love this place like I do? The money does not matter; I've made back my investment, and it wasn't ever about the dollars. The passion for it is the important thing.

As I sit by the window biting at the red, angry skin next to my nails, Faith blows bubbles up at me with her perfectly formed lips. She interrupts my fears. There is no work to do with the girls hard at it in the kitchen, so instead I play with Faith and stare out windows. I lift her from her pram and hold her thick body above my face. She erupts in a stream of squeals and laughs. She is getting heavier, her legs pumping solidly, each one ending in a stripy-socked foot. Her black hair frames her deep brown eyes.

"I love you, little Faith," I whisper into her neck, bringing her down to cuddle, head over my shoulder.

Outside there is a chattering in a foreign language that makes me lift my head. Across the road a small white tour bus empties itself of a group of middle-aged Japanese women, all pointing and taking photos. A young, prim, suited woman steps out with a clipboard. Faith makes a little shriek at the crowd from behind the glass, but they are busy adjusting visors on their foreheads, checking purses, sourcing the right button on a friend's camera, and posing. A man descends the stairs from the back. Silver-haired. Tall. Wearing a black leather jacket. I squint to make sure.

Gigi comes out from the kitchen, dish towel in hand. "Isn't he that French chef?"

I nod. "Léon."

I watch as he gathers the women together. They look up at him with wide eyes and big smiles. The young woman in the suit translates, but nobody looks at her; they are transfixed by Léon as he gestures with wide arms, then kisses his fingers. They follow his hands, his slender fingers, and his blue eyes. I imagine their ears full of French accent, their hearts skipping beats. The stories they will tell their girlfriends when they return home.

"What's he doing?" Gigi peers out the window, dish towel now slung over her shoulder.

"I don't know." Watching Léon, I feel no quickening of breath, no rushing heartbeat, no flushing in my face. Nothing. I think of Mama looking down on me, giggling and shaking her head. "Oh, my darling girl, what were you thinking?" I smile, glancing up at the ceiling as though she might be there watching. Then I lean in and kiss Faith's neck. She nuzzles against me.

Now Léon is heading toward Lillian's. Gigi steps back from the window.

"*Bonjour!*" he says as he enters the café.

"Hi, Léon," I reply with a smile.

"I'm doing a tour with a group of women from Japan, you can see." He gestures across the road.

"Yes, I can see."

"It's a gourmet tour of Macau. A new business venture for me." He beams and then lowers his voice. "The wives of the VIP players really have nothing to cater for their interests here. It's a huge gap in the market."

"I'm sure it is."

Gigi crosses her arms and seems to glower at him.

"Well, we are going to the Portuguese restaurant down the road for lunch and egg tarts, and then we will be back here for *macarons*. They must try Lil's, of course, it is famous. *Macarons* are very popular in Japan. We shall see you soon?"

"No problem," I say and thank him for the advance notice.

When he leaves, shirttails flapping from below the jacket and his strides long and fast, I wonder how many times I might see him before I leave Macau; wonder if this may be the last time. The women behind him scurry to keep up with his pace, their faces full of smiles. Whether I like it or not, he has played a part in my adventure, this wonderful-terrible, terrible-wonderful year. It feels like a full circle. Going to Aurora that night, learning to make *macarons*, my mad romantic fantasy, finding out I am in love with my husband after all. Now Léon is here to bring others to my café. My Lillian's. My *famous macarons*. I grin to myself.

"I don't like that guy," says Gigi darkly, her eyebrows drawn together, watching my smile.

"I know, Gi. I know." I laugh. You don't have to worry about me, I almost add. If only she had better radar for the wrong guys for herself, I think wryly.

When the crowd has disappeared from sight and I have placed Faith back in the pram, her head heavy with sleep, Gigi goes into the kitchen and returns with a plate, four *macarons* in the center. They are light orange brown, like autumn leaves, dusted with a gold powder. Almost the color of my hair, I think vaguely. She kisses Faith's cheek and takes a seat opposite me. She is wearing striped socks like her daughter, but hers are drawn up to her knees and paired with dark green shorts. Faith yawns.

"The new *macarons*?"

She nods and lifts her hair into a ponytail, securing it with an elastic.

"Talk me through it."

"Orange pekoe flavor, with that gold confection dust on the top." She holds one up to demonstrate. "Mascarpone filling." She bites it clean in half and shows me the middle. "Rose jelly in the center."

"Sounds good to me. What shall we call it?"

"I don't know."

I reach over and pick up a *macaron*, the texture, weight, and balance all perfect. Symmetry, lightness, both shells with excellent feet, wedded together with a smooth filling. Nodding with approval, I place it on my tongue. She is right; the orange and rose flavors melt lustily in your mouth. It's just like Mama—all bright and full of surprises. I am impressed with Gigi; she has learned so much. She has refused to leave Lillian's and go back to dealing cards, despite whatever chaos it causes at home. She is stubborn and she is talented. I know already that the *macaron* will sell out.

Gigi's eyes grow wide, waiting for reassurance. Reflected in her dark irises I can almost see myself, sitting like a customer, while she serves me in her apron. A thought falls into my mind and starts to seed.

I rock her daughter in the pram, pushing it gently with my foot. "Let me think about the name," I say slowly.

Gigi groans lightly, in mock frustration. "Yeah, okay, but tell me . . . do you like it?"

"Do I like it?" I ask, teasing.

"Well?" Her voice rises in anticipation.

"I *love* it," I say. "It's perfect."

Her tired face splits into a smile. She sighs and then looks between Faith and me. She puts her head to one side. "Grace, there's something I have been wanting to talk to you about for some time," she says seriously.

I nod, glancing at Faith. Her eyes spring open and then close very slowly.

Gigi doesn't speak for a while, playing with the edge of her apron. Her face seems older, with less makeup, worn, but still as determined as always. She is biting her lip. I want to wrap her in a hug, but instead I wait until she speaks.

"I love her, you know," she whispers.

"I know you do, Gi."

"I didn't expect to."

I say nothing.

"I thought she was ruining my whole life. Every dream I ever had." She swallows and blinks. "I've been thinking about the life I want for her. The very best. I'm not sure that I . . ." Her voice trails off, and she stares out above my head.

I wonder if she is looking beyond me, to the small framed poster on the wall. Children dancing, flames, sparks. They look like they are celebrating a new year. I think of Pete encouraging me to listen. Just listen and be her friend. And then I think of Mama, the first time I ever ate a *macaron,* sitting on the bed on a gray, cold morning in Paris. *It'll make everything better.* Mama's promise.

"Shall we have a cup of tea and finish these *macarons?*"

Gigi smiles, softly, and nods.

Marjory wears a violet-colored blouse, as dark as a jewel, sleeves floating like gossamer around her long arms. Her blond hair lifts in the breeze.

"Purple?"

"Yeah." She shrugs. "Thought it was time for some color."

"I like it."

She grins at me and looks around the café. The chairs are up on the tables, lights turned off in the kitchen.

"Who are we waiting for?"

"Rilla is out the back, changing. Pete's picking up Don and meeting us there. We're waiting for Gigi and Faith."

"Faith is coming?"

"Don't worry; there are plenty of babies. I was there this time last year. I'll stand at the back with her away from . . ." A memory comes to me. A young woman, in a sweatshirt covered in stars.

"The smoke," Rilla finishes for me. She is in a light summer dress with short sleeves. It is covered in flowers, and she has tan sandals on her feet. There is no mistaking that she is a girl. Laughing at our astonished expressions, she does a twirl on the black-and-white tiles. The dress billows out around her bare legs.

"Look at you!" Marjory squeals, grabbing both her hands. We all giggle as Rilla blushes and coyly puts her chin to her chest. The front door chimes.

"And Miss Gigi!" Marjory laughs. We wheel around as Gigi enters with the pram, Yok Lan in tow.

Gigi's face is brighter than it has been for months, and she is wearing red, the Chinese color of luck and fortune. Her mandarin-collared blouse is paired with jeans, her hair lifted off her face. Signature dark mascara. Yok Lan has on a navy blouse in the same style and what looks like a touch of Gigi's makeup—a flick of mascara and some lip gloss. She beams at us, one hand on her granddaughter's shoulder and one hand on her cane. Outside the sky is already aglow with lights and low-hanging smoke that turns green, red, orange, and yellow with the reflections of the sparks.

"Shall we go?"

Gigi passes Faith to me when we arrive, and I make a camp for us far enough back from the action to avoid most of the loud bangs and smoke. Foldout chairs, Faith's pram, nappy bag and formula, snacks for everyone. Sitting with Faith in my lap, wrapped like a moth in a cocoon, I draw her hat down over her ears. She looks up and diligently suckles on my pinkie. Yok Lan sits beside us holding tea in a thermos flask, smiling. Gigi giggles like a schoolgirl at the huge bag of fireworks Marjory drags back with her. Marjory's face is lit up with mischievousness. She doesn't seem to care about or notice the large smudge of charcoal up her arm and a little underneath her jaw. Rilla rushes to help her, and they both end up sooty and laughing.

The first few attempts are duds. They sizzle pitifully once lit, or fly out to the water instead of up in the sky. We all laugh at the failures. Gigi claps her hands in encouragement as Marjory stands over a rocket, tongue pushed into the corner of her lips in concentration. Rilla giggles, with her hand pressed over her mouth. The tail is lit; the end wriggles and sparks.

"Stand back!" I cry out nervously, hugging Faith to my chest. She burrows into my warmth. They all take two steps backward, gazes firmly on the rocket. The flame hits a crucial point; there is an intake of breath. A whine like a boiling kettle pierces the night.

Whoosh!

It is off, propelled into the black sky, through the threads of smoke and cloud. The whine grows weaker as I get to my feet, pressing Faith to me. I place my hand over the side of her tiny head. Gigi, Marjory, and Rilla lean back, heads craning skyward, their mouths dark Os in anticipation. There is a brief silence and then . . .

Bang!

An explosion of bright light, streams of champagne sparks showering from above like gold raining from the heavens. Rilla leaps into the air, Marjory high-fives Gigi, who whoops. Laughter erupts from my throat. They are dancing now, a spontaneous, wild dance, around the launching spot. Full of light and love and hope. Soot on shoes, smoke in hair, love in bellies. I can almost hear Mama yahooing.

Thick arms move around my waist, under the bundle that is Faith. There is warmth against my neck. A soft kiss. I lean back into the space between his chin and his chest. *My place.* The blanket falls away from Faith's face, and we look down at her. She blinks back up at us, her eyes deep and brown and as clear as truth.

"Happy New Year, Grace," Pete whispers.

Epilogue

I look out over a yellowed yard, bordered by a low fence whose pickets need a fresh coat of paint. A tricycle rests against them. The light is the color of ripe lemons, and a rainbow-feathered bird screeches its loud good-night song. It even smells Australian—gum trees, heat, the caramel and charcoal scent of a distant barbecue. In front of me there is my desk, covered in invoices, postcards, travel plans, photos of Lillian's new sign with Gigi standing underneath, a newspaper clipping and photo of Marjory standing among her nuns, all lined up like smiling penguins. There is an uncommon stillness in the house; I can feel peace settling into my bones. It makes me sigh. Last night, as we lay next to each other in the warm dark, Pete had whispered, "It's a good life, isn't it, Gracie?" and I had nodded and curled against him like a koala into its pouch. A good, sweet life. That's for sure.

I breathe in the humid air and sink down into the chair, which makes a wooden creak. Somewhere in the debris there is a notepad. I fish it out and pluck a pen from the jasmine tea tin that now serves as a pen holder. I think of her face as I write. Fresh, free from the heavy makeup she used to wear. She still has the same defiant chin, now more confident than rebellious. A little tired around the eyes—she is a little older after all—but the very faint lines curve out and up. From smiling. She doesn't roll her eyes anymore. Dark and clear, they still draw you in. Her good, true self shining out of them.

Dearest Gigi,

How are you?

I'm sending some drawings for you to pin up in your apartment. There's you and me, a pink sky (of course), and Yok Lan having a cup of tea. I'm told the others are of cakes.

I've been looking at my messy desk and thinking of all the things I forget to ask or tell you about when we call; I get so distracted talking about the little one. We've booked our flights for Chinese New Year; did I tell you that already? We'll be there for at least four weeks, but I might extend if I don't have any orders I should get back for. Tell Yok Lan we're going to bring over those chocolate biscuits she likes. As many as I can fit in the suitcase! I hope you two have room in those kitchen cupboards of yours.

Business is booming here, Gigi. I wasn't sure about it at first, squeezing it in with swimming lessons and playdates and everything else, but it seems to work. It's just cakes after all; although they can take a while, especially when certain people want to eat the icing or make finger paintings on the wall with the batter. I've got an order for the opening of a new Russian restaurant on Brunswick Street. I think I'll make dark chocolate with kirsch-spiked ganache, perhaps covered with the tiny gold stars I used for the Lam wedding. What do you think?

I got the article about Marjory and the Macau Samaritan award; Don sent it over. Doesn't she look like a supermodel? All white teeth and legs up to her eyeballs. You must tell her to stop wearing such short skirts when she's photographed with the nuns; I swear she is the sexiest-looking Mother Teresa I ever saw. I keep imagining Rilla off to one side, hiding behind a potted plant or something. Thrilled but embarrassed. They are changing the world together, those two, one girl at a time. When I come over, I want to see the foundation's new space.

Perhaps we can have a little office warming? Give them my love, will you, and tell them we'll be there soon.

Not long until another birthday party. I can't quite believe it, can you? Four whole years since that day Rilla picked up the phone and said you'd had a girl. It makes me catch my breath to think how big four years old is when I still have that picture in my mind of a tiny baby. A tiny baby with dark eyes and a perfect mouth. It's gone so fast. I still wish we could see you more, but we've got it just about right, haven't we? That first year was the hardest. I don't know who cried more—you or me or her. Sad tears, happy tears, grieving and accepting tears. We could have filled the Pearl Delta, couldn't we? Thank God for baking and for Lillian's. We all just had to get used to missing one another so much and find that balance. I'm glad we have. It feels so good to hear laughter in your voice.

She wants to know if she gets "moon bick-its" at Chinese New Year. She remembers them from the visit before last; Yok Lan was feeding her little slivers while she sat on her knee and watched the goldfish in the pond. I haven't the heart to tell her they're only for midautumn festival. We might have to make a special New Year macaron *instead. Actually, I was thinking of a recipe last night. It might not be appropriate for children? Lychee flavor with champagne buttercream and a sugared violet.* L'Amour et les Amis, *Love and Friends. Just a thought . . .*

I'd better go. I can see a small person and a tall person walking up the street. I think someone has a balloon in her hands. We can't wait to see you. We miss you. Hope you like the drawings. We think of you every day, Mama Gi.

Your loving family,
Gracie, Pete, and Faith

X

* * *

I put down the pen and lay the letter over the drawings, vivid crayon in energetic swirls and stripes, wobbly lines formed into cakes and stick figures. I'll post it tomorrow. I stand up and wave out the window. Pete sees me first. He shoots me a grin and lifts a hand. Faith looks up. Her dark hair falls back from her face, and her eyes catch mine. The smile stretches from cheek to cheek. The ribbon of the balloon is wound around her wrist. As she lets go of her daddy's hand and runs toward the house, her balloon bobs along with her. Her laughter lifts and catches on the breeze, sounding just like Gigi's. I press my hands against the window and watch her. She calls my name with a voice full of joy and youth.

"Mama!"

Macarons

Macarons are tiny French confections made from the finest almond powder, egg whites, and sugar. They have charmed Parisians and Europeans for centuries, their crisp, sweet shells sandwiched together with creamy fillings. They are infinitely more elegant than cupcakes, daintier than tarts, prettier than pastries. Charming, meringue-like buttons, full of French couture attitude. The delight is in the changing flavors, inspired by seasons, whims, or moods. They are best enjoyed over a cup of tea and a conversation filled with secrets and gossip. These sweets have a cult following, and it is easy to see why; after your first, you will be hooked . . .

Acknowledgments

My grateful thanks to

- the wonderful team at Scribner; especially Whitney Frick, editor and champion of this book, I so appreciate your commitment and enthusiasm. My agent, Catherine Drayton, and the good folk at Inkwell, for your support. The nurturing team at Pan Macmillan Australia who first saw potential in Grace and Lillian's and who worked so hard and taught me so much. To Brianne Collins, for all your generosity, tact, and insight. Because of your efforts, this dream is a reality.
- food writers and bloggers whose passion provided inspiration and distraction; especially Karen Chong of *Mad Baker* and Clotilde Dusoulier of *Chocolate & Zucchini*. Personal thanks to the gifted chef Anthony Poh, for patient and gracious instruction.
- my phenomenal friends; particularly those in Macau who were my family away from family, including but not limited to Gigi Kong, Veron Mok, Peta Lewis, Amanda Quayle, Monica Ellefsen, Kylie and Chris Rogers, Helene Wong, Faith and Paul Town, Lucie and Phil Geappen. A big thank-you to Deane Lam, for local information and friendship; the errors are all mine. To the people of Macau like Fran Thomas,

Marjory Vendramini, and members of the ILCM, who try to make things a little better, thank you for your service and compassion. Warm embraces to friends in Vancouver who supported me during my juggling to get rewrites and edits complete, especially all "The Mamas." I'll never forget the special time and experiences we shared. *Merci beaucoup* to Rachelle Delaney and Helene Wong for assisting me with my (terrible) French and Ria Voros for kindhearted, sisterly buoying up. Faith and Lucie, all my love for cheerleading and inspiring me; Lucie, you are such a wonderful muse.

• my amazing *whanau*: Rob, Glen, Greg, and Kendall Tunnicliffe, who have believed in me and supported me, *aroha nui* and then some (always). Special thanks to Mum for all the flying, babysitting, draft reading, unconditional love and commitment; we love you, Nonna. To my Ballesty family, especially Paul and Wendy, who have welcomed and encouraged me so lovingly; I feel very blessed to be part of your tribe.

• my precious family: Wren Lillie, your mama adores you wholeheartedly, and Matthew Ballesty, my husband, true love, and best friend—thank you doesn't do it justice. Somehow I am more me because of you. For cherishing me, having faith in me, and raising me up to the very last word, I love you very much.

About the Author

Born in New Zealand, Hannah Tunnicliffe is a self-confessed nomad. After finishing a degree in social sciences, she ventured from her homeland's fair shores to live in Australia, England, Macau and, memorably, a camper van named Fred. A career in human resources and career development has been put on the back burner to pursue her dream of becoming a writer. She currently lives in Vancouver, British Columbia, with her husband, Matthew, and their daughter, Wren. *The Color of Tea* is her first novel.

A Scribner Reading Group Guide

The Color of Tea

Hannah Tunnicliffe

Introduction

Lost among the bustling, foreign streets of Macau, expat Grace Miller is an outsider in a strange land. Devastated by the news of her infertility and retreating from her unraveling marriage, Grace finds solace in preparing foods from her childhood and from her time spent in Paris with her impetuous Mama. Inspired by the dazzling displays of light on the Chinese New Year, Grace makes a bold decision to open her own small café. Among the casinos, *yum cha* restaurants, and futuristic high-rise apartment complexes, Lillian's becomes a sanctuary of *macarons* and tea where patrons come together, bridging cultural divides, to share in each other's triumphs and pain. But Grace's dedication to the café comes at a price—propelling her to a rediscovery of what it means to love and herself.

Topics & Questions for Discussion

1. Hannah Tunnicliffe writes beautiful, tactile descriptions of food and the ritual surrounding food. What was your favorite or the most memorable passage about food from *The Color of Tea*? Did Grace's culinary efforts inspire you in any way?

2. What were your initial reactions to Grace and Pete's relationship? How was their relationship impacted by their inability to start a family? Consider how both characters individually reacted to this news. Compare their relationship at the beginning of the novel to the epilogue. What has changed?

3. "I can feel so self-conscious here. So pale and tall. Too foreign. Sometimes it feels like I've been growing more and more foreign over the years." How is Grace's identity and sense of self influenced by her surroundings? How did the setting of Macau propel the narrative's action?

4. Each chapter opens with a description of a decadent *macaron*—from the "Parisian Crêpe–Inspired Banana with Hazelnut Chocolate Ganache" to "Dragon Fruit Filled with Lemongrass-Spiked Buttercream." How did these descriptions influence your reading?

5. Many of Grace's memories of her mother, her childhood, and her relationship with Pete are connected to food. Why is food such a powerful anchor for Grace? What is your most vivid or favorite memory related to food?

6. "I guess some women have a journal; I have Mama. Ruby-red-haired Mama." Discuss the letters Grace writes to Mama.

What does Grace's habit of writing letters that will never be sent tell you about her character? What did these letters reveal about Grace's and Mama's relationship?

7. Discuss the theme of motherhood and how it affects each character in *The Color of Tea*. How does Grace act as a mother figure to Rilla and Gigi? Who does Grace look to as a mother figure or role model? How does Grace eventually come to terms with her relationship with Mama?

8. When Grace meets Linda for the first time, she thinks to herself: "I wish I were better at making girlfriends. Or at least understanding other women. Sometimes it feels like they are speaking another language." Have you ever felt this way? How does Grace's approach to relationships change by the end of the novel? Why are Grace's female friendships so important to her?

9. Discuss the moment in the novel when Grace decides to open her own café. What drove her to this decision? How does Grace's dream of running her own café help her let go of her dream of becoming a mother?

10. Which character are you most alike? Which character do you most admire? Whom do you think you would most likely be friends with?

11. When talking to Rilla about missing Australia and her previous life, Grace thinks to herself: "I hate this enduring need to make out that your life is perfectly blissful. . . . The oily lies and half-truths leave me feeling uncomfortable and queasy." Do you think Grace herself is guilty of her own complaint?

Do you think she is completely honest with herself about her own struggles? Why or why not?

12. Discuss Grace's relationship with Léon. Why is Grace so drawn to him? What does he represent? How did you react to the fight between Pete and Léon at the tennis club? Was Pete's anger justified?

13. Were you surprised by Pete's confession of infidelity? Why or why not?

14. Discuss the scene where Grace finds out that Jocelyn and Rilla have been sleeping at Lillian's. Did you understand why she felt betrayed? In your opinion, did Grace overreact? How does this discovery act as a kind of personal catalyst for Grace?

15. What did you think of the ending of *The Color of Tea*? What has Grace learned from her past? From her mama's mistakes? From her relationships with Rilla, Gigi, and Marjory? Did you have any lingering questions?

Enhance Your Book Club

1. Instruct each member in your book club to invent their own *macaron* and share your descriptions with the group. Reference the mouthwatering descriptions that introduce each chapter for inspiration! What flavors would you include? What color would your *macaron* be? If you are feeling adventurous, consider baking *macarons* for your book club's meeting. For recipe ideas and tutorials on how to make these elegant confections, visit cakejournal.com/tutorials/how-to-make-macarons/ or www.marthastewart.com/318387/french-macaroons.

2. Write a letter you never intend to send, like Grace does to her mama. It can be to anyone—a friend, a family member, a historical figure, a celebrity, or even a fictional character from your favorite book. When was the last time you wrote a letter by hand? How did knowing the person you wrote the letter to would never read what you wrote influence you? Consider sharing your letters and discussing the experience with your book club members.

3. Grace is inspired to open her own café while watching fireworks on Chinese New Year, celebrating the arrival of the Year of the Rat. For more information about the Chinese Zodiac and astrology signs, visit www.astrology.com/chinese-astrology. Which animal are you and your book club members? Do you think they are accurate descriptions of your personality?

4. Visit www.HannahTunnicliffe.com to learn more about the author and to read her blog where she shares her inspiration and passion for writing and traveling.